'Lyrical, compelling and full o̶̶̶̶̶
down.'
Katie Fforde, the *Sunday Tim*

'I hope Catherine Fox will forg̶̶̶̶̶̶̶̶̶̶̶̶̶̶̶̶̶
an angel; she writes like a human being, with immense compassion,
unsentimental faith and an impressively undisciplined humour. Not
many writers give such a vivid sense of what it is actually like to try
and live in the light of absolute mercy. Very few indeed do it with such
brilliance and freshness of language.'
Rowan Williams, former Archbishop of Canterbury

Also by Catherine Fox (all published by Marylebone House)
The Lindchester Chronicles
Acts and Omissions
Unseen Things Above
Realms of Glory

Angels and Men
The Benefits of Passion
Love for the Lost

'Catherine Fox's glorious Lindchester series is the twenty-first-century
answer to Trollope's Barchester – but Trollope was never so funny, so
fundamentally kind or so mischievously attentive to grace.'
Francis Spufford, author of *Golden Hill* and *Light Perpetual*

'These books are utterly unputdownable, gossipy, subtle and wise.
What's astonishing is that, despite Catherine Fox's sharp awareness
of the feet of clay under surplices, she somehow makes you believe
several cheering things that most modern fiction doesn't: that the
natural world is endlessly beautiful, that most people aspire to goodness even if they fall flat on their faces and that the attempt to live a
good life is worthwhile.'
Maggie Gee, novelist and Professor of Creative Writing, Bath Spa
University

'Unsure what to buy the Trollope devotee in your life for Christmas? Look no further than Catherine Fox's *Acts and Omissions* and *Unseen Things Above* for a refresher course not only in cathedral politics but also a set of profound, although lightly drawn, insights into the contemporary Anglican Communion.'
Janet Beer, *Times Higher Education*

Angels and Men

'As original as its abrasive but engaging heroine.'
Pat Barker in the *Sunday Times* Pick of the Year

The Benefits of Passion

'Fox . . . writes this provocative and witty story as if she were on springs, her exuberant style happily combining with religious argument . . . thoroughly enjoyable.'
Good Housekeeping

Love for the Lost

'Catherine Fox is brilliantly skilled as a novelist.'
Penelope Fitzgerald

Catherine Fox is an established and popular author. Her debut novel, *Angels and Men* (reissued in 2014), was a *Sunday Times* Pick of the Year. Her other books include *The Benefits of Passion* and *Love for the Lost* (reissued in 2015), *Acts and Omissions*, which was chosen as a Book of 2014 by *The Guardian*, and its sequels, *Unseen Things Above* (2015) and *Realms of Glory* (2017). Catherine lectures at Manchester Metropolitan University.

catherine fox

fox

tales from lindford

First published in Great Britain in 2021

Marylebone House
36 Causton Street
London SW1P 4ST
www.marylebonehousebooks.co.uk

British Library Cataloguing-in-Publication Data
A catalogue record for this book is available from the British Library

ISBN 978–1–910674–65–9
eBook ISBN 978–1–910674–66–6

1 3 5 7 9 10 8 6 4 2

Typeset by Fakenham Prepress Solutions, Fakenham, Norfolk NR21 8NL
First printed in Great Britain by Jellyfish Print Solutions
Subsequently digitally printed in Great Britain

eBook by Fakenham Prepress Solutions, Fakenham, Norfolk NR21 8NL

Produced on paper from sustainable forests

For James,
fellow pilot of the Manchester Writing School starship,
for steering a steady course through 2020
and keeping me sane.
Live long and prosper.

With grateful thanks to the band of readers who kept me
company as I blogged this story.

Dramatis personae

Ambrose Hardman-May	Alto, Lay Vicar of Gayden Magna
Kat	Bishop Steve's EA

Beyond the Close

Dr Jane Rossiter	Lecturer at Linden University, married to Matt
Neil Ferguson	Father Ed's partner
Andrew Jacks	Director of the Dorian Singers
Becky Rogers	Ex-wife of Martin, mother of Leah and Jess
Leah Rogers	Older daughter
Jess Rogers	Younger daughter
Mrs Todd	Father Dominic's mother
Chloe Garner	Street pastor, lawyer, lay member of General Synod, cousin of Ambrose
Madge Williams	Retired midwife, parish nurse
Lesley	Parish nurse
Star	Hairdresser – junior stylist
Miss Clarabelle Sherratt	Retired nurse, philanthropist, heir to the Sherratt fortune
Rachel Logan	English teacher at Queen Mary's Girls' Grammar School
Mrs Logan	Wedding planner, Rachel's mother
Mr Logan	Consultant ophthalmologist and surgeon, Rachel's father
Jack	Ex-army homeless parishioner of Lindford Parish Church

All Creatures Great and Small

Cosmo	Chloe's labradoodle
Pedro	Father Wendy's rescue greyhound
Lady	Father Dominic's golden labradoodle
Bear	Neil and Ed's golden labradoodle
Alfie	Ambrose and Freddie's golden labradoodle
Luna	Martin, Leah and Jess's golden labradoodle
Andy and Theo	Alpacas

Prologue

———— ✦ ————

Much has happened, dear reader, since the end of 2016, when we turned the final page on the fictional Diocese of Lindchester, vowing never to begin a fresh volume. Our task back then was to chronicle in weekly instalments the state of the Church of England in times of rapid change, as mediated through the triumphs and disasters of my cast of characters. However, like a polite afternoon tea unwittingly booked into the same venue as a stag weekend, our parochial storylines were all but overwhelmed by a larger and louder narrative.

My forebears in the craft sensibly identified a few fertile acres of the past for their serialized tales. Consider *Middlemarch*. Published in 1871–2, the action takes place between 1829 and 1832. That's forty years of hindsight. How much easier to maintain a godlike omniscience when the era is fossilized and the politics all done and dusted. The past tense instantly commends itself as the proper choice. None of this faffing about in the present, trying to capture things as they unfurl before our horrified gaze. Four decades after the event, there's only so much tension you can inject into 'Dear God, will they pass the Reform Act of 1832?'

In my early days of blogging novels – back when it was a bit of a lark – I used secretly to ask myself the question WWGED? Answer: George Eliot would never launch out on a novel without a calm controlled sense of what she was about. Still, if the good Lord had wanted two George Eliots, he could have intervened back in 1819 and blessed Robert and Christiana Evans with twins. I can only do my best, acknowledging that George Eliot is Galadriel, beside whom I'm a mere Hobbit pestering about second breakfast while The Quest stands upon a knife edge.

But for all her merits, George Eliot is dead. I and my readers are not. We must do the best we can with what we've been given. So up we go, into the loft space again, to stumble among the crates of Lego which wait for unborn grandchildren, and the boxes of crap stored for grown-up sons and daughters until that day (which will never come) when they can afford a place as big as the empty nest their boomer parents now rattle around in. Somewhere up here, under carpet oddments, Christmas decorations and knackered standard lamps, are our Anglican wings.

The wind blows outside. The polythene tacked between beams sucks, bulges, sucks, like tired old lungs. The water tank warbles. What are we doing up here, among the cobwebs and memories? Are we mad to think that it will still fly, this creaking pterodactyl of a structure? The days of a wing and a prayer are long past. A handful of feathers and the mercy of God is all the C of E flies on now. The post-industrial dioceses of England are broke. The historic ones bolstered by medieval endowments are not much better placed, with hundreds of Grade I listed buildings to prop up. Apart from in the wealthy suburbs, you'll be a youngster in the congregation if you're in your fifties. The worldwide Anglican Communion hangs by a thread.

You know what, dear reader, I'd rather be writing about something else. (So say all who live to see such times.) I have no answers for you. But I do have this imaginary diocese where I can channel what's in the air, and try to work out what I think and feel. Its lands lie between Lichfield and Chester Dioceses, which is to say nowhere. It is a Borset/Barset quintessence of Middle England. The inhabitants are a bit mad, frankly; but I love them.

Come with me, one more time, dear reader. Don't be afraid. It's a long way to fall, but underneath are the everlasting arms.

JANUARY 2020

Wolf Moon, Part I

Dawn breaks over Lindfordshire. It's New Year's Day 2020. The revels are over. Scorched firework cases lie in empty parks and gardens. In every litter-strewn town, the streets are as empty as if the Rapture has happened and only we got left behind. But the world's not over yet. In a day or two it will all start up again. Work. Brexit. Life. But for now, Lindfordshire can roll over and sleep a little longer.

By 8.30 the first dog-walkers and dedicated runners are out. A grey-haired woman plods along beside the Linden with her three-legged greyhound. On the opposite bank, a young blond man cranks out mile after mile. They call across the river. 'Happy New Year!' 'Happy New Year!'

It's nine o'clock before Jane does her perfunctory stretches and sets off on her 5K jog round Martonbury Reservoir. At fifty-eight, she's stopped kidding herself. She no longer dignifies the activity with the verb 'run'. The only time she gets up speed these days is when she's going downhill, or slip-streaming a mobility scooter. But she's out there. Facing down the New Year. She knows if she grinds on, she will outpace the pixies.

They well and truly got out of their box under the bed again last night. First it was the advance guard Catastrophizing Squadron swarming all over her (what if Matt dies? what if management closes the history department and I'm out of a job?). Next up, the Pixies of the Apocalypse (post-Brexit political meltdown in the UK, climate extinction, what if Trump blows us all up?). Finally, the Bad Person troops parachuted in behind the lines (why are you so grumpy all the time? you've really let yourself go, fatty). At this point, it was useless, and Jane had to get up and make a cup of tea.

What a way to greet the New Year. She and Matt never bothered with the 'Auld Lang Syne' caper these days. For a busy bishop, an early night felt like the highest treat imaginable. Jane was vaguely aware of the muffled crump of fireworks at midnight, and mumbled 'Happy New Year'. Welcome, 2020! Sitting at 3 a.m. with her mug of chamomile, sleepless and pixie-harrowed.

She's shaken them off now. And look, blue sky, smoky light. The reservoir is like a mirror. There goes a jay. And a green woodpecker yaffling in the distance. She can hear the rusty bawling of a donkey. Jane knows it's pure coincidence, of course, that the Hill Top Farm donkey is called Nigel. But she's still grinning as she meets a set of dog-walkers. They hail each other – 'Happy New Year!' – as they pass.

All across Lindfordshire people smile and greet strangers. 'Happy New Year!' Another old friend of ours, Chloe, is out jogging in Lindford Arboretum, with her labradoodle, Cosmo. Cosmo is on a lead, lest he ravish some innocent lady dog, and father another litter of pups. Chloe's mind turns to The Question again. Is she mad even to be contemplating it? How do you even broach the subject? Hi people! I hear your pain and volunteer? No. Forget it. Too scary.

But why is it too scary, if it's coming from love?

It's like that song – what was it? *You must be kind you must be good and something something chop the wood*? Chloe skips round a puddle, to keep her nice trainers dry. She wants to be kind *and* good. But it's like running with two dogs. You get pulled in two directions. Cosmo screeches to a halt and hunches, quivering.

'Good boy!' She fishes out a poo bag. I'm a lost cause! Never once forgot my PE kit, or skived off violin practice. Did all my homework, passed every exam from 11-plus through to Cambridge Law Finals, paid every bill on time, never been in debt or had a speeding ticket or parking fine. Street pastor. Member of General Synod!

She bends to scoop up the warm handful. (Never once failed to clean up after my dog.) Am I brave enough to be kind, if that means other people will think I'm not a good girl?

Honestly. A good *girl*? 'I'm thirty-six!'

A man jogging the other way glances. 'Congratulations!'

Oops! Said that out loud. 'Happy New Year!' she calls after him. He half turns, and raises a hand.

Chloe is still laughing as she deposits the tied bag in the proper bin. Is she overthinking it? Maybe she should be more like Cosmo, just go with her instinct. Because sometimes the heart knows the shortcut to truth.

'Come along, boy.' She jogs home, with Cosmo bounding ahead till his lead has spooled out to its full ten metres. His world explodes with scent. Takeaway box, squirrel! Pug pee, bin! He greets them all with a happy Wow! Wow!

Happy New Year! Happy New Year! On the other side of the globe, Australia burns. *Happy New Year* doesn't cut it at the edge of doom. What words are there left to us? Even the portentous old Prayer Book falls short: 'Send us, we beseech thee, in this our necessity, such moderate rain and showers, that we may receive the fruits of the earth to our comfort . . .' We're on a runaway train. The failed brakes screech. We hurtled past Station Moderate years ago.

Dusk on New Year's Day. The girls and their mother emerge from the carpet-cushioned popcorn fug of Lindford's Odeon into the hard air. They've been to see *Little Women*. You go in tense, thinks Becky, in case they ruin it, but in fact it's made her love the book more than ever – if that's possible. Oh, how she adored it as a girl. Loved it literally to bits. She still has the falling-apart copy she devoured under the bed covers by torchlight. Even now, she can remember the longing it unleashed in her. To be a tomboy like Jo, to sell her hair and save the day, to write stories, have boys in love with her and yet prefer to be just friends.

How come she never managed to infect the girls with the same passion? Maybe her very passion inoculated them. With hindsight, she'd have done better to ban Leah from reading it. Put the book on a high shelf and say, 'It's *far* too grown-up.' Honestly, that girl came out of the womb counter-suggestible. Jess has always been a dream in comparison. But Jess isn't much of a reader, bless her. Why didn't I read *Little Women* to her at bedtime? Why was I always too tired? Bad mother.

No. I'm not a bad mother. I was doing my best. *I am enough.* She repeats this mantra every time the negative thoughts intrude.

Leah has stormed on ahead as usual. There she is at the corner under a streetlight, practising her karate moves while she waits. A crisp packet scratches along the pavement. Becky feels her scalp prickle. There's a feeling, a surge of something that Becky can only just keep down when Leah is around.

I am enough.

Says who? It should be enough to say to yourself that you're enough. But it's not. She still needs external corroboration.

Jess tugs on her hand. 'Mu-u-um?'

'Sorry, darling. Miles away. What were you saying?'

'The moon!'

Becky looks up. An almost half-moon glows between the clouds. 'Lovely!'

'I'm going to keep a moon diary,' says Jess.

'Are you? Lovely!'

'So you know my new notebook Leah gave me with the moon on? I'm going to write in that every day. Plus I've got a moon app on my phone.'

'That's great! Is this something for school?'

'No, I'm just super-interested in the moon.' She swings Becky's hand in time with their steps. 'I know all these amazing moon facts, like the phases of the moon? Do you want to know what phase it's at now?'

'Yes please!'

'Waxing jibbous.'

'You mean "gibbous".'

The hand-swinging stops. They walk in silence, moon keeping pace over the rooftops.

'That actually proves you're clever,' adds Becky. 'Because it shows you've learnt something all by yourself by reading about it.' She squeezes Jess's hand. 'So well done, you. What else have you discovered?'

Jess says nothing, just looks at the moon and starts humming, sweet and high. Something from her chorister repertoire. Becky should know it by now, but she doesn't. *Bad mother*.

'What about . . .' Becky ransacks her threadbare astronomy. 'The dark side of the moon?'

But by now they've caught up with Leah, who mutters, '*Finally.*'

'I know! Shall we get a takeaway, girls?'

'NO!' Leah drowns out Jess's *Yay!* 'Have you any idea how unsustainable that is? I've *told* you like *a million times* I'm vegan and I only eat locally sourced food.'

'We could go to Diggers?' suggests Jess.

'Diggers is closed, idiot.'

'*Don't* call people idiots, Leah.'

'People ARE idiots, FYI!'

Leah storms off ahead again. Becky tamps down that surge. Right now, it seems like hatred.

'It's OK, Mum,' says Jess. 'We can have vegan mac 'n' cheese again.'

Which I *drove* to Lindchester Waitrose to buy in my *gas-guzzling planet-killing* car, Becky doesn't say. 'Good plan.'

Jess starts swinging their hands again. 'So shall I tell you some more moon facts?'

'Yes please!'

'OK! So there's like a name for each full moon? Like each month has a different name?'

'Wow! What's January?' But she's maintaining the conversation on maternal autopilot. *I am enough. I am enough.*

Even before the twelfth day of Christmas, trees are stripped and dumped beside wheelie bins. There's a surge of something across Lindfordshire – impatience? Resignation? The party's over. We may as well get on with it. It really is going to happen this time. Brexit. End of the month. But it's dragged on so long, it doesn't really feel like anything. Some people are talking about parties, and demanding that church bells be rung in celebration of our liberty. Clergy are mentally preparing boiling oil to tip from the bell tower on any would-be ringers. That's how the fracture lines go, on the whole. Remainer clergy with leave parishioners.

How come we didn't realize we were singing off two different hymn sheets all this time? It was right there, under our noses, and we couldn't see it. The other half of our nation, in the next town, the next timeline, right next door. They might as well have been round the back of the moon for all we knew.

Each morning the sun rises a little sooner and sets a little later. Minute by minute the night is chipped away. On we trudge. Rain falls at last on the other side of the world. Immoderate rain. Storms and floods. They douse the fires for now, but 500 million animals have died already. Five Hundred Million. We can't see a figure that big. It goes off the edge of our brains. What we can see is a tiny pair of koala paws on social media, clinging to the hand of the rescuer who comes with a bottle of water. We can see the details. Only the details make it real.

And quietly, with barely a jingle of harness, another horseman of the Apocalypse sets out to ride in a distant province of China.

Wolf Moon, Part II

I t's Epiphany. No biggie in the UK. Strange that the free market hasn't seized on this feast as another opportunity for a retailing orgy. Shelves of *galettes des rois* to agonize over in the supermarket, and glossy magazines telling us how to fashion silver cake charms out of upcycled teaspoons. We could even call the *galette* a king cake, so it wouldn't sound foreign.

That said, one foreign Epiphany custom has crept in, if only in church circles. Let us shake out our Anglican wings (which I fear are shedding feathers like a boa bequeathed by a dead great-aunt) and circle round the Diocese of Lindchester. We will see that here and there people are clambering on to chairs or up stepladders, holy chalk in hand, to inscribe a line of curious runes above the front door of their house.

20+C+B+M+20.

Out in the sticks, Father Ed is not allowed anywhere near the chalk he blessed at the end of the parish Eucharist. This is because he has no instinct for correct layout, and his lettering is, frankly, an embarrassment. He is to hand the task over immediately to someone who is not visually illiterate. Psht. Don't argue. If a job's worth doing, it's worth doing by Neil. The ciphers above the vicarage door in Gayden Magna are exquisite. Look! There are even little crowns above the kings' initials: Caspar, Balthazar, Melchior.

Up on Cathedral Close, one of the tenor lay clerks chalks along the beam high above the Song School door. How on earth did he get up there without a ladder or a risk assessment? Is he mad? What kind of an example does that set for the choristers? The canon precentor will give *him* 'spider monkey genes'. Brr!

Let us – still on Anglican wings upborne – glide over to Lindford, where chalking is about to happen in the vicarage of the parish church.

Father Dominic stands on a chair in his porch. Mother holds the chair, because they have agreed that this is fractionally less alarming than the other way round. If Dominic falls, he probably won't break a hip and end up in hospital, get pneumonia, sink into a decline and die.

'Oh, people were always being carried off by their hip, you know. Pneumonia, the old man's friend.'

'Ssh, Mother. I'm trying to say the prayer. "O Lord, Almighty God, bless this home" – oh shit.'

'That's never part of the prayer!'

'Sorry. "That in it may be health, purity . . ."' It really doesn't matter that the leaflet Dominic has distributed to the congregation still says 2019. Freudian slip *there*, if ever there was one. Stop the calendar! I want to get off! He chalks the letters C+B+M. *Christus Mansionem Benedicat*. May Christ bless this house. He chalks 20 in front and 20 at the end. Bookends. Lord knows what will happen in between.

In a different house in Lindford, Jess picks up her jade gel pen and starts to write.

Friday 10th January 2020
Tonight is the full moon!!! Yay! 😄 *It is called the Wolf Moon. It is called this day in the day it was the time when the wolves were all starving and they howled at the moon because they were so hungry.* ☹️☹️☹️ *I am sad for wolves in this day and age too, there habitat is being eroded. Leah and me watched 'Seven World's One Planet' and in that the wolves finally caught a deer* ☹️ *and then the dogs stole it off them so they were still hungry. Leah explained how its all humanitys fault as is her want.*
Moon facts: Moonrise 15.46 moon set 08.07
Observations: I saw the Wolf Moon when we were going to the song

school, it was jinormous, and we were all WOW!!! I so wanted to stop, only I didn't want Mr Gladwin to tell me off for being late to rehearsal. After rehearsal I glanced the whole time when we were crossing to the cathedral and then I nearly fell down the steps LOL! Me and Ellie couldn't stop laughing and Mr Littlechild went 'Girls, will you stop being silly, please!'

The entire day I was super excited for the penumbral lunar eclipse only its cloudy so I don't get to see it. ☹

It's dark when Leah walks to karate. Mum hates that Dad lets her walk on her own. *She's only a child, Martin!* FFS! Like she's five, not nearly fourteen. But Dad's cool about it, so long as Leah has her phone, and doesn't take the shortcut through the arboretum, which obviously is a lame rule, because of her *zanshin*. Like she isn't in a state of total alertness the whole time. I mean, please. She's a junior black belt now. She can handle herself.

The moon glides above the rooftops. Leah stops. How weird is that? The moon's changing shape, like a stress ball and some giant invisible hand is squishing it. For a second she's scared, because what if she's got a brain tumour? But if you stay calm, there's a rational explanation, like probably it's an optical illusion due to refraction of light through the clouds or something?

Leah does not personally pretend to be a physicist, but she does not despise physics, like the other girls in her form when they don't get something because it's conceptually hard. They would do well to be humble in the face of the universe and Gaia's revenge, and remember how fragile we are.

Leah grips the olive wood cross Father Dominic gave her at confirmation. She keeps it in her pocket for when she's shit scared because there's No Planet B and there's no point praying even, because there's no fucking words are there, and the grown-ups don't get it, they're sleepwalking, and it's down to Leah's generation to shout WAKE THE FUCK UP!

Plus right now, it's flashback time to when she was young and got totally freaked by the Black Death after they did the village of Eyam in primary school, how the people locked themselves in so the plague wouldn't spread and loads of them died. Back then the grown-ups were all, Oh, don't worry, Leah, that couldn't happen now, we have antibiotics!

Hello? Coronavirus? Wuhan in lockdown? Ring any bells, people?

The moon convulses again, like an omen. Like, nothing's safe any more.

Leah unshoulders her kit bag and gets out her phone to film it. But when she looks up again, a big cloud slides over and blocks it out. Typical. She pockets the phone and picks up her bag. Then she remembers: *zanshin*. Her heart bumps. A car goes past. You lost your focus there. Anything could have happened, idiot. Stay alert.

Up above, a camera on a pole tracks her as she crosses the road and heads towards Lindford Sports and Leisure Centre.

The clock to Brexit ticks down. Father Dominic will not be ringing the bells of Lindford Parish Church on 31 January, thank you very much. They were decommissioned back in the early 80s, and although there have been periodic fundraising appeals, none has been successful. The one remaining bell, why yes, Father Dominic is prepared to ring that, if asked. After all, it's tolled for every *other* funeral.

He is in the vicarage hallway checking in the mirror that he doesn't have toothpaste in his beard. Dominic is not a vain man, but he is wondering about headwear. Part of him would rather like to splash out on a proper parson's hat, a broad-brimmed *Barchester Towers* affair. But the vision of the wind whisking it off his head, and the ensuing Charlie Chaplin-style chase down Lindford High Street, is deterring him. Perhaps a nice beret? Or is that too foreign? Will he get pelted with Cumberland sausages after the 31st, and told to go home, Frenchie?

These are displacement worries. He knows they are. In a moment Madge will arrive to sit with Mum, so that Dominic can go out on his pastoral visits with his faithful hound, Lady. Lovely Madge. She will soon be one of his parish nurses – a scheme Father Dominic has prioritized over getting a full ring of bells up and clanging. Thank the Lord for mad wealthy Anglo-Catholic donors like Tinkerbell! Oh, I *do* beg your pardon – Miss Sherratt, of Sherratt Shoes, I mean.

He frets that Madge will get told to go home. But perhaps she has the necessary family networks to support her? Windrush-generation parents, forced to navigate the famous open-hearted 'No Dogs, No Blacks, No Irish' welcome to Britain. It's new to him, the blatant racism; but maybe it won't surprise her. If you never fell for the illusion of a level playing field, disillusionment isn't an issue. The real issue has been there all along, invisible to him. Lord, he'd assumed, as a gay man, he knew about bigotry and oppression.

Well, well. Madge will arrive, and Dominic will go through his routine of introduction and explanation for Mother's benefit yet again. Fortunately, dementia has mainly had an exaggerating effect so far. It is a distillation of Mother into her purest essence. Which essence – like the overproof Jamaican rum Madge gave him for Christmas – is proving highly flammable. Mother will keep trying to cook and iron things. The fire brigade has been wonderful, but enough is enough. Hence Madge, lovely Madge.

Ah, the doorbell.

Dominic makes his pastoral visits, then gets a haircut and beard trim at Goran's (where he will unwisely agree to getting his eyebrows and nostrils waxed). Let us take once more to the air, and cruise at an altitude of about thirty metres, among the flocks of town pigeons – clap-clap-clap, gli-i-ide – and admire Lindford in all its glory.

I call it glory. The Victorian town planners would cry Ichabod. It is glorious to me in the January sunshine. Let us wheel round the frightful sheer cliffs of fall that are the university's Fergus Abernathy building, where our friend Jane has her office. Light flashes off the windows (hold them cheap may who ne'er dangled in a bosun's chair to wash them). Lower down, Queen Victoria glares, soot-blackened and jowly, from her pinnacle among the buddleias on the old town hall. Signs jut from its facade, advertising retail units to let. The rank beery-piss smell of weed drifts from a hidden corner. This is the scruffy part of the town centre, where you'll find the charity shops, Tasty Bites café, Eden Mobility and Cash Converters; where Bonmarché is closing down and two community police officers chat to the group of drinkers on the benches.

It's lunchtime. The queue lengthens outside Greggs. Schoolchildren squawk and shriek. People buy the now famous vegan sausage roll, which so recently undermined the very fabric of Britishness in the minds of those with nothing better to be outraged about. Look down. This is Goran's. The lit-up red and white barber's pole twirls. If we peer through the window, we will glimpse Father Dominic wiping his watering eyes and trying to pay. But as usual, Goran won't hear of it. No, no, for you, free, Father!

Just outside, a South American panpipe band plays. Tassels and feathers flutter in the wind. How much more glorious the players' wings are than ours! A new tune begins. It's 'El Condor Pasa'. Who would not rather be a hammer than a nail? Though, theoretically, the impact of each blow is the same, given that every action has an equal and opposite reaction. You just feel more in control if you're the one doing the hammering.

'It should be song thrush, not sparrow,' Jane tells Dominic.

They are sitting in the little courtyard of the newly opened Lindford branch of Vespas, where dogs are welcome.

'What's she on about now, Lady?' Dominic asks.

Lady pricks up her ears and lets fly a wild bark.

'That tune.' Jane waves towards the panpipes whiffling in the distance. 'Sorry, Simon and Garfunkel, but sparrows don't batter snails on rocks.'

'She's such a blue stocking, isn't she, Lady? Such a blue stocking!' He buries his hands in the dog's fur and gives a good old rummaging rub. Lady laps his freshly barbered face.

'Are we going to conduct our entire conversation via your hound?' asks Jane.

'Tell her to relax,' Dominic says, still addressing Lady. 'We aren't going to discuss it.'

'Thank God for that.' Jane picks up the menu. 'What are we having, then?'

Smashed avocado. Sourdough bread. Vespas is the latest pocket of hipsterdom to erupt in the town. Perhaps the pockets will join up to form swathes of gentrification now that austerity is 'over', thinks Jane.

The 'it' they are not discussing is the House of Bishops' so-called pastoral statement on opposite-sex civil unions. It's too near the knuckle for both of them. Anyway, there's no point. It will blow over.

14

Like the Meeting of Primates' fiasco back in January 2016. Why, whole days go by without Twitter outrage on that subject now.

Jane feels his hand on her arm. 'Are you OK, darling?'

Her eyes brim without warning. 'Yeah. Weary. Of it all. January. Modern Britain. You, having to set up *Call the Midwife*, for God's sake. Foodbanks were bad enough.'

'I know, I know. Are you coming to the commissioning service?' asks Dominic. 'I can save a front row seat for Mrs Bishop.' Even this flagrant red rag doesn't provoke a response. Oh Lord. She's not having one of her 'That's it. I'm off to New Zealand' phases, is she?

'We're heading back to Josephine Luscombe's day,' she says. 'It'll be workhouses next.'

'Have a good old swear,' he suggests. 'Come on, give me your views on Boris.'

'I've concluded that vituperation is part of the problem, not the solution.'

'And besides, your work here is done. You've passed your swearing mantle on.'

'Leah? God, I love that girl. She called me out for striking over associate lecturers' pay but not joining Extinction Rebellion.'

'Lindford's own Greta! Apparently, the church loo rolls aren't sustainable enough for her liking.'

They both laugh. But then Jane falls silent again. She stares at the menu. It's over, she thinks. Our political system. Both parties are dead. Hollow as clay golems. They'll go on blindly functioning until someone cracks their empty skulls open and pulls the slip of paper that's telling them what to do. Then they'll crumble to dust. What comes after? Nationalism. Right-wing extremism, that's what.

The waitron appears in her Breton shirt, notepad poised. 'Hey guys, what can I get you today?'

Jane rouses herself. 'I'll have the soup, please.'

The moon rides over Lindfordshire. Maybe we can gaze at it and take heart. Is there anything more constant than th'inconstant moon? Why, we can download an app, like Jess, and find out exactly what it is doing and where it will be. There will be no apologies for the delay to the moon's journey, and for any inconvenience caused to the tides.

All across the diocese, people glimpse it as they unlock their cars before dawn on frosty drives. So do shift workers returning home. Insomniacs, jolted awake by the cattle prod of random dread, pull back the curtains, and there it is.

How strange to think that every creature that ever lived and gazed at the sky has seen the same moon, the same face looking down. Shakespeare saw it. So did Cleopatra, the long-gone pterodactyls, and Jesus on the shore of Galilee. All beasts and cattle, every salmon that ever swam upstream, young Mary Ann Evans in the garden at Griff House – the same moon.

All the soldiers who laid down their weapons to play football on no-man's-land on Christmas Day, 500 million dead Australian animals, all the people in tiny boats fleeing their homes, all the birds that ever visit your feeder, every ant in your garden. Donald Trump, Nigel the donkey, every firefly flashing in a North American forest on a summer night. All the poor dodos who didn't know not to trust humans. Every babe staring up wonderingly from its mother's arms as she soothes it in the night, walking, murmuring, Look, there's the moon, hush, hush, it's all right, little one, Mama's here. All of them – the same moon.

It's too much for me. The number goes off the edge of my brain.

See. The self-same moon hangs there now, a gleaming gold paring low on the Lindfordshire horizon, as rooks tumble out from the roost into the blue dawn. The last sliver of the Wolf Moon.

Rain falls. It blows into shop doorways where bodies lie Spice-coshed in sleeping-bag cocoons as the world passes by. It falls on the little locked garden where the statue of Josephine Luscombe, friend of the poor, stands holding her prayer book. It rattles against the vast hangar where the zero-hours contract workers walk-walk-walk the aisles to find your one-click impulse buy. It drips in through the rotting roof of Tinkerbell's summerhouse at Sherratt Manor, and trickles down the *For Sale* sign on the 1960s semi at the bottom of her garden.

The last days of January approach. The Brexit clock ticks down. Tick, tick, tick. The moon is still there, but our shadow hides it. The new moon will appear. It always does. The papers are signed in London, in Brussels. The Brexiteers get their 'far fierce hour and sweet', with flags and excruciating 'Auld Lang Syne'. Neeps and haggis fly off the shelves of M&S. And far off the edge of our little map, off the edge of our brains, vast new hospitals are flung up in China and expats begin to fly home.

Tick, tick, tick.

It's 31 January 2020, 11 p.m. Fireworks. Jane wakes. Oh yeah. Huzzah for Brexit. She gets up, crosses to the cronky old Crittall window and forces it open. Matt snores on. There's another brief sputtering volley in the distance.

An owl calls.

She looks out across the dark garden and waits for more. It's a cold clear night. Orion rides above the dark bulk of the tall tree, his starry belt glinting. The owl calls again. Then silence.

So that was it, she thinks.

FEBRUARY

Storm Moon, Part I

In a pink bedroom in Lindford, a lamp casts fairy shadows on ceiling and wall. Fairy lights twinkle round the door and window. Jess leaps on to her bed, nestles down among the sparkly rainbow unicorn cushions, and opens her Moon Journal. She uncaps a mauve gel pen, and starts to write. She dots her i's with little hearts, because nobody has yet ridiculed her out of it.

February 1st

It is February and we have a different full moon, SNOW MOON. Yay! ☺ I so hope it will snow, I adore snow plus maybe it will be a SNOW DAY!!! I don't actually mind school it is mostly OK and I am eternally grateful to be in the cathedral choir and get this amazing musical education thanks to the Blatherwick Trust like Mr Littlechild is forever reminding us about LOL.

Today the moon is 6 days old, it is First Quarter (40%). It will be Full Moon on Sunday 9th February which is Stanford in G and the anthem is the new one by Jacks when I do my FIRST EVER SOLO!!!! Ta dah! Mum and dad are both coming. Even Leah is coming (I know why LOL!!! but she gets mad if I say it so I don't). It is only 2 lines to be fair, but Mr Hardman-May says we all have to start somewhere and I will be awesome and then GREATER THINGS!!!! Ellie is singing 2 lines as well, because we are the probs.

Afterwards for a treat we get to go as a family for PIZZAAAAAAA!!! Mum said I was allowed to choose, but Leah said I will check out Pizzalands track record and make an informed decision first, and mum went We're going to Pizzaland, that's final, it's Jess's choice, but I do hope you will dane to join us, Leah, and she went FINE.

<u>*Full Moon Names.*</u>

So full moon names are traditional and come from Native America. There is not one official list, there are many and various names for the full moons. Leah warned me not all websites can be trusted as they contain made-up facts not to mention conspirasy theories. I have chosen to mainly go with the Royal Observatory website because it can be trusted like the BBC. Leah went Yeah right when mum said that and roled her eyes. Yesterday when she came for tea Ellie said No offence Jess, but your sister can be a total b**** sometimes. I get that, but I bare with Leah, she is my sister when all is said and done, she has her issues and hormones but she totally means well.

<u>*Names for February Full Moon*</u>

1. Snow Moon

2. Storm Moon

3. Hunger Moon

My favorate is SNOW MOON because I'm always super excited for snow.

It's a new month, a new moon, a new life for us, and (like the great Nina herself) we are *feeeeling* good! Or are we? I presume great swathes of Leave-voting Lindfordshire are currently upbeat, having thrown off the shackles of the EU at last. But whichever way we voted back in June of 2016, the end has manifestly not come with the decisive bang of a Hazard Type 1 professional-only firework. It was more your back garden Catherine wheel nailed to the clothes prop, all stoppy-starty, with a surge here, a snag there. There will be eleven more months of fizzling while the details are thrashed out. After that we will have a deal, or not, and everything will be clear, or not. Honestly, it's as though we've spent years trapped in a runaway car screaming at each other as we hurtle down a 1 in 3 hill. We've just ploughed to a standstill in the deep grit of the escape lane. No wonder we're feeling dazed.

Anyway, at least we've got January out of the way. We can console ourselves once again that February is short. Spring will come. If we take to our wings, we will see that across Lindfordshire there are sheep on hillsides. There will be lambs before long. Molehills splash the meadows like black freckles. Turbines turn. Horses stand in drab blankets, and in churned-up cattle fields there are fragments of sky in the hoof prints. The blackbirds are singing again. Everywhere, signs of hope.

Miss Clarabelle Sherratt looks out of her drawing room window. Her world is crystal clear again, thanks to Mr Logan (and God guiding the surgeon's hands). She crosses herself.

Oh, I say – crocuses! Why, she can even read the *For Sale* sign a hundred yards away. Oh, bravo, looks like it's been sold at last. The Grindons will be pleased. Been on the market for simply ages. A fox! Trotting down her path, bold as you please! Miss Sherratt claps her hands and lets out her trademark wheezy squeal of delight. I can see why Father Dominic likes her so much. She disconcerts people, mind you. She's so young at heart, it's like hearing Red Riding Hood squeaking from the wolf's belly. But then in a snap, she's Sister Sherratt cracking down on your sloppy hospital corners.

The fox vanishes from view behind the rhododendrons. Gosh, it's like a new world! That said, now her cataract haze has gone, she has to admit that apart from the lawn, the garden has become a . . . wild-life preserve. That's how she'll think of it. A haven for beast and bird rather than an utter disgrace.

Oh blast. Maybe the time has come to sell it off to a developer? Oh Lord, my poor old summerhouse is falling in. It's a derelict old wreck, like this derelict old girl. Maybe she should lug the gramophone out on to the terrace, then totter across with a gin, and smoke a valedictory ciggie in the wicker chair? Then have the jolly thing demolished. No, can't bear to. So many memories! (Bertie Douglas, hold your hand out, you naughty boy!) And Mummy. That's where we were sitting when the first siren went off. Shelling peas. The phony war. Age fifteen. Everyone in a screaming tizz. You gripped my hand. Wait, Belle. Sit still. This is what we do. We pray, and then we serve. *Hail Mary . . .*

Dear reader, I sense your impatience. Enough of your mad old lady philanthropists! What about Mr Hardman-May? Don't tell me

Freddie and Ambrose got married, and we weren't invited? I know, I know. How could I do that to you? It wasn't a fancy affair. It was practically an elopement, to be honest. They ran off in August of 2017 and tied the knot, before Ambrose's events-planner sister took over everything.

Mr and Mr Hardman-May still live in the sweet little house in Vicars' Court. Shall we go and see how they are getting on?

It's a while since we visited the Close. Come, seize the portkey of your imagination, and I will whizz you straight there. This is no night for flying. Storm Ciara limbering up.

Here we are. It's early evening on Saturday. Wind roars in the lime trees, and shivers across the lawn. A wheelie bin goes scampering. Look! There's the moon, the Storm Moon (sorry, Jess – not much snow forecast in Lindfordshire), rising above the Song School like a vast genial face. The cathedral is still standing, you'll be relieved to hear. Notice how the spire tower now prickles with scaffolding? The final phase of restoration is underway, after the work on the south side was completed last June.

We do a quick recce: yes, the palace, the deanery and all the canons' houses remain as gorgeous (and draughty) as ever they were. But there has been one lamentable change for lovers of impracticable nostalgia: the boy choristers no longer board at the cathedral school. Alas! They still attend, and can be seen crocodiling from Song School to cathedral in their cherry-red caps, but they are day pupils now. The girl choristers, being a recent innovation, never boarded. Those familiar with cathedral life will be able to picture the anguish that led to this reluctant decision a year ago last September. But the brute facts of finances forced the hand of Dean and Chapter.

Enough of that for now. Let's head past the quarters of the Broderers' Guild, trailing a hand along the hedge, and go through the narrow arch and into Vicars' Court. There's the little row of crooked Tudor houses, the lawn, with its venerable mulberry tree (associated in some nebulous way with Charles 1) now creaking in the wind.

Listen. Can you hear a piano? Someone is playing rippling jazz riffs, channelling his inner Fats Waller. I wish I could play like that; but even if I had taken lessons as a child, and bothered to apply myself for three decades, my hands are nowhere near big enough.

24

Someone is singing along. Not entirely tunefully, I confess. But Alfie the golden labradoodle wants the world to know he ain't misbehaving.

Freddie comes into the tiny sitting room with a bottle and two glasses. The baby grand takes up half the space.

'Dude, I can't believe it? We're actually *actually* moving off the Close?'

'Whoa, whoa, whoa. Freddie, they've accepted our offer. Let's wait till we've exchanged contracts before we open the fizz, OK?'

'Man, you're such a . . . C'mon, can't you be even like a *tiny* bit excited here?' The cork pops. Alfie barks and leaps. COOL NEW GAME! A music stand goes flying. Scores scatter. 'Fuck. Hold this? Leave it, boy!'

Ambrose takes the bottle.

'Give! Let go!' Freddie manages to persuade Alfie they're not playing tug of war with the new Jacks anthem. 'Shit.' He smooths the crumpled sheets and stacks them on the piano. 'That totally never happened. Sit, boy. This here is totally why we need a bigger place?' He spreads his hands in appeal. 'You know?'

Ambrose hears the unspoken *Especially if* . . . He pours the Crémant. 'I know.' They chink Champagne saucers. 'To future happiness, babe.'

He doesn't want to rain on Freddie's parade, but his husband's jerry-built air castles terrify him sometimes.

Yes, Storm Ciara is thrashing about the UK, churning trees, washing windows. By Saturday it's roaring in the Aga flue in the kitchen of the Bishop of Lindchester. There is no Aga in the Bishop of Barcup's kitchen, but every so often the wind blasts in an overflow pipe like a tiny enraged elephant. Jane and Matt are in the bedroom, where Matt is packing for General Synod, which starts tomorrow. They've been watching the England versus Scotland rugby match in Murrayfield. Insane, with lashing rain and wind-assisted kicks going long and lineouts a total lottery.

All of which prompts Jane to question her husband's wisdom in setting out for London.

25

'Matt, I know General Synod is important on Planet Church, but this doesn't constitute essential travel.'

Matt doesn't argue. Nor does he stop folding shirts and balling socks together.

'Why don't you bunk off? Or at least set off on Monday morning,' persists Jane. This is merely a thought experiment. She knows he's not going to change his plans for a mere Category 2 storm with winds of up to a hundred miles per hour predicted, causing widespread flooding and travel chaos. 'Why risk life and limb to get shouted at? I snuck a look at the timetable. Windrush – shouted at for institutional racism. Safeguarding – shouted at for failing to support survivors. Not to mention the so-called "Pastoral Statement".'

'Aha! Won't get shouted at for *that.*' Matt zips his case. He gives her his sunshiny smile. 'That was the Head Boy's cock-up. I'm only a prefect.'

'Whatever.' Jane can never hold the distinction between *House* and *College* of Bishops in her mind for more than thirty seconds. 'I'm going to miss you.'

'I know.' He gives her a hug. 'Ships in the night. I'll be back Thursday late afternoon.'

'I'm teaching till six. I know – let's run away to New Zealand and live in a little bach on the South Island and spend our lives fishing and reading.'

The wind does another elephantine blast in the pipe, like a derisive raspberry to Jane's suggestion.

'It's a plan,' says Matt.

The storm splits the nation. It divides us into optimist and pessimist. Some of us see SEVERE WEATHER WARNING and picture ourselves crushed by a falling tree (or at the very least, stranded in Crewe). Others assume things will in all probability go ahead, even if there's a bit of a delay. The dutiful turner-uppers, people like our friend Chloe, will always battle on rather than let other people down.

She's just nipped out in her car to the little Co-op to pick up her synod essentials (big bags of Minstrels and Maltesers to share, wine for her hotel room). It's a wild dusk, with racing clouds. She's going down to London a day early – trains permitting! – so she can catch up with her old uni friend Sarah. Maybe she can find a moment to talk through The Question? To say: Look, tell me frankly – am I mad to contemplate this? Because Sarah, ha ha, will be frank!

She gets back in the car and drives home. She slows as she passes the 60s house with the *Sold* sign. Could this work? Am I mad? She rounds the bend, and the Storm Moon pops up vast and pale gold above the trees. It looks so much like a big happy face beaming over a hedge that she laughs for joy.

Ha ha! I'm completely mad, but I think . . . *I think* I may suggest it to them?

Storm Moon, Part II

It's the Storm Moon, all right. Literal storms, church storms, political storms, storms of outrage on Twitter. Interestingly, Jane's capacity for outrage no longer functions. Somewhere along the line – last December's election maybe? – there was a terminal crunch under the bonnet, the kind that even a non-mechanic recognizes. Nothing's going to jumpstart this thing now. Boris? Dominic Cummings? Trump being found not guilty in the impeachment process? Nope, not even a spark.

In the place of outrage, what? Something like unease. She'd noticed it on election day. We've all been caught out looking the wrong way, wringing our hands in our sandbagged front doorway while the floodwater is creeping in the back. Her brain keeps scrambling the Pixies of the Apocalypse at 3 a.m. Yet there's a weird inertia too, as though she's dreaming that she's on her sofa with a book, and can see people waving frantically through her window; can almost lip-read the warning. She knows that by the time she's worked out that they're time travellers from the future of Planet Earth, it will be too late.

She knows all this, but she's got her flight booked for the lecture trip to the States in late March. She's still driving her car to the supermarket and ordering pointless crap on Amazon when the whim takes her. How much more will it take before I wake up? she wonders.

Oh, it's probably just her usual seasonal gloom. It will pass. The days are drawing out, and let's not forget our bright new post-Brexit future. HS2 going ahead, investment in the North. Coronavirus apparently slowing. Cheer up, you silly mare. She applies for her

ESTA, then goes back to her Josephine Luscombe lecture, which she will be delivering at Luscombe College. This is a small liberal arts college in the Mid-West, and it's possible she will be treated there as Dr Jane Rossiter, Leading World Expert, rather than being in receipt of emails saying, 'Hey Jane sorry i missed the session did i miss anything so i can catch up thanx ☺.'

Storm Ciara disrupted things for poor old Jess, I'm afraid. Choral Evensong on the afternoon of her first ever solo was sparsely attended. Her hands trembled slightly as she held her dog-chewed music, but she nailed her part. Her parents and sister were there to hear her, and they did go for pizza afterwards to celebrate, despite the weather.

Leah spent the service glaring at the specially printed order of service and doing everything in her power not to glance across the aisle at Mr F H-M sitting on the back row of *dec.* This was a tactical error on her part. She'd have been less conspicuous staring at him like a normal person. If we can't enjoy gazing at bright and beautiful people, what is the matter with us? The Lord God made them all. But spare a thought for her, those of you who can remember what it felt like to be thirteen years old and locked in an eternal crush on someone as unavailable as the man in the moon.

Talking of the eternally unavailable, a special stall was reserved in the quire for the composer, but it remained empty. Dr Jacks did not risk getting into his new silver Aston Martin Superleggera to grace Lindchester Cathedral with a visit. (Perhaps an example of the old adage about ill winds? I leave that for the reader to decide.) Those who did attend will remember the anthem for many years to come. Girls' voices against the background roar of the storm: 'God be with you till we meet again.'

Oh, for heaven's sake! Not another of your shocking old schmaltzy hymns, Jacksie. That was the reaction of Giles Littlechild, the canon precentor, when he first hummed his way through the musical score. Still, it was a freebie, not a commission, and Giles was never one to look a gift anthem in the mouth. He stood by his initial reaction during the premiere. This did not prevent the tears mounting as the probs' voices rang out, however. First Eleanor (a bit tight and sharp with nerves): "Neath his wings protecting hide you, Daily manna still provide you.' Then young Jessica (spot on, hairs on the back of the neck stuff): 'When life's perils thick confound you, Put his arms unfailing round you.'

Dammit, Jacks! Out-Ruttering Rutter again. This is so cheesy it's practically a choral fondue, man! The precentor delved furtively under his surplice, insinuated a hand through the special pocket slit in his cassock, and pulled out his handkerchief.

One week later, hot on the heels of Storm Ciara, comes Storm Dennis. It's like some ghastly camp song: Next verse, same as the first, a little bit louder and a little bit worse. Leah, as is her wont, explains to Jess that it's all humanity's fault. (She's been banned from freaking Jess out with the fact that coronavirus has now killed more people than SARS, by the way.)

'Windy old weather, stormy old weather!' sings Father Dominic's mum. 'And when the wind blows . . .'

It's Sunday afternoon, and she's dry-mopping the vicarage kitchen floor.

'We'll all pull together!' sings Dominic with her. He buttons his coat. 'Keep swabbing that deck, Second Mate. I'm just going to wee the dog and check on Jack.'

'Aye-aye, Cap'n!'

Dominic clips on Lady's lead, and off they go. He locks the front door after him, so Mother doesn't go a-roving so late into the night. Vile weather. Worse than last week, even. He pulls his beret down snugly (yes, he did buy one) and they sally forth into the maelstrom. Rain pecks his face and glasses. The wind roars in the tall lime trees along his drive. He crosses himself. You can't fall on me – I'm a clerk in holy orders!

They are heading round to the churchyard before it's too dark to see. Numbers were down this morning at the 11 a.m. mass. He suspects some of his flock seized on the storm as the perfect excuse for bunking off the Annual Parochial Church Meeting. He's rung round to cancel Evening Prayer as a precaution. They'd only had three brave old soldiers last week during Ciara.

'We don't want Tinkerbell skittled over by Dennis, do we, Lady? We need her fit and well for the parish nurses' service!' Mind you, it would probably take a tag-team of Dennises to topple Miss Sherratt. *Built for comfort, not for speed, Father!*

There's water spurting up through drain covers again. It's rushing like a river down the road. Please, not more floods! Lindford has barely recovered from last November. He'll have to buy a kayak to do his pastoral rounds at this rate!

A Coke can goes clanking past. They round the bend and the wind sends him scuttling sideways. Lord, have mercy! He wedges his beret down again. They fight in through the lichgate. There's a punctured foil Valentine's heart from Friday snagged on the open gate. It hisses viciously.

No, this is ridiculous! Even Jack can't bivouac in this carry-on. Last weekend was bad enough. I don't care if you're a war vet, my friend, you're staying in the vicarage tonight. Dominic and Lady press against the wind to the far corner of the graveyard, where Jack's been camping out since January. Dark clots of laurels loom and sway. Lady tugs on her lead, and Dominic stumbles round behind the Sherratt monument, arms windmilling.

'Jack?'

But there's nobody there.

February 20th

It is half term YAY! We are down at granny and gramps in Eastbourne. Eastbourne is supposably the sunshine coast LOL! Its been raining the entire whole time so me and granny have been baking. We made rock buns. Leah is listening to podcasts as per usual and doing karate in the lounge. Dad said this is actually not ideal Leah but gramps said don't worry she will be careful, Martin. Leah is totally grampses favourite. Dad always says rubbish, grandparents don't have favourites but I am cool with it. Plus I am happy for her, she is not everyone's cup of tea at the end of the day. She will get his army knife when he's gone.

MOON FACTS

Today the moon is 'waning crescent' (11%) and on Saturday it will be 'new moon' (2%). You can't ever see the new moon, it is in the earths shadow. It should be 'NO moon' LOL! (Except it is really there all the time obvs.)

MORE MOON FACTS

Here are some more facts I have researched from the internet.

1. Once upon a time the moon was part of the earth. There was this giant asteroid the size of Mars called Theia, it hit the earth and created the moon.

2. The earth used to spin faster and it was the moon that slowed it down.

3. The moon stops the earth wobbling on it's axis so we get seasons.

4. If the moon vanished most probably things would change slowly and not in our lifetime but many animals would be impacted and also the tides. (Plus I would also miss it to be fair, it is very beatiful.)

Rain falls in such quantities that even atheists reach for 'biblical' to describe it. What words are there but those of the Book of Common Prayer for these several occasions 2020 is dishing up? 'We humbly beseech thee, that although we for our iniquities have worthily deserved a plague of rain and waters . . .' Our iniquities criss-cross the sky, they fume from our gridlocked cities. We try to ship them away out of sight and bury them in landfills.

Lindford is spared this time, but all through the long rainy nights, people whose homes have barely dried out listen in fear for the war-zone throb of Chinooks again. During the day, Father Dominic stands with Martin Rogers, who organized the flood hub last November, and they watch the Linden race and plunge by. 'Send us such weather, as that we may receive the fruits of the earth in the due season . . .'

This time the Linden bursts its banks farther downstream and overwhelms the low-lying villages there. Cardingforth, Carding-le-Willow, Lingmorton. Poor old Father Wendy is the one turning her church into a flood hub. But it takes her mind off her own worries, which is a tiny silver lining. When the phone call comes announcing the all-clear, she realizes she'd barely got round to fretting about it. She and Doug can open a bottle of fizz later, when it feels more appropriate.

'Just a scare, Pedro. Just a perfectly innocent liver spot! I'm getting old, that's all.' That's all? As if getting old isn't a blessing! Pedro, dear Pedro. Perhaps he saved her life two years ago, with his snuffling at the funny old mole on her arm? 'It's a blessing, and you're a blessing, Pedro. Come along, then.' They splosh up the path to St Martin's, Cardingforth, where good-hearted people have been dropping off donations.

Come with me. The wind has dropped now. Let's trust to our tatty wings and launch ourselves from the ark like Noah's raven. Floodwater everywhere. Pylons stand ankle deep, like ladies holding their crinolines out of the water. The Linden is fierce and high. A helicopter buzzes over to our left. Look down. Every ploughed field is silver-surfaced with water. The countryside is brim-full, with more rain forecast, more flood warnings in place. Where will it end? What if all the rivers in England burst their banks? All the rivers in the world? What will we do? Oh, what will we do? Houses on stilts are discussed as a possibility. But even if we built our houses with chicken legs and ran away like Baba Yaga's hut, where is the *away* we could run to in a flooded world?

But look – a red kite! It hangs and tilts, forked tail fanned. There are sheep, and there will be lambs. The wild cherry plum is in blossom now, white and pink. Light creamy lakes seem to glow in the fields. Weeping willows brighten to gold, leaning across the silt-filled tributaries – the Marton, Whistle Brook, the Carding. The waters race by, the colour of butterscotch.

It's Shrove Tuesday. Lit-up slush flurries drift like smoke over Lingmorton, then briefly a rainbow appears. Before we even have chance to get out our phones, it vanishes. There's ashy snow on hilltops, as if to remind clergy everywhere to gather last year's palm crosses to burn for tomorrow.

Lent 2020 begins. *Remember you are dust, and to dust you shall return.* This time it's Father Dominic's turn to set off the fire alarm by accident. Knowing his luck, this fact will freakishly get caught in the wide-mesh net of Mother's memory, and she'll never let him hear the last of it. *Turn away from sin and be faithful to Christ.*

Miss Sherratt stands in the breakfast room of Sherratt Manor and looks out across her chamomile lawn. She trains her repristinated gaze on the summerhouse. It looks as deserted as ever. If she hadn't glanced out last night on her way back from the lav and spotted a torch beam, she'd have no idea there was anyone there at all. Not a police matter. But she'll have to give Father D a tinkle. Get him to go and have a word.

Back in her kitchen she gives her wireless a friendly pat. Poor old BBC under attack, licence fee to be scrapped. Do they really not know what a treasure you are? How we sat round you, hungry for news, for Mr Churchill's messages! Miss Sherratt has strong opinions about these young politicians setting about our venerable institutions. Despite what one reads in the *Sunday Times*, one holds to the unfashionable view that our peers are tireless public servants, not a bunch of idle scrounging geriatrics. Sister Sherratt – whose memory reaches back to before the NHS – has plenty of wisdom to share. She can remember her early nursing in pre-Welfare State Lindford. It appals her that things seem to be coming full circle in her lifetime. What next, pray? Disestablishment? They'll miss it when it's gone, thinks Miss Sherratt. But it'll be too late then.

'No, Leah,' Martin calls. 'This is non-negotiable. All phones and iPads stay downstairs in the kitchen overnight. Even mine!'

He hears the bedroom door slam upstairs. Good. That went well. It feels draconian, but he can't have her up all night checking the internet and scaring herself. Good thing she hadn't overheard his conversation with Archdeacon Kay just now. Lydia is absolutely fine. It's probably just a cold. But given they were in Italy over half-term, best to be careful. Queen Mary's have said to keep Lydia off as a precaution. Fourteen days, apparently. No, no, Kay's fine. She and Helene are working from home. What a nuisance. Take care!

Martin frowns. Given that Lydia was in school all day yesterday, and she and Leah are thick as thieves . . . What's the position here? he wonders. Better phone the school tomorrow for clarification. His heart sinks. He really doesn't fancy another tense exchange with Mrs Hill – not after the uneasy truce about Leah's 'School Strike for Climate' stance. He rings Father Wendy to check how they're doing over in Cardingforth, and to share his experience of the post-flood clear-up process. He'll be glad to leave his devices on the kitchen table overnight. Social media is too full of Harvey Weinstein and Jean Vanier.

The following morning, Mrs Hill tells Martin roundly that if he keeps Leah off school, it will be treated as truancy and he will be fined. Up on the Close, the Bishop of Lindchester has already had the first trickle of anxious enquiries about the common cup and communion in one kind. The World Health Organization is advising a 'state of preparedness' for coronavirus. Share prices slump on Wall Street, in Japan and London. In Korea, infections rise to 977. Italy and Iran struggle to contain the virus. Globally, cases pass 80,000. We must wash our hands. We must sneeze into our sleeves on crowded trains, if we have no tissues, and stay at home for fourteen days if we show symptoms. (How worried should we be?) The death toll in China reaches 2,663. In Italy, cases rise from 3 to 229 over four days. Parts of Lombardy and Veneto are in lockdown. People sing opera from balconies. There are cases in Northern Ireland. Tourists are quarantined in a Tenerife hotel.

For the first time Jane wonders whether to bother finishing her Josephine Luscombe lecture.

All across Lindfordshire we divide once again into optimist and pessimist. The optimists are not unduly worried. Apparently, it's very mild. We've probably already had it without realizing! It's only the old or those with underlying health problems who are at risk. The pessimists are watching the horror unfold in slow motion. They feel like that ten-year-old schoolgirl on the beach in Phuket, who had learnt about tsunamis in geography. Except the Brits on the beach won't listen to their warning! The government's doing nothing!

Time will tell who is right. For now all we can do is wash our hands and talk about it. We can't not talk about it, as we congregate in church or at work, in schools and colleges, in cafés and pubs, on buses and trains.

February draws to a close. Waterlogged fields gleam after sunset like brushed steel. It's a leap year. Over in the vicarage at Gayden Magna, Neil goes down on one knee and pops the question to Father

35

Ed again. Not because there's been a change in canon law to make marriage possible. But he wants Ed to know, all the same.

Ed smiles down at him. 'Know what?'

'You may *think* you've ducked the big fat gay wedding bullet, pal, but I've not forgotten.'

Oh God, thinks Ed.

'I heard that!'

A waxing crescent moon hangs in the electric blue dusk, with Venus bright above it. There's a stripe of rose gold along the western horizon and blackbirds everywhere are singing of summer. But this is just a lull. Third verse, same as the first, a whole lot louder and a whole lot worse. Storm Jorge is on the way.

MARCH

———◆———

Worm Moon, Part I

ell, March certainly brought breezes loud and shrill to stir the dancing St David's Day daffodil. By Sunday morning, the worst of the storm had died down, but there were roads blocked by landslips, and streams that burst joyously across country lanes as though the landscape belonged to them. Cables were down. There were power cuts. But miraculously, the derelict summerhouse at Sherratt Manor still had its roof on Sunday morning. In the lower pane of the left-hand window there was a green card. Miss Sherratt spied it when she opened her bedroom curtains. Good. Provided her system of signals was adhered to, and the carbon monoxide alarm she'd bought for Jack was used at all times, Miss Sherratt was happy to live and let live. And now the prinking and titivating for the Big Day.

She crossed to the wardrobe and began rustling through her dry-cleaned suits. Heliotrope or scarlet? Really ought to get rid of these jolly furs. But no charity shop would sell them – they just got ragged. Genuine astrakhan, sable, a fox complete with poor little dangling paws and glass eyes. What a ghastly race we are, when one stops to think of it. Lord, her mad aunts with their grebe feathers, those humming-bird hats, butterfly-wing necklaces. But soppy old thing that she was, she couldn't bear the thought of them being bunged in some landfill. So many memories. She plucked out the heliotrope suit – it was Lent, after all – and closed the wardrobe door again.

The main route between Gayden Magna and Martonbury was closed again. Neil Ferguson, licensed Reader to the Hollyfield estate church, did the wise thing this time round. He'd tested his conviction that flood signs did not apply to him during Storm Dennis, and ended up abandoning his Porsche window-deep in what had proved not to be a wee puddle after all. He'd agreed years ago to keep out of Father Ed's liturgical hair, so he set off in the courtesy car, resolved to attend the first place of worship he found open.

This turned out to be the tiny gem of a Baptist chapel in Itchington Episcopi, the one Neil had frequently cast greedy eyes over, in case it ever came on the market. Ooh, he'd up sticks from the Britannia Business Park in a heartbeat and relocate his business here! He went up the brick path between the tombstones and in through the porch. An electric organ was warbling. He joined a congregation of seven octogenarians, who greeted him like the little brother who'd emigrated decades before and they'd never expected to see again in this life.

The pew had a red carpet on – and a place at the end for your umbrella or walking stick. There was the *Baptist Hymnal* on the ledge, and one of those wee clips for your communion glass – non-alkie, of course. He checked the hymn board and looked the numbers up. To his delight, he knew them all from childhood. All those Boys' Brigade parade services had not been wasted. Number 334: 'Blessed Assurance, Jesus is Mine!'

I will admit, for all his good intentions, Neil's attention wandered during the long stream-of-consciousness intercessions. He opened his eyes. Sunlight streamed through the windows. The pastor had reached Kenya now, locust plagues, famine. Neil could see ivy tendrils scrolling up the window frame, bird shadows flitting past. He clamped down on a yawn, and began a sneaky read of the next hymn, number 337. 'I know not why God's wondrous grace to me has been made known!' In the pause between prayers, there was the tick of the chapel clock. Measuring the steady seconds, tick-tock, since before these oldies were youngsters.

Suddenly he felt all the decades of prayer crowd in on him, the ghosts of all the hymns ever sung here, all the deacons' meetings, baptisms, Lord's Suppers, weddings – and then came a heart-breaking sadness. They love their Lord, he thought. They love this special place. But it's going to close. Some greedy bastard like me will snap it up and convert it. What we need is a revival in this country. Like the pastor was praying right now. But would it come in time? Sometimes Neil wanted to give the Lord a shake. He stared at the hymn: 'But "I know whom I have believed, and am persuaded that he is able to keep that which I've committed unto him, against that day"'. Aye, he is able, bad man. I'm the one that needs a shake.

March 1st 2020

It is a new month (March) so that means . . .

A NEW FULL MOON! Yay! 😄😄

Goodbye and good riddance to the STORM MOON!!! Lol. Storm Jorge (pronounciation Hor-hay) meant hardly anybody came to the service this morning where the Cathedral Girls Choir were singing YET AGAIN!!! In warm-up Mr Hardman-May said THE CURSE OF THE NEW JACKS ANTHEM in a movie trailer voice. We were literally ROFL in the vestry and Ellie had to go to the toilet super quick. Bishop Matt roled his eyes, he said well looks like you get the choir you deserve, Freddie.

   To be fair some people came, eg Leah and mum was their, so was Jane and Star who cuts me and mums hair but not Leahs, she goes to Gorans and gets a buzz cut. It was the service for the new parish nurses, and I am sad for Father Dominic, because it is his dream ☹ Miss Sherratt herself aka Tinkerbell was there. Mr Hardman-May when he said it instantly went I should totally not of told you that girls, delete it from your memory! But . . . TOO LATE!!!! Ha ha ha! When Father Dominic said a round of applause for Miss Sherratt Ellie whipsred 'Clap if you believe in fairies!!!!' and Mr H-M shot us with his finger because we couldn't stop laughing. But it is totally his own fault.

Moon Facts

1. Tonight the moon is First Quarter (33%) it is 5.7 days old.

2. Moon rise 09.33 moon set 00.03.

3. Moon distance 397,841km.

NAMES FOR THE MARCH FULL MOON

So March will be another SUPERMOON clouds permiting. There are many and various full moon names like I wrote before, the most common one for March is WORM MOON, but I am going with LENTEN MOON because it is now Lent in the C of E when all is said and done. Plus worms are icky, even if they play a vital roll in the soil ecosystem by recycling organic material blah blah blah (says guess who lol). Leah then preceeded to read me all these gross worm facts, like how they mate, and I was screaming, EW that is gross Leah, I'm actually going to be sick here, and she said, its not gross, FYI sexual reproduction is a totally natural thing. Then dad made her shut up FORTUNATLEY.

LOL LOL LOL she just came into my room and said Guess what, I'm making us SPAGGETTI WORMS for dinner!!! She did her evil overlord laugh MWA HA HA! Then she went, seriously though Jess, it is not gross and if theres anything you want to ask me about puberty and stuff, you can totally ask me. And I went Thanks.

PS Obvs I am not going to ask her, we allready did it PHSE, but it was kindly meant.

PPS She has her issues, but she is a pretty cool big sister, she looks out for me 😄

PPPS plus she is a good cook for a vegan.

Poor old Father Dominic. I'm sad for him too. This was the biggest service he'd planned since the Santa Lucia extravaganza of last December, with one thousand Christmas lights lining the old pilgrim route through Lindfordshire, and a trailer load of light-bearing maidens riding through the streets. He needed a little lie down after *that*, believe me.

This day had been even longer in the planning, but Father Dominic has more Tigger than Eeyore in his DNA, and he was philosophical about Storm Jorge. His two parish nurses, Madge and Lesley, were duly licensed by the Bishop of Barcup, in their retro bespoke *Call the Midwife* capes and hats (Father Dominic can never resist a trip to the ecclesiastical outfitters). Though he said it as shouldn't, the liturgy was a triumph. He'd enjoyed pulling together a suitable form of words. Jane had been full of her usual helpful suggestions. 'Bless these nurses to our use, and us in your service.' 'In a world where so many parishes go without, we give thanks that *we* have *two* nurses.' Yes, all right, fuck off now, dear. Numbers had been down, yes, but it had all gone off beautifully, with their glorious benefactress Tinkerbell – a vision of lilac loveliness – leading the prayers, the girls' choir singing like little angels, and the Prosecco corks flying before the procession reached the sacristy, as is only proper. (Prosecco in Lent, Father?! Why yes! Sunday is a feast day.)

There were flowers in church too, I'm afraid. Just a bunch of garden primroses in a tiny vase at Our Lady's feet. Gladys of the flower guild was about to sweep them away in horror, but Dominic forbade her. Star, the junior stylist from Hair Works, brings flowers every week, lights a candle, and kneels. Sometimes sunlight comes in through the side window and lights her hair like a turquoise candyfloss halo as she prays. Dominic sees her lips moving and longs to know what she's saying, but he never asks.

He didn't ask what Madge was praying either, as she sat there in the Lady Chapel looking up at the statue, while the glasses were chinking at the back of church. Was she all right? She was so still, almost another statue herself, in her new uniform.

Madge wasn't praying exactly. She was still rather new to all this high-church stuff. The Pentecostal church of her childhood hadn't been big on Mary. And this statue! Classic English Rose. Left her cold. 'She is holding out her son to the world,' Father Dominic had said. Suggested she and Lesley pray and light a candle each time they visit. That was his image for what the parish nurses would be doing – holding out Christ to a needy world. So that's my template? Right. Madge frankly hadn't had the energy for yet another of *those* conversations. Tiptoeing round his feelings, as though offending him was a bigger offence than . . . Oh well. Another time. He was a lovely man, bless him. Not his fault old Jorge had brought down the overhead power lines and prevented her relatives coming up to support her. She'd been looking forward to the bishop getting a spot of holy heckling in his sermon!

You need this, she reminded herself. You know that voluntary work and gardening never quite filled that nursing-shaped hole. Remember that day when Father Dominic came along with his scheme? Ding! The world suddenly lit up. Coming out of NHS retirement to a brand new vocation, a new calling. Working with Lesley in the local schools, visiting the housebound, staffing the little health advice stall in the covered market.

43

But that was last June. What about now? Madge had been keeping an eye on the spread of COVID-19. Something in her wanted to shout, 'Hang on a minute – I did not sign up for this!' Except she just had, hadn't she? Been blessed by the bishop and everything. Huh. A fine time to pick a new vocation.

She got to her feet. There was the box of candles waiting. Take the light and share it. Take Christ into a needy world. All right, all right. I just wish my folks were here. She lit a candle and wedged it in the stand among the others. She glanced up at the pastel template of her new vocation. Great. Now she'd got Kenny Rogers in her head. 'Well, you picked a fine time to call me, Lucille.'

Madge turned abruptly.

'Oof!'

No! There was a brief flailing of arms. Madge seized a lilac coat sleeve. Heaved the figure upright again. Lord, don't let the Queen Mother have heard that Lucille thing.

'*So* sorry, Miss Sherratt. Didn't see you there.'

'Yes, I'm rather easy to miss, aren't I?' Miss Sherratt patted herself back into order and beamed a horsey smile.

'Ha ha! Um . . .' Help.

'Are you all right, my dear?'

Madge turned back to the statue. Blinked back tears. 'Oh, I'm . . . sizing the job up. Right. I'd better . . .'

She made to slip away, but the older woman laid a hand on her shoulder. 'Wait.'

They stood a moment without speaking, looking at the flickering candles. Out of the corner of her eye, Madge could see Miss Sherratt's lips moving. Then she crossed herself and gave Madge a brisk pat.

'Good. Good. That's it. We pray and then we serve, Nurse Williams. Now go and get yourself some bubbly. Shoo!'

Miss Sherratt is a force to be reckoned with. She bent Bishop Matt's ear about intincting (filthy habit). He and Bishop Steve should be introducing communion in one kind immediately, ordering the use of hand sanitizers at the altar as a precaution, as they'd done in previous epidemics. Forward planning, Bishop. She informed Jane (sitting beside her on the front row like a proper bishop's wife for once in her life) that she'd heard all about Jane's research and forthcoming trip to the States, and was available for a conversation about Josephine Luscombe's nursing legacy in pre-NHS Lindfordshire, should Jane wish to call for tea sometime.

'When I grow up, I'm going to be a hatchet-faced old besom too,' says Jane in the car home. 'Forward planning, Bishop. Chop-chop. No more of this double-dipping in the chalice.'

'House of Bishops is taking advice from the chief medical officer,' replies Matt. 'There'll be an announcement, I expect. Sharing the Peace is a far bigger risk, to be honest.'

'Combine that with "social distancing" and you've got the introvert's dream church.'

'Well, the extroverts have had their way up till now.'

Matt drives them through the waterlogged world in the episcopal Skoda Superb, because this is work. (The sporty black Mini is now Jane's to drive like a nobhead girl racer.) It's a bright day. Snow lingers on distant peaks, and the north side of each roof is still white with frost. The Marton rushes in blinding meanders through glassy meadows. All the lane edges are eroded. On either side, there are submerged fences.

'Welcome to the Lindfordshire Everglades National Park. Look! Lambs!' They totter on black-stockinged legs beside their ewes. The pussy willows are fuzzed with yellow. 'Nearly spring. I'll stop being an old misery when the clocks go forward,' she promises him.

Matt reaches over and squeezes her thigh. 'Don't go changing,' he sings, 'to try and—'

'What do you mean, you don't want clever conversation?' she interrupts. 'That's my entire modus operandi.'

They pass the sign to Cardingforth. Giant shadows from the cooling towers lie in long bands across the landscape. Jane thinks of all the sandbagged doorways. Skips full of carpets. Thank God her own house is up a hill. Hadn't even crossed her mind to worry about that when she'd bought it back in the 90s. Three hundred yards farther down Sunningdale Drive and she'd be struggling to rent it out now.

What a grim year. Bush fires, storms, floods, plagues of locusts, epidemics. Certainly looks like old Gaia is giving her mighty hide a twitch to dislodge the gadfly human race. That said, the roadside is a glory of daffodils. And look, there's a second field full of lambs. The canal lies like a ruler of sky across the fields. Round the next bend is the Anglers' Arms. Scene of their first date.

'I know,' says Jane. 'What about a pub lunch as a reward for being a model Mrs Bishop?'

Matt smiles. 'Already booked.'

Jane laughs her filthy laugh. 'Now that's what I call forward planning.'

They pull into the car park. In the distance, flocks of crows drift down on to a ploughed field among the whirling bird-scarers.

Miss Sherratt pays the cabbie lavishly and heaves herself out of the taxi. Steady as she goes! She's three sheets to the wind after a nice pub lunch of her own with Father Dominic, his mum and both parish nurses; but she steers majestically into the harbour of her front porch without shipwrecking herself on any low-lying planters. She rummages for her key in her crocodile handbag. The taxi is still there on her drive. She glances round and sees the cabbie wringing his hands as he sits. Hand sanitizer. Sensible chap. At least *somebody* is taking this seriously.

I'll tell you someone else who is taking this seriously: the other Mr Hardman-May. I admit I don't know much about house-buying, but even I realize that to go from having your offer accepted to picking up the keys to your new house in twenty-one days is little short of a conveyancing miracle. Despite cautioning Freddie to hold his horses, Ambrose has been busy since the middle of last month, calling in favours and, by patient polite persistence, making it easier for people in the Lindford business community to do what he wanted than not to. It was a question of making sure his stuff was at the top of the right pile in the right office at the right time – and praying nothing dodgy came up in the survey.

Like the Rogers family, the Hardman-Mays have a 'devices down-stairs overnight' rule. This is a good rule. I admire this rule, although

I don't adhere to it myself. It stops us checking news channels in bed, and watching the national id frolicking naked in the witches' Sabbath of social media, and generally making our cortisol levels spike just when we should be winding down to sleep. But abiding by the 'no phones in bed' rule doesn't mean that you are automatically granted a quiet night and a perfect end.

Ambrose can't sleep.

It's now 6 March. Friday. On Monday, he'll pick up the keys. Some superstition made him decide not to tell Freddie until he could hand the bunch over with a ribbon attached. Ambrose can see what he's doing here. He's going to make it look like he planned it as a surprise, to deflect Freddie from the truth: after nearly three years of marriage, Ambrose still can't one hundred per cent relax into treating his husband like an adult.

The cathedral clock chimes midnight. Ambrose can hear Freddie's light breathing. Alfie is lying across their feet. That's one battle Ambrose lost. The small room is too full of man and dog. If Ambrose stretches, he can almost touch either wall. He props himself on an elbow and looks out across the jumbled roofs of the Close. There's a bright half of moon in a fuzz of frosty clouds, and bright glints of stars.

It's coming. He knows it's coming. London Book Fair cancelled. The rest will go like dominoes. First panic-buying has started. Hand sanitizers, tissues, loo roll. Freddie teaching his girl choristers to sing for twenty seconds as they scrub their hands ('I'm gonna wash that man right outa my hair'). All this talk of herd immunity, control, contain. Ambrose finds himself remembering foot and mouth, back in 2001 when he was seventeen. The culls. Bonfires. That smell. Soldiers digging graves. Exclusion zones – he sees himself wrapping gate after gate with yellow *Keep Out* tape. People out for a country walk just not *getting* it. The impact on tourism, on farmers – his own family included. And the silence of the countryside that whole summer.

One thing's for sure: no way is he spending weeks – months? – cooped up here, working from home with a lunatic dog and hyperactive husband. Freddie will be bouncing off the ceiling after forty-eight hours. No. He's already booked the day off work. Moving date is next Friday. He'll tell Freddie when he hands him the keys.

In another house over in Lindford, Ambrose's cousin Chloe is sleepless too, and looking at the moon through her bedroom window. She's waited almost a whole month, like Sarah had wisely counselled. Don't rush in. This is not one of your humanitarian missions to save humankind, Chloe. Do your research. Check with your GP. Think how you'll play this with your family. At work. How resilient are you? Can you cope with negative reactions and shaming? If you're going to get cold feet, get them on your own, Chloe. Cruel to raise their hopes, then back out.

In the distance she can hear music from the clubs. A house alarm going off. She's done her research. Podcasts, journal articles, blogs, scientific papers. Technically, it would be a virgin birth, ha ha! Plenty of boyfriends over the years, but nice girls saved themselves for the wedding night in Mum's book (which was Granny's book, and nobody argued with Granny Gno!).

This is not me trying to save humankind. This is me wanting to be a mum before it's too late. So why am I waiting?

The cathedral clock chimes one. Ambrose finally drifts asleep. Downstairs, on the baby grand piano, two phones vibrate in the dark.

Worm Moon, Part II

Leah is sitting outside Mrs Hill's office on Monday morning. It's like old times, when she was sent to Mr Crowther's for being rude and silly in assembly back at Cardingforth Primary. Leah is not being rude and silly this morning, but she is wearing a surgical face mask and latex gloves, which she declined to remove when Mrs Jessop, her form teacher, told her to. As this is her third Pink Slip misdemeanour this term, it has been automatically escalated to the Head.

Here is Mrs Hill's PA now. Leah gets up and follows her into the Head's office.

Mrs Hill finishes an email, then turns. 'So, Leah. Would you like to explain?'

Leah glares at the Head over the top of her mask. She exercises her right to remain silent. Mrs Hill very nearly exercises her right to sarcasm. *Very sustainable – single-use face masks and disposable latex gloves!*

'Look, I can understand why you're anxious, Leah. These are challenging times for everyone. But Mrs Jessop is right. So long as we're all washing our hands and being careful about covering our nose and mouth when we cough and sneeze, we're doing all that's necessary.'

More glaring.

'Leah, you do realize there's no scientific evidence masks protect you?'

'They're to protect *others*, not the wearer, for your information. People wear them in the Far East when they're ill, so other people don't catch it.'

'I see. And *are* you ill, Leah?'

'I have a cough.'

'If you're ill enough to need a mask, can I ask why you're in school?'

'Oh, I have to come to school, Mrs Hill. Because each day's learning is important for my life chances and my potential to go out and change the world.'

Mrs Hill stares. Nothing feels real. The Year 9 from hell mock-quoting her – no spare bandwidth to react! It's 9.25 a.m. and things have already gone ballistic. Staff calling in sick and having to isolate, supply teachers ditto, anxious parents demanding to know why she hasn't closed the school. Not to mention keeping up with briefings and directives, scrambling a switch to online teaching, and worrying what the hell's going to happen with exams. Frankly, her favourite thorn-in-the-flesh is barely on the radar.

A knock at the door. The PA looks in. 'Sorry to disturb you, Mrs Hill. I've got the Head of Governors on the line.'

'Thanks, Caroline.' Mrs Hill picks up the receiver. 'Leah, I haven't got time for this now. Go and see Miss Logan.'

I daresay my readers don't have time for this right now, either. I left you hanging after those two phones buzzed on the baby grand piano. *What was the message?* I won't toy with you by pretending it was NHS-NoReply telling them DO NOT go to a GP surgery, pharmacy or hospital if you have symptoms. The first COVID-19 text won't ping in until Monday, and we are rewinding back to Saturday, first thing.

You guessed right. The text was from Chloe. We will join Freddie and Ambrose after the first storms of happy tears have died down.

'Oh man, this is so . . . Ah, wish wish *wish* I wasn't going to London this weekend!'

Alfie has been shut in the kitchen, but he's still barking like a crazy thing.

Brose is giving Freddie the *I see what you're thinking* look. 'But hey, Dorian Singers? Can't disappoint the great man.' He stoops and grabs his holdall.

'Can we maybe agree some ground rules first, Freddie?'

'Naw! What? Why? Gonna miss my train. What is *with* you and ground rules?'

Ambrose does that *Eyes – look into my eyes* thing with his fingers, like Freddie's some kind of ADHD toddler?

He tosses the holdall down and folds his arms. 'Fine.'

Ambrose waits. Alfie is scrabbling at the door now and whining.

Ah, nuts. Guy always cracks him up. 'Stop trying to make me laugh, dude. So the rules?'

'OK. Two thoughts. First, can we only talk about it between ourselves for now? Just you, me, Chloe. While we're still deciding.'

'Deciding? C'mon! What, like we're gonna say no?'

'No-ooo, but Freddie, it's a massive step. We need to think what it would look like, long term. Your singing career, my job, Chloe's work—'

'Dude, we went through all this when we talked about adoption. It'll be fine!'

'This is different. Look, the whole Close is going to have an opinion. Do we really want their input? Because there's probably going to be a lot of negative judgemental stuff in the mix.'

'No way! Seriously? But this is such a beautiful thing she's doing here! Make sure you take her flowers, OK?'

'I know, babe. I will. But it's . . . unconventional. People will judge.'

'And? This is *so* not other people's business!'

'Exactly. That's my point.'

'Hnn.' Freddie rumples his hair. 'OK. Cool. I agree that rule.' He checks his watch. 'Look, listen—'

'Second rule?'

Freddie sighs and refolds his arms. 'Hit me with it.'

'Maybe *don't* swing by Chloe's on your way back from London and tell her we've agreed, and there's no time like the present—'

'Dude! I totally would not do that. I can't believe you're even saying this!'

Ambrose waits.

'Gah!' He ducks his head and smothers a grin. 'How do you even *know* this stuff, like, before I've even thought it?' He grabs his holdall, blows him a kiss. 'Gotta run.'

Ambrose catches his arm. 'Promise me, Freddie?'

There's Alfie still scratching at the door. Cathedral clock chiming six. Suddenly, shit gets serious. Something like a movie trailer flashes through Freddie's head – Chloe expecting, him trying to explain to Brose this total betrayal of trust? Not good.

'Yeah, OK, I promise.'

'C'mere.' Ambrose gathers Freddie into a hug. 'Thanks.'

'No worries. And just so's you know, I almost one hundred per cent would not have done that. It's just, man, you're always so fucking *cautious* about everything? I mean, if we're all cool with me as donor, why *not* start now? Coz it could take for ever? It's not like twinkle in my eye, boom! Ladies everywhere get pregnant. I mean, Chloe's what? Thirty-five, thirty-six? Shit, I'm gonna be thirty this August! Can you *believe* that? Thirty! Man.'

Ambrose rests his cheek on Freddie's head. 'Promise I'll still love you.'

'I've wanted this *so* much – to be a dad? From when I was little, way before I got that it was never gonna happen, because, yeah? So yeah. You know?'

'I know.' Ambrose squeezes him tight, then lets him go. 'Look after yourself in that London. Wash your hands. Don't touch your face.'

Freddie does his trademark slutty smile. 'Don't lick any knobs?'

'*Specially* don't do that.'

So Freddie goes to London for the Dorian Singers' recital. Ambrose goes online and orders a henhouse for the new garden. He rings home and begs four Plymouth Rocks off his mum as a housewarming present. And then, because he can't put it off any longer, he bundles Alfie into the car and drives across to Lindford, stopping to buy flowers on the way. Chloe is just setting out to walk Cosmo. They all head to the arboretum together. As if this is an ordinary Saturday and she hasn't just turned the world upside down.

'Is this too weird?' she asks. 'Be honest, now.'

'Well, it's pretty weird,' he says.

52

'You don't feel . . . I don't know what the word is!'

'Can't help you there.'

'Left out? I mean, it's because of the first cousin thing. It would be genetically risky, so . . .'

They stop by some exciting bushes so the dogs can sniff and wee.

'Yes, risky,' he says. 'And weird.'

'Very, very weird.' She laughs. 'OK. Well. I'm glad you think that too.'

'Plus Freddie's a whole lot better looking than me.'

'Well, there's that too.' She bends down to stroke Alfie. 'By the way, this is the exact spot where this good boy was conceived. I don't know why I'm mentioning that.'

They fall silent.

'I'm guessing Granny Gno will turn in her grave,' he says.

'So long as she stays put in there, we'll be OK, ha ha!'

'How's Aunty Claire going to react? But I guess you've thought that through.'

'Have I ever! Mum will just have to deal with it. If we get that far.'

'Yeah.'

In the trees all around, there are wood pigeons crooning. The Park Run is just starting. People are feeding the ducks. It's just an ordinary Saturday.

Far away, northern Italy quarantines sixteen million people.

Neil drags Father Ed to the reclamation yard to pick up a load of *perfect* teak block parquet flooring salvaged from an old church hall (reason not the need). Becky takes Jess swimming. Leah goes to karate to work towards her second dan grading next month. Clergy prepare their Second Sunday in Lent services. Bishop Steve works on his statement for Diocesan Synod in two weeks' time, because he won't have chance next week – it's the Northern Bishops' Mission. People with flooded houses go out to escape the noise of the industrial dehumidifiers. Father Wendy changes all the publicity for the Holy Week holiday club in Cardingforth to Scarecrows (her original Noah's Ark theme now seems tactless).

Northern Italy closes all schools, gyms, nightclubs, cinemas, swimming pools.

53

Just a Saturday in March, and all across Lindfordshire we get our hair coloured and cut, we go to pubs and clubs, plan holidays. Couples argue in IKEA, children go feral in Wacky Warehouse parties, gardeners pootle round garden centres. We play football, go to the gym, watch the rugby. Trains hurtle north and south. Planes criss-cross the sky.

Of course, we wash our hands. Our hands are raw from twenty-second scrubbing in hot soapy water. In public toilets, we engage in competitive endurance washing. 'Happy Birthday, Our Father' – front, back, between fingers, palms, tips, wrists, thumbs, repeat (in case anyone is judging us) – 'Happy Birthday to you, Amen!' We thrust our hands into the screaming jet engine that is the modern hand-drier, open the loo door with a sleeve or an elbow, job done. Off into the wide world to pick up a tray in a café or hold an escalator rail, press a lift button, grip a shopping trolley, scratch an ear, rub an eye, lick a finger to turn a page on the crowded train home.

We still keep going to shake hands when we're introduced to people. We remember just in time, and do an awkward wave instead, ha ha. Yes, it's meant to be serious, but it feels silly. It goes against the grain of British piss-taking. We sneeze into tissues (*Catch it. Bin it. Kill it!*) on public transport, in libraries, museums, charity shops, foodbanks, churches, indoor markets and shopping malls. We talk-talk-talk about coronavirus. (Wow! Northern Italy in lockdown now. That must be so weird!)

All the time, cases of 'It's probably just a cold, but' multiply. In far-off Italy, confirmed cases of COVID-19 jump from 1,200 to 5,883 overnight. The death toll there passes 230. Weddings and funerals are suspended.

Father Dominic adds northern Italy to his intercessions, and empties the holy water from the stoop by the church door as a precaution.

By the time Freddie is halfway to London, the holy dusters are wielding antibacterial spray on all the stalls, chair backs, door handles and handrails of Lindchester Cathedral. They will be back to respray first thing on Sunday, because the Lindchester Community Choir are in this evening to rehearse the *St Matthew Passion*.

The dean finishes saying Morning Prayer, and walks through the cathedral to the side exit nearest to the deanery.

The dean? Please tell us it is still the same Dean Marion we know and love? Yes, it is. Those of you who understand the inner workings of the C of E, I'm afraid this information will give you pause. Surely a woman of her gifts and experience should be a bishop somewhere by now? Don't say the cloud that hung over her after the Lindchester CNC fiasco never dispersed?

It did indeed disperse. I happen to know that Marion has been through three CNC processes of her own. In the first two, she was not the preferred candidate. In the third – nearly three years ago – she was. Our Most Reverend friend Rupert Anderson Archbishop of York got as far as making the happy phone call one Friday. But by then Marion was sitting with her husband in the consultant's room, reeling from the news that Gene had acute myeloid leukaemia, and treatment would begin on Monday. Marion withdrew her name. Now and then Gene still moans about this. His ambition to turn the palace of the Bishop of X (my lips are sealed) into a Berlin-style cabaret, with himself as Sally Bowles, dashed, forever dashed! 'Yes, dear. You do womble on sometimes,' says the dean.

Marion pushes open the cathedral door, glad to escape the hospital whiff of sanitizer. It still yanks her back to those chemo sessions, the horrible tunnel vision of those months, life lived an inch at a time. She fills her lungs with fresh air. There are daffodils on the cathedral lawn. She can hear the soft tooting call of a bullfinch.

Ah, folk are just trying to be upbeat, but it's like a slap each time someone blithely says, 'It's only the elderly or people with underlying health conditions who are vulnerable.' She's pretty much got Gene under house arrest. The first thing she'll do when she gets in now is wash her hands. The soap will sting in the cracked skin, reminding her that she's alive, that he's alive, that all time is borrowed, not owned.

Are we doing enough, though? This feels to her like the lull before the storm. If the virus was circulating for weeks in Italy undetected, how can this not also be the case in the UK, and across the whole of the EU? The whole world? For all the talk of herd immunity, lockdown has to be coming, doesn't it? Dear Lord, if we have to close the cathedral! We'll go bust without visitor revenue and bookings. Will it come to that? How can it not? There's a senior staff meeting on Monday. Jo, the new diocesan secretary, will be on it. She's already been warning them everyone will be working from home. But what would that even look like for clergy?

As she climbs the steps up to the road that loops the Close, Marion wonders if this will prove to be a severe mercy; if we'll look back on this as a dress rehearsal for a truly deadly pandemic in the future.

I'm conscious, dear reader, that we left poor Leah rather abruptly back there. By the time she knocked on the head of Lower School's office door, she was more than ready to take the stupid mask and gloves off. Her face was boiling. Her hands were sweating, and the sweat was getting into her eczema, which totally killed. Plus she was nearly crying. For no reason at all! She couldn't get Mrs Hill out of her head. Staring like that. On and on, just staring with her eyes all glassy, like she was having some kind of fit.

'Come in! Oh hello, Leah. Sit down.' Miss Logan smiled. 'What's the problem?'

Stupid tears. Leah ground her teeth. Hello? The *problem* is there's a global fucking pandemic happening, and nobody's taking it seriously!

'I expect that mask's hot, Leah. My dad's a surgeon, and he says they can get pretty uncomfortable. Look, if we maintain social distance, I think you're OK to take it off for a bit. What do you think?'

Leah removed the mask. Then she peeled off the gloves. The olive wood holding-cross clattered out on to the floor. She bent to pick it up. Something weird was happening. Like she couldn't see her hand properly, except obviously she could. Then when she looked at Miss Logan, part of her face was . . . missing.

'How's Luna?' Miss Logan was asking. 'I'm thinking of getting a dog. Do labradoodles make good pets?'

Leah went to say, *Luna's a companion animal, not a pet.* But there was a pattern in her left eye, bright, like a ring of tiny snippy zigzags, like goblin teeth in *Harry Potter.* Oh God! Now *I'm* having a fit too!

'Miss, not to worry you, but I can't see properly.'

My fellow migraineuses will know to be deeply sympathetic but not too alarmed for Leah. Miss Logan fell into that category. She was able to reassure Leah, find the school nurse to dispense her some paracetamol, and ring for Becky to pick her up. Well, she was able to reassure Leah about migraines. Pandemics, not so much. The stuff she was hearing from Dad was pretty sobering. Global share prices plunging, the whole of Italy was in lockdown now. UK cases rising: 319 this morning, up 46 since yesterday. Not looking good, frankly. If it weren't for the sheer number of NHS workers with school-age children, she'd be all for closing the school right now, if not two weeks ago.

Tuesday *10th March*

Tonight is 'FULL <u>WORM</u> *SUPERMOON'. I have decided to go with Worm Moon out of respect for Leah because that is her choice of moon name and she's been ill with a migrain, she has been sick and says it is the worse thing ever, you think you're head is literally going to split open.* ☹

Worm Moon

It is the Worm Moon because the ground is getting soft after the winter frosts and the worms are on the move again. Me and Leah will do some digging this weekend to make an allotment in the garden to grow vegetables and be self-sustainable, dad says we can and he will buy us seeds if we agree to do the work. I went Yay! Let's grow flowers but Leah said don't get me wrong, flowers are beatiful Jess, but we need to prioritise. Then she went, but we can if you want. 😁

Moon Facts

Moon age: 15.1 days

Moon Rise: 19:08 Moon Set: 07:21

I saw the 'FULL WORM SUPERMOON' after 'Sing-up' when we came out of the cathedral, 'Sing-Up' is the big concert for all the primary schools that do 'Sing-up' and all the little children get super-excited because the parents come. I remember when we did 'Sing-Up' at Cardingforth, it was awesome. Nowadays the Girl's Choir sometimes go with Mr Hardman-May in the minibus to do choral outreach but we did not go to Cardingforth. That would be so weird!!! Guess what, we sing the <u>exact same songs like back in the day!!!</u> *LOL.*

Afterwards we were waiting outside school for our mums and the moon was in two haloes, a gold haloe and a silver haloe, it was beatiful.

Me and Ellie sang 'Pokare kare ana' again, I did the top part, and Mr Littlechild who was also there went, My poor heartstrings! Then he pretended to have a heart attack and everyone laughed.

How light the mornings are now. The moon starts to wane in a cold blue sky. Jane sees it from her train to work. Her backdrop is dread, despite the coming spring. The conspiracy theorists are having a field day. Modern-day Gnosticism – only *we* know the secret truth. Helps you feel in control, probably. A hammer, not a nail. Doomsday planning is kicking in at Poundstretcher University. Technical learning support people, your hour has come! All those emails we deleted about Kaltura lecture capture and Skype for business! Yeah, we're crawling back now. Jane's head of department is in spreadsheet heaven. The US trip has to be dead in the water, although it's not officially cancelled yet. Pity she bothered buying that ESTA. And to think we worried about Brexit.

And we divide again. Tigger, Eeyore. Pollyanna, Cassandra. Freddie Hardman-May, one hundred per cent proof Tigger, is high all week. It may be Lent, but his veins are fizzing with alleluias for *the secret*, and the house move on Friday. On Thursday evening it's Gibbons, 'Drop, drop slow tears', and it feels all wrong. Freddie is a stunt kite freestyling high over Lindchester.

'Guys,' he says afterwards, as they head to the lay clerks' vestry, 'I know they're not advising it yet, but I just did an *epic* pre-Apocalypse chest wax?' He's in the power zone, doing 540 flat spins. Way down below, feet firmly on Planet Earth, Ambrose gives a tug on the lines. The choristers?

'What? O-oh! Did I over-share?'

I am the moon looking down on Lindfordshire. I can see the fields still ribbed with floodwater, though nobody is talking about that any more. Patches of blazing gorse bloom on Lindford Common. The air is full of the foxy smell of flowering currant. There are giant pincushions of mistletoe high in treetops, and silken trails of weeping willow lifting in the breeze. The blackthorn is out in the hedges. There's a fisherman by the Linden. Dozens of swans gather in Martonbury

Marina, and in an old neglected vegetable garden in Lindford, a homeless man starts to dig.

Flights to the US have now been cancelled. The first universities announce an end of face-to-face teaching. Ladies in the busy Lindchester Waitrose are shopping in gloves. Madge and Lesley offer advice to worried shoppers from the parish nurses' stall in Lindford's covered market. In the cathedral vergers' vestry, the hand-sanitizer dispensers are under lock and key, so they don't get nicked before Sunday's Eucharist. Ounce for ounce their street value is more than smack.

Tomorrow, on moving day, local and mayoral elections will be postponed. So will the London Marathon. Britain will move from the 'containment' to the 'delay' phase. Premier League football will be suspended. Great swathes of busy Outlook calendars will open up in the coming days, as events get cancelled. And briefly, it will all be weirdly energizing; briefly (for the lucky ones), it will feel a bit like a furtive sabbatical.

And the moon, nearing its last quarter, will ride round the sky, slowing us down, keeping us steady, face still bent patiently towards us.

Worm Moon, Part III

rains go to and fro across Lindfordshire on Sunday 15 March. Let's take to our moulting Anglican wings and fly along above the track. Just higher than roof- and treetop – that's my favourite altitude. From here, we can see enough to infer the big picture, yet we are still low enough for human detail. There are pink magnolias and pear blossom in back gardens, and the Easter blaze of forsythia. There are trampolines in ragged nets, closed patio umbrellas, rotary clotheslines. Beside streams, we glimpse the lovely drifty-waft of weeping willow fronds in the breeze.

The train below us races away from Martonbury now. This is the stretch Jane knows from her commute to work. Spirals of razor wire coil along a wall top. That is the Britannia Business Park; home to Neil's design company until such time as the perfect gorgeous little chapel comes on the market. Graffiti artists have been industrious along the trackside, though we will not see these nocturnal creatures at work. Let us put on our David Attenborough voice for a moment and ponder the expense of their materials, the risk to life as freight trains rumble by. What drives them to spray these huge bulbous or jagged tags? Some are veritable works of art with love poured in, others mere hasty scrawls. I exist, they all seem to say. I was here. This is my patch. I am hammer, not nail.

Jane was unplugging her work laptop after her 3 to 5 p.m. seminar (as sparsely attended as you might imagine), when some presentiment overshadowed her. I won't be back here for a very long time. She crossed to her window in the Fergus Abernathy building and looked out across Lindford. It lay spread below her. True, the official line was that the university would continue face-to-face teaching on campus for two more weeks, then switch to online in the final week of term. But each day, as the coronavirus update pinged into her inbox, Jane was less confident this was going to happen. Other universities had already announced campus closures.

She watched a train pull out of the station. People milling about like little beetles. Students. *Big Issue* seller. Cars. Buses. Town hall, old town hall. Spire of Dom's church. The arboretum trees over to the left. To the right, the gentrified Lindford Riverside. In the twenty-odd years she'd worked for Poundstretcher, she'd seen this view change from the death throes of heavy industry to derelict wasteland to partial regeneration. It was meant to be an academic stepping-stone, but here she still was, cynical and semi-detached.

Well, semi-detached until this term. Even Jane could see that this was no time to be pissy and uncollegial. It was all hands on deck, reassuring panicky students, scrambling to work out what exams and graduation might look in These Unprecedented Times. Finally, I'm a team player! *And* a bishop's wife. The kind of person who meets High Sheriffs and Vice Chancellors socially. Bloody Nora.

Jane lingered, staring out. Daylight was fading. There was nobody to mark this moment with – if indeed it turned out to be A Moment. Her one real pal in the faculty, the person who would immediately get it, was Spider, and he wasn't in on Fridays. The only History colleague who'd still be in her office on Level 6 at this time on a Friday was Jane's dear friend Dr Elspeth Quilter, queen of passive-aggressive timetabling, whom Jane had to thank for this late-Friday seminar slot. Collegial though she now was, Jane felt she could take her leave of Poundstretcher, nay, of this vale of tears itself, without saying cheerio to the Quisling.

She went back to her desk and unplugged her keyboard and screen. Was it overkill to lug these home on the train too? On any other Friday she could've rung Matt and asked him to collect her on his way back from William House. But he was off on the Northern

Bishops' Mission in Newcastle Diocese. Clearly, the C of E was less nervy than the universities. Maybe Dommie could rescue her. Admittedly, it was his day off (sorry, 'Rest Day'), but she could bribe him with Deliveroo or an offer of mum-sitting. She sent a text, then sat waiting in her office chair. Her noticeboard still had last year's calendar of New Zealand open at December. Photo of Danny's graduation – which she'd missed. List of useful university phone numbers. That Mars bar wrapper – hah!

She spun the chair and looked at the window. A pigeon waddled along the ledge. Waiting. We're all waiting. The slo-mo tsunami is still rearing to its full height on the horizon, she thought. The US had suspended flights from the UK and Ireland now, so even if Poundstretcher hadn't instructed staff to cancel foreign trips, she wouldn't have been able to go. She looked at her hands. What had she touched today? Lift buttons, doors, desk. Data projector in the seminar room. Was she already infected? Had she already had it – that cold back in January? We know the drill, but we still can't take it seriously. Witness the sneezing episode downstairs in the foyer earlier. There were cries of 'Bless you!' then 'Quarantine!'

Waiting for the next stage. Constantly checking news feeds. Braced, poised. So-called 'delay' phase, now 'containment' was over. We don't need lockdown like weaker nations; we've got the Ready-Brek glow of Englishness to protect us, so way-hey, let's all go to the Cheltenham Festival for a flutter on the gee-gees.

What would land next? At some point in the coming weeks, people over seventy were going to be asked to self-isolate, apparently. Well, good luck with trying to persuade the likes of Mr Tyler senior to stay at home. Also those with 'underlying medical conditions', whatever was included under that heading. God, poor old Gene must be really high risk, she thought. He might be her main competitor for the Most Shocking Clergy Spouse award, but she hated to think of a world without him. (Or his wine cellar.)

Her phone buzzed.

Dominic: Be there in 15/20min. Bringing mum. Pizza at the pally after? X
Jane: Deal. Outside sweet FA at 5:45? xxx

Bless you, Dominic Todd. Wait. How the hell's he going to navigate the coming weeks with his mum? He'll go bananas, having to explain every five minutes why she can't go out. Jane put her phone down. Another shiver of presentiment. What will happen to us all? Do I still think my house is far enough up the hill to avoid the rising waters? The pigeon was staring in at her like a nutter. Or like god. A tiny mad little god. Time to bury the hatchet, Jane? Get up, and go and knock on the Quisling's door, Jane. If not now, when, Jane?

Europe goes into lockdown. The UK goes to the races. Or Twickenham, or Murrayfield. Freddie Hardman-May gets on another train – to Barchester this time – for another Dorian Singers concert. This will be the last. The director has pulled the rest of the tour. Freddie totally gets it has to happen, but man. All his gigs vanishing like bubbles? St John the Evangelist in Handel's *Resurrezione* – pop! *Magic Flute* – his first major outing as Tamino in June – pop! *Please* let the Edinburgh Festival still be on! This is seriously gonna derail his career plans. His singing teacher (La Madeleine) has cancelled face-to-face lessons until further notice. So he's standing by for alternative virtual teaching arrangements.

A new word enters the national vocabulary: Zoom. Previously confined to retro ice-lollies and irritating C of E primary school worship songs (as if small children needed encouragement to zoom-zoom-zoom around the room-room-room), Zoom zooms from 0 to 2,000 mph in a few weeks. If only we'd bought shares in the company! Elderly parents – who hitherto had reserved their mobile phones in bottom drawers with flat batteries for 'emergencies' – surprise us by mastering the rudiments of Zooming, in order to bend over screens and allow their great-grandchildren an uninterrupted view of the tops of their heads.

Ah, those virgin days of Zoom, or Teams, or Skype for Business. With these platforms came the dawning realization that working from home did not mean we could let ourselves go, and live unwashed in pyjamas with half a croissant stuck in our hair. Those early meetings, where the first ten minutes consisted of: Is this working? Can anyone hear me? I can see you all – can you see me? Hello (excited waving). YOU'RE MUTED! There was many a gormless close-up and lingering cleavage shot, and hilarious experimenting with touched-up appearance and Golden Gate Bridge backgrounds. The mesmerizing sight of our tiny selves in the corner of the screen. (My hair's sticking up. Is my face really that wonky?) The thrill of seeing our colleagues' bookshelves and studies! Their coffee mugs! (And occasionally their children, dogs and naked partners.)

Ambrose, always a strategist and forward planner, arranged his workstation in the new house while Freddie was in Barchester. He placed the desk so that the wall was behind him and it was physically impossible for his husband to wander accidentally into the background of Skype sessions with clients. What a spoilsport. (In the weeks before the Hardman-Mays bought new curtains, their neighbours in Lindford, Miss Sherratt included, were rather more fortunate.)

You remember all this. You remember that weekend. Or you don't remember it. It was nothing special at the time. Perhaps you were off somewhere on a train yourself. Or out shopping, playing football, visiting relatives, going to the cinema. Like Jess and Leah (with the help of Becky, whose flat has no garden) you might have been doing some digging in the sunshine and seen the worms on the move. Maybe it was you who led that camping trip with a group of hyper primary school kids, the ones Freddie grinned at on the little stopping train to Lindford on his way back. It was gonna be tight, but Brose was meeting him, and they'd just make it to Evensong. He ran through Parry's 'Lord, Let Me Know Mine End' in his head. (If the Song School library went up in flames, you could probably reconstruct the entire repertoire out of Freddie's memory banks.) 'Thou hast made my days as it were a span long.' Maybe it was you who went through the crowded compartment of that train with the giant bottle of sanitizer, a squirt into each outstretched hand, while the children coughed and squeaked, impersonated the bleep of the closing doors, blew raspberries or played rock, paper, scissors and clapping songs. *Charlie got hit by a UFO, on the way to Mexico!*

Third Sunday in Lent. Maybe you went to church. Maybe you meant to, but then you rolled over and went back to sleep, resolving to make an effort next week on Mothering Sunday.

Chloe had a lie-in after her late night street pastoring, but she was there at the 6 p.m. mass. So weird, being greeted in the porch by the churchwardens doling out a squirt of hand sanitizer (yow, that stuff stung her poor over-washed hands). It was still communion in one kind, of course, and no Peace. Not hard to stay two metres apart when there are only seven people!

Afterwards Chloe went and sat in the Lady Chapel to light a candle and see if she could get her thoughts under control. Her head was cluttered with all the How-To tutorials she'd watched on YouTube. The fertility tracking, the awkward–tender–hilarious paraphernalia (soft cups, syringes, aargh!) and the staying-propped-up *logistics*. Was she almost laughing, or almost crying? Hard to tell. Did it still feel a bit sinful? Surely not! Ssshh! Focus on Our Lady, holding her son out like a gift.

Like I might be doing? No, not giving her baby away, not surrogacy, more . . . co-parenting? They were all adults. They'd work it out. Except, when it came to it *would* she be able to share, to let the baby out of her sight for one minute? Would a sword pierce her own heart? If there ever was a baby. Captain Careful was reading the entire internet and doing his relational risk assessment, his emotional number-crunchy stuff, love him. Physically restraining Freddie from buying all the baby toys and painting a rainbow unicorn nursery, ha ha! Well, let Ambrose do his thing. Let him take his time and *own* this. Maybe she could ask St Joseph to intercede for him? Joseph, patiently standing by, always a part of it while not being *biologically* part of it.

Here came Star from the salon, with her little bouquet. Sweet girl. Best scalp massages in Lindfordshire – must remember to book a trim. They exchanged smiles as Chloe left the chapel.

Father Dominic looked at his watch. Star was still kneeling in the Lady Chapel. 'It's OK. I'll lock up,' he told the wardens. Most of the lights were off. He sat halfway back and waited in the silent building. Outside he could hear the wind in the big trees in the graveyard. Then a bus going past, the rumble of someone putting out a wheelie bin for tomorrow. Car alarm. Music from the Abernathy estate. Siren in the distance on the ring road.

He didn't want to hurry Star. Well, that's what he was telling himself. The truth was, he didn't want to hurry himself, either. Mum was fine with Jane. A few more minutes' peace. I bet Mum thought that often enough when I was a tot. How the big circle of parenting turned!

He watched Star get to her feet and cross herself. She walked towards him, the light behind her, and her turquoise hair haloed round her head.

'I left her some violets, Father.'

'That's lovely, Star.'

'Will the church have to close, Father?'

'Well, we're waiting to hear. We might have to stop public worship for a bit,' he said. He switched off the last light, armed the alarm, and they went out into the night. 'But we'll stay open for private prayer. You'll still be able to come, don't worry.'

He closed the door, and locked it. They walked through the grave-yard towards the lichgate.

On Monday night we'll be told to work from home where possible. We've been expecting something like this. No unnecessary travel; avoid pubs, restaurants, theatres. Campuses will close. People in at-risk groups will be asked to 'shield' for twelve weeks. If anyone in a household develops a 'persistent cough or fever' everyone living there will need to isolate for fourteen days. Schools will close on Friday, apart from for the children of 'key workers'. So far, 1,500 people have tested positive, but lurking behind that is the shadowy other number, the guessed-at figure of between 35,000 and 50,000. Already that's too big. It melts into white noise. On the other hand, UK deaths stand at fifty-five on this beautiful warm spring day, with blackbird song, flowering currant, and lungwort vivid blue and purple. Fifty-five is sad. But it's small. We can still get our heads round it.

'Lord, let me know the number of my days, that I may be certified how long I have to live . . .' Freddie broke off. 'Dude, don't get me wrong, I appreciate how you busted your ass so we could move, only I'm kind of, Whoa! That was fast. We didn't get to say goodbye properly? To the Close? Like it was . . . I thought we'd maybe have a party, or. You know, not just . . . leave? End of an era, you know?'

'I know.' It was Sunday evening. They'd just finished assembling the henhouse. Ambrose put an arm round Freddie. 'Well, maybe we could have a housewarming. When we're sorted?'

'Awesome! We should so do that!' Freddie ducked his head and got inside the henhouse. 'I love this! Here's where they sleep, here's their little ski slope.' He made some chicken noises. 'So when are the girls coming?'

'Wednesday. It's OK, I'll be in.'

'Cool, yeah, you're working from home.'

'We may all be by then.'

'Not me. Not like I can be a waitron from home, babe.'

Ambrose hesitated. 'Freddie, you've got your head round the possibility of Vespas closing, right?'

Freddie stared at him through the wire. 'Well, whatever. Guess I'll do the garden. Paint stuff, look after the chickens? Could be I'm over-identifying here, but seriously, no cock?'

'No cock.'

Freddie shook his head. 'Man.'

Ambrose laughed. 'Trust me, the neighbours wouldn't thank us for the noise.'

'Yeah no, still though. Do you miss the bells?' He wove his fingers through the chicken wire and leant back, letting it take his weight. 'I miss them. In the night?'

'A bit. How about pizza?'

'Sure. Isn't this kind of small? Can we let them out in the garden? Like free range?'

Ambrose shook his head. 'Not safely. Foxes.'

'Really? Man, foxes are such dicks.' Freddie climbed back out of the henhouse. He latched the door shut. For a moment he stood, fingers woven through the wire again. He gripped tight. 'End of an era.'

'It's going to be OK, Freddie.'

'Yeah.' He let go. 'I guess.'

67

It was fast, that end of an era. A long time coming, yet it still caught us by surprise; water racing in behind us on our little island, as we stood gazing the wrong way waiting for the incoming tide. It felt untimely, like a ruthless stripping of altars one day halfway through Lent. *How doth the city sit solitary, that was full of people?* Every church in Lindfordshire. Every church in England. Doors closed. Locked. *The ways of Zion do mourn, because none come to the solemn assembly.*

In Lindchester Cathedral, they rang the bells down after Choral Evensong. The tumbling chimes dropped, dropped, like slow tears, one by one into silence. Then Great William was tolled twenty times. The sound spread out across the Close, like ripples in a lake, out across the Lower Town, the streets, trading estates, water meadows, villages, towns. Out. Out. Fields. Hills. The evening air, the golden hour when the sun has gone but the world is still charged with radiance.

In the heart of the cathedral, the girls' choir sang the ill-fated Jacks anthem one more time: 'God be with you till we meet again.' 'For these things I weep: mine eye, mine eye runneth down with water.' And the people departed in silence.

Worm Moon, Part IV

Gene heard them ringing the bells down. He was sitting in the deanery drawing room. It was Lent, but there was a bottle of 2008 Pol Roger waiting in the ice bucket. He'd selected the Sir Winston Churchill, because Gene was getting a distinct Second World War flavour unfurling in the complex bouquet of 2020 Britain. Marion would probably tell him that now was not the time for Champagne. He would counter with, 'Now is *always* the time for Champagne.' It was a hill he was prepared to die on – all the more so since the miraculous resurrection of his taste buds post-chemo. Even hen party spumante was to be rolled on the tongue and savoured! Well, nearly. (Well, no.)

One by one, the bells chimed themselves silent. He waited for the last stroke. That, surely, was it. But then, after a silence, came one more. And one more. Like Dame Nellie Melba's final farewell appearances. Gene broke into his warbling rendition of 'Home Sweet Home'. He'd only got as far as 'pleasures and palaces' when Great William began to toll, and realized that he'd missed the last chime after all. It was like waiting beside a deathbed, bending close to the slow rattling breath. In, out, pause. In. Out. Pause. Thinking repeatedly that it was all over, but then agonizingly, in . . . out . . . His first wife had finally died when he slipped out for a coffee. As if he'd been tethering her there by his watchful presence.

On mature reflection, while now was certainly a *good* time for Champagne, it was perhaps not the *best* time. He would save old Winston for Mothering Sunday, which was also Refreshment

Sunday, when he'd be able to bring pious reasoning to bear. This evening, he'd brew up a nice pot of tea instead, which was all his deanissima would really be wanting. If he moved fast, he could rustle her up a batch of scones. He whisked the Champagne out of sight and set to work.

'To every thing there is a season, and a time to every purpose under heaven.' A time to drink Champagne and a time to refrain from drinking Champagne. May the Lord grant us the wisdom to distinguish in these Unprecedented Times.

A time to break down, and a time to build up. All across Lindfordshire the latter feels appropriate. It is a time for neighbourliness. For reaching out, getting back in touch, affirming our colleagues. A time for wondering what on earth will happen to foodbanks and our local *Big Issue* seller. A time for sending parcels and cards. Texting old friends. R U OK? Setting up sibling WhatsApp groups to compare notes on elderly parents. And a time for retiring old feuds. Even Jane sensed that on her last day in the office. Later, working from her desk at home, she wished she'd heeded the mad little pigeon god and walked the ten yards down the corridor to make her peace with the Quisling. She is one good deed in arrears now.

Looking back, it's simple to spot the right moment for doing something. We may have realized it was time to rush out and panic-buy all the pasta and paracetamol, but other significant seasons escaped us. With hindsight, how obvious to identify this as the week to get a haircut, or to buy a set of clippers before Amazon sold out.

This is the problem with the Days of Noah. Even if some lunatic neighbour is building a large boat on the front lawn, we will carry on with our daily life, marrying and being given in marriage, until the flood sweeps us away. Because we simply can't believe it applies to us. Epidemiologists have been warning us for years. Leah Rogers was warning us back in January. Italy is warning us now, from their vantage point of two to three weeks ahead. But this is a week of strange limbo, of mixed messages. Of suspended public worship, but clergy still allowed into their churches for private prayer. Of 'stay at home' and 'social distance' but with pubs and restaurants still open. Of shopping for 'essentials' only, but having to make a judgement call on what is essential. Is this a time to shop for mini eggs, or a time to refrain?

Talking of Noah, little Noah Frederick, the canon chancellor's three-year-old son, patrols Cathedral Close proclaiming a prophetic word to anyone he deems to be at risk.

'BISHOP STEVE! YOU'RE OLD! GO INSIDE!'

Bishop Steve is taking a turn round the Close to clear his poor head. The diocesan secretary found she had no option but to close the diocesan office and instruct staff to work from home. Therefore Bishop Steve is not walking to William House for a meeting when he is admonished by young Noah. If you want to know what the bishop has been up to in recent months, you could do worse than check the website of the Diocese of Lindchester, click on the COVID-19 tab, and read his *ad clerums*. This is a Latin phrase which means 'to the clergy'. There is doubtless a correct plural *ad clerum*, but I'm afraid it lies beyond the grammatical scope of one whose Latin never really advanced beyond observing that in the picture is a girl, she is a small girl, the small girl is called Cornelia, and being endlessly amused by the word 'superbum'.

The bishop's EA, Kat, has not yet worked out that she needs to schedule down time between Zoom meetings and phone conversations. Steve is missing the equivalent of driving between appointments and services in the episcopal car. Hence the need for a stroll round the Close. As he walks, he weighs up his wife Sonya's suggestion that they invite the children and their families to come and stay with them in the palace, in the event of a total lockdown. The palace is vast, but will it still feel vast when populated with tiny Penningtons?

Thursday 19th March

SCHOOLS ARE CLOSING!!!!! Tomorrow is our last day of school!!!! Well, it will be our last half day to be fair, we finish at lunchtime and I will get the train home. Leah will meet me at the station and we will walk home together because QM is closing too.

It is so so wierd, we do not know what it will be like. We will be HOME-SCHOOLING next week, then it's END OF TERM!!! Yay!!! I will be tactfull though. Leah is mad because QM does not break up till a week on Thursday (aka Maunday Thursday.) Dad trolled Leah and me, he told us he is a key worker and we have to go to school. But then he went Gotcha! (Because he will not be taking advantage of it.) I laughed but Leah yelled THAT IS SO NOT FUNNY, DAD, she slammed the door and he went Oops.

Mum will be our home school tutor because she doesn't have a real job, she will come to dad's house to supervise us. It is all very amicable.

New term aka HOME SCHOOL starts on 20th April. The cathedral is shut too so no choir and no evensong. The 'Girls choir' prerecorded the DREADED JACKS ANTHEM so it could be in the Mothering Sunday Service which will be 'ONLINE' and then us and the 'Boys' all waved and said 'Happy Mothering Sunday!' so that will be online too. Mr Littlechild says these are unpresidented times but we can still sing every day and do our vocal excercises. Mr Hardman-May was crying and he went, we will sing through this, girls, and we will still be singing on the other side. And we were all crying too.

I will miss my friends ☹

<u>Moon Facts</u>

Waning crescent (24%). To be frank I am a bit tired of the Worm Moon so I am not sad it is waning. I am super excited for the next full moon, it will be PINK MOON yay! N.B. pink is my favourate colour.

Let us take a journey, dear reader. (We will deem this essential.) Let us shake our tired old raven wings – somehow, this is how I picture them – and flap ponderously over Lindfordshire. I'm afraid it's not all soaring on thermals, this flying caper. Sometimes we have to slog at it, holding on to the belief that we are clocking up air miles in heaven.

A bird's eye view of the diocese would not lead us to conclude that much has changed. The streets are still busy with people. The roads are fairly busy too, especially during the school run. The shops are open. From up here, all looks normal. But we are too high to see the detail. Swoop down and you will see how empty the cafés are, how the attendants stand in the doorway of Specsavers looking out because nobody has booked an eye test. Will they all keep their jobs? Will it mean a three-day week? Will they close for a month, take stock?

Most of the charity shops are closed, now that so many of the volunteers are isolating. Takings are down in all the shops. In Eden

Mobility, Cash Converters, the newly opened Lindford branch of Vespas, Debenhams, Clarks, Topshop, Greggs, M&S, H&M. And in all those little independent shops that line the Pilgrim Road up the mount to the cathedral. Business owners lie awake at night. How will they pay their staff?

What will happen to all the little stalls in all the markets of Lindfordshire, all the small businesses on all the trading estates: Lee's Workwear, Dale's Vac and Electrical Spares, NDF Design, Lindford Wado Ryu Karate Club, J&L Hot Tubs? What will happen to the sports and leisure centres and swimming pools, the libraries, the cinemas and theatres? The hotels, all the big blocks of student accommodation? The golf courses, the garden centres?

And the hospitals. The care homes. The crematoria.

The taxis wait, wait, at the rank. Buses go by almost empty.

If we flutter down and perch on house windowsills, we will see people working from home. Their heads ache from staring at computer screens all day. All those expensive ergonomic chairs with inbuilt lumbar support curvature are still in the work office, so the workers slump and slouch. They poke their heads forward and squint at laptops, because their posh flat-screen monitors are still on their work desk, not the dining-room table. But it's only temporary.

And we divide again. Tigger, Eeyore. Studiers of graphs, la-la-la lookers-away from graphs. Introvert, extrovert. The extroverts will only be able to live camel-like on their social humps for a few days before they start going crazy with hug-deprivation. The introverts were born for this hour. Jane enjoys her first Skype for Business departmental meeting on Friday morning. She knows she has peaked too early, and nothing will ever match up to the experience of being present yet unable to get the sound working. To see her colleagues' workstations without being able to hear a word they are saying! And, with a clear conscience, log off and drive to Martonbury Reservoir for a run.

There are far more walkers and joggers than usual. Everyone keeps their distance, but the greetings are warmer than on her New Year jog, even. It's bright and wild today. The water brims with blue sky. She hears the first chiffchaff and the joyous drum of the woodpecker. A flock of Canada geese flies over, with screechy honks and wings buzzing like freewheeling bikes. Hawthorn leaves juicy green, blackthorn blossom. Willows silvered with pussy willow buds.

Jane notes them all as she slogs along the path. There's a disconnect between the world and her feelings, but she doesn't know what it is, quite. Now and then she gets absorbed in her work and forgets the backdrop, but then she comes to: this is not a dream she can wake from.

She passes a family group, who stand aside for her. Loving messages shoot back and forth from eye to eye: *Stay safe, look after yourself!* All these flashes of silver lining. Neighbourliness, kindness, uncomplaining cooperation at Poundstretcher. Our poor planet getting a rest from our restless travelling and consumption. Fishes reappearing in Venice canals. But this is just the false glamour of novelty, thinks Jane. The much-touted Spirit of the Blitz we fetishize, when in fact the Blitz was numb misery and dread and many loved ones lost and no certainty we would win.

Nobody can see the far side of this, she wants to shout.

She feels like such a cheap, inadequate person, as if her responses are rubbishy replicas and not fit for purpose. (Argh! Should have made peace with the Quisling!) Maybe she's still not scared enough? Will there be a moment when we realize that all bets are off? There was a before, but this is now *after*.

'Miss Clarabelle Sherratt is isolating.' She says this out loud as she waits for the kettle to boil. It sounds like the title of a modern novel, one of those feel-good ones she can never be fagged to read. She will take her cup of coffee and little radio and sit on the terrace. No point lugging the old wireless out. Doesn't work. It's just an exhibit in the Sherratt Manor museum. Mother's famous thriftiness followed by Clarabelle's famous idleness – result: an unspoilt Arts and Crafts gem! If it ain't broke, don't fix it. And if it is broke, keep it anyway, *in case it comes in*.

Miss Sherratt claps her hands and lets out one of her squeaks of delight at the vision of all her broken things *coming in* at last, like a flotilla of merchant ships across a treacherous ocean. 'Home is the sailor, home from the sea!' And there are all the lost friends and loved ones riding the waves astride garden rollers and clothes horses, all waving. *Yoo hoo, Belle! Do join us, slow coach! It's such fun!* Well, the day can't be far off. Maybe this pesky virus will send her packing?

Except for the fact that *Miss Clarabelle Sherratt is Isolating.* She picks up her cup of coffee, tucks the radio in her housecoat pocket, and parades to the terrace. A green card is showing in the summerhouse. Marvellous! She can hear Jack digging somewhere in the old veg garden. A wren trills. The blinds are down in the house next to the Grindons' old place, as always. Is that a chicken she can hear? And someone playing a piano. Oh, I *say*! Stark naked! She gives him a cheery wave, but he whisks out of sight. The new neighbours. Lay clerks from the cathedral. Must pop round and invite them— Except one is isolating, of course. Bother.

She leans back on her bench. Everything is sparkling. In a moment, she'll have to turn the ruddy wireless on, listen to the news and spoil everything. Then she'll say her rosary. We pray, and then we serve. Perhaps prayer *is* her service now? She'll pray for those who can't pray. She'll pray for mothers everywhere, this Mothering Sunday, when children are being told not to visit. She will pray that the NHS will not be overwhelmed, that there will be enough ventilators when the hour comes. For nurses and cleaners and doctors, for hospital porters. She'll pray that hotels and student accommodation will be made available for the homeless to self-isolate. And she'll pray for the politicians, giving thanks for the chancellor's unprecedented intervention, for the relief it will bring to all those businesses and workers. She'll pray for the ill and the dying, the grieving, the feckless who still don't understand what lies ahead. And she knows she will not pray alone or in vain. The terrace is already crowded with saints; it is stiff with angels, with loved ones, all bending close, as the beads pass through her fingers.

'Man, I am IN LOVE with him, I can't tell you. I'm whoa, this is like, what, Tory socialism? Everyone's gonna get paid. Rishi and his incredible package. I— Fuck!' Freddie springs away from the window.

Ambrose pauses, mid-chord. 'What?'

'Tinkerbell. In her garden.'

'She probably can't see you from there.'

'Dude, she full on just waved at me!' Freddie grabs his dropped towel and wraps it round his waist. ''K. Gonna go and check the girls. Aw, can you hear them?'

They both listen. Through the open window comes the broody chook-chook. There's also a steady humming sound. Coming through the party wall. Like an industrial fan-heater.

Ambrose plays a thoughtful riff. Hmm. 'Let's call round on the next-door neighbours again,' he says. 'Take them some eggs. See if they answer this time.'

'Telling you, nobody lives there,' says Freddie. 'Blinds are always down. Let's go see Chloe instead. Take her some Mother's Day flowers? Aw, g'wan. See how she's doing? That's essential travel, no?'

Mothering Sunday 2020. The first Sunday with no public worship in the UK for five hundred years. I wonder how many bulk orders of daffodils had to be cancelled at the last minute. That was the first Sunday of Zoom, of services livestreamed via Facebook, of amateurish muddling through. It was the day we placed a lit candle in our windows at 7 p.m. to show that although our buildings were closed, hope had not been extinguished (until the fire brigade begged us not to leave naked flames unattended).

Oh, Times Unprecedented! Will we be remembered for closing our buildings? Or will this opening of new and virtual doors rejuvenate a declining church? It is not the business of this narrative to adjudicate on the rights and wrongs of directives and decisions. We must remember that we are finite, that even the wise do not see all ends, and instead leave all judgement to the Supreme Arbiter and Fount of Eternal Knowledge: Twitter. That is where you will find all the right answers, dear reader.

Ah, how we default to our factory settings in these days of Noah; how the secrets of the heart are laid bare. The worriers worry. The carers care. The ranters rant. The writers write. The piss-takers take the piss. The Pollyannas play the glad game. Haters hate, bakers bake. We all fall back on our preferred methods of fixing stuff. We are only trying to help. We are all doing our best, even if our best is dangerous, or draconian, cavalier, full of calories, and gets on other people's tits.

Like Jess, I am tired of the Worm Moon. By the last Sunday in March (did you even notice the clocks go forward?) it has all but gone. And with it, an era. Were we caught looking the wrong way again? Perhaps not, this time. Perhaps we stopped what we were doing on Monday evening at eight in order to find someone else to watch with. Maybe we felt a bit like an earlier generation of Brits, gathering round the wireless. Twenty-seven million of us, one of the most-watched TV events ever, all staring at those clenched fists on the desk, all hearing the same words at the same time: Stay at home.

Father Ed watched it with Neil. Bishop Steve watched it with Sonya. Jane watched it with Matt, Freddie with Ambrose. Others were alone. Father Dominic felt alone, although Mum was in the sitting room watching an old episode of *Call the Midwife*. He leapt up after the broadcast. His feet stuttered this way and that in his study like a cartoon character not knowing which way to run.

He forced himself to calm down. In a moment he'd give Jane a ring. Or Ed. Yes, Ed. Jane might be snarky, and he couldn't be doing with that now. But first, he'd step outside for a breath of fresh air. He paused to listen in on Mum. Terrible bovine groaning. *Well done! One more big push!* Another baby on the way. Yes, there was the little thread of a cry. Lady was in there with Mum. They wouldn't notice him sneak out. He pulled the front door closed quietly, and set off up the drive.

There was no moon, but Venus hung above the trees, incredibly bright. As he walked, he got whiffs of night-scented shrubs. A dog barked in the distance. He reached the end of the drive and looked right and left. Nobody. The underground river was rushing on deep beneath the road. He looked up. The church spire was black against the sky. Frozen in time, frozen in Lent. He supposed by now Star's little bouquet had withered. Our Lady would be standing there in the darkness, still holding out her son.

How bright Venus was, like the star of the Magi. Oh, I don't know if I can do this! Dawn on our darkness and lend us thine aid. Brightest and best. I can't do this. Lend us thine aid. Now, and at the hour of our death. Dearest heart, don't abandon us now.

He walked back to the vicarage, slipped inside and closed the door behind him.

APRIL

Egg Moon, Part I

We live in precedented times, dear reader. They only feel unprecedented because *we* have not lived through them before. There is nothing new under the sun – or, for the purposes of this narrative, the moon.

Oh, the moon has seen it all before. War, famine, plagues, you name it. I dare say George Viccars looked up at the moon from his cottage door in the village of Eyam, on the evening of that unremarkable day when he hung out his bale of London cloth to air in front of the hearth. We can Google and discover that the moon was in its last quarter on 24 June 1666, when the villagers went into voluntary lockdown. It was a full moon on 1 November when Abraham Morten died. All Saints' Day. He was the last of the 260 Eyam villagers to succumb, and the eighteenth of the Morten clan. I think we can say that they were all of them saints, staying put, locking themselves in for the sake of others. We know Abraham's was the final death, although it wouldn't have been obvious at the time. There would have been more waiting. More fear. More spikes of dread when someone coughed.

The moon rose and set above bustling Camp Funston in Fort Riley too. It shed silvery light on the city-like grid of streets, with the theatres, libraries, schools, stores, social centres, coffee roasting house, sleeping barracks. Soldiers drilling, relaxing, writing letters home. Maybe they saw the moon in the Kansas night through the infirmary windows, those first flu patients in 1918, lying on their metal-framed hospital beds.

Fly me to the moon. Let me see what the moon has seen; all the pale riders of history, mounted on their pale horses. China, five millennia ago. Athens, 430 BC. The Antonine Plague, AD 165 to 180. Plague of Cyprian, AD 250 to 271. Plague of Justinian, AD 541 to 542. The Black Death, AD 1346 to 1353. What more can I say? Time would fail me to Google the Cocolitzli epidemic, the American Plagues of the sixteenth century, the Great Plagues of London, Marseilles and Russia, yellow fever, polio, Spanish flu, Asian flu, HIV, swine flu, Ebola, Zika. What is the total number of deaths from pandemics? We don't know. The Black Death alone probably killed between 75 and 200 million worldwide, and thirty to sixty per cent of the population of Europe. How can we get our heads round numbers this large? What kind of yardstick is there? All our normal units of comparison are useless. Double-decker buses, football pitches, an area the size of Wales, to the moon and back. Suppose we ask instead: what is the mortality rate of our current human condition? Now, that one we do know the answer to: it stands as ever it did at one hundred per cent.

From the vantage point of the moon, we are very small. Our times are precedented. Our mortality is incontrovertible. However, our name is not Aiken Drum. We do not have the luxury of isolating up here, playing on a ladle. We live on the uneven playing fields of Planet Earth, in places fraught with crazy and glorious detail, with people to love or hate (and an infinity of shifting nuances between). Our lives are contingent on a complex web of happenstance. Yes, we will all die, but how and when we go still matters. Oh, it matters *so much* we can hardly bear it.

When we tread the verge of Jordan, bid our anxious fears subside. But what happens if the whole planet is hustled to the verge of Jordan at the same time? Who is left to bid our fears subside now?

We must love you and leave you, Aiken. We can't see anything interesting from up here. Even the Great Wall of China isn't visible from the moon. (File that one away in the cobblers drawer, along with bats nesting in your hair and catching COVID-19 from 5G.) Let's head back to earth, like a different Man in the Moon, the one who came down too soon to ask the way to Norwich. I dare say

Norwich is a splendid destination (if you avoid the cold plum porridge), but we are going to enquire the way to Lindchester instead.

After the first scramble for places, Lindfordshire – like the country at large – has settled down, as if in some vast communal air-raid shelter, with joshing and grumbling and the inevitable spats breaking out over other people's perceived selfishness. When lock-down was announced, they raced to the shops and lugged back carrier bags bursting with crisps, booze and chocolate in response to the subliminal memo – presumed to be from God or Downing Street – announcing the abolition of Lent and diets. We will join them in the heady era of online Zumba and Zoom cocktails – you remember that time? Back when people made sourdough starters and still knew which bin to put out.

Flying is exempt from lockdown. We continue to go where we please, dear reader. From vicarage to palace. From Arts and Crafts manor house to thin-walled flat. From closed church to rural river-side, where a heron stands patient on the bank. From overstretched hospital to busy crematorium. Our route will have little logic to it. I had a few plans for this narrative, but there is no plotline to 2020 apart from COVID-19. All I have is a line of words to follow, and my characters. Perhaps if we stay close to them and their stories, we will feel less abandoned. We might be able to catch hold of the coat-tails of faith and cling on.

April 1st 'PINK MOON'

It is April so it is a new full moon, the 'PINK MOON'. Pink Moon is Native American and we are not supposed to say it, because it is cultural approbriation. Says guess who. She KNOWS pink is my favourite colour and she ALWAYS SPOILS EVERYTHING I LOVE.

IMHO she is a vegan and you would of thought vegans could not say 'EGG MOON' even if that is the English name, it is illogical. I complained to mum. I love that Mum is living with us again. She is staying in the spare room because this makes sense, she is our home school tutor at the end of the day, they are not getting back together even if it is all very amicable. Mum said I know Leah can be a pain,

83

but these are unpresidented times. We must all bare with one another as best we can.

That is why I did not prank Leah back for April Fools even though she pranked me first, she came in super excited and went Jess, your sunflowers have come up! I ran down to the garden we've made and she was totally lying.

I had eggy bread for breakfast which me and mum made, we used the eggs from Mr Hardman-May, that he left for us on our doorstep from there own hens, then he rang the bell and social distanced on the drive. I SO felt like saying to Leah Oh what a shame you were still asleep when you know who came and brought us eggs, big shame you missed him!!!! It is nice to be important but it is more important to be nice in these unpresidented times, so I did not say that. Plus she probably would of slapped me to be fair.

Moon Facts

Pink Moon meaning

You would think the Pink Moon is going to be pink. Sometimes the moon is orangey red, right? Anybody would think pink means pink, they would not be a moron for not realising it means all the pink flowers and blossoms that bloom in April.

I miss my friends. There is no school because it is the hollidays for me. QM does not break up till Friday but Leah does exactly what she wants and mum let's her, and dad is out the whole time with his work or he would totally tell her to stay in Zoom.

I AM SOOOO BORED. It is pointless to say that to grown ups, they will only go I will FIND YOU SOMETHING TO DO. Like 'tidy your room'. My room is tidy it is Leah's room that's a total mess. I keep checking Mr Hardman-May's YouTube channel but he has not posted today. I wish we could keep hens as companion animals like him, he is so funny when he sings to them.

Moon Phase

First quarter (46%) It is confusing that it is called quarter because actually when you look at it it is more like half. It is waxing aka growing bigger, it will be full on 8–9th April right before Easter. This Sunday will be Palm Sunday when normally the choir processers with big palm branches all the way round the Close and the congregation all follow. We learnt the Agincourt hymn tune, it is very

84

ancient and the tune made me shiver, but we will not be singing it this year. ☹

P.S. everything is wierd, an owl is hooting in the garden and it is not even night time.

Oh dear. Looks like my poor Pollyanna is struggling to play the glad game right now. Maybe it's just because she's bored, she's missing her friends, and everything is weird. Or maybe, somewhere in the vast complex of Hormone Central, someone has just checked the puberty files and realized it's high time to pay Jess a visit and catch her up with her big sister.

I'm glad for the Rogers household that they live in a four-bedroomed detached house, with a sizeable garden. Not all our characters are so fortunate, and even the least fortunate of them are not too badly off in the grand scheme of things. But the grand scheme is not always easy to hold on to when we feel as though our own small schemes are being systematically thwarted.

Leah is out digging in the garden now (having substituted her Zoom presence in maths with an image of herself concentrating). The little strip they dug last month is fully sown with carrots and early onions.

And fucking *sunflowers*. Leah is determined to grow potatoes too. And beans. She is trying to dig with love and respect for Gaia, but her spade keeps hitting fucking bricks and rubble, which sends a jolt right up her arms, which is obviously not Gaia's fault. Gaia didn't exactly make bricks. Plus the earth is hard because there hasn't been enough rain. Everyone is excited for the lovely weather. Morons. Like climate change is going to say, Oh look, poor humanity are having a pandemic, time out, guys, give them a break.

Leah hasn't said a word about her cancelled second dan grading last Sunday. Not. One. Word. You'd think people would NOTICE how fucking mature she's being, but no. They probably didn't even remember it was her Big Day, because it's all about Jess missing all her special fucking choir services, isn't it?

If only she could go out somewhere. Anywhere! The arbo, even. Meet up with Lydia and hang out. Obviously she gets why she can't, she's not exactly stupid, even though Lyds probably already had

COVID back in February. Knowing Leah's luck they'll still be in lockdown on her fourteenth birthday on 15 May. And now she can't even take Luna for a fucking walk, because she's in heat and has to be kept in the house. Leah *knows* what Mum and Dad are thinking. Hello? That incident was nearly *four years* ago FYI. I can be trusted to be responsible for my own companion animal, fuck you very much.

And another thing! *Everyone* has TikTok FFS. It's so *embarrassing*. I mean, what is even the *point* of having a smart phone if your parents treat you like a baby? Leah, put your phone away. Leah, who are you messaging? Well, Father, mainly I am messaging random older guys who ask me to take my top off and meet up with them and I say yes. Duh. Like I don't know how to stay safe.

And now the fucking spade's fucking stuck!

For one second, Leah nearly screams. Like she used to scream at stuff and at people, before she learnt how to channel her rage.

Focus. We've got this. Breathe. *Zanshin*. Total awareness.

She hears an owl in the big tree. Sees the tree's shadow like a skeleton on the lawn. A bee buzzes past. Her hands relax. They let go of the spade. She turns. Breathes in. Earthy smells. The seed drills in lines. Wait! She squats to look – no joke, no April Fool! – she can see the first feathery tops of the carrot seeds. Very gently, she runs her fingers over them. And something inside her whispers, 'It's OK, Leah.'

Spring comes to lockdown Lindfordshire. It creeps across fields and along hedgerows and riverbanks. Sticky buds grope out pale fingers from their tip-tilted twigs in parks and gardens. Doves brood on branches. Even on grey days, the sun breaks through occasionally, and there are fierce glints on the dark water of Martonbury Reservoir, like stars on a frosty night.

Listen! The chiffchaffs are back. There are patches of violets, drifts of celandines. Owls call, night and day. Lindfordshire is quiet. Cars stay on drives. Planes stay on tarmac. The shutters stay down on shops and clubs. The municipal tips are all closed. Ducks and geese waddle through the deserted centre of Lindford as bold as any goat in Llandudno. But it's not as quiet as you might hope, what with lawnmowers and pressure hoses drowning out the birdsong, your neighbours having a BBQ and playing their music. Jays screaming in branches, children screaming in gardens. The roar of angle grinder and earthmover on building sites (are those workers *really* maintaining social distance?). And on Thursday nights at eight it's #ClapForCarers, just when you've got the baby off to sleep. How fast that escalated from scattered clapping to a cacophony of saucepans, car horns, fireworks. Roosts empty of panicked rooks, cats flee in terror. ('And damn'd be him that first cries "Hold!"')

Up on Lindford's Cathedral Close, the precentor's wife Ulli is notably absent from this nonsense. What is this – sodding Peter Pan? Clap if you believe in the NHS? *Um Gottes willen!* In Germany, we support our health service by funding it, not by clapping.

The rest of the Close plays the game. Even Gene (now shielding as well as isolating) comes and stands on the bedroom balcony in his lavishly frogged velvet smoking jacket. He gamely dings his Edwardian silver-topped cane on the wrought-iron balustrade.

'I like to imagine we're taking part in a global skimmington ride,' he says to Marion (also shielding, to keep him company), 'which will culminate in the glorious burning in effigy of Trump and Boris Johnson.'

'Don't.' Marion dings her wooden spoon. 'Johnson's in intensive care, and regardless of what you think of him, now is not the time.'

'Oh.' Gene ends his rough music performance with a jangling flourish. 'There. All done for another week. I'll tell you what this *is* the time for, mind you.'

'Champagne?'

'Brava! But *apart* from that, now is an excellent time to pick up a couple of dioceses on the cheap. If only we had some spare cash!'

Marion gazes across the deanery garden. The magnolia is almost out. Tulips blaze in the borders. From near and far comes the tink-tink-tink, the tonkle-tonkle-tonk. Someone (mercifully distant) lets out a blast on a vuvuzela. 'Look at all our beehives!'

'She says, deftly turning the subject. You don't need to rein me in any more, Deanissima. There's nobody to hear.' He leans in, leering like the Childcatcher. 'There's only thee and me.'

'Shall we buy another?' she persists.

'Diocese, or hive?'

Marion deals him a smart rap on the head with her spoon. 'Stop it.'

'One final thought: if this pandemic is the bishops trying to bury *Living in Love and Faith,* one can't help feeling it's overkill.' He dodges the second blow. 'Heavens to Betsy! I'd better buy myself a nice colourful fez. For protection.'

'If you carry on like this, you'll need a crash helmet,' says the dean.

Round the Close, the clapping and banging peters out into silence. Then come the calls of 'See you next week!', 'Take care!' And doors closing.

Gene and Marion continue to stand looking at the garden. The rooks and pigeons settle down again. How our worlds are shrinking, she thinks. Dwindling to the size our forebears knew. House, street, village. And far off the edge of our known world lies Birmingham, or London, where we have never been.

'There's only thee and me,' repeats Marion.

Gene puts his hand on hers. 'And all the company of heaven.'

She waits for the inevitable wisecrack. But it doesn't come.

The last tenacious events of summer vanish from the calendar. Lambeth Conference, Tokyo Olympics, Edinburgh Festival. Through some perverse piece of mismanagement, the hay fever season still goes ahead. We are warned not to confuse the symptoms with coronavirus. New etiquettes emerge. Amazon leaving parcels on the step, ringing the bell, stepping away. Deliveroo unloading our pizzas on to the drive. The new normal. Like livestreamed church. Like the long queues in supermarkets, where we encounter one-way systems and taped-out two-metre zones on the floor that keep shoppers safely apart. Woe betide anyone who forgets the spring onions and tries to backtrack from frozen foods. The dry goods sections still look as though locusts have swept through. No flour to be had for love nor money (unless you think to go to your corner shop). Even the lentils and wholemeal fusilli have all gone. A lone pack of organic wild black rice remains, like a sprig of bent watercress after a church bring and share buffet.

And the moon rides round us once again, waxing towards full. It has made this journey over 40,500 times since 1666, not counting blue moons. How much longer? When will it end? What will happen afterwards? Is that what Aiken Drum wonders, adjusting his hat of good cream cheese? Round and round and round, playing on his ladle, tink-tink-tink, rough music for the human race.

Miss Sherratt wakes at 3 a.m. Moonlight comes through the crack in the curtains. She can tell that all hope of sleep has vanished, so she gets up and makes herself a cup of Horlicks. The museum of Sherratt Manor is ghostly. All the exhibits are bathed in silver light. Very carefully, she wraps herself in a blanket, unlocks the terrace door and steps outside with her drink.

Careful, careful now. We don't want to trip. Somewhere in your early seventies you stop falling over and start *having a fall*. Can't risk that, even with her protective padding fore and aft. *Skinny women – bane of my life!* She can still hear her older brother Dickie saying it. Decades as an orthopaedic surgeon. *Don't go getting skinny, Belle. Healthy bones need meat on them.*

She stays on the terrace, though she longs to wander the garden among the memories. Ah, how the garden throngs with loved ones. But now is not the time to be pestering the emergency services through one's own selfish folly. The moon casts shadows on the lawn, even though it's not full yet. The stars are bright too. She still hasn't got over her delight at being able to see them again. Everything smells of summer, almost. But what a sense of pause, of waiting. And goodness, tomorrow is Palm Sunday. To think Our Lord would have seen that very moon, the night before his triumphal entry.

'The last and fiercest strife is nigh.' Yes, he knew what lay ahead. And so does Miss Sherratt, if the graphs are to be believed. The peak, coming over Easter weekend. She thinks of overwhelmed morgues and mass burials. Of exhausted medical staff. Of all the people unable to sit beside their loved ones. Of heartbreak. Of dying alone.

A fox barks in the distance. She looks up at the stars again. 'The winged squadrons of the sky.' Ah, she can never sing that line without a tear welling. All the pilots who never came back. How can I still be here? It can't be much longer now, can it?

'All right, Miss Sherratt?'

For a moment she thinks it's another waking dream – the borders are wearing thinner all the time – but then she remembers. 'Yes, thank you, Jack. Couldn't sleep, that's all.'

'Me neither.'

Now she knows where to look, she can make out his shape under the big cedar. The wind stirs softly. It sounds like the sea.

'If you need anything,' he says, 'I'm here.'

'Thank you. God bless, Jack.'

Later, as she falls asleep at last, she can still hear the sea through the open window. How extraordinary. It's not far off at all. It's just over there, behind the hill.

Egg Moon, Part II

The grains of sand trickle through the hourglass. Minutes, hours, days. If we pay attention, we notice the moments as they pass. Carrot seedlings getting a bit taller. Scent of grass as the council mows the verge. The moon waxing to full and the cherry blossom coming out. We spot hopscotch grids chalked in the middle of quiet roads. A hawk flies over, and higher still a lone plane passes in the blue. Somewhere on the far side of the estate, a dog barks, barks. Or perhaps an ambulance arrives in the street, paramedics get out in PPE and go into someone's house, poor soul. Rainbows appear in windows. The Queen in her green dress reassures us we will meet again. We can always try to be in the moment, be mindful, grateful. But what we can never know is how many grains there are left in the top of the hourglass. We don't know how to pace ourselves in lockdown. How to *be*.

This doesn't mean we don't know how *not* to be. We are quicker than ever to air our views and admonish one another. How can people go into their church building/not go into their church building at a time like this? Support/decry the government? Lambast/not lambast the bishops? Clap/not clap? In short, how can other people be other people?

Lord have mercy, we still have sharp elbows as we tread the verge of Jordan.

It's Holy Week. The sands of time are sinking. They sink at different rates, depending on how old you are. If you are three months old – as

Bishop Steve's youngest grandchild is – a fortnight is a sixth of your life. A sixth of Miss Sherratt's life, on the other hand, is more like sixteen years. Sixteen years is two years and one month longer than Leah Rogers has been alive. She *aches* to be sixteen. Her moments treacle past. Sixteen years is like *almost half* of Freddie Hardman-May's life? Omigod, how can he be so *old*?

The speed at which the sands sink also depends on what you are doing, and who you are doing it with. There are now three generations of Pennington living in the palace on the Close. Each hour might seem interminable (especially to the middle generation trying to entertain small people), but somehow the days are flying past. Can it really be two weeks already?

The palace household now includes Steve and Sonya, their daughter Hannah and her family (husband and two children), their son Dan and his family (wife and three children), and their youngest son Ben (separated from his fiancée by lockdown). That's a lot of Penningtons in one house, but they all get on. They are all churchy extroverts, so this feels a bit like a New Wine family get-together, only without the tents and mud. There's lots of friendly joshing round the big kitchen table at joint mealtimes. There are Bishop Steve impersonations (with tea-cosy mitres), and Post-it IOUs in the episcopal wine cellar until the next Naked Wines order arrives.

The palace is so vast that there are enough rooms for those working from home to get a bit of P&Q. Mercifully, there's always an extra pair of hands to grab the baby when the toddler goes into meltdown over the spaghetti hoops touching the fish fingers on the plate. And there's the garden, of course. Lawns, walled vegetable garden (sadly let go), orchard, the laburnum walk, the safely fenced pond, which used to be cathedral canons' fish stew in medieval times.

There are still spark points, and the odd outbreak of silent passive aggression over chores. These morph into competitive 'Brother/sister, let me serve you', before finally being repented of. A palace WhatsApp group has been set up to head off the major sources of logistical aggravation. Each day messages are exchanged:

Dan: Hey guys, just to give you the heads up. Soph and I are livestreaming our all-age at 10am in the downstairs lounge.

Steve: Hello everyone, I've got a House of Bishops Zoom in my study this morning.

Ben: Hey lovely people. Planning on recording a worship sesh in the attic 6–8pm ish tonight. Let me know if this works for you guys.

Sonya: Food's ready!

So, all is well in the palace. Bishop Steve never loses sight of his good fortune as he Zooms, writes *ad clerums*, liaises with Kat his EA, and makes pastoral phone calls to his clergy.

Shall we snoop? Steve is in his private chapel praying. This morning he's pondering his godly forebear, William Brownlow, the first Bishop of Lindchester to live on the Close, in what is now the cathedral school. Back in the 1860s, this constituted a major downsizing. Brownlow sold off Ingregham Palace, with its deer park and Capability Brown landscaped grounds, and ploughed the funds into projects to serve the poor. The Brownlow Fund is still relieving misery to this day. And what is Steve doing? Not that this house is in his power to sell, and even if it were sold, the diocese wouldn't benefit. Oh, how this pandemic operates like a searchlight, laying bare the cracks, the rift between haves and have-nots.

Steve prays for the Prime Minister in intensive care. He prays for the new Labour leader. That wisdom may be given to all in authority. But his mind keeps straying back to the footage he saw on the BBC website of a group of low-paid manual workers in India, squatting huddled together in a street, being hosed down with disinfectant by men in hazmat suits. After long years on the coalface of intercession, Steve has learnt that when his thoughts stray like this, it is not a distraction from the task. It is the task.

His English words run out. The Spirit groans with prayers too deep for utterance while Steve intercedes in unknown tongues for all the clergy and lay people in his care. For the haves, yes. But above all for the have-nots. And for those working alongside them, not hosing them down with policy and advice from afar. For Martin Rogers and Virginia, working so tirelessly in Lindford. All those folk across the diocese reimagining the foodbanks, the soup kitchens, school breakfast clubs, all the volunteers. The carers (Father Dominic and his mother), NHS workers, delivery guys, shop staff. The crematorium staff and undertakers. The new Nightingale hospitals going up, the grim sight of mass graves in New York.

It's Maundy Thursday. There will be no Chrism Eucharist this morning, no foot-washing and stripping of the altars tonight. He can hear the children playing under the chapel window. Sonya's got the paddling pool out for them. Splosh! Sploosh! The cathedral clock chimes the half-hour. This evening Sonya will join him in the chapel for a short act of worship. They will listen to an old recording of the cathedral choir singing Bairstow, and afterwards he will blow out the candle and fold away the cloth on his communion table. That's all. But it will be enough to break his heart. O Jerusalem!

Steve closes his eyes and sees the Indian workers again in the dusty street. The utter misery. Herded like animals. The blast of the hose from a safe distance. All they can do is endure it, until it stops. 'He emptied himself, taking the form of a slave.' The words form in Steve's memory. 'He humbled himself, and became obedient to the point of death, even death on a cross.'

In my mind's eye I see Steve's intercessions radiating out, like ripples in a lake, like the sound of cathedral bells being rung down, out across the Close, the Lower Town, the streets, trading estates, water meadows, villages, towns. Fields. Hills. The whole diocese, the nation, the globe. And everywhere there are other ripples, raindrop-rings of prayer, out, out, intersecting, never-ending, as the gentle rain of heaven falls, until justice rolls down like waters, and righteousness like an ever-flowing stream.

'Are you off to church?'

'Not today,' says Father Dominic. 'I'm just going to wee the dog. Here, Lady.'

'Shall I come?'

'If you like. We're only going into the garden.' Please don't come, please don't come. Just give me a few minutes alone before I try and livestream my little service.

'Oh. I'll just finish my Sudoku, then.'

'Goody-good. Won't be long.'

He unlocks the back door. Lady races out into the vivid scent-scape, hot on the trail of fox and cat. Dominic breathes in. Flowering currant and warm creosoted fencing. Another glorious day. He can see that it is, though it feels like he's watching spring through a rainy window. How the moments smudge past. This ferocious boredom tethering him to the here-and-now. There's a chiffchaff singing in one of the big trees. Leaves coming out. Before long, the tower blocks of the Abernathy estate will be completely screened off. Only his church spire will still be visible. Oh, my people!

'I can't help you!' The words burst from him. I have to let myself be helped instead. Let Madge bring our shopping and leave it at the end of the drive. Let Virginia and Martin take all the funerals between them. He's already poured all this out to his bishop. He wishes now he'd managed not to sob, 'You don't know what it's like!' Trying to ring round parishioners, or put together and livestream services, with Mother wandering about like a lost soul. Endlessly having to remind her that he's not David, her long-dead husband; he is her little boy Dominic all grown up. Round and round the mulberry bush explaining about coronavirus and lockdown. And above all, not to be able to minister to his flock. He can see the windows of their flats now.

It's Good Friday. How can he not be in church during Holy Week?

He wants to sob that even Jesus can't know what this is like! You never had to cope with a doolally mother in a pandemic, did you? Dominic bends his mind to that best of all disciples. Did Mary end up looking after St Anne? He sees her holding her son out. Ha! Maybe she's saying, Take him! For God's sake, take him, will you, so I can get a moment's peace!

And here comes Mum now. Slowly down the steps, holding the handrail that the diocese kindly had put in for them.

'What's that she's found, David?' she calls.

'What?' He looks. 'Oh Lord! Looks like a dead pigeon. Lady, *leave*!' He hurries over the lawn. The dog noses about in the explosion of feathers. 'Leave it!' He hauls her off by the collar.

Mother joins him. They stare down at the headless carcase. Downy feathers stir in the grass.

'Sparrowhawk got it, I expect,' he says.

'Nature red in tooth and claw. Is that actually a pigeon?'

'That's just what I was thinking. The feathers look too brown.' Dominic toes the body and flips it over. Furry feet.

'It's an owl!' they cry together.

'Why's that so much worse?' he wonders.

'I don't know,' she says. 'A tawny owl. Tu-whit-tu-woo, a merry note.'

'While greasy Joan doth keel the pot.' He bends and picks it up gingerly by one wing. 'You take Lady in. I'll give this a decent burial.'

'Thanks, love. Before Dominic sees it and gets upset.'

'Oh, we can't have that,' he says.

He has to put it in the wheelie bin, of course. Pointless burying it. The foxes – or Lady – will only dig it up. Besides, there's no time for digging. So much time, and no time at all! He can't leave Mother safely for more than a few minutes.

He closes the wheelie bin lid. *I can't do this!* And yet, there it is – just enough strength and courage to go back into the vicarage and do the next thing. Just enough manna in the wilderness to last one day, even while the tears are sliding down his cheeks.

All around the parish of Lindford, people log on to Facebook and join Dominic as he livestreams his brief Good Friday service. His faithful Iranian parishioners are there. So are his two parish nurses, and stall owners from the covered market. Star is there with her parents. Students scattered back to their parents' homes around the country, the parents of children he has baptized, relatives of those whose funerals he has taken. In tower-block flats, in part-gentrified Victorian terraces, in Arts and Crafts manor house and in a dilapidated summerhouse; on laptop, tablet and phone, they watch and pray with him for one brief hour. Complete strangers log in too. Later, when he comes to check the number of views, he'll see that today's virtual congregation exceeds any real one on Good Friday in recent memory. Nobody minds when Mum comes in to bring him a cup of tea and they have to listen in as he goes through the lockdown explanation again.

'Yes, that's right. Everyone's staying at home. Goody-good. Well, we're just going to sing "There Is a Green Hill" and say a prayer,' he says, 'and then we're done.'

'Ooh, I know that one,' she says. She stays and sings with him.

Oh dearly, dearly has he loved!
And we must love him too,
And trust in his redeeming blood
And try his works to do.

Chloe is one of those who logged in to join Dominic. He's so tender and patient with his mum, she thinks. Bless him! She wipes her eyes and texts him.

You might think you're doing nothing, but you really are doing his works xxx

Time for the daily exercise, she thinks. Jog round the arboretum with Cosmo, dodging the other runners and walkers. Must remember to switch off her inner head girl, ha ha! and not judge people for sitting on benches or lying on the grass sunbathing.

She goes upstairs to get changed. But as she sits on the edge of the bed, a wave of tiredness washes in. How can this be so *exhausting*? All she does now is work from home, really. Skyping and phoning and emailing. She's not sleeping well. She's forever fending off the fear that their little three-person practice won't survive this; that legal aid won't survive this. Maybe that's what's so exhausting – the anxiety? This is supposed to be a bank holiday. But what does that amount to? Not checking work emails, that's all. Everything's blurry now her schedule has vanished. No office, no court, no church, no appointments, no entertaining. No people! She almost wails aloud. Nobody to hug. Well, apart from Cosmo.

She needs to pull herself together and establish some new routines. Get back into violin playing. Join in with Freddie's online singing lessons. Read some good books – isn't she always lamenting that she has no time to read? There's *The Mirror and the Light* waiting on the sofa arm downstairs. But she can't seem to concentrate; can barely make it through an entire episode of *The Crown* without getting restless.

There's a thump through the wall. Voices. She goes tense. New upstairs neighbours next door rowing again? Still no reply to her 'Welcome' card last week. There's a child screaming. Then music. Chloe relaxes. She heard the wife weeping a couple of days ago. But haven't we all wept in the past few weeks? Over anything and nothing. Over another month going by, and not knowing if that was the last chance.

Come on! She laces up her trainers. No moping. Count your blessings. No point brooding over what could have been if only you'd got your courage up a bit earlier. It's for the best! You wouldn't really want to be expecting *now*, would you?

She closes her front door quietly, because the downstairs neighbours will be asleep after their long shifts. Cosmo tugs at his lead. They set off over rainbows chalked on the pavement, past homemade paper rainbows in windows, under rainbow flags, by rainbow-painted rocks heaped beside gates, and jam jars of flowers. Little wayside shrines to the saints of the NHS, she thinks. And somewhere over the rainbow, out on the other side, all this will be over and we'll be singing again.

Bluebells will soon be out in the woods, but we can't drive to visit them. There's so much we won't see this spring. The sea, the airport lounge. Our distant loved ones.

Most of us won't see the cows coming home morning and evening, or the thousands of gallons of milk poured out and swilled down the drain, when the tankers don't arrive. We won't see the crows mustering black on a green hill where new-born lambs lie torn apart, because the man coming with his gun to shoot the foxes was turned back by the police.

Holy Saturday passes. The number of COVID-19 deaths approaches 10,000 in the UK. We can only wait, and do everything by doing nothing. *Stay Home. Protect the NHS. Save Lives.*

Those lucky enough to have gardens plan Easter egg hunts. Clergy families gather moss to make their Easter gardens for tomorrow's livestreamed worship. There will be no Easter lilies in the churches this year, but vases are filled with tulips and daffodils ready to adorn makeshift chapels in studies and vicarage kitchens.

The locked churches are silent. Sunbeams, then moonbeams, slide round over the altar and the pews, the statues, the pipe organ. Or maybe the sound desks, the drum kits, data screens and stacked chairs. Dust motes drift in the shafts of light. Sun, moon, sun, moon. In the little Baptist chapel in Itchington Episcopi, the clock has ticked itself silent.

The buildings look dead and empty, but they are full. Brimful of waiting. They are repositories of all the centuries of prayer, of all the ghosts of all the hymns ever sung there, all the meetings, baptisms, Lord's Suppers, weddings, funerals. Every tear, every hope. Listen. We are not alone. Voices everywhere. I can hear the old saints singing in the little Baptist chapel long before any of us were born.

> Dark, dark hath been the midnight.
> But dayspring is at hand.
> And glory, glory dwelleth
> In Immanuel's land.

Don't be afraid. Tonight is dark, but it's Sunday tomorrow. All the churches of Lindfordshire are crowded with saints, with our lost loved ones, all bending close, even if we can't see them yet from where we are standing.

Egg Moon, Part III

The moon is setting over Lindfordshire. A robed figure waits in the dark under the west front of the cathedral. Blackbirds begin to sing around the Close. Up above, the clock chimes half past. There's the click-click-click of a lighter. A taper flares. Then a hand (quaking with excitement) holds the flame to the brazier.

Will it catch? Shredded service sheets doused in lighter fuel. Last year's dried-out Christmas tree twigs. Pyramid of kindling. Yes! With a joyous *whoomph* the Easter fire blazes. Gavin the verger steps back with a smile. Job done for another year.

In the fire's light, we now glimpse another figure in robes, tall and thin, with wild hair. He stands at a distance of two metres from Gavin at all times. There's a rustle of paper, a ding of tuning fork. Then he starts to sing in a nasal churchy tenor:

> Rejoice, heavenly powers! Sing, choirs of angels!
> Exult, all creation around God's throne!
> Jesus Christ, our King, is risen!

The dean and her husband, standing on their balcony, can just hear him. All around the Close, on drives and in doorways, the scattered congregation strains to catch the words; while in the palace garden, the bishop livestreams the lighting of the 2020 paschal candle. Dawn brightens the eastern sky. There will be no full peal of bells this year to greet Our Lord's resurrection, no choir, no crowds of churchgoers, no crashing organ voluntary. But away with sin and sorrow! The

Champagne's in the fridge, the lamb's in the Aga. In a moment, the lay clerks from Vicars' Court will sing from their dispersed spots, and we will join in: 'Christ the Lord is Risen Today, Alleluia!' Alleluia anyhow. Our Lord is not locked down by death.

Over in Lindford, Freddie pulls on his sweats and creeps downstairs. He steps out through the patio door and lights a candle. He doesn't need the score, doesn't need a tuning fork – he *is* a tuning fork.

This is the night when first you saved our fathers.

The moon is setting behind Tinkerbell's big cedar tree. He can see it gleaming through the branches. The girls are still asleep in their coop, so he sings softly. He could totally wake half of Lindford if he let rip, but no. He's just one part of the dawn chorus, blackbirds, pigeons, wrens, little bats twisting and flickering there, the sun coming up red.

This is the night when the pillar of fire destroyed the darkness of
   sin.

The wind chimes Brose ordered for him ring softly from the cherry tree, like cathedral bells in the distance. God, Freddie *hates* lockdown! Even the word gives him flashbacks, like he can literally taste it, smell juvie on his skin and in his hair again? And he's all, Get me out of here, get me anywhere, up on a mountain with nothing but sky over me? Which is dumb, coz he's in his own home with his own husband, here's the garden, he can go running, so why's he whining?

Ah, he just can't, I mean, it's everything? How's he gonna keep it together? In his head, the universe is a massive choir making this truly *horrible* noise, it's all falling apart, and everyone's yelling, I've lost my place, what even *is* this shit? You guys are messing up, can we get a director here? Except, you keep on hearing how it *could* still all come together? In your bones you just *know* there's a score, there *has* to be, because when you stop panicking and listen, isn't that a *basso ostinato* going on underneath it all, like a giant heartbeat? You can feel it going through everything, even though it's way, way too deep to hear, and then you can believe it's still a work in progress even when it falls apart.

101

> This is the night when Jesus Christ broke the chains of death and
> rose triumphant from the grave.

But Jesus. Singing in the dark, nobody to hear him? Was that ever a symbol of his life right now? And this was gonna be the big break-through year.

There's a rustle and scratch in the henhouse. He stops singing to listen. He hears the first brooding chook-chook. 'Hey, girls! Morning! Aw.' They're snuggled in there, safe and warm. He wants to gather them all up in his arms. He loves those girls. So. *Much.* Gloria, Fabiola, Dolly and Mae. Chick-chick-chicken, lay a little egg for me! Man, who'd've thought his doofy songs would take off like that on YouTube and TikTok? Just messing, filling the time now he's furloughed. Trying to work out what to do. I mean, he wants to volunteer to drive people and stuff, only La Madeleine is all, Are you mad? This vile plague targets the lungs, Frederick, that's your priceless irreplaceable Stradivarius! Yeah, he gets that, but still. To do *nothing*?

He rolls his shoulders, stretches and gazes all round him. It's all turning gold – lawn, trees, the fence there. 'Hey, it'll be fine, OK? Don't worry, it's Easter now, it's OK, it's all gonna be fine.' He whispers it over and over, like he's talking to the hens, but it's to himself mainly? Then he starts singing again, even if there ain't nobody here at all.

But Ambrose can hear through the open bedroom window. Miss Sherratt, sleepless on her terrace with a cup of tea, can hear. Jack in his sleeping-bag cocoon in the old summerhouse can hear.

> Night truly blessed when heaven is wedded to earth.

And next door, in the house where the industrial fan thrums day and night and the blackout blinds are always down, someone else is listening. And as he listens, it's as though a tiny flame gleams in his endless traumatized night. It lingers, even after the last note fades.

You'd be surprised how many people got up before dawn on that first day of the week in Lindfordshire, how many candles shone like good deeds in a naughty world. We must hope that those little flames fared rather better than Bishop Steve's paschal candle. He balanced the

Light of Christ in the vase Sonya had put there ready, then stepped prayerfully away. Behind his back – watched with dismay by his helpless online congregation – the candle and vase toppled in slo-mo, to land with a vast crash on to the York paving stones, plunging everything into darkness once more. I feel Steve did very well not to say *bollocks*! Those of you who have seen the video clip will have heard the stifled mirth of the Pennington clan in the background, though.

Over in Martonbury, in the house of the other bishop, Jane finally paid off that good deed in arrears by joining Matt for communion in his spare-room chapel. She had consented to be the congregation, so that he could say mass for the first time in weeks. It was not livestreamed. She was not going to receive communion, but her presence made it possible for Matt to preside. She agreed to join in the hymns (provided they were pitched low enough for her to growl along) and to do the Bible readings. When it came to it, however, her particular contribution turned out to be floods of tears throughout the entire service. What a rubbish congregation you are, Dr Rossiter! Though you are a surprisingly good flower guild. That vase of informally arranged spring flowers is worthy of Susanna Henderson herself.

Easter week goes by. How can you be on leave in lockdown? At least working from home gave a bit of structure and point to the day. What does it mean to be on holiday at home when we launched our normal holiday repertoire of eating, drinking and Netflix-binging back when lockdown started? Will we get that refund from Ryanair?

Hot on the heels of these questions comes another: why are we moaning when we are fortunate enough to be able to work from home, when we have homes to isolate in? How dare we not be grateful, how dare we not be content? On Thursday at 8 p.m. we clap again. Wooden spoons on saucepans, car horns, fireworks. This is followed by outrage over car horns and fireworks, on behalf of nesting birds and small babies. Ah, Newton's third law of social media: for every parade, someone to rain on it. Thus equilibrium is maintained in our land.

And now the government has extended lockdown for another three weeks. The idea of getting back to normal is unravelling at the edges. What if there's no normal to get back to? What if *this* is normal, not temporary? We are busking our way through, sight-reading this impossible relentless score as we go along. Certain motifs start to recur. Jarring discords in the nation's rough music. *Half of us can work from home. The other half should be paid more.* What can we do? Too many people are dying. We saw it coming, why were we unprepared? Oh, what should we do?

Was it not Gandalf himself (or possibly Rowan Williams) who so cogently remarked, 'You do not have to make every kind of difference. But you do have to make the difference only you can'? All round Lindfordshire, we find people doing what only they can do, even if it feels small and rubbishy, and they wish they could do more. We never know in advance the good we can achieve, setting out, like ninety-nine-year-old Captain Tom Moore, to walk a hundred lengths of our small garden, modestly hoping we might raise £1,000 for the NHS.

Some do what only they can do by asking questions, investigating, holding the powerful to account, campaigning for change. (Would that all God's people were prophets.) How have we come to this, that a ninety-nine-year-old war veteran needs to fundraise, not for an extra kidney machine for his local hospital, but for basic PPE for doctors and nurses? Everywhere, the cracks running through our society are lit up by the searchlight of COVID-19. The years of austerity and underfunding are laid bare.

Such matters exercise Jane as she jogs. She has to plod round Martonbury Golf Course now that she can't drive to the reservoir. So far, Captain Tom has raised nearly one tenth of the fabled bus slogan £350 million sent each week to the EU. Jane doesn't come to the end of the palace drive to clang her saucepan, by the way, for fear she'll break social-distancing rules and go and clang the skulls of her Tory neighbours for their sheer breathtaking hypocrisy in clapping for the NHS 'heroes'.

The nation divides again into ragers and those who go more gently. We can only do what we can do.

Over in Cardingforth, our gentle friend Father Wendy gets her sewing machine down from the loft. Between funerals, online services and phoning parishioners, she spends every spare moment making scrubs. It's her small thank you to the NHS, for the cancer treatment that saved her life. Her husband Doug, a design and technology teacher at Cardingforth Comp, spends hours with a 3D printer making face masks. Mr Crowther, the Head of Cardingforth Primary School, wheels his garden trolley (a donation from Willow Tree Nurseries) round five miles of streets, delivering meals to his disadvantaged pupils, even though it's the holidays. The children wave at him through their windows as he leaves the brown paper carrier bags of food on their doorsteps. The Cardingforth foodbank moves from the church hall into the main church building – which only last month was operating as the flood hub.

Everywhere, the good folk of Lindchester Diocese do what they can. William House on Cathedral Close has been closed for weeks now. Staff have been furloughed. The COVID Response Team runs now from a virtual equivalent of the diocesan offices, under the eye of Jo, the diocesan secretary. Bishop Steve signs legal instruments to get round tricky technicalities in these Unprecedented Times, the details of which need not detain us. You may check them out on the diocesan website among the *ad clerums*, if that's your bag. Bishop Matt pastors the ordinands whose training is disrupted or whose ordination has been postponed. Three of the archdeacons (there is a vacancy in Renfold Archdeaconry following the retirement of the Venerable Alan Bowes) gather up good news stories from their different areas, and have set up a centralized system for funerals across the diocese. The finance team responds to desperate parishes, as common fund contributions tank and income from lettings has vaporized.

Tomorrow is Low Sunday. Last year's dead leaves patter along the empty pavements of Lindfordshire, like tiny crowds trotting by. The first swallows and willow warblers have arrived. In the garden of a Lindford apartment block, retired couples sit wine-sozzled on their patios, apart (obviously) but sharing companionable conversation with neighbours over the white fence. Their loud chat and laughter carries in the evening air. No secret gossip now. Nearby there's the thump of a football against a wall. A teenage boy wanders past down the hill, earbuds in, talking, talking on his phone, while he juggles three red-and-blue balls. In the arboretum, the police disperse groups of teenagers sitting on the grass.

Some days it seems as though the whole world is out walking, running, cycling in their household groups. We catch ourselves trying to solve little domestic puzzles. Mother and middle-aged daughter? Or gay couple? Father and sons. Grandpa and toddler. We notice people getting into cars. Where are they going? Essential shopping? To work? To deliver medical supplies? From our windows, we can see who's having a BBQ, who's coming and going, who's standing too close. Yet again, we divide: school prefect/skiver. Do we dob in our neighbours, or turn a blind eye?

Saterday 18th April

Moon Facts

Moon Phase: waning crescent (22%)

Moon age: 24.9 days

More Moon Facts

The moon allways rises in the east and sets in the west same as the sun. This fact might surprise you. I for one did not know that fact, I thought the moon appeared in random locations. Not true!!! It only looks like it does because it does not rise and set at the same time every day like the sun does, so sometimes you see the moon in the day time. The other fact is that sometimes the moon is high up and sometimes it is low down in the sky aka 'moon altitude'. Your app will tell you the moon's altitude but to be fair I don't really know what this means.

'Egg Moon' v 'Pink Moon'

IMHO pink moon is still a nicer name but I am going with a mash-up name PINK EGG MOON!! It is a win-win situation. I had seven Easter eggs this year not counting mini eggs!!! People gave eggs to dad to give to me and Leah when they found out he has two girls, because he works so hard, he does there shopping for them and picks up there proscriptions if they are isolating, they are greatful for his help. It is not my fault none of the eggs were vegan eggs is it. Mum sent off for vegan chocolate eggs for Leah online, they taste gross. Leah went, It's not about how they taste, and I went what is even the point of Easter eggs then, why don't you just tie a ribbon round a potatoe? Then I sang thank you baked potatoe which she hates and she yelled SHUTUP

SHUTUP but I kept on untill dad went *girls, I have a headache could you dial it down please?*

I feel bad now because he went to bed, I only hope it is just a stress headache like mum says and not CORVID-19. Leah and me made up and then we did some more work in the garden. We weeded the carrots and onions and my sunflowers and then we watered them, there has not been enough rain. You might think hot sunshine is nice but it's not, it's global warming (says GUESS WHO).

Me and Leah have a 'new thing', it is 'Moon phase gardening', the moon effects plant growth like the tides, so you should plant some things when the moon is 'waxing' and other things when it is 'waning'. Leah explained it to me, she has researched it all. Because it is waning now she says we should plant things that bare their crop <u>under the ground</u>. Then she glared at me and went, *don't even DARE sing thank you baked potatoe again I mean it I will kill you,* but she was only kidding.

When we finished gardening we went inside, I made some vegan rock cakes. She is a good sister to me at the end of the day, she sets my mind at rest. Like just now I asked her *does it hurt when you start developing?* And she went *god yeh to start with it totally KILLS, but don't worry, it's normal plus it stops.* And I went *oh cool thanks.* We have a pact, the pact is that I won't tell mum and dad that she's got TikTok on her phone if she lets me see Mr Hardman-Mays posts too. We both totally agree it is just a misunderstanding, mum and dad don't get that TikTok is fine, they have just read negative stuff about it, is all. It is a kindness to shield them, it is not dishonest. Oops Mum's just told me it's lights out now. When I asked she said dad's doing ok, I can say a prayer for him if I want but not to worry.

P.S. Mum sent off for some seed potatoes. Yay!!!

P.P.S. They better come before the moon starts waxing!!!!!!

It's 3.15 a.m. on Monday and Father Dominic can't sleep. That's why he is sitting on a bench in his garden, with a coat over his pyjamas, eating Vietnamese iced coffee cookies. If Mother gets up and starts wandering, he'll see the landing light flick on. He can't stop her roaming, but at least the motion sensor bulbs mean she won't be falling over in the dark.

It's not really dark out here. The sky seems to glow pale grey from all the security lights of Lindford. It's not really silent either. He can hear the hum of a street sweeper toiling away along the empty roads. Owls call. A freight train rumbles by. There's a flapping and settling in the big trees.

He's down to the last cookie. The sugar rush isn't going to help him sleep, is it? Oh well. He licks his sticky fingers and crumples the paper. Bless you, Chloe. Driven to distraction and baking her way through Granny Gno's old recipes! He let out a whoop of joy when he saw her on the drive. Oh Lord. This is what it's going to be like for the foreseeable future. Standing two metres apart, flailing the poor arms that ache to hug the other person, laughing and crying at the same time. Envying Cosmo and Lady their lavish father–daughter reunion.

Well, he's awake, so he prays. For Chloe, and her upstairs neigh-bours and what sounds like possible domestic abuse, for wisdom to know if and how to intervene safely. He prays for his tireless parish nurses running their phone surgeries, ferrying people to appoint-ments, collecting medical supplies. For his colleague Virginia doing so many funerals. For poor Martin, ill with a raging temperature (Lord, have mercy!). For all his elderly parishioners in care homes, whose names he recites faithfully each week in his intercessions, now slipping categories too fast, one after another, from sick to RIP. He would have been by their bedsides! Oh, world, you poor world! It all rushes up, his helpless love and pain.

The sweeper is coming up his road now. Dominic shivers and gets to his feet. Cup of chamomile, then bed. He turns to the vicarage. Somewhere, he realizes, somewhere in China there was a specific moment when COVID-19 first skipped from animal to human. There was an actual first person, a human body, the site where all this started. And because he keeps having to explain it to Mother, Dominic knows that a virus is tiny, unimaginably tiny. Roughly ten million times smaller than you and me, Mother dear. How can it be that such a teeny-tiny thing has brought us to this – half the world in lockdown? If only there could be a reverse virus. One that drives us into one another's embrace to catch the good from one another. That rips round the globe through every human host, repairing cells, reversing dementia, restoring hair and teeth, easing our pain, wiping every tear away.

Yes, I know, I *know*, thinks Dominic. There was another site, another human body, where all this ended. It's just that the outworking is so slow and ah, so so painful.

Egg Moon, Part IV

The he cherry is in flower across Lindfordshire. Petals flutter like confetti on to lawns and pavements. It is the Pink Egg Moon's wedding and we are all bridesmaids – but that is something to write in your secret journal. Never say it out loud, or people will laugh at you.

Becky catches herself. She shuts Jess's Moon Journal and slides it away. Honestly, what was Jess thinking, leaving it lying open on the kitchen table, like a bit of homework? What if Leah finds it? Becky can just picture that. Exactly like what happened to her when she was ten. For weeks, Sarah kept reciting that one line: 'We had netball today, I played goal defence.' Mum never really *got* it. Just take no notice, and she'll stop doing it.

I still haven't forgiven either of them, Becky realizes. No wonder she identifies with Jo in *Little Women*, when Amy burns her novel. Marmie didn't get it either, did she? Then *the story itself* punishes Jo, by having Amy nearly drown because Jo doesn't forgive her! Funny that you never notice how preachy books are when you're a child.

The washing machine churns away. *Little Women*. That's what this feels like. The invalid lying upstairs. Home entertainment. Staying brave for the girls. Praying. The kindness of everyone. She can't believe all the cards, cakes, offers of cooking and shopping and dog-walking! Was it only *this* New Year that I took them to see the film? Could have been last century! Time's gone strange. Nearly a week since Martin started to show symptoms. A blur of leaving drinks and meals outside his door. Bundling load after load of bedlinen and pyjamas into the machine with rubber gloves. Spraying door handles and taps. The upstairs reeks of anti-bac.

God, she's exhausted. She pours the last of the coffee from the cafetière. It's like being back on maternal autopilot 24/7. Hyper-calm in those crisis moments, then jittery afterwards. Like when the girls fell and hit their heads, or that time when Leah found the Calpol bottle with the lid off. Last night she was poised to ring for an ambulance at 3 a.m. But he's breathing slightly better now. Temperature down a bit – assuming he checked properly, and texted her the number correctly. They're tracking his oxygen levels too. Madge brought an oximeter when she called last Sunday. Maybe he's through the worst.

And here's another school day to get through, hooray. Leah's asleep. She'll be late logging on again. It would be nice if QM Girls could send one letter of support, along with the complaints. Just one! Honestly, if the school's going to use these online platforms, shouldn't staff be properly trained? Surely the responsibility lies with the teacher, not the parents, for ensuring that pupils don't seize control of the session and upload Freddie's chicken videos?

A snort escapes. Becky clamps a hand over her mouth. It's not funny. Oh, she's such a rubbish home-schooling mum. Well, at least Jess is doing some vocal exercises. Becky can hear her in the dining room. The washing machine swishes. Luna is snoozing in her basket. The smell of toast lingers from breakfast. In a moment, Becky will go upstairs with some more Lucozade and see if he's up to eating anything. Spray around with the anti-bac again. Bang on Leah's door.

Oh, don't let him die. She breathes in, out. Reminds herself that Martin's fit, he has no underlying health conditions. He's through the worst.

She finishes her coffee and starts loading the dishwasher. Back in January, her head would have *exploded* at the thought of being quarantined with her ex. How weird to be enjoying their text exchanges, the phone conversations. Laughing over that Ann Summers penis pasta bake someone brought round. Maybe it's because she's starved of adult company. Or because she doesn't have to pretend with him. Nothing to hide, no fucks left to give – as Leah is so fond of saying. But you can't mend a broken marriage, really. Not without

111

a valley-of-dry-bones miracle. All the scattered vow fragments twitching – love, honour, cherish – scraping through the dust, clattering themselves back together.

No, just keep plodding on. It's nearly the halfway point of their fourteen-day quarantine. So long as she and the girls don't develop symptoms, they will all be able to go out for a walk again at least. In the meantime, there's the garden.

The new moon rises. Jellyfish pulse languidly in the crystal clear canals of Venice, but we Lindcastrians will never see them, land-locked as we are. Facebook trolls us with 'On This Day' memories of previous holidays. How ill-suited we are to patience and staying in one place. Lockdown's a jigsaw with no box. Thousands of pieces, but we don't know what it's supposed to look like. We haven't even found the corners yet, let alone the edges. A dullness settles, quilting our minds even as we lag our bodies with extra fat layers to see out the COVID winter.

Unless you're on the other side, of course, viewing 2020 through face masks and Perspex barriers, rather than the kitchen window. Forget jigsaws – this feels increasingly like Russian roulette for the woman at the till. For the guy spraying the trolley handles in the supermarket car park. The care home workers, intensive care nurses, paramedics. Bus drivers, pharmacists, undertakers, clergy taking funerals, teachers in schools open for key workers' children. Doctors, emergency service personnel, hospital porters, cleaners, postal workers, delivery guys. Has the number gone off the edge of our brains yet? How many animals was it, again, that died in the Australian bush fires? (Can that possibly have been only this January?) Around 480 million. It's white noise. Humankind cannot bear that many zeros. We cannot even take in the 20,000 registered COVID-19 deaths in UK hospitals. But we can all see in single figures. When the world is burning, we can see one koala clinging to the hand of the person bringing water. One death is always a tragedy.

April is almost over. At dusk, half a waxing moon lies in a shallow puddle like a fallen petal. Take heart. We may not be very deep, but we can still reflect the heights of heaven. Horse chestnut candles blossom. Bees drone. Eggs hatch. The first hints of lilac waft from gardens. All across Lindfordshire, the church clocks, the town hall clocks, chime out the passing quarters. Chiffchaffs in big trees chip away at the minutes. In shafts of sunshine mosquitos dance like tiny fire fairies. Perfect, perfect April days. Revision weather, but nothing to revise for. There are no exams this year. Unless 2020 is our life's Final, and how can we revise for that? Study to be kind? Be patient? Be grateful?

The moon goes round. The earth turns. On 29 April an asteroid a mile wide passes us at a distance of around sixteen times as high as the moon. Astronomically speaking, this constitutes a close shave, one that might justifiably put our current woes into a rather different perspective – that of the dinosaurs.

The US oil price drops to negative. Billionaires come cap in hand for government bailouts, offering tropical islands as security, and 140,000 companies apply for the government furlough scheme. There's still upbeat talk of a short V-shaped recession, but U-shaped is being whispered. The knife-edge balancing act: lives/livelihoods. We begin to notice more cars on the roads. Anti-lockdown protests break out across America. Some different theme tune must be playing over there – 'Land of the Free', not 'We'll Meet Again'. We ache for everything to go back to normal, too. But we know the drill: *Stay Home. Protect the NHS. Save Lives.* If only we had proper testing and tracing, enough PPE, a vaccine! We still have this in the same category as storms. We think we will wake up one day to find it's stopped, thank God. That there's still a *normal* to get back to.

And in the meantime, there's the garden – for the lucky ones. How lockdown mocks us. Garden centres binning millions of plants, just when we are itching to buy! Lockdown mocks Brexit too, as Romanian fruit pickers are flown in to ease the problem of 'continuing recruitment in the agricultural sector'. How selectively we embrace the spirit of the Blitz! Where are the Land Girls digging for Britain, I wonder?

Over in the vicarage at Gayden Magna, a potagerie is being designed. Raised beds (to be constructed out of reclaimed timber), handwoven willow fencing, wee hammocks to cradle the marrows and melons that will flourish. Oh, the fresh asparagus, the artichokes and cardoons! The Heritage strawberries, Malabar spinach, amaranth – what the hell is that? Och, well never mind.

Yes, Neil has a new lockdown project. Business at NDF Design is slow. He's working from home, rather than in his unit at the Britannia Business Park. He still nips across to Martonbury twice a week, to do a stint at the foodbank, and maybe some shopping for the housebound. He puts on his reader cassock first, so the polis don't give him grief over non-essential travel. The rest of the pastoral stuff he can do from home on the phone. Ringing round, checking up, Zooming. That still leaves a lot of time to persecute poor Father Ed with advice. Screaming has occurred in the vicarage, I'm sorry to say. So the potagerie, with all its minuscule origami-folds of micro-decisions, is proving a godsend. Long may this lovesome spot exist purely at the planning stage!

Father Ed is about to livestream Morning Prayer from his study. He hears the wincing clash of a metal tape measure from the garden and smiles. When life gives them lemons, Ed can count on Neil to make lemon-drop U'Luvka vodka martinis in hand-blown art deco crystal glasses.

Freddie's in the garden too. Going through all his karate katas. Mental how he can still remember them all? But that's muscle memory for you, I guess? He winds the session up with a Sun Salutation, coz yoga's less fighty, and he needs to calm himself, focus, we got this, it's gonna be fine. Standing Mountain. Breathe. Upward Salute. Stay mindful. Inhale. Exhale. Upward-Facing Dog, Downward-Facing. It's gonna be fine. Mountain Pose. Aaaaand . . . Welcome warmth.

Yeah. See? We got this. He fills his lungs. Opens his mouth.

Well, I think half of Lindford heard him yell *FUUUUUUCK!* The chickens certainly set up an almighty squawk.

Brose looks down from his home office window. 'Everything OK, babe?'

'Yeah, no, sorry. It's just . . .' Freddie shrugs.

'Well, I think you spoke for the whole world there.' He disappears back to his desk.

Gloriana is still flapping against the wire, so Freddie sings 'Summertime' to soothe the girls. Maybe do this for YouTube? He gets his phone out. Sees a new email arrive.

BOOM!

Shit-shit-*shit*! His face burns.

Andrew Jacks is inviting you to a scheduled Zoom meeting. Topic: Come lie with me and be my love.

Gah! Freddie knows it's just some Dorian Singers thang, but Jesus. Andy just *has* to do this, every time he *has* to try and fuck with Freddie's head or wind Brose up. Like Brose even cares these days. He'll be all, Why are you even telling me, babe? I trust you, you know that. But Freddie still feels he's got to run it past him, to be not hiding anything, even though there's nothing to hide? Stopped carrying *that* torch years ago, it's just emotional muscle memory?

But still. Asshole.

He takes another calming breath, and whoa, there's the smell again. Someone's seriously mellowing out round here. He'd love to think it's Tinkerbell on her terrace, ha ha. He's seen her with the cocktail ciggies. What a girl.

Brose is at the open window again, looking down.

'Hey.' Freddie spreads his hands. 'Not me, dude.'

Brose jerks his head. *Next door.*

Freddie looks at the empty house. Nada. Blinds all down. His eyes widen. 'O-ohhhh! You reckon . . .'

Brose nods. Puts a finger to his lips. 'Talk about it later?'

'Cool.'

April ends. We've stopped counting lockdown in days. We're on to weeks now. In the terraced streets and quiet cul-de-sacs of Lindfordshire, a real community spirit has burgeoned. We learn our neighbours' names at last! There are socially distanced coffee hours every morning, and community singing after the weekly #ClapForCarers. People chalk botanical messages on pavements to help children identify the urban trees. There are themed cooking nights even, when every household experiments with the same ethnic cuisine. This is not true in the posher postcodes, where walls are high,

115

drives long and gates electronic. The bigger your house, the further your neighbours.

Some neighbours are too close and the walls too thin. Father Dominic can still just see the windows and tiny balconies of the Abernathy estate between his trees, and his heart yearns towards the families he knows. The ones trying to home school four children with a single mobile phone and no computer. There's nowhere to escape when tempers fray. One walk a day to the arboretum, no sitting on benches or lying on the grass. There and back. Lord have mercy. He longs to offer them the run of his big house and garden. But rules are rules.

Virginia, Father Dominic's fellow priest, and Diocesan Officer for Social Justice, has been obliged to start sleeping in her spare room at the front of the house, because her left-hand side neighbours – who had always seemed so pleasant pre-lockdown – are turning out to be really inconsiderate. Sitting out on the patio drinking, shrieking with laughter and playing their music till all hours. Virginia's had more than one quiet word, and every time they're full of remorse. But one bottle of wine in and the promises all come to nothing. If only it would rain and drive them indoors!

Poor Chloe lies awake too, listening to the voices rising and falling next door. Some nights she takes her duvet and pillow downstairs, and curls up on the sofa with Cosmo. So far, it's not felt right to call the police. With lockdown, she can't catch a word with the wife on her own, and mention she's worried for her. Offer to put her in touch with the right agencies. Let it be OK, she begs. Visit this place, O Lord, we pray. Drive far from it the snares of the enemy. May your holy angels dwell with us and guard us in peace.

She hugs Cosmo tight and weeps into his soft springy fur. He's the only living creature she's touched since 23 March – five weeks ago. He whines and laps her face. 'I'm sorry,' she sobs. And now it looks as though her poor senior partner Simon is going to have to furlough her. Even that probably won't save them. From next week she won't even have her caseload and clients to keep her going.

It will pass. There's no shortage of things she can volunteer for to fill the hours, especially with Martin still poorly. But the year had felt so full of promise. The big yellow moon smiling down the night

116

before General Synod, seeming to bless her crazy plans. Oh Cosmo! Another month, another egg gone. How many have I got left?

Her phone buzzes. A text from Dominic. It's almost midnight. Her heart thumps. Bad news?

> Hope all's well. Prayers for Martin, if you would. Just heard from Becky. They're admitting him to Lindford General. Ambulance on the way. Bless you. Dxx

MAY

Milk Moon, Part I

I t's raining in Lindfordshire. Listen. Water trickles in gutters and downpipes. Drops patter on roofs. Yesterday's sudden downpours have washed away all the chalked rainbows, the hopscotch grids and helpful botanical annotations on town pavements. The whole world is rinsed and ready for May.

Far off, beyond the reaches of this tale, there is no choir on Magdalen Tower to sing *Hymnus Eucharisticus*. Oxford ('lovely all times she lies') is silent. May Morning is virtual this year. Not that we'd be able to leave our homes and drive there to listen anyway. Here in Lindfordshire there are no merry lads and bonny lasses playing, either. No spring games on the greeny grass in 2020, apart from with members of your own household for the purposes of exercise.

How sad this all is. Nights full of strange dreams and owls calling in the dark. Days all blurry. We could fly, I suppose, if we could remember where we'd put our wings. We could climb the skies with sad steps, like the moon, and visit the far-flung farmlands of the diocese, and listen out for the first cuckoos calling. We could watch the cows come home twice a day to be milked. Will the tanker arrive? Or is all this going to waste again? Oh, where is that army of land girls? Gone to their long home, most of them. Perhaps a very few remain, in sheltered accommodation or in care homes, where they won't have to witness the sight of thousands of gallons running like a white river down the gutter into the drain. Yes, twenty-first-century England, a land flowing with milk.

I'd forgotten how pretty it is out here, this overlooked part of the country. A gentle landscape, like the kind found in the pages of an old sincere Ladybird book before all the spoofs came out. A region full of ancient hedges and meandering rivers, haunted by the ghosts of long-gone elms. The stitchwort is out, and the yellow archangels. Crab apple blossom, bluebells. The rape fields are just reaching full wattage. Every mile or so you'll see churches on small rises, tower and steeple visible among mature trees. There are pastures rippled with ridge and furrow, where cows and sheep graze; and blackbird song coming slow and relishy from every tree- and rooftop. You can still pick up an old farm cottage in a tiny village round here for a fraction of what it would cost you in the Cotswolds.

The second homes stand empty this year. I hope their owners are not contemplating sneaking off for a bank holiday break next week. *Stay Home. Protect the NHS. Save Lives.* I can tell you something for nothing: if you do decide the rules don't apply to you, your arrival will be noted. The locals aren't overfond of offcomers at the best of times. Swanning in and buying up property, forcing out families who have lived here for generations. And these aren't the best of times. The farmer may see your car sneak up on Thursday evening, and decide that 7 a.m. on bank holiday morning is the time to spread a load of celebratory VE Day slurry on the field beside your property.

Monday 4th May

I have not been keeping up with my journal I regret to say. It is a new month and a new moon, and I should of written that, it is now the 'FLOWER MOON'. *But it is hard to write when you are sad and scared for your own dad and keep thinking he might die of CORVID-19 even if he has no underlying health issues. Leah says your meant to journal all your feelings, that is what a journal is for, but this is supposably a MOON JOURNAL at the end of the day, not a feelings journal. But she means well. She loaned me her wooden holding cross to hold in the night because I couldn't get to sleep, it has been a comfort to me in my hour of need.*

Fortunately dad is out of intensive care, we FaceTimed him this morning, he said 'Sorry I scared you, girls' and we were all crying, and

122

mum was hugging us tight, I know it is going to be OK, but we still kept on crying for some reason. But I have decided to 'accentuate the positive' like the song says that Mr Hardman-May and his chickens do on his YouTube channel 😄 I will try hammer tooth and nail to think about nice things and bring gloom to the minimum.

Names for the May Full Moon

As per usual, there are many and various names for the May 'full moon'. I am going with FLOWER MOON because that is the nicest, I am aware it is Native American and I am not, but it is still my choice. If you are a vegan and say 'Milk Moon' that is illogical, so its swings and roundabouts. Another name is Hare Moon, I would love to see a real live hare, I have only ever seen rabbits.

Flower 'SUPERMOON'

So the Flower Moon will be a 'SUPERMOON', it will be the last supermoon of 2020. It is called a supermoon because it looks so big. It happens when the full moon coincides with 'perigee', aka when the moon is closest to earth on it's orbit. The moons orbit is ellyptical, it does not go round earth in a circle. The moon will be full on Wednesday and Thursday, hopefully it will be a clear sky. It is cloudy today. We will get deliveroo fish and chips tonight, well mum and me will, Leah will have vegan suasage and chips, and then . . . BEN AND JERRYS!!! Yay!!!!!!!!!!!! I'm having cookie dough and Leah is having dairy free chocolate fudge brownie. Mum said to me when Leah went into the garden to do her karate Vegan chocolate ice cream? She might as well just eat a mouthful of cocoa powder. LOL LOL LOL.

So because Leah was not there I said, Don't get me wrong I am very grateful to God and Jesus and all the people in the NHS who looked after dad and risked there lives, but a part of me thinks none of this should of happened? Mum went, Well a lot of it didn't have to happen, the UK has not done as well as other countrys like Germany and New Zealand, our government has not handled it well. (Frankly I do not need Leah to explain AGAIN to me it is all humanitys fault and global capitalism that we have pandemics.)

Then I went, I totally get your reasons, but you would think God could of stopped it if he is all-powerful? I get that its something to do with free will, but still. She said, You'd better ask your dad when he gets home!

Not long to wait finger's crossed. Now I am going to do some singing practise because singing is good for mental health, I will do Mr Hardman-Mays online lesson. His lessons are super popular, he is 'the Joe Wicks of singing' (says mum).

PS Mum still hasn't found out about Leah having TikTok!!!!!

PPS Leah warned me some of his songs on TikTok are inappropriate, she says do not and I mean not go around singing them like you always do. Like in 'Have you seen my chicken' the words roosting pole has 'another meaning' and I went like what? then I went OH! And she said Yeh, so DEFINATELY don't let on I've got it on my phone!!!!

There you go, gentle Anglican reader, you who are so full of the milk of human kindness you found yourself adding Martin to your intercessions list. He is on the mend and will be out of hospital soon. It is not the intention of this narrative to make 2020 more harrowing for you than it already is. We aim to tread that tricky line between faithfully chronicling these times via our narrow squint in the church wall, and seeking to console the reader (perhaps in the manner of a Ravilious painting) that, in spite of everything, 'not as orphans are we left in sorrow now'.

Martin is drowsing in his propped-up hospital bed on the COVID ward. He will forget almost everything about those four days in the intensive care unit. Even now, it's fading. Memories of drugged delirium, the Thing – abyss? monster? – coming closer, closer, tongue like a whale's, head thumping, pistons pounding, can't breathe – *something* looms, impossibly vast yet terrifyingly tiny, and he knows he's done for. Being turned on to his front? Machines bleeping. Tubes, needles. Drip stands. Other people in other beds far faraway. Curtains being drawn. The sound of a long zip being done up. And kindness. All the time, kindness. How are you feeling, Martin? Can you tell me where you are, Martin? We're just going to change your sheets. Kind hands in gloves, kind eyes behind masks. And one night (was it only last night?) a hand on his shoulder, recalling him from the abyss of pistons, and a voice at his ear: *Do you know that I love you?*

They're bringing breakfast now. He can smell toast. Normal. Things are getting normal again. Blessed normal. He draws a crackly breath, and coughs. So tired. In a moment, he'll reach for his glass and sip more water. Tears slide from his closed eyes. He feels them trickle down through his stubble. *Yes, Lord. I know that you love me.*

'Martin's out of hospital, Matt says.' Jane sits down illegally on a bench.

'Yes, thank the Lord,' says Dominic. 'Where are you? I can hear birds.'

'By the seventh tee. It's a willow warbler. Listen.' She holds the phone out for a moment, towards the tree where the bird is rippling down its silvery song. 'There's a grass bank, and the sun's shining on the dew. It looks like a forest of tiny rainbow-coloured lights. Extraordinary.'

'Ah, I wish I could see it all. Not that I'm not grateful for the garden. Blackbirds – listen.'

Jane hears one carolling away.

'And I get owls at night-time,' says Dominic. 'It's all lovely – lovely.'

'Apart from the decapitated owl corpse on your lawn. With its little furry feet.'

'Oh thanks, Jane. I'd almost forgotten that.'

'Well, I'm enjoying this while I can. I bet golf courses are among the first things to open again.'

'I hope you're not trampling the greens in your stilettoes.'

'I'm in my farting Birkenstocks, I'll have you know. But I'm keeping off the greens. I did have a brilliant idea for when this is all over. I'm going to buy a dog and call it "Fore" and let it off the lead up here every day.'

He laughs. 'Oh, Janey. I miss you so much. I miss everything.'

'Yeah. It's shite, isn't it? How are you doing?'

'Well, the big news is, we've rediscovered the jigsaws Mum brought with her when she moved in. I was on the very brink of buying her a new one on Amazon, but then I spotted it won't be delivered till August! The whole world's buying jigsaws!'

'We were such stockpiling innocents!' Jane marvels. 'We'll know next time. Jigsaws and hair clippers.'

'Don't! I may have to self-barber with my beard trimmer. Mother's offering to do me a pudding-basin trim with the kitchen scissors.'

'Ha ha! Looking forward to the pics.'

'My spies tell me that if you go round the back of Goran's, you can still get a cut,' whispers Dominic. 'But it'll cost you twenty-five quid, instead of nine.'

'What? The price-gouging bastard!'

'I know! But seriously – who risks their life for a haircut?'

'People who don't believe it's a risk,' she says. 'To themselves or others.'

There's a pause. The willow warbler ripples on. Jane watches the wind stirring the silver birch trees in the distance. Spring forging ahead, regardless. It all feels like a dream.

'I'm so worried for Madge,' Dominic says at last. 'Oh, Jane! What if she gets it too? I can't bear the thought. Should I insist she stops going out? She can still carry on doing her phone surgeries.'

'Have you asked Madge what *she* thinks? Or does Father know best?'

'Of course I've asked her! She says it's her vocation, and she's being careful. But the risks seem so much worse for BAME people. Oh Lord. Never mind *Call the Midwife* – it's turning into a dystopian Florence bloody Nightingale horror film! Frontline nursing, no proper PPE—'

'And Mary Seacole,' says Jane. 'Everyone forgets her.'

'*Damn!* Of course.' Silence. 'Now I feel bad.'

'Feel bad, then move on,' recommends Jane. 'Otherwise we end up doing that white privilege thing of making it about how bad we feel, rather than about systemic racism.'

There's another pause.

'Well, that worked,' says Dominic. 'I've moved on to being mad at you.'

Jane laughs her filthy laugh. 'Sorry. You can take the girl out of the academic seminar . . .'

'But you're right. I probably don't get it, do I? Oh Lord. I used to think I had good antennae for discrimination.'

More bird-filled silence.

'You know what,' says Jane, 'I actually caught myself missing my little tin-can train to work the other day. And I keep thinking about my office, frozen in time like Sleeping Beauty's castle.'

'I know! It's all so— Oops, sorry, I can see Mother in the kitchen. Have to go, darling. Thanks for ringing. My love to Matt.'

'Your love? Didn't you get the memo saying all bishops are lickspittle quislings for banning you from going into your church building?'

But Dominic has already hung up.

Jane mooches back across Martonbury Golf Course, feet farting occasionally in her flatbed sandals. All this C of E argy-bargy over whether the church has retreated to the kitchen. Oh, for God's sake, take a reality check. You're like the English Folk Dance Society quarrelling over whether schoolchildren should be dancing 'The Dashing White Sergeant' or 'Strip the Willow'. Nobody cares!

There's a sprinkler on one of the greens. It sends out smoky spray and rainbows on the breeze as it rotates, *tk-tk-tk*. She passes a clump of gorse by the clubhouse, and gets a waft of coconut, like old-fashioned suntan oil and holidays of yore. Well, that's her daily exercise over. Back to the inbox. She scuffs through carpets of pink under the cherry trees. I'm going quietly mad, she thinks. Term has started, but nothing has proper edges. Normally she'd be buried alive in marking now, but the deadlines have all been extended. Poor kids. No exams – well, no real exams with invigilators in sports halls, just a 'takeaway' equivalent. No graduation ceremony in Lindchester Cathedral, either. No proper goodbyes.

In some unimaginable future, they will be setting seminar and exam questions on the 2020 pandemic. Reflecting on the role of politics and popularism. Teasing out why the UK was so shite and incompetent, why the impact on BAME communities was so devastating, and why we weren't angrier about it all. No proper antennae for racism – well, that's her. She can only carry on listening and educating herself. Being called nig-nog at primary school for having dark eyes and hair – that hardly counts. Oh, this country. Cool Britannia RIP. She feels . . . contaminated. Thank God Danny's safe in New Zealand!

Jane is not skilled in eliminating the negative, it has to be said. Not for her the old school Ladybird innocence of *Things to Do and Make*. She walked past swathes of wild garlic earlier without a thought of gathering it for pesto. She has not started making her own bunting for VE Day with a trusty old Singer sewing machine inherited from Grandma (which, in any case, she doesn't own). She will not bake scones and have a cream tea with Matt at the end of their drive beside the pampas grass, community singing 'The White Cliffs of Dover' with their socially distant neighbours. No, if Jane had a Ladybird book, it would probably be called *The Eton Tory Abomination of Desolation: How it works*.

The lilac is in bloom. Bracken uncoils. The official number of COVID-19 deaths in the UK is the lowest for some time. We hear the first hints of a staged easing of lockdown, details to be announced next Monday, after the bank holiday weekend. And yet the UK death toll is now higher than Italy's. But how are we counting, how are we comparing? Facts smack into us like insects on a windscreen. Prof Neil Ferguson resigns after being exposed for breaking the lockdown rules. The UK economy is facing the deepest turndown in living memory. Cases in Russia and Brazil start to climb exponentially. The House of Bishops announces that clergy can now livestream from inside their church buildings. The NHS tracking app is launched in the Isle of Wight.

All the time, these perfect May days glide past. Not a cloud. Now and then, a jet tows a V of vapour across the blue, like a swan on a lake. Willow fluff drifts. We can wander down the middle of roads, where the hopscotch grids have been redrawn in fresh chalk. Oh, if only we could silence the news, come off Twitter, maybe we could enjoy this glory. But we can't. Lockdown will be eased, but we have no sense that the worst is over. How can it be over, when nothing's really changed?

In supermarkets desperate mothers queue, and load their trolleys. But at the checkout, the school meal vouchers won't scan. They have to leave with no food for their families. Mr Crowther still pounds the streets of Cardingforth, delivering packed lunches to his pupils. Volunteers make up parcels at the foodbanks. Half the world is forced to play uphill on this sun-baked playing field where the virus gets in through every crack.

In the house next door to Chloe, one of her downstairs neighbours – Bethan – falls ill. She and her boyfriend Zach, a hospital porter, both have to isolate. Bethan works in a local care home, but also does shifts at Lindford General, trying to make ends meet, saving for their postponed wedding. Has she passed the virus on? Next week, all the old people in the home will be tested for COVID-19. But not the care workers. And in the upstairs flat, angry voices still erupt. Sometimes the woman sobs, and Chloe still doesn't know what to do.

She tells some of this to Virginia, as they stand two metres apart on a street in Lindford, having met unexpectedly. They haven't seen each other since the last mass at the parish church. (When was that?) Remember General Synod? They both shake their heads in disbelief. Like another world. Remember planning for Lambeth? She tells Virginia she's been furloughed, but Virginia has already heard this from Dominic, of course.

They talk about poor Father Dominic and his mum, about how relieved they are about Martin. Then they talk about the virus in general, and how *sick* they get of people moaning about their kids, their spouses, when single people literally haven't touched, or been touched by, another person since lockdown started. How tired they both are, and isn't Zoom exhausting? They wonder why this is.

Virginia tells Chloe about the anguish of taking funerals, with siblings weeping for the parent whose deathbed they couldn't sit beside, brothers and sisters standing two metres apart sobbing, and Virginia just having to watch. What it feels like not being able to console them. And then to do another funeral like that. And another.

Oh, it's so sad, it's all so sad!

Virginia and Chloe are crying now too. They flail their arms at one another, semaphoring hugs across an invisible river. A river that runs through everything now, breaking every heart as it goes.

Milk Moon, Part II

'So how was your Zoom?' asks Ambrose. 'What did Svengali want this time?'

Freddie comes and perches on the edge of the desk. His shoulders slump. He fidgets about with his phone. 'Ohh, it was just this new commission thang. BBC? Wants me to sing a . . . Hey boy!' He starts foot-wrestling Alfie. 'So it's like another of those old hymns he does? "Sands of Time".'

Ambrose knows the signs. But he also knows to take it steady. 'So . . . that's all good then?'

'Yeah. I guess. Yeah, it's good. He's gonna send the score across, so yeah.' Alfie jumps up and plants his paws on Freddie's shoulders. 'Wanna dance? Yeah?'

Ambrose watches them as they waltz round his home office. Alfie's claws skitter on the bare wooden floor. 'How's he finding lockdown?'

'Seems fine? Listen, I'm gonna go for a crazy long run, clear my head? Unlimited exercise, way hey!' Alfie barks. 'Aw, sorry boy, can't take you this time.'

Ambrose clicks his fingers. 'Here boy. Good boy.' He gets hold of the collar. 'Want to talk it through first? So you have my take, as well as whatever narrative's going through your head?'

Freddie closes his eyes. Sighs out through his nostrils. 'Shit. How can you always? OK, here's the thing. Naked guy?'

Ambrose waits.

'Walks past? Totally saw his reflection in the mirror behind where he's sitting, and I'm all, Whoa! Who's that? And he's, Who's what?

130

Dude, only the naked guy? And he's, I'm sorry? There's no naked guy here.' Freddie flings his hands up. 'Wow. I mean, none of my business, but wow. Then he starts in gaslighting me. Making me think I'm seeing things? So.'

'OK. Which bit of this is upsetting you?'

'All of it! Man. He lives alone, and this is still meant to be lockdown and all?'

'And?'

Freddie laces his fingers behind his neck. Looks up at the ceiling. 'Gah! None of my business, right? But, yeah no listen. I can't stop thinking how shit life must be for sex workers right now? The risks to earn, what, probably fifty a hundred quid tops, depending on?'

'OK. That's one possible scenario,' says Ambrose. 'Any others? What about, he's sharing lockdown with an old friend? Or one of his cousins?'

Freddie flings up his hands again. 'He flat out denied there was anyone there! Why would he lie?'

'Um, let me see – to mess with your head? Because this is Andrew Jacks?' He strokes the dog's ears. 'Babe, I've told you before, he's never going to change. He can guarantee getting a rise out of you every single time.'

'So it's my fault for being dumb? Thanks for that.'

'It's not your fault. I'm just saying, you can't control him. You can only control *you*.'

'Yeah? So what's that smile for?' Freddie comes across and flicks him on the forehead. 'Is it maybe because you're as big of an asshole as he is?'

'Maybe.' Ambrose fends him off, laughing. 'But I've sworn to use my powers only for good.'

'Fuck you.' He knuckles Ambrose's scalp. Then he stoops for a kiss. 'Thanks for . . . yeah. So I'm going for a run.'

'Remember to stay alert.'

'Whatever.' Freddie heads for the door.

'He probably wasn't lying,' says Ambrose.

Freddie turns. 'I. Saw. A. Naked. Guy.'

'Sure he wasn't *half* naked?'

131

A pause. 'Dang. *Dang!*'

'Here's a thought. What if he's finally found someone, only he's not ready to talk about it yet?'

'No! Aw, that is so sweet?' Freddie grins. 'Ha ha ha! The girls and me are *so* going to dedicate our next song to him?'

'Do that. He can't control you either, babe. Enjoy your run.'

Freddie runs through Lindford. Cherry blossom rusts in the gutters. The chalked bunting zigzags the streets from Friday's VE Day celebrations. He's heading for the river. It's his old running route between Lindchester and Cardingforth, just configured differently. Everything's configured differently now. He'll run from here to Lindchester, then back on the opposite bank, through Lindford and on to Cardingforth, over the bridge, then back home. When it comes to it, he knows he'll probably skip the end loop – the old cobbled pilgrim road that winds up the mount – because he'll find he can't face running round the silent Close, with the empty locked cathedral.

Tuesday 12th May
I keep on not writing this journal and today I nearly gave up, but then I thought, it is not like there is 'a law' that says you have to write it every day. It is not schoolwork, I can do what I like. This made me feel happier. 😊 *If you can choose for yourself what you do it is 'empowerment'.*
'FLOWER SUPERMOON'
It was the full Flower 'supermoon' on 7th. Leah and me watched it rise from her bedroom window, she let me because her room faces the right way – east. It was super dramatic because there were dark clouds and the moon looked all made of fire. Then when it rose higher it was pale and beatiful and very big. We stood watching it for ages, we could hear some people in a garden playing there music and talking in the dark. Then Leah went 'Oh f***!' and her tone of voice freaked me out, I went 'What?' and she said she had another migrane. She's OK again today and she explained to me it is a classic trigger for migranes when you have 'release of tension'. There is a lot of tension when your dad is in hospital with COVID-19 and then when he comes home your mum gets it, so you have to look after her. We both looked after mum and dad but mainly it was Leah, she felt responsible because she is older.

132

Fortunately mum did not get it badly and she is nearly better now, it is OK. That is the 'release of tension'. It is when things are OK again that you might get a bad reaction. I looked after Leah when she had her migrane, I took her some toast and marmite after she stopped being sick. She's OK now, I was super prepared for a reaction, but so far so good finger's crossed! I am totally fine. We missed VE day because only I was well and I didn't want to do stuff on my own, I just watched the Queen and 'We'll meet again' and I sang it too, but it was not the same.

It is Leah's birthday on Friday, she will be 14, but I can't buy her anything, obvs the shops are shut and if I get mum to get her something from Amazon she will TOTALLY FREAK, because he is a trillionnaire and doesn't pay tax so I don't know what to get her. She just wants money from mum and dad and granny and gramps so that she can make her own informed choices about what to get and be empowered. Its good to be empowered but I still like getting real presents. Me and mum will make her a vegan chocolate cake with vegan buttercream icing, we have done a shopping list and Chloe says she will get the ingredients like almond milk and chia seeds 'come what may'. Leah and me are in quarantine, we can't even take Luna for a walk which sucks. I have a plan, but it is 'a secret'. It is not an actual present but she will so like it, trust me.

Moon Facts

Moon phase: The moon is 'waning gibbous' (75%) For ages I was saying gibbous wrong (with a J), I did not know it was like as in 'gibbon'. Mum told me and I was embarassed. Then she said it proves you have learnt it from reading so I felt better. That was back in January (Wolf Moon.). It is so wierd thinking about that, it feels like the time before lockdown is 'abroad', like holidays abroad in Portugal. Lockdown is being lifted in stages, it is known to be an 'omni-shambles'. Leah says this is because nobody knows what their supposed to do now and more lives will be lost.

N.B. I do not always know what is a fact and what is Leahs opinion. I get that some facts are made up on google but how do you know which is which?

I suspect Miss Logan, Head of the Lower School at Queen Mary's, would endorse Leah's opinion here. Judging by the government directives schools have been spammed with, omnishambles is a pretty good description. A free-market approach to the pandemic, she thinks. You don't want a lockdown? OK, just wash your hands instead. Sorry, you *do* want a lockdown? OK, everyone, lockdown. You're getting fed up? All right, we'll start lifting it for you. Schools, prepare to reopen on 1 June. As if we've been closed all this time, thinks Miss Logan. Everyone forgets we've been open for key workers' and vulnerable children.

We last glimpsed Miss Logan 'abroad' in that pre-lockdown era, when Leah was sent to the Head for refusing to take off her face mask. Since then, Miss Logan has been the friendly face of QM for the Rogers family. She's begun phoning Leah each week, to check she's doing OK, and gently encouraging engagement with schoolwork. Off the record, she's felt all along that the Head's dealings with Leah have been cack-handed and disproportionate.

Let's go and visit Miss Logan. Unlimited flying now, remember. You know the drill. Fly to work if you can't work from home, *don't* fly on public transport, control the virus, fly in groups of up to six but stay two metres apart, fly on a bench and sunbathe unless you live in Wales, fly to clean someone's house, *don't* fly to visit your relatives, stay alert, take away the number you first thought of, and to sum up, fly to work if you're low-skilled, *don't* fly to work if you're professional. Above all, fly indoors where possible, save lives.

Emboldened by these guidelines, we will take to the skies, away, away, away. Oh, Lindfordshire in May! You break my heart. Frothing with cow parsley, may and rowan; buzzing, fizzing with spring, like homemade ginger beer bottles about to explode in the garage.

Look, that's Miss Logan down there. Her name is Rachel, by the way. She is out for a walk to clear her head between online lessons. We will glide along at our preferred altitude of two double-deckers, close enough to be nosy, high enough to maintain a bit of perspective.

Rachel knows she's one of the very lucky ones. On that weird Monday night, she bundled a load of stuff in the car, and fled her tiny two-up-two-down terraced house in Martonbury. She headed out here to the sticks to share lockdown with Mum and Dad, in the Old Rectory in Gayden Magna. Kind of infantilizing to move back home at the age of thirty-four, but at least this isn't the house she grew up in. She's not in her childhood bedroom, thank God. No, it's more like an en suite room in a boutique country house hotel. She gets to walk for miles along country lanes and footpaths, and eat breakfast on the terrace, smelling the wisteria and the roses. Glass of wine with Mum in the evenings, looking at the craft projects she's filling her time with. They'll all come in once the wedding industry is up and running again, and she can hire her venue out. All those poor couples with their Big Day micro-planned, your heart bleeds. But it's all pretty idyllic. So long as you don't pan out. If you do, it's like playing Sylvanian Families on the plain of Armageddon.

Today's another hot day. All the horse chestnut trees are a mass of candles. Rachel can feel the heat radiating up off the grassy footpath. Ah, there's the cuckoo again! She spots a runner approaching, so she climbs up the bank out of his way. Oh look, it's Gayden Parva. He labours past, giving Rachel a thumbs-up.

She slithers back down on to the path, and plucks the goose grass off her dress. It feels like some updated Jane Austen. 'For what do we live, but to make sport for our neighbours, and laugh at them in our turn?' The vicarage Gaydens certainly keep life interesting. Rachel smiles, remembering Monday night. That spectacular anti-Boris swearie Scots rant wafting across to the terrace, punctuated by the occasional murmur from Gayden Magna. Rachel and Mum with hands clamped to mouth. Dad nodding. 'Yep. What he said.'

The cuckoo calls again from a different patch of trees. Everywhere, thinks Rachel, everywhere there are good people doing their level best in impossible conditions. Dad, still doing emergency eye ops for cancer patients, but knowing people are getting missed, because GPs and opticians aren't referring them. Everything taking longer. Putting on the gear, checking, checking all the time everything is sanitized, that you've done everything possible. Staying positive, eating healthily. Trying to find ways of treating patients safely in routine ops. The backlog is already unimaginable. Knowing that however careful he is, he could still get infected. And then all the dickheads who got drunk and ended up in A&E after the bank holiday – thanks, guys!

But still, there's goodwill, mostly. All those people clapping, making scrubs, knitting ear savers. Some arrived in the post only this morning from the Archdeacon of Martonbury, along with a lovely card. Yes, most people are doing everything they can. You *have* to assume goodwill, good intentions, or you'll go mad. That's the problem with the government. You can't assume it. Your faith wavers. (Take that *Panorama* programme.) She thinks of Dad's weary face when he comes home, the sores across his nose and cheeks, his cracked hands.

Suddenly she works out what it is about Johnson's announcements that really gets her. It's not just the mixed message, it's his soft hands. Those fists plumped parallel on the desk, like he's playing spuds. Like it's a random lockdown counting game. One potato, two potato. Who's out this time? Seven potato *more*! It's you, schoolteachers! Ah, she's being cynical. Don't let's go there. There are other news feeds and timelines, of course there are, where people think the government is doing the best it can, where people #ClapForBoris.

Rachel sees an older couple approaching, hand in hand. They have a three-legged greyhound with them. She steps aside and leans on a gate. They nod their thanks. Both are in face masks. Overcautious? Or will this become normal? She turns and gazes across the meadow, where white cattle are grazing. Such a perfect, perfect May day. The kind of day when the Bennet girls might walk to Meryton to flirt with the officers, eliding any mention of the Napoleonic Wars. It must have hung in the air, though, the dread. Like the smell of may blossom now. The smell of corpses, according to Dad. It's everywhere. It creeps into everything. But you have to keep going. See another patient. Knit another ear protector. Teach another online *Macbeth* lesson.

The playgrounds of Lindfordshire are still eerie and silent. The swings move in the wind, like the ghosts of vanished children playing. A badger is seen wandering through the concourse of Lindford Station at night. But the garden centres are open at last. When he's back from his run, Neil sets off to stock his potagerie. He has to queue for forty-five minutes just to get in. Heaving with auld grannies! Golf courses open again too, spelling an end to Jane's fairway wandering. But she can now drive to the reservoir to exercise again. In far off London town, trains and buses are packed with people who can no more go to work without using public transport than French peasants could eat cake.

The days pass. Everything hurts. In the vast hangars, the workers walk, walk, walk the aisles, find the item, parcel the goods. The drivers drive, drive, drive, ring the bell, leave the parcel, back away. What is a trillionaire? How many zeros? If you laid all those workers end to end to the moon and back – as many as that?

Oh! What would George Eliot do? George Eliot would wait till 2062 to write this. She'd be brainier and do her research properly. She'd be able to discern what is what in the fact wars of politics and social media. Her plotlines would join up properly. It would not look like this; like our lives have fragmented into a vast mosaic. Vignettes of work, queuing, shopping, walking, weeping, gardening, Skyping, home schooling, fighting, worrying, praying, nursing, cleaning and failing. Failing. Failing, with nothing but the moon to steer by. Thousands of little Zoom tiles of anguish on the screen of this hot green May.

However, in 2062, dear reader, your author will be as old as Miss Sherratt. I'd like to think I'll be like her, still going strong with my wits about me, wrestling novel number twenty-five into shape. But I'm not betting on it. No, I'll just have to keep going. What else can any of us do? We can only look after one another as best we can, and keep going.

In the gardens, the first young carrots are ready to be picked. Miss Sherratt comes down to find a dusty bundle of them on her terrace. She bends – oof! – to pick them up. Later she will put out a plate of warm fruit scones in their place. *Same spirit of national endeavour.* Miss Sherratt resents this Johnsonian twaddle. The audacity of requisitioning our efforts – after years of underfunding! This isn't the war. In the war, we could hear the doodlebugs coming.

The copper beeches are settling into their deep wine colour. A wood pigeon coos. All the tight beads of peony buds are showing pink. Someone is using an angle grinder on a Martonbury construction site. In Abbey Grove Nursing Home, Renfold, a resident dies – the second this week. In the maternity ward of Lindford General, three new babies are born. In Lindford cemetery, an orange-tip butterfly flutters among the gravestones, and lands on the one that Jane photographed for her cancelled Josephine Luscombe lecture in the States. It lists the names and ages of all the orphanage children who died in the cholera epidemic of 1849. George Fenton, aged 12 yrs. Anna Fenton, aged 10 yrs. Eliza Greatrix, aged 12 yrs. William Dobson, aged 11 yrs. And so on, and on. All dead, for the want of clean water and proper washing facilities – and a vaccine. Oh, for a vaccine. How can we be safe without one? The butterfly flits on.

We will flit on too, away over the cemetary wall, through the arboretum, where a group of teens are playing Frisbee, and Chloe is out jogging with Cosmo. She delivered the shopping to the Rogers' household, and the cake has been made. Even now, we can peer in through the window and watch the family gathered round the kitchen table. They're singing Happy Birthday. The fourteen candles flicker, lighting up Leah's face. So young, so radiant. Make a wish, make a wish!

I too will make a wish. I wish it didn't have to be like this. I wish we'd made a better world for you to live in when we're gone.

But for once Leah isn't blaming the boomers as she blows out the candles all in one go. I don't know what she's wishing. Never tell, or it won't come true. But I think she'll play that doofy clip a few more times tonight before she falls asleep. Freddie and the girls singing her 'Happy Birthday', as requested by Jess.

Milk Moon, Part III

The Milk Moon wanes over Lindfordshire. On this bright breezy May morning, all that remains is the top left-hand crescent, like a paring of cloud. Father Wendy sees it as she walks with Pedro beside the River Linden. Oh, it was so lovely to be able to drive out somewhere with Doug, and finally wander along the footpaths in the bluebell woods near Gayden Parva last week. Bluebells!

'I thought we'd miss them this year, Pedro!'

Pedro stops to be a good dog. Wendy didn't get the memo saying you don't have to pick up after your dog during a pandemic, so she's come prepared with biodegradable bags. They set off again. To walk here is a blessing, too, she reminds herself. An everyday blessing, like daily manna in the wilderness. How quickly we get fed up with our everyday blessings and forget how lucky we are. Like the children of Israel, grumbling that they had cucumbers in Egypt. Yes, we were slaves, but at least the food was good. Not this miserable old manna. We're sick of it!

'Cucumbers in Egypt syndrome – that's what it is.'

She's been walking this stretch of river for over a decade now. First with Lulu, now with Pedro. Two years ago, she was in the valley of the shadow of death – not knowing if the cancer was everywhere, or if it would be treatable. And now the whole globe is walking through that valley. She recognizes the feelings from 2018. It's like wearing a motorbike helmet. You're encased, closed down to your immediate surroundings. There's only the next hour, the next thing. But a gift

139

was given two years ago too – the gift of suddenly seeing how glorious life is. Like a diamond placed on black velvet.

They've reached their bench. 'Here we are, Pedro. I need to rest my old bones for a minute.' She sits. Someone's coming on a bike, so she pulls up her mask until they've passed. It feels foolish, but you never know. Nobody really knows all the ways of this terrible virus yet. People's cavalier approach hurts so much. Calling school-teachers work-shy. Protesting in Hyde Park against lockdown. It's like . . . what is it like? Spitting at key workers? Something like that. Watching partygoers kick funeral wreaths about in front of the grieving families. Father, forgive them. She sends a blessing chasing along the bank after the cyclist – *Stay safe!* – then pulls her mask back down.

Even this bench is an everyday blessing, restored to her after those weeks when it was taped off. *In loving memory of Ronnie Farrell, 1913–1990. True gentleman and loving dad and husband.* Thirty years ago. They would have been able to sit with him at the end, gather at the funeral, grieve together, have a wake, choose this bench. Everyday manna. Nobody thought, nobody could have imagined the funerals of 2020. Wendy has three more this week.

The Linden flows by. There goes a moorhen with a brood of chicks. Pedro watches intently. May blossom and cow parsley. Bird's-foot trefoil growing beside the dusty path. Everything's so dry. Goodness, those February storms. A distant memory for most people now. But not here in Cardingforth, where the flooded homes still haven't dried out properly. Oh, her poor parishioners! For lock-down to come just as work was getting underway. Everything's on hold. Waiting for floorboards to be replaced, for walls to be replas-tered. There are still sandbags piled in the streets. Well, things will start moving again, now lockdown's been eased a bit. The builders should be back soon. Is it safe, though? Will they be able to maintain social distance?

Oh dear. She's trying to carry the whole world again. Time to lay the burden down, Wendy. Down by the riverside. And face the next hour, the next thing. She gets to her feet.

'Come along, boy. On with life.' The next thing is a deanery Zoom meeting. Well, assuming Zoom isn't on the fritz again like it was on

Sunday. Some people were joking the Church had caused the outage. 'My word, if the World Wide Web went down, we'd all be in bother, wouldn't we, boy?'

Hush! Don't say that out loud, Father Wendy! Don't even think it, or you'll jinx us. Lord have mercy – imagine lockdown without the internet! Odd to reflect that it's a mere thirty years old. Back in the time of Ronnie Farrell, *double you double you double you dot* was scribble talk. We all had landlines and analogue TVs. Everything plugged in. *Wireless* was what your aged grandparents hilariously called a radio, and mobiles hung over cots.

Is there anything that could wipe out the internet? Delete the Cloud? I realize I've been picturing the Cloud as magical, like a repository of Christmas wish lists shimmering over the North Pole. But the information must be stored *somewhere* real, mustn't it? There must be an actual infrastructure of cables and hubs and satellites. I daresay there are safeguards, and back-up systems to safeguard the safeguards, and back-up back-ups to safeguard those.

Now I'm thinking of Fukushima. The failsafe system that automatically closed down the reactors when it detected an earthquake, then the diesel generators that took over automatically when the electricity went down, and kept the coolant circulating. Everything anticipated, contingency plans in place. Only one question wasn't asked: is there anything capable of taking all this out in one go? With hindsight, it looks obvious. Who hasn't seen a print of the Great Wave, with Mount Fuji dwarfed beneath it?

Ah, but it turns out the question *was* asked in 2000, and again in 2008. Both those tsunami studies were ignored, because they would only create anxiety, and anyway, the plant's sea wall was ten metres high. A wave bigger than that? Not likely to happen. I bet it came down to money in the end. Planning for an almost unimaginable disaster that almost one hundred per cent probably isn't going to happen anyway, fingers crossed? We'll deal with any fourteen-metre tsunamis if and when they come along. In the meantime, we've got an economy to run.

How hard it is to feel any urgency about theoretical disasters. And if you do feel the urgency, you're like the lone voice agitating to buy snowploughs on a hot May morning when there's barely enough money for mowers. Permanently stockpiling and replenishing supplies of hazmat kit and PPE in vast warehouses, safeguarding supply chains, funding the NHS, all on the off chance of a global pandemic? Not scrapping the Threats, Hazards, Resilience and Contingency Committee? With hindsight, it's obvious. We'll know next time.

There goes Father Wendy now, through the little kissing gate. She opens it with her sleeve, and sets off along the path home, depositing the poo bag in the overflowing dog waste bin.

Are we losing the plot in lockdown? That's what it feels like. But plot is not always linear, like the Linden flowing authoritatively from Lindchester to Cardingforth. The mainstream is not the only thing that counts. There's always a network of tributaries – the Marton, Whistle Brook, the Carding; and all the tiny meandering brooks and hidden culverts, the water meadows, quaggy and cow-churned, with kingcups and ladies' smock. From high above, where the last scrap of Milk Moon looks down, the waters of Lindfordshire feather out like roots and ferns. Or like the tracery of veins in your eyes when the optician shines a light in; like your lungs, their bronchi, six-fold dividing, small, smaller, ever smaller, fanning out into your terminal bronchioles, respiratory bronchioles, and your 300 million alveoli, so fearfully and wonderfully made.

Martin and Becky sit on the sofa. They have blankets over their knees, like an old, old couple on the seafront. Now and then they laugh weakly – look at us! Sometimes their eyes leak weary tears. Through the open French windows, they can see the girls digging the plot ready to plant the seed potatoes at the new moon. Every breath they take – in, out, oxygen, carbon dioxide, in, out – is a miracle, a 300 million-fold miracle. A blessing so tiny, you could easily miss it.

Ascension Day 2020. In spite of everything, God went up across Lindfordshire with a merry noise, in birdsong and sunshine, in kindly acts, in every faithful heart, and via Zoom. But not, sadly, in the form of giggling choristers making their way up the spiral stone steps to sing from the base of Lindchester Cathedral's spire. In the sound of the trumpet, yes. At 5.30 p.m., one of the lay clerks stood in front of the cathedral's west end and played a specially composed Ascension Day fanfare. Sing praise, sing praise, sing praises out! It echoed round the whole Close. If you were there to hear it, you will have felt the two-edged sword of music piercing even to the dividing asunder of soul and spirit.

Gene heard it, as he stood hulling strawberries in the deanery kitchen for the rococo confectionary ravishment he was constructing for Deanissima's Ascension Day supper. Dean Marion, in her study, waiting prayerfully for the livestream service to start, also heard the notes float down like flakes of glory.

It was still resounding as Giles, the canon precentor, made his way through the cathedral towards the quire – it fell to his lot to livestream the short act of worship. How his soul had been longing all these weeks of lockdown to enter into the courts of the Lord. This was his third time back since the regulations were eased and, as always, he was alone. But oh, as the trumpet sounded, the cathedral had never felt more full. Tears streamed down his cheeks. He might have been crowd surfing the entire communion of saints up the aisle, in heart and mind thither ascending, with the tinnitus of glory susurrating in his ears.

I would love to tell you Father Dominic felt something similar the first time he entered his church again. He had to take Mother in with him (permitted, because they're in the same household). I wish he'd been transported by glory too. But he had no time to spare for his own feelings. He was too busy explaining to Mother that they were in the middle of a global pandemic.

'Goodness! You mean like whatsername, that village in Derbyshire, the ones who shut themselves in?'

'Yes. Eyam. A bit like that,' agreed Dominic. 'Everyone's staying at home, so that the virus can't spread.'

'Well, blow me down with a feather.'

It wasn't until later, when they were home and Mother had nodded off in her chair, that it all caught up with him. He wept silently in his study, rocking back and forth. His only prayer was *Oh dear. Oh dear.* It felt as frail an offering as Star's tiny bunch of violets, standing desiccated at Mary's feet.

All across the Diocese of Lindchester, individual clergy have to weigh up matters of safety and decide how to respond to the new guidelines. There's no one size to fit all. Some clergy are shielding, or living with vulnerable people. Not all church buildings are conveniently right next door to the vicarage. Travelling there is low risk but not no risk. Quite rightly, everyone has an opinion about the way the government and the House of Bishops have handled the situation. Emergency COVID-19 regulations have made it mandatory to express those opinions on Twitter, so that the world is a nicer place for everyone. If you ever dip a toe into Twitter waters, you'll have noticed how soothing it is. Like those fish spa pedicures, with the Garra rufa fish replaced by piranhas.

Oh dear. Oh dear. But at least everyone is staying at home. Every household a mini Eyam. Everyone is staying home so that the virus can't spread. Public figures caught out breaking lockdown rules must fall on the sword of resignation, like Prof Neil Ferguson and Scotland's chief medical officer. Unless, of course, they are above the law and the rules don't apply to them.

A blustery storm whips through Lindfordshire. In Gayden Parva the thin trunks clack and clatter as the wind kneads the bluebell wood. Every path and pavement in the diocese is lurid green with snapped-off tender leaves. A freak autumn in May. All that hard work for nothing.

In Gayden Magna, the Logan family gather on the terrace to eavesdrop on the swearie Scots rant against yon evil Gollum-weasel Scummings. I honestly believe that if Neil were silent, the very stones would cry out. Every stone in every road that has laid itself down to make the way ahead possible for others; every stone that has stayed put in its place in the wall, cobbled itself together and stayed in its place with all the other stones, to keep the building standing, come hell and high water. Every stone in the land.

'Cummings won't resign,' says Jane. 'You watch.'

'Well, if the whole driving to Barnard Castle thing is true, he should,' says Matt.

'You're assuming they've got quaint old-fashioned values like integrity and accountability,' says Jane. 'They won't even apologize.'

23rd May

It is the weekend nearly YAY!!! Plus it is another <u>Bank Holiday</u>. Me and Leah are going to plant the seed potatoes tomorrow because it is the NEW MOON. This is when you should plant potatoes and things that grow under the soil so the moons gravity helps them grow. It is to do with the tides, Leah explained it to me, but I was not really listening.

The Next <u>FULL MOON</u> will be the <u>STRAWBERRY MOON</u>. We should of planted strawberries but it is to late now ☹

Frankly I will be glad for June, May has been somewhat stressful. Mum and dad are getting better and Leah and me will boost there immunity with our garden produce. Leah is doing my head in making me to learn a new song, the Diggers Song, she has been researching the Diggers. Miss Logan set her some work, it is voluntary. Leah is doing the work because Miss Logan is cool (according to Leah) plus she will ask Jane for resources, Jane is actually a historian.

Don't get me wrong, the Diggers song is cool, but 'major problem' I can't exactly sing when Leah sings, she has her own take on the tune. Leah says we've got to sing it when we dig, it is our literal history, if we are ignorant of our history the govament will carry on p****ing on us like Dominic Cummings and the Prime Minister who flaunt the rules.

FORTUNATLY I came up with a plan and Leah went for it, like I knew she would LOL. We are going to ask Mr Hardman-May if he will sing it on YouTube for his next online music lesson. FINGERS CROSSED.

Well, if you follow the Joe Wicks of singing, you will know that Jess did not cross her fingers in vain. 'You noble Diggers all, stand up now, stand up now.' How often music cuts to the quick, giving us a vehicle for all our pent-up rage and heartbreak. 'The gentry must come down and the poor shall wear the crown.' But that rallying cry for justice was not the only piece Freddie uploaded this week. You may also have enjoyed Freddie and his girls singing 'I'm in Love with a Wonderful Guy'. The performance was dedicated to his former mentor, and cut with rare footage from 2016 of Dr Jacks tap-dancing.

Many miles away, and well beyond the scope of this tale, his former mentor watched it. 'You little shit.'

Someone laughed and ruffled his hair for him. 'Busted.'

Milk Moon, Part IV

Week Ten of lockdown. Not a cloud, not a drop of rain. If we were to put our candle of hope in the window at 7 p.m., the way we did back in March, nobody would see it. Long golden summer evenings, when the trees all sparkle and insects dance high up like specks of light. Wisteria is in full mauve glory on mellow sandstone walls. Look at the vivid reds and hot pinks of rhododendrons in parks and gardens, and out in fields and woods, the wild strawberry flowers and dandelion clocks, speedwell and buttercups. Bees fumble their way up the Fragonard frills of aquilegias; everywhere, the scent of roses, the velvety purr of wings as small birds flit to and fro. Winter-white feet develop sandal stripes, and Neil sets about the anguished task of buying the world's most expensive Panama to tend his potager in.

These are the days of waiting between Ascension Day and Pentecost. Waiting to be clothed with power from on high. Praying #ThyKingdomCome. How long, O Lord? Limbo of limbos in unravelling lockdown. We are fishing all night and catching nothing, *nothing*. Maybe at dawn Jesus will be there on the shore, calling to us. Maybe the catch will be miraculous.

It's the marking season. Jane is deep in Turnitin, in the land of rubrics and assessment criteria. She worked through the bank holiday, because what else was she going to do – skip off to Barnard Castle for an eye test? Rose gardens and innocent parish-hall tables are forever smirched by association with the Dominic Cummings press conference.

Even when thirty-five Tory MPs call for Cummings to resign, the Prime Minister stands by his spad. Jane relishes that word. It smacks of those shocking playground insults from the 60s that nobody dreams of saying any more. And it appeals to her mordant humour that in railway speak SPAD means *Signal Passed At Danger*. Johnson refuses to throw his spad to 'the dogs'. And who are these dogs of which you speak, Prime Minister? Every heartbroken weary outraged soul in the UK, that's who. This is on you, if people stop keeping the rules. Let the record show who bent the bars of lockdown and let the dogs out.

For twenty whole minutes at a time, Jane gets engrossed in her students' work and forgets the backdrop. Forgets that her study window in the palace looks out across the plains of Mordor. Loses sight of the fact that she swallowed a chunk of ancient filling yesterday, and therefore fails to worry the gap with her tongue, or pray that the emergency filling she ordered from Amazon arrives today. *Temporary tooth repair. One-step formula. Ideal for travel.* Travel. Yeah right.

She comes to the end of another assignment. *There is much to admire in this clear and thoughtful dissertation. Here's what you've done well. Here's where you might improve.* Jane gives it seventy-five per cent. This is probably generous, but she is applying the university policy of 'contextualized marking'. She takes this to mean 'We can't help noticing that COVID-19 has blighted your university career and hopes for the future, depriving you of a social life and the company of your peers, preventing you from visiting the library, sleeping at night, and overall has turned your undergraduate years into Munch's *Scream*'.

Her tongue finds its way to the absent filling. It was one of those vast 1980s amalgams, like a chunk of gravel. On the plus side, it's not hurting. On the negative, it's not an emergency – hence the repair kit. And the moral of the tale, boys and girls, is never eat Bombay Mix during a global pandemic. Jane can't see dentists reopening safely any time soon. Not after they handed over all their PPE to bail out the hospitals.

She does a quick check of her inbox between Final Year dissertations. Stuff about planning for next year, mainly; and what campus teaching might look like with social distancing. Invitations to webinars to learn how to navigate the useful tech she's been ignoring for years. Flagrant COVID phishing attempts caught and quarantined in the university's 'You must think I'm an idiot' filter. There's an email from a random stranger. Title: *Family History*. She gets them now and then. People hoping she can help them research their family tree.

Dear Dr Rossiter,
Apologies for contacting you out of the blue like this, but I think we might be related. I know this might come as a shock, but I've been thinking a lot about it during these strange times. With the death of my dad last month, I've been wanting to reach out. His name was Elliot Robinson, born 1936 in Liverpool, and he lived his whole life here.
Apologies again, because I have no idea how much you know already about your father. I will understand if you don't want to take this further. I won't trouble you again, but as I said, I just wanted to reach out.
With best wishes,
Sandra O'Brien

For a wistful moment or two, Jane entertains herself with the idea of having a family of long lost relatives. Obviously, she'd prefer them to be raffish and decadent, descendants of ramshackle Russian revolutionaries, perhaps; drunken musicians and poets, rather than a pack of Scousers – but a tantalizing thought all the same. It's a clear case of mistaken identity, however. She rattles off an email saying sorry for your loss, and explaining her dad was Ray Rossiter, of solid East Midlands mining stock, etc. etc. *During these strange times.* That would make an interesting study – the weird 'only connect' urge to reach out. There was quite a wave of it in March. Getting back in touch with people, mending walls. Why, Jane herself very nearly buried the hatchet with the Quisling.

But on to the next assignment. Seven more to mark, then it's Second Year 'takeaway' exam scripts. She sees the post arrive. Perhaps there will be a death threat for Matt today. Some of the other bishops have received them for speaking out against Dominic Cummings' lockdown law finagling. She wouldn't want Matt to feel left out.

It's half-term, whatever that means. Lindfordshire is tinder dry. The moss on walls and roofs is frizzled. Everyone is out for walks and picnics. The car parks at the region's beauty spots are rammed. People paddle and swim in the Linden. There they go, with buckets and spades and wooden swords, and not a face mask to be seen. They scramble up wooded banks under the outrageous green canopy, sandalled feet slipping on the dusty soil. They try to stand aside for one another on narrow paths. Giant wood ants are busy everywhere. Sometimes a cuckoo calls, hollow, mellow, as if the sound were amplified by some cunningly crafted wooden box.

The fire brigade works round the clock putting out blazes on heathland sparked by disposable BBQs and dropped cigarettes. People play golf – if they are lucky enough to bag a tee time. They're only supposed to play one- or two-ball games, socially distanced or with members of their household, but if Cummings can drive to Durham, fuck it. The train has whistled through the red light. All bets are off now.

In Lindford, Virginia finally flips. She calls the police at 2 a.m. People, dozens of them, have been arriving all evening next door. The party music in the back yard is blaring so loud, even earplugs can't block it out. Eventually, car doors slam. She hears voices shouting away off into the distance, and it falls quiet. Early the next morning, her yard is full of beer cans and takeaway cartons. Only the Lord himself will ever know how close she comes to chucking it all back over the wall. Screaming, *Have your fucking rubbish back, you fucking trash!* Virginia, who has dropped neither the F-bomb nor litter in her entire life. Instead, she walks to church. She will sit in the silent building and pour it all out, weeping like Hannah in the Temple, not caring that she looks like a daughter of Belial. Then she'll pull herself together and drive out to the crem to take another funeral.

A few streets away, Chloe blots her tears and ties her trainers. It hadn't been hard to text Freddie back with a clear *No* to his suggestion.

'Walkies, good boy!' They head to the arboretum, past scattered silver bullets of nitrous oxide. The pavements are dusted green gold under the sycamores.

No, I'm really sorry, but I just can't, Freddie. It doesn't matter what other people do, the regulations haven't changed.

Oh, it's all just so sad. It feels like a waste. Ten weeks of keeping the rules, not even a handshake, just waving and wailing across the horrible two-metre abyss of heartbreak.

This Thursday is the tenth and final #ClapForCarers. The sound rises all across Lindfordshire, like reverse rain pattering upwards. Then comes the usual ding and clang of wooden spoons on saucepans, car horns and firework volleys, and birds scattering in panic, cats bolting, babies waking. Ten's a good round number, and the woman who started it has said this should be the last one. We'd been wondering how we'd ever stop. Would the nation still be clapping every Thursday centuries from now, the way we burn Roman Catholics in effigy four hundred-odd years after the Gunpowder Plot?

When to finish has been awkward all along. The start was clear: 8 p.m. But each week we eyed one another. Is this enough? Then we hear someone on the next street still clapping, so we carry on. We knew what it was about at the start, too. It was heartfelt and spontaneous. A simple narrative: Thanks, guys. We're with you. Now it's a tangled mess of ribbons round the national maypole, with shouting, recriminations, and different groups tugging for control. Enough.

'So, I'm gonna message him, say I can't do it?'

'OK, babe.'

The hens chook-chook and dab and scratch in their run. Fabiola has a fluttery dust bath.

'Aw,' says Freddie. He unlatches the door and reaches in. 'Come to Daddy, here c'mon.' He scoops up a speckled armful. Ah, he should fess up. Coz Brose knows there's something, and he's mad, only inside; he's a nuclear reactor, not a volcano. Except maybe he's mad at the world, at the government, at black people getting killed, people dying of COVID, the economy tanking, and not Freddie at all. God, that's probably it, so Freddie can't ask, coz it will be like back at the referendum, when Brose was all, This is a nightmare of global proportions and you're stressing that I'm mad at you?

'Oh God, listen, are you, you're not mad at me?'

'What? No!' Ambrose ducks to get in Freddie's eye line. 'Should I be?'

'No. Maybe? Probably not.' Freddie gazes away to next door. For a second he thinks the blind moves upstairs, but no. 'Gonna put this girl back, and yeah, text Andy?'

Ambrose watches him. 'Why can't you sing it?'

Freddie shrugs. 'Just not feeling it right now is all.'

'OK. Get you a beer?' He heads back inside.

'Nah, I'm good.' Freddie latches the henhouse door. The swifts are flying high, *shwee-schwee*. He's not feeling anything right now except homesick? Like when he was six, boarding for the first time. Or when Mum and Dad split up. Or juvie. Oh God, he misses Miss B so much, and Brose is mad? That feeling when you're curled up inside, and the only voice you've got is a scream, and only a razor blade can express it? Jeeesus. Can't believe you're even thinking that. There's only this tiny place he's found between speaking and singing? That's all he's got right now. And in no way does that fit the Dorian Singers' brand?

Saterday 30th May

This is not to do with the moon as such but Leah and me have been wattering the garden, it was hilarious. It is a drought, and humanitys <u>*fault*</u> *yeah yeah. Leah is opposed to hosepipes, it is waistful, so we are using a special system of recycling bathwater. The system is called 'Syphening'. So you have to put one end of the hose in the bathwater and put the other end out of the bathroom window. Gravity will then suck the water out and you can water your garden sustainably!!!! Leah told me, and I went That is so cool! I will have a bath right now!!!!! And she went DO NOT use your pink fairy unicorn bath bombs I mean it, you will chemically kill the potatoes.*

I had a super quick bath, we had to wait till it cold so we looked at <u>*'you know what'*</u> *on her new phone she got with her birthday money to see if Mr Hardman-May has uploaded anything new yet. But there is* <u>*still*</u> *nothing new* ☹ *I hope he is not ill with 'THE VIRUS'.*

So I through the pipe out of the window but I let go of my end of the pipe and Leah got mad, then I slipped and my foot went in the bath and my trainer got soaked and I literly could not stop laughing and mum was going are you OK in there, because she thought I was crying in there LOL.

Long story short we tried again and it should of worked but it did not. I was super disappointed and Leah was <u>really</u> mad then dad came into the bathroom and explained about gravity. You have to help the water get up the pipe from the bath uphill to the window first, the pipe has to be full of water before it will work, it is physics.

So I shouted down 'Dad says you have to suck your end'. Leah shouted back up to me 'I am not sucking the f****ing pipe I do NOT want to drink you're gross bathwater, YOU f***ing suck the f**ing pipe.' And this old couple was going by who looked at her so she yelled WHAT? And dad called down 'I am SO sorry' to the old people. Then Dad was laughing then he was coughing and he sat on the edge of the bath because he is still not up to full strength, (caused by the virus, it is terrible trust me).

At the end of the day it was mum who saved the day! She came in and roled her eyes and she put the pipe on the tap and ran the water and then we heard Leah scream when cold water went on her. Then mum put her thumb on the pipe end and then put it in the bathwater. Long story short, it worked. Then I said to mum and dad, I do not totally 100% get why this is sustainable? I mean normally I like, have a shower? And dad said ours is not to question why. And mum went ours is but to do and die, it is a poem, don't worry Jess. They smiled at eachother in this really nice way.

<u>Moon Facts</u>
First quarter (49%) not long now to the STRAWBERRY MOON!!!

The globe is tinder dry. The pale horseman still rides, but he looks smaller now, silhouetted against a backdrop of fire. Far away, Minneapolis burns in the night. Then another city, another. Metal barriers go up round the White House. *When the looting starts, the shooting starts.* Twitter hides the president's words, but they cannot be unsaid. We can never wind back. It only goes one way; the grains of sand trickle down from the top of the hourglass, down, down. It's gravity, it's physics. There's no going back to 25th May, to the hour before George Floyd walked into the grocery store. We cannot unsee what we saw, those eight minutes and forty-five seconds of white knee on black neck, the full weight of the law bearing down, the full gravity of the situation. We cannot unhear the words *I can't breathe.*

Pentecost Sunday. The world is baptized with fire. What will be left of us? Jane picks armfuls of red rhododendrons to put in Matt's chapel. Bumblebees have made a nest under the eaves. She can see them swirling outside the window. Sometimes there are buzzings, like distant voices on a faraway phone. Jane weeps her way through the service of Holy Communion again. This is my superpower, she thinks. My tears. I would prefer the ability to fly. I'd fly to New Zealand, to my baby boy, just to hug him. Jane will never unhear it. The way George Floyd called for his mama.

The tiny bee voices murmur on in the eaves. Blackbirds sing, and goldfinches, and everything is mad and everything is normal. Curled in an empty room, his arms hugging his knees, Freddie hums softly, in that tiny space between speaking and singing. 'Amid the shades of evening, while sinks life's lingering sand, I hail the glory dawning from Emmanuel's land.' It's all wasted, all his talent, this year that was gonna be the big breakthrough, the year he was maybe gonna be a dad, gone.

But curled on the other side of the wall, where the fan hums day and night, someone is listening. He's less than a foot away, though Freddie doesn't know it.

JUNE

Rose Moon, Part I

I t's raining in Lindfordshire at last. Pattering on leaves, chuckling down drains. Jack hears the first drops in the night, falling on the ancient summerhouse roof in Miss Sherratt's garden. He goes and stands under the cedar tree.

The sky's pale, although it's three in the morning. Nearly midsummer. Never really dark this time of year. There's the moon through the branches. It's setting, fuzzy behind the clouds. He breathes in the smell of rain, and the honeysuckle is pumping out scent for the moths and other night insects. The peonies seem to glow, but on a dull wattage about to go out. Like night-vision goggles, only more ghostly. There's a splosh in the old pond. If there were kids here, you'd need to fence it off, but it's OK, there's only him. Even Miss Sherratt doesn't come down this far. Just a frog or something else restless, and now it's quiet again, apart from the pattering drops. It's fine. Nobody's going to drown in this garden. There won't be any fatal three minutes of distraction. Sometimes wonders about the au pair, poor lass. Nineteen? Whether she ever got over it. How would you? He never has. Should've told them to get a self-closing hinge on the swimming pool gate. Twenty-three years on, and he still thinks that.

There are no lights on in Sherratt Manor. He hopes she's sleeping tonight. Not sleeping's a killer, he knows that. You go chasing sleep to give your head a break, throw your chemical weaponry at it, pills, booze, but the more you chase the faster it runs. Better to stalk it gently, or give up, let it come to you if it's going to, the way birds come, or not. Robins, when you're digging. Always friendly, robins. Comes from when they followed the pigs rooting in the forests. They mistake us for pigs. So the story goes. Jack doesn't buy that. They're friendly because you'd never harm a robin, nobody would. Something about a robin. Christmas cards. The old tales. How he got his red breast trying to pull thorns out of Christ's head on the cross.

Jack runs a hand over his own head. Shaggy. And his beard. Like the Wild Man of Borneo – can't say that. His grandma always did. Get your hair cut, Jack, you look like— The things we used to say, no harm meant, they were just words. But he's been called so many things now, scum, hobo, retard, paedo; he's been spat at, robbed, kicked awake by kids, pissed on – never really just words, is it? He rubs his hair again and thinks about Star, the lass who cuts it for him, won't take any money. How's she getting on in all this?

The pattering stops. Not enough for the thirsty garden. Total silence, except for the faint hum from the weed house. Thirteen years sober now. Not often tempted these days, not even when the smell's so strong he can't believe the bizzies don't come swarming like bees. All over the show people must be falling off the wagon, he guesses; lockdown doing their heads in. But for him, no. He's got everything he needs, finally. Peace and quiet. Nobody hassling him. A garden. Someone to look out for, who also looks out for him. Hard to believe – here in the stillness – that America is burning. He scans the headlines once a day to keep abreast, otherwise steers well clear of the news. He's seen enough burning. Hardly gets the real flashbacks any more. Mostly it's like ancient footage. It plays across his brain-screen as if he's a civilian watching old clips and going, Oh yeah, Kuwait. I remember that, terrible.

A light goes on downstairs in the other house. Sometimes one of the lads, the blond one, comes out and sings in the dark. Another insomniac. Other times he goes for a run, and then Jack hears him coming back maybe an hour later. The distant beat of his trainers through the empty streets. The sound gets gradually closer, like the rain coming in across the town. Miles, he must run. Looks like he's just getting a drink this time, because the kitchen light goes out again. A lot of yelling earlier, but seems as though things are OK now.

Silence. The hum of the fan. High up, he can just hear the quiet rumble of a jet slowly passing. All OK. All tucked up, safe as the chickens. Good bit of kit, that henhouse. Fox isn't going to get in there. Jack goes back into the summerhouse and settles himself down again.

'Where are we going again?'

'To visit Jane and Matt, Mother dear.' Lord, it feels strange to be back behind the wheel after all these weeks. Not too much traffic this evening. He navigates the big roundabout like an Edwardian dowager. He practically needs a man with a red flag walking in front! He's praying that poor old Lady doesn't get carsick after all this time, and puke on the upholstery. 'We're off on a frolic at last.'

'Ooh! I like a good frolic.'

Has she any idea how long we've been cooped up? Some days she's got hold of the concept of quarantine, other days she's bowled over afresh. Well I never! It's like Eyam! Yes, Mother, like Eyam.

'Is Jane the Spanish one?'

'Spanish?'

'You know. Isn't she a whatchamacallit? At the thing, the academy.'

'University, you mean?'

'Yes! Is it her?'

'Yes. Jane's a history lecturer. Oops!' He crunches the gears turning right. Embarrassing! The motoring equivalent of a public fart. 'Pardon *me*. And she's married to the Bishop of Barcup. Matt. You remember Matt? He took the parish nurses service. No? Well, anyway, we're going to have fish and chips in their garden. And she's not Spanish.'

'Well, she's *something*.'

'Oh yes,' he agrees. 'We're all something.' He's given up following the convoluted red-herring-strewn path of her thought processes. He checks the rear-view mirror. Lady seems fine.

Cow parsley. Wild roses. Everything so green! Oh, don't let him spend the whole evening sobbing into his Prosecco. But perhaps it will all seem calm and totally normal? He hardly knows what he's feeling any more. Lockdown's scrambled the dial on his emotional barometer. Pity it's not warmer. The pally garden is gorgeous, but it's not *quite* sitting out on the terrace weather. Still, them's the rules. Jane's got rugs to wrap Mother in. Lady can chase the episcopal squirrels and everything will be lovely, lovely, lovely.

Well, it's taking Father Dominic an unconscionably long time to make this journey. I propose we fill the time, dear reader, by flying over Lindfordshire to see this week's small easing of lockdown taking effect. There are many small socially distanced meet-ups and reunions going on in gardens. Come, come! It's always worth it. Let's blow those cobwebs away.

We'll head out to the sticks, where Neil and Father Ed have invited the Logan family to come and sit on the vicarage terrace. They admire Neil's exquisitely appointed potagerie. It looks stunning from our bird's eye view. He's worked hard. It lacks but the finishing touch: plants. (Far be it from me to suggest that Neil invited them in order to scrounge cuttings from the Old Rectory garden.) The Logans have brought their own wine glasses. The bottles of St Émilion and Pouilly-Fuissé stand on a socially distant table for the guests to help themselves. No hugs or handshakes, no food. It just doesn't feel very hospitable, does it? But at least they have a garden to be inhospitable in.

Father Wendy is deeply conscious of her many blessings in a diocese where so many live in gardenless rented property, or who are homeless and in temporary hotel accommodation, and have been separated from their beloved dogs. She reaches down to stroke Pedro's silky ears. She and her husband Doug are shivering on their patio chairs on the vicarage drive, waiting for the Cardingforth churchwardens to arrive. Two more patio chairs stand ready sanitized on the other side of a chalked line. Doug was out with his measuring tape early, making sure it was two metres. 'Doesn't that look a bit rude?' worries Wendy. (There is no greater manifestation of Englishness than to lay down your life for fear of looking rude.)

At last, children can go and spend time on their parents' patio. Lockdown babies can be shown to shielding grandparents through French windows. The national right to BBQ in the rain can be exercised. No going inside though, unless it's for a wee, and then it's the whole sanitizing the door handles and taps folderol, just in case. (Even though we've all been isolating for eleven weeks.) Behold, how good and pleasant it is to see one another again. A bit fatter, a bit hairier, but still here.

Up on Cathedral Close, the canons may now sit collegially in one another's gardens. The precentor and his wife take a bottle of Riesling across the Close. They sit in their coats on a bench on the lawn of the canon chancellor and his wife. The two benches face one another across a flowerbed where the black poplar towered until the Halloween storm of 2013. Time has not filled in the gap left behind, but it has softened its edges. A tulip tree grows in its place. In another thirty or forty years, who will remember any of this?

There are gaps all across Lindfordshire now. Homes where absence is so intense, it feels like presence. Unsaid goodbyes, unvisited bedsides. All the edges bleed, with no proper funerals to staunch them. In hospitals and care homes, nurses sit and hold the hands of the dying. They put phones to dying ears so family can weep *I love you. I love you.* The UK death toll reaches 40,000. One day it will be in the past tense. It will be like old footage. COVID-19. I remember that. Terrible.

Father Dominic's car has pulled up on Jane's and Matt's drive at last, beside the clump of waving pampas grass. We will give them all a chance to get settled and tuck into their Deliveroo fish and chips. Then we'll join them on the patio.

'I feel like I've got masses to tell you,' says Dominic. 'But literally nothing has happened!'

'Apart from the global pandemic,' says Jane. 'And the wave of protests and rioting currently sweeping the world. That's enough for anybody's bandwidth.'

'It feels different this time,' he says. 'Is it just me? It feels as though we're finally waking up to white privilege?'

'From sourdough starters to defunding the police,' marvels Jane. 'Lockdown has radicalized us all.'

'What are we talking about?' asks Mum.

Dominic explains briefly – because Mum will only forget – yet also wokely, because he's all too aware of Jane's sardonic ears flapping. Not to mention the fact that his bishop, an ex-copper, is sitting right there with his IPA, as Dominic skates swiftly over institutionalized racism in the police force.

'So that's it, basically. Black Lives Matter.' He fans himself and swigs some Prosecco. This is fun!

'Well, of course they matter!' says Mum. 'All lives matter!'

'Ye-e-s, but that's like saying . . .' Dominic flings up his hands. Some help here?

Jane screws up her fish and chip wrapper and wipes her mouth. 'It's like a bunch of blokes waylaying a busy midwife to say, Men get stomach aches too.'

'There, Mother. Imagine saying *that* to Sister Evangelina. You'd get a right earful.'

'Ah, she's dead, though,' says Mum. 'It was a stroke. A long time ago now.'

'Yes, I know.' He pats her hand.

They fall silent. Lady is off nosing happily about in the borders. There's a wood pigeon calling lazily. The scent of mock orange drifts. Mother is starting to nod off.

'Well, time we were making tracks,' says Dominic. 'Can I have your blessing, Father?'

Jane and Matt stand on the drive and wave them off.

'Ah, lovely to see him.'

'He's one of the best,' says Matt.

They go back to the terrace to clear away.

'Apparently, I'm Spanish,' says Jane.

'News to me.'

'Mrs Todd thinks I'm Spanish. Or *something*. Do I look *something* to you?'

'You look stunning to me.' Matt eyes her. 'Is that the right answer?'

'Yes. Gold star!' Hmm, thinks Jane. That *family history* email seems to be niggling more than I realized. Tapping into those childhood fantasies about having foreign blood. Of being anything other than plain Jackie one hundred per cent English Rossiter.

High above the clouds, the moon waxes again. This Saturday it will be full. Half the year has passed. *Plus ça change, plus c'est la même chose.* Yet we are still swayed by the idea that this time it could be different, that these days of ours are unprecedented. That history is tending in some direction. 'Nearer and nearer draws the time, the time that shall surely be.' Our creeds affirm it. 'He will come again in glory to judge the quick and the dead, and his kingdom shall have no end.'

The moon has seen it all. The horsemen riding. The end not coming. Another June with rain and roses. If we are spared to a ripe old age, we might live to see a thousand iterations of the lunar cycle. Same old, same old. And same new, same new. Each time another chance. For all that time's arrow flies one way, while we live and breathe there's another chance.

Rose Moon, Part II

The full moon rises above inky clouds. Madge watches it from her bedroom window in Cardingforth. She's just driven back from a socially distanced drink with Father Dominic in the damp vicarage garden, to talk about how she's doing, parish nursing, the virus and how they can safely open the church building for private prayer again on the 15th, who'll be on the cleaning rota, all that.

And Black Lives Matter, of course. Madge opens her window and leans on the sill. It's nearly dark. The rooks are all going home, swirling and tumbling towards the roost.

Have a difficult conversation. Lots of that going round at the moment. And yes, it's good to do, but bless you, Father Dominic, I think the idea was millennials trying to talk to boomer relatives. Madge sighs. Now she's ruined the Blessed Virgin Mary for him. The statue, not *herself*, obviously. It's just so exhausting, talking to nice white people. Bet he's on eBay now, trying to source a black Madonna for the Lady Chapel, as though it's down to him personally to put everything right. I just need you to understand, that's all.

The scent of honeysuckle creeps up from her garden. The rooks are settling. A fox trots across the building site next door, past a huge tower of earth. Look, don't feel bad, Father. Why would it occur to you, why would you see it, if you've not lived it? Same old. Except he surprised her by saying he knows not to make it all about his hurt feelings; his friend Jane had been educating him.

Well, Jane would know!

That's what she said. Madge frowns again over the silence that followed. His expression. Uncertain, like he couldn't tell what she meant, if she was being sarcastic, or what. And then – can you believe it? Madge herself suddenly got tangled up in awkwardness! Must be contagious. She shakes her head. Come on, how hard is it – why is it hard at all – just to ask? To say, Sorry, what, I'd always just assumed Jane was . . . Like assuming it would be a faux pas, a slur? For heaven's sake, Madge. Anyhow, she missed the moment, because there he was, talking to the dog, glossing over it: Oh yes, Dr Jane Rossiter, never knowingly under-informed, is she, Lady?

Ah well. The moon glows red through the bank of cloud, but it never quite breaks free. Madge closes the window.

June 6 Saterday
Tonight is the night of the full 'STRAWBERRY MOON!!!' Aka the ROSE MOON, they are both cool names so I don't mind which, me and Leah have a new pact not to argue. I said Cool, but no offence, it's not me that argues the entire whole time, it's you. And she went No it's not! LOL LOL LOL. She has promised I can watch moonrise from her bedroom again. My app says 'Cloud Coverage' but finger's crossed.
Moon Facts
So there is a 'perigee' and an 'apogee' in the moon's orbit round the earth. This means nearest and furthest points. If it is something going round the sun (e.g. the earth or another planet going round the sun) it's called 'perihelion' and 'aphelion'. Helion means sun in Greek. There are also words for moons going round Jupiter!! They are 'apojove and perijove', Jupiter and Jove are one and the same thing in Latin and Greek mythology, it is the Father of the Gods and god of thunder and sky. This is cool IMHO and probably quite a lot of people care in actual fact, like for example astronomers and scientists. You would think that a vegan who is all about Gaia and the environment would not think this is boring, they would think its amazing. When I said that she went See? Your the one arguing. I said nothing, I did not fall into her trap!!! GO ME!!!!

But at the end of the day, I will cut her some slack because she has her ups and downs like everyone, plus she is missing her freinds. I so wish school would start, only reception and Y1 and Y6 are back, it is *very sad and impacts on 'mental health.' FORTUNATLY 'you know who' has posted another song (it is on Youtube not on 'you know what') we watched it on Leah's laptop, its a sad song IMHO. In actual fact we did it at 'sing-up' back in the day, but I was young then and did not know it was sad, it past me by. It is called 'sometimes I feel like a motherless child' he sings it in this very quiet voice and it is dedicated to #BLM which Leah has explained to me <u>as is her want</u>. Mum and dad did not let her go to London to the 'peaceful protests', she says she totally would of to stand up for justice, but she respected there reasoning and did not argue with them either. She can go to the Lindford one if she wears a mask and maintains social distance says mum, plus she's to keep out of trouble. Leah roled her eyes and was all Like I've never been on a protest before, mother, but quietly (because no arguing LOL)*

Maybe we all need a pact not to argue. There have been so many arguments in Lindfordshire. Arguments of all stripes, from minor bickering through to thundering rows. For those who have never learnt to communicate via the medium of slammed doors and flying crockery, there is always recourse to the vast smouldering Yellowstone Park of passive aggression, where you can camp out for days at a time. There are face-to-face arguments in kitchens and gardens – like the one that carried from the Hardman-Mays across to Jack in his rickety old summerhouse last week – and virtual ones on Twitter (redder than ever in tooth and claw).

Everything's scratchy and volatile. Spats expand to fill the lockdown space available. There are arguments over who's not stomping properly on the cans before recycling them and how many biscuits you're allowed. Over text messages that should not have been sent, and illegal raves that should not have been attended and arrests narrowly averted (oh, Freddie!). Over social bubbles – who to ask, who will feel left out. Over how to pronounce COVID (does it rhyme with Ovid, or is that just BBC snoot?). Over who's racist and which lives matter. Over the rights and wrongs of peaceful protests during pandemics. Over how much is too much to spend on a new sunhat. Over whether tumbling statues from plinths is a prophetic act, or utterly disgraceful, completely unacceptable and sheer vandalism.

Interesting question, that last one. Do you recall similar debates raging over the toppling of Saddam Hussein's statue in 2003? But that's a long time ago. We might have forgotten.

Colston, what would you say about all this, if your (Grade II listed building) bronze lips could speak? (Reason for designation: 'A handsome statue, erected in the late C19 to commemorate a late C17 figure; the resulting contrast of styles is handled with confidence.') Perhaps you would assert – as charitable websites still do at the time of my writing this – that you were 'a renowned and respected philanthropist, giving immense sums to causes in and around Bristol'. That at the time, the slave trade was promoted by the king and pursued by other European trading countries as a legitimate trade.

But your bronze lips are sealed. Not a single bubble rises from the bottom of Bristol Harbour where you were so abruptly baptized. You died full of years in your London home in 1721, and were carried back in a week-long solemn procession and buried with monument and effigy in All Saints'. There you recline in the closed church, marble hand to breast, in your curly stone wig. *This great and pious Benefactor was known to have done many other Charities, and what He did in Secret is believed to be not inferior to what He did in Publick.*

Perhaps by the time your statue was cast and erected – some sixty-two years after the Slavery Abolition Act – you would have come to see that it was complicated. That you were no longer straightforwardly 'the brightest Example of Christian Liberality that this Age has produced'. After all, the entire nation had undergone a change of heart by then. Did the British people not lead the way, with Wilberforce at the helm, sailing gloriously into the harbour of abolition? Odd then that such considerations did not appear to strike James Arrowsmith when he proposed the statue, or the mayor and Bishop of Bristol when they unveiled it on 'Colston Day' in 1895.

Bristol lies far beyond the borders of the Diocese of Lindchester. We may safely banish Bristol. Oh, lucky Lindfordshire, as far from the coast as it is possible to be in England! We are surely at the apogee out here in our little backwater, as the nation tentatively orbits this nettlesome issue. We are remote from the major slaving ports, far from the plantations, from the sugar warehouses, those dubious merchant venturing societies, the tobacco and cotton trades. There are no statues to slave traders in our public squares. Our streets are not called Milligan and Codrington. Those were different and terrible times. It's all very difficult and sad, but it's not that close to home, fortunately. Besides, if we take down statues and change street names, isn't there a risk of erasing our history? There needs to be a proper discussion about these things, of course. It's probably long overdue. But acts of hooliganism and vandalism are not the way to go about it. Please, the debate needs to be conducted quietly and politely, preferably so that we can't actually hear it from where we're standing.

Meanwhile, all across the Diocese of Lindchester the rain falls. It falls on the gracious eighteenth-century stately homes, with their stately parks and rose gardens, and on the roofs of the former dairy or stables, now the tearoom, where in happier times we could enjoy some of the world's most expensive cakes and scones. Where did the money come from to build the homes of Sir Edmund This or Mr William That Esq? From 'Trading extensively in various commodities'. From having 'Interests in the West Indian Island of St Kitts'. From being a 'Shareholder in the Royal African Company'.

The rain also falls on the picturesque rows of almshouses, on town libraries and galleries. But which great and pious Victorian benefactors funded all those, finding themselves plump in the pocket after the Slave Compensation Act of 1837? There's no sheltering from it. The rain falls everywhere. On a village school here, a steeple there, on that strip of disused railway, now a cycle path. There is no perigee or apogee. What we did in secret is not inferior to what we did in public. Everywhere that the rain falls in this green and pleasant land, it falls on blood money.

'The nations no-ho-ho-ho-hot so blest a-as thee!' Gene warbles 'Rule Britannia' in his legendary Peter Pears voice. 'Must i-i-i-i-i-i-i-i-in their turn to ty-eye-eye-eye-rant fall!'

They are sitting in the deanery garden under the rose trellis, where a Rambling Rector twines rather enthusiastically with the Lady of the Lake. It's rest day eve. They've just embarked on a bottle of Nyetimber 1086 rosé prestige cuvée, because Gene does like things to match, it's a weakness of his. They are ostensibly celebrating the forthcoming reopening of the cathedral for private prayer. And besides, why not pop a cork? This very night our souls might be required of us.

'Interesting that "Britons never-never-never shall be slaves" was penned at the height of the transatlantic slave trade,' he says.

'I can never bring myself to sing it, to be honest,' says Marion. 'Or "Land of Hope and Glory".'

'Ah, but you are sui generis among Englishwomen. For the most part, the English are deeply shocked at the idea that they aren't God's favourites. They're in total denial of the legacy of empire.'

Marion laughs. 'Says the man clad in colonial linen and the most expensive Panama in the diocese.'

'Why, thank you. But honesty compels me to admit that that *particular* laurel goes to the rector of Gayden Magna's consort.' Gene leans forward and whispers, 'I'm embarrassed to say I baulked at the Montecristi bespoke prices. Baulked, I tell you! Like a fat pony shying at a gymkhana and dashing poor little Gwendolen's hopes of a rosette! I plumped instead for the Montecristi Rollable Superfine. I do hope this isn't being widely spoken about.'

The dean shakes her head. 'You're hopeless.'

'And yet you drink my wine! You're complicit in my wickedness.' He raises his glass. 'Here's to the bold iconoclasts of Bristol! I gather old Churchill's been boarded up for his own safety.'

'Mmm.'

A blackbird whistles. Gene whistles too. It's his COVID-19 theme song: 'Enjoy yourself'. Bubbles rise in the Champagne. Scent of roses and mock orange, of June, an English June. He admires the weak sunshine through his raised glass.

'I hereby grant you permission to enjoy yourself, Deanissima. You don't have to dismantle systemic racism singlehanded this week.'

'True.' She reaches for his hand. They twine fingers. 'If I mine deep enough, I hit a seam of gratitude. And then it's possible to be happy, in spite of everything.'

He squeezes her hand. 'And I'm honoured to be a humble dwarf with a pickaxe, assisting Snow White in her excavations. Ooh, I wonder which one I am.' He bats his eyelashes at her. 'Bashful?'

'Sleazy. Definitely.'

'Brava!' He tips his Panama. 'And may I just confide a tiny thought? Much though I'd relish the prestige and cultural razzmatazz of capital city life, I can't help being glad you are not Dean of Westminster or St Paul's right now.'

'Amen to *that*.'

Over in the bishop's office, Kat, the bishop's PA, gathers her things up before Steve can come in and tell her to stop working and go home. He's being extra-solicitous. Alert to the dynamic of her being the only non-white person on the senior staff, and making sure she's not the default spokesperson on race matters. That she's not being called on to educate white people on racism – he's heard that narrative loud and clear. Yeah, for a straight white guy he pretty much gets it.

But with the best will in the world, he's always going to be *in* the establishment club looking out. He's asking, Who's not being heard, who's excluded, how can we widen the doors and make the club more hospitable and inclusive? Never, What if the club's rotten to the core, maybe we should actually dismantle the club altogether? Because how would that be imaginable? What would it even look like not to have the club?

'I'm off now, Steve,' she calls. 'I'll be back in on Thursday.'

He comes and stands in the door of his office, two metres away. 'OK, bye. Thanks, Kat. Say hi to Jo.'

'Will do. Bye.'

She leaves through the main entrance. Steve will leave through the private door in his office that leads into the palace. That's the agreement. Kat comes in twice a week to sort through the post and do anything that can't be done from home. Blue file stuff. The historic cases that don't go away, even in a global pandemic.

She gets in her car. Better swing by the Tesco garage for milk and bread. The strict weekly shop routine is fraying at the edges a bit. But she's got a face mask. Feels a bit of a tit wearing it, but hey, it keeps Jo happy. Compulsory in hospitals from the 15th, even for non-clinical staff like Jo – thanks for the advance warning there, Mr Health Secretary. Another time it'd be nice to consult the health bosses first. Masks on public transport too. We'll get used to it. It'll gain traction. We got used to handwashing and social distancing, didn't we?

Oh, what song should we sing in all this? 'Enjoy yourself, enjoy yourself'? Or a sad song, like Mr Hardman-May's 'Sometimes I feel like a motherless child, a long way from home'? But singing will simply spread the virus further. Allegedly. Who knows? Well, apart from everyone on social media. They know all right. They'll soon tell you how mistaken you are. Unless we're to run mad, we have no alternative but to mute mute mute, until we can only hear the voices of people like us. But there are different narratives out there. Far-right groups assemble in London. Old footballing rivalries are dropped as the armies can unite against the common enemy of our way of life. They pledge to fight and protect our statues from the Black Lives Matter protesters.

In Lindford a group gathers to protect the town's war memorial. To protect our history. Not a counter-protest – they are not opposing Black Lives Matter – they are just concerned citizens. Many are ex-servicemen. They stand in the rain, watching the hundreds that gather in front of the town hall and take a knee. Socially distanced, in masks. *The UK is Not Innocent*, say the placards. *Stop Police Brutality*. There's Leah, with a cardboard banner. *White Silence is Violence*. The police stand and watch.

Slowly the rain seeps in, cold, through all the cracks of this land of hope and glory. Is this the truth getting in – not political correctness gone mad, not trendy woke-ness, not some dangerous agenda bent on destroying everything we hold dear, but the quiet persistent rain of truth? Will it set us free? Free from what, though?

'How shall we extol thee, who are born of thee?'

It's stopped raining. The long grass beside the roads is bowed down and spangled with tiny drops. Homemade bunting still draggles along walls here and there from VE Day. Freddie and Ambrose are sitting in the garden. Freddie's got Fabiola on his lap, and he's crooning to her softly.

He raises his head. Looks up at the treetops over the fence. Miss Sherratt's garden. There's this one tall pine, with a rose grown right up to the top. Maybe thirty metres? Sweet. And he knows there's a homeless guy living in the old summerhouse, but Freddie's saying nothing. He's not doing any harm, and maybe Tinkerbell knows and she's cool with it?

'Hey girl, it's fine. Who's beautiful?' He loves the weight of her, the plump silky feathers you can work your fingers into. Oh man, he's so in love, he's always so in love. 'I love you.'

'Me?' asks Brose.

'Yeh.'

'Back at ya,' Brose says. 'Babe, you . . . got Chloe's text?'

'Yeh.' The wind blows. The raindrops on the chicken wire all shiver. 'It's cool,' says Freddie. 'I get that she needs to bubble with her mum and dad, so.'

'She's not seen them since February, to be fair.'

'Yeah no, I totally respect her choice. Hey. It's fine. We've got Alfie and the girls, we've got us. We're cool. Ah, Jesus. Sorry.' He wipes his eyes on his sleeve. 'Sorry.'

'Don't be. This is going to pass, Freddie. It is. It's going to pass.'

'Yeah.'

Rose Moon, Part III

oday is the big day. Monday 15 June 2020 – the reopening of non-essential shops. There was thunder yesterday evening, as though the gods themselves were rumbling about overhead, shifting barriers to prepare for the safe reopening of retail heaven. From today we may *Shop with Confidence*. Alternatively, we may stay safely at home and sneer with confidence at those who queue three-quarters of the way round the block for the chance to visit Primark. Imagine risking your life to buy a cheap T-shirt! It's not like COVID-19 has gone away. How can people be so thick? (And so fat. And so poor.) Look at them! There will be queues outside Harrods too, but that's a different matter entirely.

Shop with Confidence. Everything's getting back to normal. The COVID-19 threat level in the UK has been reduced from 4 to 3. Hand sanitizers, face masks, gloves, one-way systems, *Keep Your Distance* stickers on floors and pavements, Perspex screens, contact-less payment, no changing rooms – everything screams normal, now that we can confidently shop again. Lockdown has felt like an endless Sunday afternoon in the 60s.

Let us take to the air and clock up a few more air miles in heaven. Visibility is patchy, what with all this cloud. Even the swifts and swallows are forced to fly low and skim the treetops. The elder is in blossom now, and the pale pink of bramble flowers sprinkles the hedges. Was the oak out before the ash this year? I believe it was. But splash or soak, who knows? Trees are no more proficient than St Swithun when it comes to long-range weather forecasts.

We are approaching Lindford. That's the historic Victorian arboretum there, planted by selfless souls who never lived to enjoy what we see below us now. A lesson to us all in forward-planning. Plant trees while you may, for night cometh when no man can work. Trees, so many mature trees, hoovering up our carbon dioxide, sustaining biodiversity, offering shade and shelter. Look down – there by the vast tulip tree. Do you see that pink umbrella? We will track its progress as it exits through the wrought-iron gates and heads into Lindford.

Star is walking through the almost empty town at quarter to nine. Rain still patters gently on her pink umbrella, but maybe it's brightening up over there? The shutters remain down on most of the small shops. It's not business as usual after all. Every few metres she passes a sign stencilled on the pavement. *Stay Safe. Keep your distance.* Boots has been open all along, so has the Co-op and Spar, Bargain Booze, the essential shops. You can get a takeaway coffee in Costa, if you go in one way for your flat white and come out the back where the wheelie bins are. She's sometimes done that after her stint at the foodbank. The charity shops are mostly closed still, and Hair Works. That's where Star works, or where she will work when it opens again in July, fingers crossed. Their shutters are down. Someone has sprayed *Fuck Boris* across it in red, and that makes her sad, because probably he's doing his best? Like everyone? And even if he's doing a really crap job like some people say, what good's spraying that going to do? Not like he's ever going to come to Lindford and see it. The salon's only going to have to clean it off, or maybe get something nice sprayed over the top, like a rainbow for the NHS maybe?

Ahead of her, a fox trots by the old town hall. It disappears round the corner. She once saw a badger outside Debenhams – about a month ago, that was. Thought it was someone's little dog, until she saw its cute stripy face. That made her think of all the stories of talking animals, or of St Francis with the birds, and she wonders sometimes if we're not kind enough to animals, and maybe we should all be vegans? Maybe in the future people will be. Seriously, they like ate animals, and kept them locked up, and everyone thought that was OK? The way we had bear-baiting, or torture and slavery, and everyone was OK with that back in the day because it was normal? If it's normal and everyone does it, how do we know if it's not OK?

Star passes by Goran's. The barber's pole is not lit up, it's not going round and round, but everyone knows you can still go to the back door and get a cut. Star's not judging. It's people's livelihood at the end of the day. You've got to carry on somehow, and try to make ends meet. She's seen the people coming into the foodbank for the first time, literally blinking like they can't believe it, because here's where they always dropped off donations, and now here they are themselves needing help?

And Mum and Dad's business – who knows if they're going to make it? Even though everything's always deep-cleaned, plus the Hot Tub Association says coronavirus would be inactive with those levels of chlorine. It's the social distancing that's the problem. Hen nights, the eighteenths and twenty-firsts, graduation, all that. Bookings have nosedived. Yes, you can carry on servicing people's private hot tubs, but all the spa and holiday rental tubs have to stay closed, so that's not going to cover the costs on its own. Touch and go, Dad says. And maybe Hair Works won't be able to keep her on? You just have to stay positive, one day at a time.

She goes down the High Street. There's barriers all along outside the shops. People are already queuing outside Primark, but Star's heading for church, because yay, churches can open again today too! Just for private prayer, but still. Her heart does a little skip, like it used to when she was little and it was sports day, and the dads' race, and she *so* wanted Dad to win, but he never did, ha ha! Once he pulled a hamstring trying, aw, bless. Hero. No school sports day this year, she guesses.

All across the Diocese of Lindchester the churches are opening. Or not. Opening your church building means a lot of extra work – work to be done by whom? Who will sit at the door and make sure people stay safe? Who will clean and sanitize everything? So many places have relied for years on the cheerful service of volunteers in their seventies and eighties – the very group who have been isolating because they are vulnerable. Father Wendy's church building in Cardingforth has temporarily been housing the foodbank, and before that it was the flood hub. Can they combine this with opening for private prayer? Or will they have to move the foodbank back into the parish hall first? Wendy herself is potentially vulnerable, after her cancer treatment.

And why say that churches are opening, as though church hasn't been going on all the time, online and through the networks of help and support? What if we have been more open than ever, more inclusive of those who can't, for whatever reason, get themselves across the threshold of a physical building? And what if these buildings of ours are a collection of glorious white elephants? We inherited them and are now obliged to dust them, glue back any bits that drop off, prop them up where a leg has gone missing, endlessly, endlessly maintain them without any help from the state, and with the dawning realization that the magic money tree of endowments that's flourished for centuries in the quad of church history, well, it's almost dead. Apologies. Asking 'what if?' is something novelists are legally obliged to do.

'It's Mr Hardman-May!'

Leah springs to her bedroom window just in time to see the blond head disappear behind next door's privet hedge. Her heart thumps. Footsteps approach along the landing. She slips back to her desk.

Jess taps on the door and opens it. 'Leah, I just saw Mr Hardman-May and Alfie go past!'

'And?'

Jess shrugs. 'Nothing.'

'FYI I'm actually in an English lesson here, Jess.'

'Sorr-eee.' Jess shuts the door.

Leah darts back to the window. He'll reappear in the gap by the Nisa shop. She waits. Come on, come on. Please let him come. If he doesn't appear in thirty seconds, she'll give up. The English lesson drones on from her laptop. *I think of thee! – my thoughts do twine and bud/About thee, as wild vines, about a tree.* What if she missed him? Perhaps he's already gone past? Thirty more seconds.

'Now we're going to do a free-writing exercise, girls. Think about the imagery, come up with some mutually beneficial relationship in nature . . .'

Blah blah whatever. She touches her tingling fingertips to the window. Please please please.

It looks as though Star isn't the only one heading for church. That's where Mr Hardman-May is going with Alfie. After they pass the Rogers' house, they cut down to the river and run along the bank, under the trees, which is why poor Leah waits at her window in vain. It's warm, everything's dripping, then the sun comes out and everything sparkles, the holly trees are a light show, every leaf glints. He runs through the smell of smushed-down wild garlic, then honey-suckle. Whoa, intense! Plan was to head up to Lindchester, go back in the cathedral, but he can't face it? Knows it would hurt too much. He can feel it in his throat right now, how much it hurts. Like a fractured bone?

So, it's the parish church instead. Not been in since – when? – the parish nurse service back in February? The girls' choir singing the Jacks anthem. Jesus, that anthem, like it's hexed. Still kills even to think of it, little Jess, singing her heart out. We had no idea, literally? 'God be with you till we meet again' – but when's that ever gonna be? Getting them all recording themselves, piecing it together, putting it out there – not the same. Plus he's not meant to be doing that anyway, he's furloughed, has to leave the girls' choir to the director of music now? God, he misses the back row. It's *so long* since he sang with anyone apart from Brose. Well and Alfie. 'Hey boy, good boy, you can sing too, yeah?'

It's so long since he did *anything* with anyone apart from Brose. So the rave? He was there like five minutes, ten minutes max? Then the police arrived, and he was *out* of there, still got the old parkour skills, upstairs window, across the roof, drop down into the alley, then walking, la la la, nothing to see here. And yeah, the roof *could've* been asbestos, he *could've* gone right through, but it wasn't, he didn't, so hey, no harm, no foul?

But Brose is all, I'm not doing this, nu-uh, not playing this game, Freddie. I forgive you, but I'm not going to be cast as headmaster in this marriage. You need to work out what's driving you in all this.

Man. I just wanted to cut loose, is all. Have a blast for once, lose myself, dance.

But why now, Freddie?

They reach the arboretum. Alfie gallops ahead, far as the lead lets him, past the rose garden, greeting the other dogs. No chance of running into Chloe and Cosmo today. She's still away in her bubble with her parents. I mean, why wouldn't she be? Not like there's anything for her in Lindford, not now Freddie's fucked that up. His whole body winces at the memory. The three of them sat in the garden, their first socially distanced drink, the sudden silence – boom! – after Chloe apologized for disappointing them. Brose not saying anything, but Chloe's face going red, suddenly getting that Freddie must've sent that text behind Brose's back.

Hey, we're thinking why not start now, we're cool with trying if you are?

Wanna know what's driving me? The same old turbo-charged self-destruct booster rockets, is what's driving me.

But why? Why now? Why? Why, Freddie? Why?

Jesus, Brose, I don't know? Because I'm a total melt? Because lockdown?

Sure Brose has forgiven him. But that's not the same as forgiving yourself? Maybe talking to someone outside it all's gonna help, and Father Dominic's the only person he can think of. Not like he can talk to Andy, with the history and all, plus anyway, been ignoring his emails, so Andy'll be mad as well, soon *everyone* will be and, gah! *Seriously* going backwards here.

Freddie and Alfie pass through the big gates and down the street, under the plane trees. There's the new Lindford branch of Vespas, looks like they're open again. God, he even misses waiting tables, how the original Vespas kinda saved him back in 2016, becoming the singing waitron? He misses the climb up to the cathedral from the restaurant. You could follow the road, or take the steps, the crazy steep back way on to the Close.

It comes to him unexpectedly, how he collapsed that time and got this weird paradigm shift, where he was flat on his back looking *down* on the sky? Like up was down, down was up? Before the whole Paul Henderson thang. Right now he's got this whole new acrophobia going on – how deep the drop is, how thin the earth's crust is, like maybe one per cent, and underneath it's ninety-nine per cent pure fire? I mean, what are we even standing on?

Moon Journal
Moon Facts
So the most dissapointing moon fact I have discovered so far is that the moons surface is made up of dark grey rock and dust aka 'lunar soil', I mean how is that even possible when you look at the moon, it is so bright!!!! (Answer: the moon actually only reflects 12% of the suns light) It's a true fact that moon dust is dark, the astronauts bought some dust back from the moon landing. Some people think the moon landing was fake but that is 'a conspiracy theory'. It does not make sense to say its fake, IMAO. If you were going to fake it no way would you have faked this boring grey dust. You would fake this amazing shiny dust to make people go wow, that's totally GOT to be from the moon, for definate! I personally would prefer lunar soil to look like crushed diamonds but facts are facts at the end of the day, you don't get to choose. It can be 'an inconvenient truth' like Leah says.

Today's news: Leah has moved everything round in her bedroom, her desk is under the window now, because she wants to see the sun and the moon rise. This made me jelous because I love the moon. So she went, I get that, but think Jess, you can watch 'the sunset', that is even more beautiful and cool. Then she helped me move my furniture round too. Dad shouted, What on earth are you doing up there girls? But him and mum are cool with it. Leah explained it is good for our creativity to change things up once in a while, we do not want to atrophy our brians. I wish my room faced west too but it is what it is, like she says I can watch the sunset, its swings and roundabouts.
Moon zodiacs: ARIES. (Tbh I do not know what this means).

What are we standing on? Jane has been asking herself this for years. Sometimes she tells herself we're standing on the deck of a slaver, like the newly converted John Newton, who conducted his first acts of worship with a human cargo still stashed in the holds. She hears the timbers creaking on the good ship UK (formerly *The Empire*), and she knows the story is not over, even though the holds are empty now. Theoretically empty. What are we standing on? The legacy of our airbrushed past. Our whitewashed past.

Jane is taking a break from her work inbox. She's wandering in the wet garden with a mug of coffee. Today is Thursday. So far she has not seized the opportunity either to shop or to visit the parish church of Martonbury for private prayer. The end of term is now in sight. She's been pleasantly surprised by how few of her students have been in touch complaining about their marks. Matt initially reported a downturn in the number of complaints as well, though they're creeping back now. Nature is healing in the Church. Odd phenomenon all the same. As if some cosmic parent has given humanity something real to complain about.

She paces up and down with her coffee, resolutely not eating biscuits, even though there's still half a packet of Aldi Biscoffs in the cupboard. Miserable weather. Massive thunderstorm the night before last, crashing and ripping the sky. She stood at the open window watching the rain cascade over the gutters and pound the garden. A solid wall of white noise. Then it eased, as though some hand had turned the volume down. In the silence, a wren sang. Another storm last night too, but not as intense.

Yep, Jane is permanently pacing the deck of life, looking out. Always alert, but apparently fated always to be looking the wrong way, always to be worrying about the wrong thing. Here's her latest worry: her own past, and the erasure of her working-class roots. How could she – a historian, for God's sake! – not have wanted anything from her childhood when family were clearing the house after Mum died? What about your old school books, Jackie? What about the photo albums? There's your mum's letters that she kept – what about them?

A whole archive chucked in the skip. Nineteen years back, she'd judged that the only person likely to have any use for the Jane Rossiter Files was Jane Rossiter. Well, Jane Rossiter wasn't interested, and besides, she had no storage capacity in her little two-up two-down in

Cardingforth. Wrong decision? Who could say? The thought of the lost photos costs her a pang now. They're really gone, those old prints. Gone for good. No back-up on the Cloud.

It would be interesting to leaf through her history exercise books, come to think of it. To see if it's possible to take off your Postcolonial Studies glasses, and capture what you'd genuinely believed at the age of thirteen when you were taught about Gladstone and Ireland; or the partition of India. Jane knows there's a narrative going round at the moment that the English know more about the wives of Henry VIII than the transatlantic slave trade. But it's not quite that simple (is anything?). We were definitely taught about the British Empire, but dustily, boringly. And definitely uncritically.

Jane can just about summon her 4th Year. Start of O-levels. Teaching was just a dreary matter of dictated notes and filmstrips (wasn't she once sent out of class for farting about in the dimmed classroom with a Tunnock's teacake? 'These filmstrips are for your benefit, Jacqueline Rossiter!') 'The Scramble for Africa'. Presented as though it were some kind of Olympics that we did rather well at, actually. Germany and Belgium were only in it for 'prestige'. Jane can almost picture herself underlining that. As if that were a bad reason to compete, as opposed to our nobler motives.

Here's what she most remembers about school: earnestly taking notes and committing dates to memory, swotting for tests and exams. Yes, it was a comprehensive school, but the grammar school ethos still clung to everything. Consume enough facts, regurgitate them in the right way and you'd get into university. Homework every night after school in the village library where Mum worked. Jane has a sudden vivid picture of Mum smoking at the desk, stamping the books, *snickerty-snickerty*, tickets in the wallets, wallets in the box. Her heavy black-rimmed glasses, coarse grey hair, yellow smoke patch in her fringe from bending over her book. Always reading. Smoking and reading. Upstairs, in the room above the library, the thumping of the ballet class, the tinkle of the piano: 'And one and two and jump and turn.' No point wishing she could do ballet. No money for that. Her only escape was books. Enid Blyton. Andrew Lang. *Anne of Green Gables. Little Women.* Boy, how those novels reinforced the message that a clever girl's only chance of escape and independence was education. So she read enough, regurgitated enough, got into Oxford.

Yeah, yeah. She got out. Became that cliché. Stopped being Jackie, became Jane. She's been telling herself she made peace with this back in 2016, when Danny pestered her to know more about his Rossiter relatives, and she finally made contact again, went 'home'.

So what is it, this new creaking under her feet? Is it the ancient timbers of Britannia herself, beached on the sandbank of lockdown? Probably. The creaking must be pretty palpable, if Greene King pubs and Lloyd's of London are apologizing for their slaving links and making amends.

Matt comes out into the garden with a coffee of his own. In shorts and polo shirt. Not much call for the purple shirts in lockdown. He's a happier bunny now the Premiership has started again. Jane finds the empty stadiums make it eerie, though, despite the canned crowd noise.

'How's it going?' he asks.

'I'm trying to navigate and comprehend what feels like a dangerous simulacrum of normality, cynically constructed by scofflaws in Westminster out of manipulated nostalgia and appeals to English "common sense", in the knowledge that it will probably become normalized – if, indeed, it hasn't already – thus leading to more deaths.'

Matt nods. 'I thought that's what you were doing.'

A blackbird whistles from the rooftop, easy as an old farmer leaning on a gate. As if everything's fine.

'Spanish flu took over two years to run its course,' says Jane. 'Four waves. Fifty million dead.'

'Yep,' says Matt. 'We're in it for the long haul, I'm afraid.'

Jane finishes her coffee and goes back into the house. But instead of going to her study, she goes and stands for a moment in the spare room that's become a temporary chapel. She can hear the steady clomp of the soap thing in the washing machine. An unlit candle stands on the table. This Sunday is Father's Day. Jane has no truck with this consumer-driven Americanization, and besides, it's not a straightforward day for Matt, who never got to be a father. In the biological sense. Spiritually, well. It's possible Matt might want to say mass, so maybe she should volunteer to be the congregation again. A double celebration. Triple, even. It's also her birthday and midsummer. What a Deliveroo jamboree there will be.

She stares at the candle. Why did she evade the issue in the garden back there? Why couldn't she tell him about that skip full of memorabilia that's started troubling her after nearly twenty years? Interesting. The tiny bee voices converse in the eaves, on and on, like a radio turned right down and almost forgotten.

Rose Moon, Part IV

If Leah was still a pagan, she would totally have hitchhiked to Stonehenge, no matter what Mum and Dad said. Or she would totally have got up at 4.52 a.m. and watched the English Heritage livestreaming of the solstice on Facebook. As it was, she had a lie-in like a good Christian girl. Enjoy it while you can, young people. Sleep through as much of this as possible. Oh, that we could fast-forward and get this pandemic over with.

Term at Poundstretcher University has ended. Perhaps there will be some kind of online knees-up to mark graduation, but nothing has been planned yet. Jane is sensibly lying low, in case someone asks her to organize it, and she ends up in a Zoom party with balloons tied to her daft *Two Gentlemen of Verona* doctoral hat. School term limps on; and so do people working from home with no childcare provision. They limp on, like people ordered into a cross-country race with no warm-up, and in the wrong shoes. They're muddling through, shouting, bribing with biscuits, weeping, giving up, then starting all over again the next day.

Are we still imagining an end to all this? Do we still catch ourselves thinking that if we can just hang on till the end of x or y, everything will be fine? Because if the end's in sight, we can probably carry on running. Even if it's a marathon not a sprint, and the end is miles away, we could keep going. We could walk – crawl even! – over the finishing line. But what if there's no real finishing line? What if we stagger through street after street, town after town, no crowds, no flags, endlessly chasing a rumour that it's possibly over. Oh, but what if another worse virus comes along before we've emerged from this one? What if Yellowstone Park goes up, and we don't see blue sky for three years? What if a giant asteroid hits the earth – boom – game over?

There. I believe that's fulfilled my contractual obligation to what-if. Acorns are raining down faster than ever on us Chicken Lickens. It's worth noting, however, that although Chicken Licken was wrong about the sky falling, he was right to be worried about *something*. The whole gang – Henny Penny, Cocky Locky, Turkey Lurkey, Ducky Lucky, Drakey Lakey, Gander Lander, Goosey Loosey – they all got eaten by Foxy Loxy. The End. Sleep well, boys and girls.

There are other narratives besides *Chicken Licken*, happily. The government has a much more upbeat one, in which Our Long National Hibernation is Beginning to Come to an End. The daily infection rate has fallen to 1,000 new cases a day, compared with 100,000 at the end of March. So from 4 July, pubs and restaurants can open again. (And libraries and museums, but mainly PUBS!) Social distancing is slashed from two metres to one! Two households of any size can meet, inside or out. Outdoors, people can meet in groups of six. Holiday accommodation can reopen. So can outdoor gyms and children's play areas. Huzzah for Winston Johnson and the spirit of the Blitz! Even the weather turns happy and glorious. Crowds flock to the coast to celebrate, and tempers flare. We shall fight each other on the beaches, we shall fight on the gridlocked Dorset lanes and in the rammed car parks.

Despite the lovely weather, Jane is inside folding clothes so that they won't need ironing. If anyone entertains a different opinion about what needs ironing, they know what they can do. She hears a faint tapping at the utility room window and glances round to see pale peachy roses curtseying, like crinolined flirts. Didn't she once have a ball gown that shade? Bad choice, with her complexion. Bad sartorial choice all round, really, because the dress had rather a lot of Lady Di rah-rah frills going on, and Jane's not a frilly person. Dim memory of walking back to college blistered and barefoot through the dawn chorus, carrying her stilettos. She picks up the laundry basket, takes it upstairs and drops it with a thump on the bedroom floor.

Right, emails. Her study is stuffy, so she opens the window. Danny's graduation photo looks up at her from the windowsill. She salutes him. Jane is proud to say that she reared a young man with zero domestic expectations of women. That is her offering back to the universe. Nobody ever had to take Danny to one side and explain that the magic washing machine isn't real. Not once did Jane iron his school shirt, or lovingly sew a name tape inside a collar. If the good Lord had wanted mothers to use Cash's woven name tapes, he would never have created laundry marker pens.

Jane's mum had been very much of that opinion too. Which led to trouble with the PE teacher, when Jane was supposed to have her name tape sewn on to the left breast of her aertex shirt. 'I don't have any name tapes, Miss.' The idea was that the name tapes prevented girls borrowing someone else's shirt if they forgot their own, thus evading a righteous bollocking. As if Jane cared about that. Never could understand the girls who stood red-faced and humiliated, or who cried when they got told off.

Why, I've probably still got that expression on my face, she thinks, all these years on. How many years now? With a jolt she realizes that it's forty-one. Forty-one years this July since she left school. She doesn't have any photos of the final day. Picnic on the school field with Tessa and Yvette, illicit cider. She can sort of remember it. No uniform in the sixth-form, so jeans – 'straights' – and granddad shirts and Kickers, probably. Perhaps she's fortunate. She doesn't have to look at that dewy version of herself, so fresh, so thin, so beautiful. Jane's carrying a couple of stones more ballast these days, but in her defence, she's turned fifty-nine, she's had a baby and she's eaten a lot of cake.

She sits at her desk and turns on her laptop. Another fierce pang of longing for the Fergus Abernathy building. She shakes her head. The things we end up missing.

The first stealthy breath of lime blossom is on the breeze now. Father Dominic smells it while he's out in the garden weeing the dog, and it distracts him from worrying about how and when to restart public worship in the parish church. The scent wafts him back to the happy throngs outside the cathedral at his deaconing and priesting, those spanking white surplices, the joyous tumbling of bells and that smell, oh rapture! Petertide ordinations. Postponed, of course, this year.

Shit! He forgot Janey's birthday. Even with a calendar alert, he managed to forget. He gets his phone out and starts Googling florists. He's deep in hand-tied bouquets when there's a shrieking squawk. He looks round. A fledgling rook.

'Lady! Leave!' He scoots over and grabs her collar. The bird shrieks again, then flutters a few more yards. There's an answering caw from a treetop. The parents.

'You poor darling!' He can keep Lady off, but the bird needs shelter, cover. He tries to shoo it into the bushes, but it gets in an even bigger flap, and now it's right in the middle of the lawn. Oh Lord. A cat will get it. Or that nasty owl-murdering hawk. The adult birds are still calling.

'Come along, darling, this way. No, *this* way!' It squeaks pitifully. 'I'm trying to save you!'

If we were up in the treetop too, we could have enjoyed the comic sight of a flapping black-clad priest chasing a small black flapping bird round the lawn. At last, he herds it towards the undergrowth, thinking, This will preach, this will preach, and the draggled black bundle scuttles safely in among the Canterbury bells and dock leaves. The parent birds up in the lime trees settle again.

'Well, we made a difference for *that* one, Lady.' He goes back into the house, where he can smell something burning. Jane's belated birthday bouquet is forgotten again.

Yes, the Petertide ordinations have been postponed this year. This doesn't mean that there will be no new curates arriving in the diocese, though. They will move into their new houses, and in these unprecedented times the Bishop of Lindchester will license them as 'lay curates', so that they can at least begin their ministry. What times we live in. How our vocabulary has been enlarged. Which of us, a year ago, would have been able to decipher the phrase 'I'm doing a Zoom licensing in my study tonight'?

But the bishop has other things on his heart today. His family, gathered under the palace roof for the last thirteen weeks, are dispersing again. Lockdown restrictions will be eased next week on 4 July, and it feels as though things are edging back towards normal, so they're all heading home. What a mad time they've had! And what an unexpected blessing. Back in March, when the prospect of lockdown loomed, he and Sonya were reconciled to three months without seeing family, and watching those littlies growing up via iPad screens.

Tonight is the final family meal. There will be a final crazy game of sardines throughout the entire house, attic to cellar, with the little ones hilariously clueless about the art of hiding quietly. As if the point of the game was to be found! (*Sermon illustration, sermon illustration.*) Then will come the final bath- and story-time. Sonya's already in bits. But we'll thank him for all that is past, and trust him for all that's to come. The bishop presses on with his *ad clerum* about the reopening of churches for worship (which is also due to be announced on 4 July).

There's a crunch of feet on the gravel drive. He looks up. Sonya stands at the window, holding up little Jonah, so he can wave at Grandpa. But Jonah can only see his own reflection in the glass, until Steve gets up from his desk and comes closer. The baby's face breaks into a slow gummy smile.

'Hello, Grandpa! Let's let Grandpa get back to work. Say "Bye-bye, Grandpa!"' She takes hold of his chubby arm and waves it for him. 'Bye-bye!'

Steve watches them go. They stop and wave at Kat through the office window as well, before going to watch the butterflies in the buddleia on the drive.

We've seen that window before, dear reader, the one where Kat stands waving. It's the very window that the former bishop's chauffeur once plastered himself against and snogged, to taunt the former bishop's chaplain. Oh, long, long ago. Who even remembers? Not a cell, not a scrap of Freddie's DNA remains at the scene of the crime. Many rains have washed it since then, to say nothing of the contracted window cleaners who come once every three months, which is often enough for anybody. You don't want to clean your windows too frequently, or you'll get birds hurtling into them. Think how many bird lives you could save by having dirty windows. Think of the good we do simply by doing nothing.

'Freddie, got a moment?' Ambrose stoops to look into the henhouse. 'Can we talk?'

Ambrose sees his expression, the default thought *Shit, am I in trouble?* Four years in, and that's still what goes through his husband's head. But Ambrose has to take some of the rap for that.

'Something nice,' he says. 'Well, potentially. And I've made breakfast.'

'Aw, sweet man! I'll just, yeah.' He puts down Ella and picks up the old carton with the day's eggs in. 'Bye, girls. Daddy's gotta go now.' The girls scratch and chook round him.

'Maybe I need a T-shirt with "I'm not mad at you" on.' Ambrose holds the henhouse door open as Freddie steps through, gently steering Fabiola back inside with his foot. 'Only I'd end up wearing it ninety-nine per cent of the time.'

'I'ma get one which says "Sorry I fucked up" and I'll be wearing it every fucking day of my life. Because I always fuck everything up.'

'Did I just hear the A-word?' Ambrose latches the door.

'Yeah, well I *do* always fuck up.'

They go into the kitchen. Freddie puts the eggs on the worktop and washes his hands. 'Aw, you made pancakes!'

They sit and start to eat. Ambrose has made everything Freddie likes best. Bacon, maple syrup, sourdough toast, poached eggs, smashed avo, smoked paprika.

'So what have you fucked up so far today? If you're always fucking up.'

'Idno.'

'This last week, then?' Ambrose pours him some coffee.

Freddie rolls his eyes. 'Yeah no, I'm always fucking up, as in *ongoingly*, like it's a condition? So I went to that rave, I blew Andy off, texted Chloe? – that's like the symptoms.'

'And my hair,' adds Ambrose. 'You comprehensively fucked my hair up.'

'Nu-uh.' Freddie jabs a fork at him. '*You* bought those clippers, my dude. Not my fault the number three's more like number one. Anyway, looks cool, it's like a fade?'

'It's not. It's *Peaky Blinders*,' says Ambrose. 'Not the best look for an accountant.'

Freddie snorts his coffee. 'I could maybe blend it in a bit?'

'Er, no thanks. You can give Alfie a trim. He's looking a bit— Did you just slip him some bacon?'

'Me?'

'Didn't we talk about that? About not feeding him from the table?'

'Oops.' Freddie grins. 'Guess I fucked up again.'

Ambrose shakes his head and sighs. 'Listen. Thoughts aren't facts, babe. You're not always fucking up. Sometimes you make mistakes. Like everyone.'

'Yeah yeah. So anyway, what's this "potentially" nice thing you've got going?'

We will leave Ambrose to show Freddie the architect's drawings of the proposed extension above the garage, which will be converted into a self-contained apartment for Chloe to move into, so they'd be an extended family unit and could start trying for a baby.

During this conversation, it will emerge that Ambrose too is capable of fucking up. Of thinking he gets to have it both ways – refusing to play headmaster, while at the same time totally infantilizing Freddie by going right on ahead and agreeing something as major as this with Chloe, and keeping Freddie out of the loop? He's fucking employed an architect *already*? Is he *serious*? He'd better not've got a builder lined up— He HAS?? Ambrose needs to take a long hard look at himself, at this pattern of total control-freak asshattery. He needs to trust Freddie to manage his own disappointment and not be always shielding him, like he's six years old? And pre-emptively cooking breakfast to keep him sweet? Hello? Ambrose better be planning on cooking breakfast for the next *year*.

And when's the builder starting?

Moon Phase
First Quarter (69%).
Tomorrow is a new month and you guessed it, there will be a new full moon. As per usually there are different names you can choose for it. For example it could be 'Buck Moon' which is for male deer, 'Hay moon' for harvesting the hay, or 'Thunder Moon' for obvious reasons (THUNDERSTORMS!!!!)

Buck Moon is Native American so out of respect I will not culturally approbriate it. I have done some research and its because male deer shed there antlers each year and in July they start growing again. This makes me sad for the bucks because what if it hurts them to grow new antlers? I sympathise wholeheartedly with them, because it might totally kill like when your developing? Maybe they bump their antlers on trees and stuff and there like YOW! That REALLY HURT.

Today Leah told mum to buy me some 'bras' and mum was like all in good time, and Leah was all Do it NOW, she could have a cropped top, do not put her through the MISERY I went through, and mum went What misery? And Leah went, The misery, plus you should make sure to celebrate when she gets her period, and not be all Oh, here are some towels for when you need them, like the menstrual cycle is this SHAMEFUL SECRET dad's not meant to know about. She only shouted that!!!! In my head I was OMG Leah! Because Dad was literally in the room at the time, he was lying on the sofa, he is still not recovered from COVID-19, fortunatley he didn't say anything so I'm guessing maybe he was asleep.

P.S. IMAO it can still be 'a bit' embarrassing at the end of the day even when your sister explains that it is not embarrassing, it's natural not gross, women's bodies are natural. I get that she means well.

P.P.S I do NOT want a 'moon cup'. Like ever.

P.P.P.S I don't care if they are more sustainable!!!!!

The last day of June. That's half the year done. In places where there's a porch to shelter the door lintel from the rain, we may still read those chalked letters: 20+C+M+B+20. Christ bless this house. The writing was on the wall back then, blindingly obvious, now that the optician of experience has slotted the correct lenses into place in front of our eyes. Already a new swine flu has been identified in China. Would we peer and frown second time round? Would we still manage to turn the blindingly obvious into a baffling *Magic Eye* picture?

But as we noted above, there are other versions of 2020. You might prefer the one where the whole of the pandemic is invented. It's a myth fabricated for arcane political reasons that only the Gnostic can fathom. Freedom of choice! It's *your* truth that matters. If you don't believe in something, you can't die from it. Just like if you don't test for COVID-19, you won't have any cases.

In the US, the number of cases starts rising exponentially again. People protest against wearing face masks. The government's tracing app still isn't working here in the UK, but fortunately, Boris Johnson does press-ups for the *Mail on Sunday*. A local lockdown is reimposed in Leicester. Job Centres are to reopen, and sanctions reimposed on those who fail to turn up. Parents will be fined for not sending children to school. Because National Hibernation is coming to an end. The government's principle is to trust the British public to use their common sense. In London, the police disperse illegal street parties. Worldwide, the number of cases rises to 9.6 million. In my version of 2020, the pale horse is currently quietly cropping grass in an English meadow, but the horseman will ride again. He will ride, but Christ will still bless the house.

It's been raining again. The *Peppa Pig* pictures chalked on Bishop Steve's terrace have all been washed away. The evening is grey and cool. Lime blossom tinges the air round Father Dominic's vicarage. At the end of his drive a passing car runs over a fledgling rook. We cannot save everything. Things will get lost and broken. Oh, will the rain wash it all away in the end? The rain falls. The sap rises, up, up, to the top of the tallest tree, where Miss Sherratt's Rambling Rector has climbed.

Miss Sherratt sits on her terrace with a pink gin. She enjoys her roses, and the sight of her young neighbour standing on his garage roof. (He's wearing clothes – swizz!) He'll be trying to imagine what the building work will look like. Good for them. The planning notice has come through her letterbox, and she won't object. How things go round and come round – she remembers all the umbrage and protest when the houses were first built, back in the 1960s. Oh, Miss Sherratt can remember when half of Lindford was fields, but people have got to live somewhere. Time marches on!

Jack's dug out the ancient push mower and got it going again. There he goes, bless his heart. Gaining confidence. Starting to trust she won't make him talk, won't fuss over him or turf him out. She just needs to see the green card in the summerhouse window every day. Up and down he goes. Up and down. That rattle-whir. Soothing, compared to today's petrol mowers bellowing away. If she closes her eyes, she's time travelling. Smell of clippings. Roses. Can almost hear the clack of croquet balls. Clop of horses along the road.

The wind blows in the treetops. It might be the sea.

And Freddie, standing barefoot on the garage roof, sees Jack mowing, Miss Sherratt dozing, the girls peck-peck-pecking, and in the distance maybe it's clearing up a little? Maybe he didn't fuck it up terminally? Maybe he'll get back to doing the doofy songs? Check in with Andy, and explain, ah, the stuff, how his heart's been breaking the whole time for everything, every lost little thing in 2020?

But this here will be a whole new baby house? He stretches out his arms wide. Breathes in. The wind stirs. The rose that's climbed all the way up to the top of the pine tree lets go a handful of petals, and they stream down along the breeze and out over everything.

JULY

Hay Moon, Part I

I s it true, that story of children in a school with no fences, who huddled near the building at playtime? We heard about it in many a motivational context – sermons, school assemblies. Even if someone made it up, the moral rings so true that nobody questions it: children need boundaries to feel safe. As soon as a fence was erected round the perimeter of the school field, off the children went, frisking like lambs to the far corners, liberated by the kindly limits.

There are probably long chopsticks in the afterlife too. You'd think the inhabitants of hell would have the wit to say, 'Screw the chopsticks. I'm eating with my hands.' In heaven, they'd be too polite. They'd carry on feeding one another for all eternity, endlessly apologizing for poking one another in the eye or dropping food down their white robe. Heaven's arches will ring with sorries, for as we know, heaven is mainly C of E. While being properly inclusive and ecumenical, of course; in the traditional English sense of: 'If at any stage you'd care to join us, you'd be most welcome.' Because what *is* heaven, frankly, if not an extrapolation of this land of hope and glory? It's the paradise everyone is desperately trying to get into, and from whom gratitude is expected if they're lucky enough to be admitted.

Come, fly with me over my green and pleasant Erewhon. Look down, when a gap in the clouds permits, and you'll notice that the hay has been mown, and lies in long windrows. From up here among the larks we can see the corduroy folds of medieval ridge and furrow, and the ghosts of erased hedges in vast fields. Lone oaks sail like galleons on wheat oceans. They escaped the hedge-uprooting of the 50s, undertaken to maximize field size and increase profitability. The ancient oaks were just too big to grub up, unless you had access to some surplus wartime TNT. Who are we to judge? People need to make a living. People can do what they like with their own property, provided they're not breaking the law, provided they've got planning permission. They can sell off half their lawn as a building plot, extend their house, rip up their front garden and make a parking space. Chop down any trees that don't have preservation orders on them. Fair enough. We might deplore your taste, but your home is your castle.

If we look down as we fly, we can see the unmistakable signs of what belongs to whom. The fences and boundaries tell us. England is all parcelled out. It's not all registered, but everything belongs to someone, some house owner, farmer, or the church, the Crown, the aristocracy, the National Trust. There isn't any no-man's-land. Even so-called common land – village greens and so forth – is owned by someone. You might have the right to roam or walk your dog (but not to camp or BBQ). Contact the Lindfordshire County Council and discover whether you have any more exciting historic appur-tenances – pannage or estover – in that woody patch down by the Linden at the edge of your property.

4 July
Today is 'Independence Day' in the USA, it is problematical because of racial inequality and sexism and the genocide of indiginous people who's land was stolen by European settlers who land grabbed it. Leah was explaining it to me when dad said 'It was actually a Great British Victory, it was English settlers throwing off the yolk of a tirranical German king.' Leah went Ignore him and carried on telling me stuff as is her want. She has been researching it as a special topic for Miss Logan, Miss Logan let's Leah do a whole bunch of stuff not on the syllabus the WHOLE TIME, which is not fair IMAO. (It is because you can lead a horse to water but you can't make him eat marmite sandwiches.) (According to dad).

Right now Dad is laying on the sofa again because he still get's tired, he went down to church with mum to see how they are getting on and *it wiped him out he says even though they drove there. There are some people who think COVID-19 is a made up fact, this hurts your feelings when your own dad has been so ill and he still is. It is because some people are <u>morons</u> (says me not Leah lol). Mum went with him in case he got too tired and she is appaled by all the people in town. She was like Honestly, it's like the week before Christmas out there. This is because today is also <u>SUPER SATERDAY</u> (so called). It is called 'super Saterday' because today pubs and restaurants are allowed to open. Everyone has to <u>socially distance</u> and mum went well good luck with that after people have had a drink or two!*

Moon Facts

The moon will be allmost full (98%) tonight and it will be 99% full on Sunday and Monday but it is so cloudy I'm scared I won't get to see it ☹ My ambition is to see every full moon of 2020, I will be gutted if I miss the 'Hay Moon!!!!'

We divide again in Lindfordshire this Super Saturday – those who huddle at home, scared of the sudden removal of safe boundaries, and those who laugh in the face of motivational stories and head out to frolic. Hospitals and emergency services are braced. They're treating this like New Year's Eve. Pity the poor inhabitants of Leicester, back in lockdown and unable to get to the boozer. Unless their house happens to be on the right side of the temporary boundary round the city. One street away and they wouldn't be as lucky.

But here in Lindfordshire we are free to drink as responsibly as ever we did. Pubs can open from 6 a.m., not because we are all gasping for a pint before breakfast, but to head off any midnight openings. By lunchtime, there will be queues outside Wetherspoons, which gives us an opportunity to lament the billions funnelled into propping up the hospitality sector, when the arts have been left to languish unaided. France has stumped up 7 billion Euros, and artists will be paid a wage until August. Germany has earmarked 1 billion. UK, zilch. (Another divide: Philistines, and those of us whose taste is valorized as objective universal truth.)

Becky Rogers was wrong to say it was like Christmas. I think her own scary experience of the virus has skewed her vision. The town is busier than it was when she last ventured out, but it's not heaving. People are maintaining social distance as best they can. They wait patiently in the drizzle outside the smaller 'Only 5 at a time' shops, until someone comes out. They use the hand sanitizer at the door. They queue outside Goran's – where the lit-up pole now twirls – for a legal haircut. Will Ambrose be visiting to get his *Peaky Blinders* cut blended into a proper fade by someone who knows what they're doing? Or will the cash-only rule (and Goran's BMW) set his accountant's antennae twitching?

Hair Works is more compliant at every level than Goran's. There's no queuing outside the salon today. You arrive for your appointment and wait outside until your masked stylist invites you in. If we peep in the window, we will see Star, in a visor, sweeping away the lockdown locks from the first clients back. Her feet in their turquoise Converse trainers almost dance. (If anyone makes the drudgery of sweeping divine, it's Star.) All the home cuts and home dye-jobs, bless. Oh, it's so great to be back at work. Nobody at the salon's had the virus, thank goodness. The boss has had a new door put in, so people can come in the front and go out the side into a little courtyard. Keeping people safe, that's the thing. Disposable towels, disposable gowns – ha ha, like we're cling-filming our clients! She keeps an eye on the front door, to see if Jack appears. How's he been managing in lockdown? she wonders. Maybe he's been in a hotel room, or one of the uni rooms? Let him be OK.

She goes to empty the clippings into the bin on the courtyard. There are giant hollyhocks, taller than her, way taller. She gazes up at them. The pink and dark red flowers are like Barbie skater skirts. Which reminds her – don't forget to buy some roses, because yay, tomorrow she gets to go to church! Star wants to click her turquoise heels together right now – there's no place like church, there's no place like church! Ha ha, they all think she's crazy, but still, they're like, 'Say one for me, Star!' She'll go to the evening mass, not the morning. Father Dominic asked her to, so it doesn't get too crowded. Mum will come too.

The rain falls very gently. It sounds like someone rustling tissue paper, getting something out of a box, something new and amazing.

'Well, Mr Bishop. What say you we nip to 'Spoons for a quick pint?'

'Is that what you'd like?' asks Matt. He looks up from his computer.

'No. I'm allergic to their carpets. Those "explosion at Axminster" patterns.'

'Apparently, each one's different,' says Matt. 'There's a book about it.'

'I don't care. They all give me flashbacks to my nan's front room.' Jane wanders across to Matt's study window and gazes at the wet garden. 'I acknowledge I'm an elitist snob in flight from my roots.'

Matt logs off. He looks at his watch. 'Well, we could tootle out to our old favourite instead. And then potter along the canal.'

'Why, you old romantic softie! Are they open?'

'Yep. I checked.'

It won't be the same, thinks Jane, as they drive through the Lindfordshire countryside. Nothing will ever be the same again. Even though the lanes are full of foxgloves, vetch and speedwell, and the rosebay willow herb is nearly out. The wild carrot, the honeysuckle. She realizes that this is the furthest she's been from home since her final day at Poundstretcher. It should feel weirder than this numb ordinariness.

Matt pulls into the almost empty car park. They get out. Immediately, there's the scent of lime blossom from the vast trees, as though heaven has tilted to slide all its perfume down on to Jane's upturned face. She feels the fine rain like the gentlest of cool pinpricks. And there's the fig tree where Matt stood waiting for her on their first date.

'Are you sure they're open?' she asks.

'From midday. According to Google.' He heads towards the pub door. 'Yep.'

They sanitize their hands. Matt goes up to the bar to give their contact details, while Jane finds a table. There are only three other groups. She picks a far corner. This is so weird. Is it weird? She's scanning round with some kind of emotional dowsing gizmo, trying to locate her subterranean feelings. There has to be more going on in her than this, surely. She reads the sign on the wall: *Resocialize Responsibly*. Social distancing. Contactless payment up to £45. And the pub promises never to touch the top two-thirds of her glass.

Matt comes back with two pints of Lindford Hoppy Days IPA on a (sanitized) tray.

'Cheers, Janey.'

201

'Cheers.' They chink rims. 'Uh-oh. You're dead. You're holding the bottom third of your pint.'

He picks up the photocopied menu. 'Am I holding this right?'

'It's single use. I'll have a bacon and brie baguette.'

He puts the menu back down. 'Already ordered.'

'What? But I might've wanted something different for a change, you paternalistic bastard!'

He just smiles and drinks his pint.

'Are we doing OK?' she asks.

'Yes. Considering.'

'No death threats this morning?'

'Nope.'

'Is Fuckwit still trolling you?'

'Probably. I muted him.'

'Ah! I love the way Twitter has a built-in passive-aggression button,' says Jane. 'What's happening with churches opening tomorrow?'

'Church *buildings* opening.'

Jane rolls her eyes.

'Some are, some are waiting till September,' he says. 'There's no "one size fits all". Look, do you actually want to talk church?'

'Well, it's that or the government.'

'Or holidays. Fancy a trip to Spain in early August? Seville? Granada?'

Once again, Jane's gizmo draws a blank. What does she want? It's like hallooing down a deep dark well. Nothing. Just her tiny reflection at the bottom, shrugging back at her.

'I have literally no idea what I want,' she says. Apart from for everything to be *not like this*.

'All righty. Happy for me to go ahead and book stuff?'

'Knock yourself out.' She takes a long pull from her first proper pint in months, and wipes her mouth. 'I mean, of course, yes please, Spain would be amazing. Thank you. And sorry. For being a grumpy old bag.'

'Yes, about that,' says Matt testily. 'If I'd known, I'd never have married you.'

She smiles. 'Aha, I lured you in with my sweet girlish ways. Then BAM.'

Matt is about to make a deeply inappropriate remark for a bishop, when he clocks a member of the clergy with his partner. Ho hum. It'll wait.

Father Ed freezes in the pub entrance. Neil cannons into the back of him.

'What? What? Oh God! Want to go somewhere else?'

'Too late. He's seen us – hello, Father!' Ed waves. The bishop raises his pint. Do they need to go over and have a chat? Yes, unavoidable.

'Hey, guys!' says the barman. 'How are you today? So I'm gonna need some contact details from one of your party?'

'Me!' says Neil. 'I volunteer. What? You go and find a table, I'll get us a drink. G'wan. Shoo.' He flaps Ed away and turns to give his name and number to the hottie behind the bar.

Never fear, dear reader. Neil has not relapsed into his old ways since we last saw him. It would be idle to pretend that there are no transferrable skills when it comes to being a fisher of men, however. A moment or two later, he comes across to extricate Ed from all the awkwardness natural to a priest who has had the ill luck to run into his bishop in a remote country pub.

'Bishop! Mrs Proudie! Mwa mwa, air hug!' He spreads his arms wide, drink in each hand. 'Och, I'm welling up! This is ridiculous, but never mind, how are you doing? Here, darling.' He passes Ed a Brewdog Barnard Castle Eye Test, then raises his own. 'Cheers. Down with the Tory bawbags! And now we'll be on our way. Come along, Eds. Leave them to their tête-à-tête.'

Super Saturday draws to a close. There have been meetings happening all across Lindfordshire; some planned, some accidental. Virginia, lying awake in her terraced house, can hear the distant sounds of merrymaking in the centre of Lindford. Perhaps she'll sleep tonight, now her noisy neighbours can go out to the pub. Please let this spell the end of those late-night garden gatherings that have caused her so much misery. A quiet night and a perfect end – how those words are now etched on her soul.

But sleep is playing hard to get. Too much rattling round her mind. Everything's ready for mass tomorrow. Surely! She and Father

203

Dominic have been over it so many times. He will preside, and trust that the routine of church is so deeply ingrained in his mum that she will stay in her pew. And if she wanders, well, he'll deal with it. Is this wise? But Virginia bowed to his preference, and his deep need to be back at the altar, which really isn't in Virginia's DNA, though she's come to respect his Catholic piety.

Is it really safe, though? Are they fully compliant with the guidelines? Covered ciborium – no speaking over the elements. Communion in one kind. Administration at arm's length. No Peace. There's tape on the pews to show people where they can sit; not yellow-and-black hazard tape – green tape for Ordinary Time! Bless Dominic and his fussy ways. Stripes of tape at two-metre intervals up the aisle, sanitizer at the entrance, and Madge all set to take contact details. They'll be livestreaming the service, for those who can't come in person, who are vulnerable or shielding. Oh, will it be safe? This rush to get everything open again – her heart warns her that it will end badly. Father Dominic pulls her leg about being an Eeyore. And he's probably right – it's safer now than it was back in February, when the virus was freely circulating.

Gradually, the thought of Dominic bids her anxious fears subside, and Virginia drifts asleep.

Super Sunday comes with rain and sun. Rainbows arch over Lindford and Cardingforth, over Martonbury and Lindchester. Out in the sticks, church towers blaze against inky clouds. The mown hayfields are luminous yellow-green, and there are heart-leaping double rainbows. Church doors open, or not, depending on so many variables: the risks, the available personnel, the wishes of the congregation when surveyed by the churchwardens. Lindchester Cathedral will remain closed for public worship for a further two weeks. Even if we don't actually know the ins and outs of this decision, it's important to wade in with an opinion.

How strange this all is. To get in our car and drive to church. To pay for parking and find the last ticket we bought still on the dashboard, faded by the sun. When we peer closely we can just make out the date: 15 March. What is it that we are feeling as we cross the familiar threshold again, with sanitizer standing in for stoop of holy water? The candles flicker. The windows are bright, dark, bright, as clouds pass. A bird shadow crosses the glass. Some people are wearing face masks, although this isn't mandatory. We are few and far between, dotted at each end of alternate pews. Is it good to be back? What is it that we are feeling? It should be joy, but we weep into our masks as we sit in hymnless musicless silence. Bright, dark, bright.

> Turn again our captivity, O LORD, as the streams in the south.
> They that sow in tears shall reap in joy.

The Hay Moon hides behind the radiant-edged frill of cloud. A cold wind, autumnal almost, swirls the trees of Lindfordshire; all the limes, the creaking sentinel oaks sailing in their lonely seas, the vast tulip tree in Lindford Arboretum, all the swaying poplars, the leylandii hedges that mark the boundaries. It whines in wires and round chimney pots.

Jess is asleep, so she doesn't see the moon suddenly appear above the scalloped clouds. Bright enough to make you blink. It blazes through the curtainless window of a house in Lindford. Freddie wakes with a jolt. For one heartbeat, he thinks it's a security light and he's back in juvie.

Aaaaand breathe. He gets out of bed and pads to the window. The moon's casting long, dancing tree shadows across the garden. There's the henhouse. Girls all safe, safe as houses. Kinda funny, how being fenced in can sometimes be good, no?

Hay Moon, Part II

St Swithin's Day 2020. Grey, but not actually raining at this precise moment. For forty days it will be iffy. For forty days it will be umbrella and sunglasses weather. Old Swithin, patron saint of mackerel sky. We squandered a summer's worth of sunshine in April and May, and now we're probably looking at a rainy holiday in Blighty. Unless it's safe to fly? What are the rules again, where can we go, what's on the safe list, the non-quarantine list? The prime minister's father breaks the rules. Or does he? No, of course he doesn't. He just does what any normal person who owns a luxury villa in Greece would do. He deploys the trademark blithering bonhomie. A cudgel disguised as an ostrich-feather duster, capable of laying about any rational discourse and ruthlessly derailing it.

In far-off Bristol town they're up at 5 a.m., erecting a statue on Colson's empty plinth. A resin-and-steel figure of Black Lives Matter protester Jen Reid. She stands, fist raised. *A Surge of Power.* She won't be there long. Tomorrow at dawn, Bristol City Council contractors will come and remove her. She will be driven away in a blue lorry, fist still raised. Her removal will reduce the number of public statues of BAME people in the UK to . . . what? Nobody knows. There's no centrally held register. There aren't any examples here in Lindfordshire, I'm afraid. But we do have some statues of women. We have Queen Victoria – but who hasn't? We will discount Victoria. This leaves us with Josephine Luscombe on her plinth holding her prayer book, in a little locked garden in Lindford. So phew, we have at least *one* statue celebrating a minority group. We use 'minority' in a technical sense here, in case pedants point out that women make up fifty-one per cent of the human race. We mean 'minority' in the generally accepted sense of 'not mainstream'. Minorities are not properly representative or universal. Unlike the white educated middle-class male norm, which is what we all understand when we say (with a flourish of ostrich-feather duster) 'majority'.

15th July

I love love love that my desk is under the window and now I can see the garden! I can see my giant sunflowers 😄 Leah did her karate and now she is picking her beans that have grown, she is meant to be in a geography lesson but she already knows everything due to 'research'. She wants us to take some veggies to Mr Hardman-May because they gave us some eggs, and this is what community is about (ha ha ha sure it is Leah (I did Not say)). It is only two more days of school then QM Girls breaks up. I have already broken up but dad says this is like Voldemort it is The Injustice That Must Not Be Named lol.

It will be a wierd holiday, we don't even know if we will go away, it is all still up in the air. It is wierd to be on holiday when its no different to being at school or not much. True there are online lessons but school is also about the social aspect. I have not seen my BFF Ellie in person since March. Leah has met up with Lydia in the arbo, they socially distanced obvs. Ellie does not live in Lindford, she lives in Martonbury so we cannot meet up in person, we can only FaceTime. Mum said she could drive me to Martonbury so Ellie and me can socially distance in her garden but Ellie's mum is 'shielding' she has rhuematoid artheritus so they cannot be too careful.

I try to keep my spirits up, it is bad enough for mum and dad to have Leah having issues the whole time. I try not to get bored and moan but sometimes it is boring to be fair. Mum understands so today we will be making facemasks, yay!!! (It will be compulsery to wear a mask in shops from 24th.) Disposable facemasks are not sustainable and Leah has been doing all of our heads in and we are like, WE KNOW THEY ARE NOT SUSTAINABLE DUH BUT WE STILL HAVE A WHOLE PACK! I mean are we like supposed to throw them away????

Mum and me are going to drive to her flat (which she still has) and pick up her sowing machine and fabric and me and her will make loads of masks which we will donate to charity. Mum says she has some cute fabric with animals on from when she did patchwork. 'We can make a pink one for your sister' mum whisperd. And Leah went I HEARD YOU! And mum went well that is surprising considering you did not hear me say will you empty the dishwasher. Then Leah fully yelled MAKE HER DO IT! SHE'S BROKEN UP, I STILL HAVE SCHOOL FYI. (This is due to hormones and PMT, Leah explained it all to me so when it happens to me I won't be scared when my emotions are up and down. IMAO Leah is like it 24/7 but I did not mention that fact.)

<u>*Moon Phase*</u>

Last Quarter (31%) I won't lie, the weather has been cloudy so I have not seen the moon much, and part of me thinks, why do I even bother? I almost gave up writing this moon journal and I would of if I'd mist the Hay Moon but I did not miss it. I woke up in the middle of the night on Sunday. Long story short, I was hungry so I went downstairs and got a banana, I happened to look through the kitchen window and lo and behold the moon came out from behind a cloud. And I went hey! Then I thought, 'The <u>HEY</u> moon geddit?' but there was nobody to tell, so I just ate my banana and went back to bed.

P.S. THERE IS AN ACTUAL COMET AT THE MOMENT, IT IS CALLED NEOWISE!!!!!! It is not often you see a comet in your actual lifetime, I so hope I see it one night soon before it vanishes. In the olden times they thought a comet was like a prophesy and meant bad stuff would happen, but that was a made-up fact.

Freddie latches the henhouse door. The wind chimes ring softly, like church bells away off on the other side of town. Rain patters down from the leaves. He stands with the day's eggs, and threads the fingers of his free hand through the chicken wire and grips hard. He gives it a shake. Yeh, strong. Saw a fox earlier from the bedroom window.

'What do we say to Mister Fox?' he asks the girls. 'We say, Not today, god of chicken death.'

Then weirdly he's remembering this toy his mum gave him, when he was maybe six, seven, this wire and bead toy from India? He unthreads his fingers from the coop. He's guessing now it was a mandala? You could fold it all these different ways, into a globe or a chalice, or this other shape that was either Saturn with the rings or maybe a spaceship?

Why's he remembering that, after like for ever? Sometimes he tells Brose this random stuff. Maybe the story ends with a shrug, something like, Hey, and then my stepbrothers stomped on it? Or, Then they tied me in a sleeping bag and pushed me down the stairs, and my dad was all, You're not hurt, don't be such a girl. Then he catches that look on Brose's face again. Ri-i-i-ght, so that would be . . . off, yeah? But you grow up with stuff, hey, you think all families are like that?

'Man, they were sooooo mean to me?' he complains to the chickens. 'I mean, Mum literally had to get me into chorister school, so I'd be safe?' She only told him that like last year? And he was all, Right, thanks for that, Mum. You couldn't've like stood up for me more at home? Except to be fair, standing up to Dad? Seriously, sometimes Freddie wonders if his dad is a literal psychopath? Even now, you push back, he does some number on your head, and *you're* the problem, the one overreacting and getting hysterical?

'Not gonna let anything bad happen to you girls. You hear me?' The hens are busy pecking up food. But they know. 'Catch ya later.'

Coz talking of psychopaths . . . He goes and sits on the bench he dried off earlier. Puts the carton of eggs down carefully beside him. Deep breath. Just do it, then get on with the day. So he pulls his phone out and calls Mister Dorian. His heart's going crazy. It rings once, then switches to voicemail.

Declined? Wow. Freddie's face burns. 'Leave a short coherent message—' He hangs up on the drawling voice. The wind chimes peal again. Well, probably he deserves that. I mean, why is he even surprised? Fully dicked him around over that recording, then ghosted him. Ah, don't be crying. Freddie blinks. Another petal comes fluttering from the high-up rose in next door's garden. Like a white moth. OK. So. Call back, leave a message, move on.

Shit! Freddie scrambles, half drops the phone.

'Yo!'

'Mr Hardman-May. Did you just butt-dial me at this unchristian hour, or are you finally reaching out?'

'Um, reaching out?'

Silence.

Great, we're going there, are we, the whole pulling-wings-off-flies game? 'So look, listen, my bad. I just wanted to—'

'Can I stop you there, and remind you that love means never having to say you're sorry?'

'Say what?'

'It's a quote.'

'It's bullshit, is what it is,' says Freddie. 'Coz actually, love means being accountable?' Freddie just *knows* he's smiling that smile at the other end. Like an asshole cat letting the mouse escape, then oops, sorry little buddy, not finished killing you yet.

'Can I assume from this that you didn't read my caring messages telling you these are unprecedented times, and not to beat yourself up and so forth? Not a single one?'

'Uh no. I . . . kind of assumed you'd be mad, and so yeah?'

'*Courage, mon brave.* Behind a frowning providence, I hide a smiling face. And how are things now? How are you doing, sweetheart?'

Gah! The switch from fuckwittery to kindness. Kills Freddie every single time. Breathe. He waits till he's sure his voice isn't gonna crack. 'Ohh. Hanging in there?'

'Well, that alone is quite an achievement. Come. Tell me what's on your heart.'

So Freddie talks about all the things, the disappointments, missing Evensong *so much* it hurts? How his career path is shot, being let go by Vespas, how maybe this is good – not having to expose himself to the virus, or to La Madeleine, coming to Lindford in person to remove his boys with her pinking shears, for playing Russian roulette with his precious instrument (her words). And how it's scary times for choirs everywhere and the whole cathedral choral tradition, because who knows where this'll end, if it ever will, and what in God's name is Freddie gonna do now, it's all so sad?

We will leave Freddie to unburden his soul to his former mentor. His voice carries up to the open bedroom window, in order that Ambrose can check Freddie's not over-sharing about Chloe and The Plan. Open window is the deal, so Freddie can stay accountable, because that's what love is. Love, however, also means trusting your beloved. Ambrose isn't listening. There was a time when he couldn't endure the sound of Mr Dorian's name even, but that was years ago. So Ambrose is in the kitchen, grinding garlic and spices with pestle and mortar to make Turkish eggs for Freddie's breakfast. (Goodness, there are so many manifestations of love going on in this paragraph, I may need to fan myself.)

But someone is listening to Freddie's conversation, though he doesn't understand a word of it. He has found a way of opening the locked upstairs window just a crack. He can get it closed again quickly, if They arrive suddenly to check on him. He daren't raise the blackout blind, but he can use a bamboo pole to hold the blind a little way out. Then he can stand and see a slice of outside. He can breathe air, real outside air, and sometimes the nausea goes away. But never for too long. The window must stay shut so the plants stay warm. He practises. Window shut, pole back in earth. Quick. And again. So that They never catch him. Garlic! His mouth waters. He has nothing but what They put in the freezer for him to microwave.

Sometimes when he squats listening, he hears bells and the hens scratching and talking. The leaves rustling might be the rice getting tall, and he's tiny again and soon he'll be going to search for the eggs . . .

Most days he sees the man with yellow hair who sings to the hens, and sings in the house, sing sing sing all the time, but sometimes there's shouting through the wall, then the man is sad and then he weeps. Some days he throws a red ball for the big brown dog. He digs the garden and plants. His sunflowers are growing well.

There's another man. This one is tall. He has to be careful when the tall man is there, because he always turns and looks up for a long, long time. He shades his eyes and looks up. Like this man knows someone is in here watching, and maybe this man will call the police, like They warn him every time They visit. If the police come, he's going to prison and never getting out, because he's a criminal, he's illegal. If the police come, he must try to run away. He must tell them nothing. Trust no one. No one will help, because the English hate foreigners.

All across Lindfordshire, there are other prisoners. Before lockdown, many were there in plain view, but we did not see them. In nail bars, washing our cars, working in hotels and takeaways. And there were children too young to drive, riding the trains from Birmingham or Liverpool, heading to Lindfordshire in expensive trainers, no ID on them, working the county lines. Where are they now? They are beyond the reach of teachers and social workers, of the caring professions. But not of the gangs.

Jane ponders some of this as she's out running round Martonbury Reservoir. What happened to the sex industry? Or the dodgy vape shops? Can't be easy to launder money by contactless payment, can it? Won't somebody please think of the criminals? She read somewhere that drug dealers have taken to trading in empty car parks, looking official in high-vis vests. Plenty of new scams popping up. Crime adapts like a rapidly evolving virus. To say nothing of creepy guys hitting on women after taking their contact details at bars for tracing purposes.

Foxgloves tower beside the path, and a wren flies so low and fast across the path in front of her that for a second Jane mistakes it for a vole. Not too long till their holiday. Looking like a small villa in a village not far from Seville. It'll be hot, but Jane is part lizard. My Spanish genes, she thinks. Dominic's mum is right. At a deep psychological level, I'm Spanish. I like Rioja, don't I? Well, there you go. There's a gust of wind. It shakes drops from the branches overhead. The ropes ping against the masts on all the little yachts. Presumably, people will be allowed out sailing again soon. Jane eases up the slope to where the car's parked. Already the early days of lockdown feel like a different era. They're taking on a sort of gem-like clarity, like beads of water suspended in lady's mantle leaves.

There. Duty done. She leans on the car, heaving for breath. Has she managed it? She checks her phone. Yesss! Smashed her Personal Worst! And now home for a slap-up breakfast. She's freewheeling towards her holiday now, when all dietary bets are off.

While we are on the subject of breakfast, perhaps you are wondering about those Turkish eggs Ambrose was cooking. What's he up to now? Let's join the Hardman-Mays in their kitchen and find out.

'So yeah, it's all cool? His point is, think of your online audience? You're like reaching literally thousands with each post? So yeah. I'ma concentrate on that, not like think of it as just this doofy thing while I'm waiting for real life to start up?'

'This is real life, babe.'

'I know. And hey – ha ha, you'll like this – we were just finishing up and I was all, So how's the naked guy? And he was, There's no naked guy. And I'm, So how's the *half*-naked guy? And get this – this voice in the background goes, I'm fine? Ha ha ha! How sweet is that? Wonder who he is?'

Ambrose shrugs. 'Who knows? Listen, can I float something past you? Just a possibility.'

'Sure.'

'How would you feel if Chloe moved in here while the extension's being built?'

Freddie pauses in the act of mopping up egg yolk. He looks at Ambrose. He looks down at his empty plate. 'Wait just one moment, mister. Is this already arranged? With Chloe? It is! You fucking— You . . .' He balls up his napkin and throws it at Ambrose's head. Alfie piles in, barking. New game!

'It's not arranged,' says Ambrose. 'I may have mentioned it to her and then caught myself, and told her to forget I said it until I'd talked to you—' He fends Freddie off. 'Look, can I make a suggestion?'

'It better be good!'

'Lockdown's been really tough, OK? We're both tired. So how about we skip the fight and go straight to making up?'

Freddie thinks about it. For maybe one nanosecond? 'Fuck yeah.'

Lockdown eases another notch, like a belt being let out. Nail bars can open, as can tattoo parlours. Church bells may be rung again. (The Bishop of Lindchester circulates guidelines.) Each morning we wake from stress dreams, and here comes another day, on with it, on with life. Is it nearly over? Are we nearly there yet? Goldfinches twitter past in charms across Lindfordshire gardens. Thistles crowd lay-bys, where brown butterflies and their shadows go flitting. There's hammering on building sites. Someone is wielding a chainsaw somewhere. A funeral cortège leaves a country church. Two girls put homegrown veggies on a doorstep, because nobody answers the door. Buses pass. Jets rumble overhead. Lawns and verges are cut, hayfields are mown. Cows graze in meadows. The sleepy sound of wood pigeons broods over everything. Lime trees hum with bees. July. Same as ever. Weird as ever. The moon wanes back down to nothing, ready to start all over again.

Ah, if only we could escape! Or fast-forward. We're getting our wellbeing (such as it is) on the never-never. Endlessly putting off dealing with it, this spiralling-out-of-control emotional debt. If only there was an *away* to get to. Thousands are still fighting for those Easter holiday refunds. The economy recovers more slowly than expected. UK payrolls shrink. True, we can get our nails done and go to the pub. Everything feels like the low season, though. Like a ghost town, a sleepy backwater.

There are other ways of looking at it. You might prefer the version that says we've turned a corner. That the hard graft of lockdown has paid off. A further batch of easing is promised for 1 August. Live theatre and concerts can resume. Skating rinks and casinos can open. Wedding receptions with up to thirty guests can take place. From September, schools, nurseries and colleges will open for all ages. From October, large sports stadiums will reopen. Well, it's been a long haul, but we're getting out of the woods now. We must continue to stay alert and socially distance. But there will be a significant return to normality by Christmas, says the Prime Minister.

Under the fizzing pylon, a white horse switches its tail in a Lindfordshire field.

Hay Moon, Part III

H ow weird to be back. Except, how weirdly normal. Chloe takes the Lindford exit from the motorway. How many times has she been round this roundabout, then down the slip road on to the old Roman road to Lindcaster? But normal-weird is the new normal. Like General Synod on Zoom last weekend not actually seeming that strange after all. Was it last weekend? That's all part of the new normal too. Events from last year feeling as close/distant as last month. Ha ha, and that email telling us what to expect! Like they were explaining to a decrepit high court judge. *Zoom*, m'lud. It's an *online video conferencing platform*. On the *internet*.

Her windscreen wipers start creaking, so she turns them off. Is the sky lightening ahead?

'Maybe the sun's coming out, Cosmo!' We can go out for a jog in the arboretum later. She knows not to say this aloud, or he'll go crazy in the back. Mostly her ramblings are a foreign language to him. But occasionally a lone word leaps out that's the same in canine. *Jog. Home. Ball.*

'No!' She accelerates with a lurch, so the combine harvester approaching from a country lane can't pull out in front of her. Cosmo whimpers. She glimpses his spanked expression in her mirror. 'Not you – the tractor! Aw, it's OK, baby. Good boy. Lie down.'

Ambrose always calls her out for moaning if she gets stuck behind farm traffic. Tells her to relax and enjoy the countryside, be grateful

215

for agricultural labour putting food on her table. You get caught in town traffic all the time without whinging, he says. Yes, yes, all right, Farmer Boy. Good job she loves him! And Freddie, bless him, who's been decorating her room ready for her, apparently. But she'll love that too, whatever it looks like. Hopefully it's not a mural of a giant cock, ha ha! (She's heard about his painting exploits from Madge. Neither of them has ever dared tell Virginia, though.)

Her heart starts to thump. Is this really a good idea, Chloe? This is the first time she's knowingly set out to do something her parents disapprove of. They simply can't give this scheme their blessing, even though they always give *her* their blessing, and they would bless and love any baby she had, of course they would! Oh, the sense of strangulation as she tried to explain. As if a panicky hand was gripping her throat, screaming, 'No no, you can't tell them! I won't let you!' Mum's tears. Dad's silence. Thank God she doesn't have to contend with Granny Gno telling her she's no better than a little prostitute!

You can't control them, Chloe. Remember, you can't control other people. You're telling them for *you*, not in order to change their minds. (Thanks for the life coaching, Brose!) She tries to enjoy the countryside. The big trees. Black-and-white cows that Farmer Boy would be able to tell her the name of. The patches of wild flowers the council have sown along the verges. White daisies, poppies, cornflowers, some type of yellow flower – corn marigolds, maybe.

Here's the Lindford turn. Three more miles. She can feel the dread closing in. All the things that drove her to run away back to her parents. Her oppressive little house. Lockdown showed her that she'd basically been camping out in it all these years. She'd never bothered to make it into a nice space – because she was hardly ever in it, she was so busy! Then there was the horrible situation next door. Domestic violence? Or not? Intervene? How? Job under threat once the furlough scheme winds down. Not knowing when they'd be able to progress The Plan. All adding up to . . . depression? Never! How could she, Chloe the little ray of sunshine, be *depressed*? She's always secretly despised people with depression – while being kind to them, obviously. Could they really not get a grip? But she ticks enough boxes. Low mood: tick. Feeling helpless and hopeless: tick. Loss of appetite, disturbed sleep patterns, tearful, anxious.

216

Oh, what if it all comes flooding back? Her hands grip the steering wheel. She's hunched over like a learner driver worried she won't get through a gap. She makes herself sit up and relax.

The countryside gives way to industrial estates and 80s housing. Concrete flyovers. Suddenly she sees her beloved town through an outsider's eyes. No wonder people think she's noble to live here! After all that time at her parents' place – suburbia with nice hedges and lawns – Lindford looks rundown and ugly. Graffiti everywhere. Litter. Abandoned mattresses. She leaves the big roundabout, drives past the parish church and the end of Father Dominic's drive – how is he doing? She should have been better at keeping in touch! (Feeling guilty: tick.) Here we go. Rows of Victorian terraces, parked solid on both sides of the street. *To Let* signs bristling – would the students be back this autumn?

'Nearly home now, Cosmo!' The dog shakes his head, ears flapping, collar jingling, and sits up. He pants happily. *Home! Home! Treats?*

Is she just being pedantic to insist on isolating for two weeks before moving in with the boys? You're not meant to swap bubbles, but two households can meet indoors, we can all go to the pub, so who really knows what the rules are any more? If she moved in straightaway with Ambrose and Freddie, couldn't she argue she was *extending* her bubble? Was that allowed? The boys say they'd be OK with that, but having told them she wasn't coming for another fortnight, maybe they won't be ready for her yet? It would be rude and inconsiderate to mess them around, now they've got holiday plans. (Wouldn't it?)

(Difficulty making decisions: tick.)

Oh God, here we are. 'Hail Mary, full of grace, help me find a parking space!' Miraculously there is one, right outside her house. Chloe crosses herself and parks. Turns the engine off. Rain patters on the windscreen again. She does her careful breathing to ward off a panic attack. In, two three four. Out, two three four.

It's like the last two minutes before an interview. Or a violin grade. Can she really not get a grip? *What would getting a grip look like?* Ha ha, another Ambrose question! It would look like . . . well, making a start. Tucking your violin under your chin, putting the bow to the string and playing the first note. And realizing that you can play the next one and then the next; that the tune is there, you *can* do it.

One day at a time.

Suddenly her head floods with Freddie's voice. His latest YouTube song. Sweet Jesus. Help me. She undoes her seatbelt and turns round. 'We can do this, Cosmo. Let's go, boy.'

Chloe is not the only one struggling. All over Lindfordshire, people are failing to get a grip. COVID-19 has dealt us a massive staggering blow. The nation has emotional concussion. Feeling stunned, dazed, confused. Memory loss. Clumsiness. Mood swings. Headaches. Feeling sick. What we need is a break. We need to get away from all this completely. Except whither can we flee from thy presence, COVID-19? If we take the wings of Easy Jet and flee to the uttermost parts of the globe, even there you will be waiting in your face mask to give us a welcoming elbow bump.

Ah, summer hols 2020! What a scaling down. What a mish-mash of dashed hopes, of making do and last-minute improvisation. We divide once more: those who are lucky enough to escape abroad and those obliged to make do with a staycation (with a further subdivision over what 'staycation' actually means: it does *not* mean holidaying somewhere in the UK, you posh git – that's what we call *a holiday*, like 'wild swimming' is just swimming, and 'wild camping' camping).

The Logan family, sitting with a well-earned glass of wine on their terrace of an evening, overheard a swearie rant along these lines, with much animadversion about the government thrown in along the way. Once again, Mr Logan (who hasn't had a day off work since the end of February and is dead on his feet) nods in agreement. Rachel Logan, with A-level results drawing ever nearer, also nods. So does Mrs Logan, who is wondering if her wedding planning company will go under, and has been going mad trying to navigate a way through the restrictions with distressed brides and grooms. They all nod. Yep. What Neil said.

What the Logan family did not hear was the swearie rant about the shit-for-brains idiot who failed to renew his passport when it expired back in March, thereby causing the cancellation of the expensive non-refundable trip to Provence, because there was a backlog of 400,000 applications, and not a chance of the Passport Office turning the renewal round in time. Such a rant never took place. I would love to tell you, dear reader, that this is because the gentle work of the Holy Spirit has so transformed Neil that he forbore to lambast poor Father Ed for this oversight. Alas no. It was Neil's own passport that had expired, leaving him with nobody to lambast but himself (and possibly God, for allowing the global pandemic that caused the Passport Office to shut). Neil is now hunting for the perfect luxury cottage, maybe in the Welsh borders? Something tastefully restored, stunning views, private garden, pets welcome, hot tub. He dismisses Ed's ignorant Sassenach suggestion of Mull. Hello? Has he no heard of midges?

Jane and Matt are in Spain, making use of that lacuna in the episcopal diary created by the cancelled Lambeth Conference. I will not deny that there were outbreaks of Schadenfreude across the diocese when the government put Spain on the list of quarantine countries. But as some of those smirking about the Bishop of Barcup's bad luck have booked themselves holidays in France, we will in due course (with the Dean of Lindchester Cathedral's husband) be able to relish the idea that there's probably a German word for 'ill-fated premature indulgence in Schadenfreude'.

It occurs to me that we have not paid Gene a visit for a while now. I miss him. He is the uncompromisingly dreadful clergy spouse I secretly long to be. He and Dean Marion have been shielding together all this time. They have not left the deanery since 29 March, except to walk or sit in the garden. Even if your house has eight bedrooms, a drawing room, gracious hallway, dining room, a study larger than that of the Archbishop of Canterbury himself, a well-appointed kitchen, breakfast room, scullery, numerous pantries and outhouses, a well-stocked cellar, attics, to say nothing of a huge garden with its own beehives, this is a long time to be stuck in one place. With one person.

'I actually find myself hankering for the hustle and bustle of a busy chemo session,' says Gene. They are in the deanery kitchen, just finishing their breakfast of homemade sourdough French toast, with homemade strawberry compote and homemade yoghurt. Gene cannot believe that *two whole months* of lockdown passed without it occurring to him that an Aga was the perfect place for coddling his own live yoghurt cultures!

'You don't mean that,' says Marion sternly. 'That's cabin fever talking.'

'True. I know – let's go on a mini-break to the small guest bedroom and pretend we're having a torrid affair. I'll check YouTube and find out how to fold the hand towels into swans, and we can stock the en suite with the toiletries you've thieved from the many hotels you've visited in the line of deanly duty.'

'It's not *thieving*!' says Marion. 'They're complimentary.'

His eyes gleam. Petty larceny of midget shampoos is one of her few foibles. 'Ah, but you don't *need* them, do you?'

'Well. They're useful when we have visitors.'

'But think of the planet! Think how many tiny plastic bottles would not end up in the blowholes of innocent dolphins if everyone exercised restraint in hotels!'

Marion opens her mouth to cite her scrupulous habit of reusing hotel towels (unlike Gene, who tosses them on the floor with the words 'Screw you, environment!'). She catches herself in the nick of time.

'Still,' Gene persists, 'it's good to know that if we live to a hundred, we will never want for a disposable shower cap.'

She makes no reply.

'Or a teeny, tiny sewing kit.'

'Oh, shut up, you horrible man!'

He smiles, as though he's finally compelled her to admit she loves him. 'Never mind. Not too long to go now, Deanissima. Shielding ends on August the first. What's the first thing you'll do when you're free of me?'

She shakes her head at him. 'It's not like that, and you know it.'

'I do know it. I have plagued and tormented you non-stop for four months, and you still don't long to be set free!' he marvels. 'Patient Griselda was a screechy old hellcat compared with you. But what will you do on the first of August?'

'You know what I'll do, Gene.'

Right on cue, the cathedral clock chimes the hour.

'Yes. You'll be up at the crack of dawn, to tread your well-trodden path. You'll go through the dean's door into your beloved cathedral. Then you'll sit in your stall and cry a river over the state of this poor world.'

Her eyes are already brimming. 'Yes. And what will you do?'

He's silent. Rain patters on the window. The kitchen is warm, and full of toast smells and the faint baby-sick whiff of the yoghurt. Strange what one misses. Places that barely registered at the time. The egg section in Lindchester Waitrose. Euston Station in the evening, with the crowd under starter's orders gazing up at the departures board, waiting for the platform number to appear. Or some half-forgotten hotel car park, where a hornbill perched on the car and pecked angrily at its reflection in the windscreen. And over and over, as he drifts asleep at night, the same long straight stretch of empty road somewhere between Joburg and Bloemfontein. It plays out like a film clip across his brain: blue sky, the veld stretching to the horizon on both sides, and the road spooling out under the wheels, mile after mile.

'I'll probably go for a drive,' he says at last. 'If I can remember how to work the gears.'

There are many in Lindfordshire who will get no break this year. No escape from home, no escape from work, or the lack of work and the looming prospect of homelessness, once the ban on landlords evicting tenants is lifted. No escape from the kids, love them. Not until school starts – please let them open! Don't let there be another lockdown.

In the farthest reaches of the diocese, on the edge of the Peaks, paragliders circle again. Parings of red and blue, high above towns and fields. They've got the right idea. Let's join them. Let's disappear into the sky one bright day between rain storms. Up, up, up, nineteen times as high as the moon, like the old woman tossed up in the basket. But for heaven's sake, let's not repeat her blunder. Leave the broom behind. Imagine mounting to the starry heights with the sole intention of doing housework. Give yourself a break, old woman. Leave the sky cobwebs to the angels.

221

Easier said than done. How holidays catch us out. Our subconscious seizes the opportunity to download months of stress every night in the form of dreams about running late to deliver a lecture on a subject we know nothing about and haven't prepared for, with a new phone that inexplicably folds out like a map, then won't fold up again. Our progress is impeded at every stage by a small child clamped on each leg. We are unable to find the venue, which has now become a wedding for which we have failed to call the banns, with the archbishop due to arrive any moment, and obviously we are naked, apart from our school hockey socks.

July is nearly over. One day we will be looking back on all this. We will be like those paragliders seeing the big picture. We will be able to say how long it lasted, what the final figures were. Eventually, we will be able to put an end date on COVID-19, and close the brackets; like Spanish flu (February 1918 to April 1920). All the stencilled circles on the pavements – *Stay Safe. Keep your distance* – will eventually wear away. But for now, the total number of cases globally carries on rising: fourteen million. Sixteen million. Seventeen million.

July 31st
We are on holiday!!!! YAY!!!! We are staying in bishop Paul's house who was dad's boss when he was bishops chaplin back when I was young, it is in the Peak district which is very beatiful IMAO even if there are too many sheep and not enough trees (says guess who).

We are all immensely greatful to bishop Paul and Susanna his wife for there generosity, we did not think we would get a holiday this year. My room is sweet, it has a little window that looks out over the purple heather, like in the song 'Wild Mountain Time' that we sang in sing-up back in the day. We have to be careful and not use gel pens when we are sitting on the sofa because it is cream. Dad is laying on the sofa now, he is tired from the journey.

Today is the last day of July. Then it's august, then its new term. New term will be wierd, it will not be like last year when I started at The Cathedral School and everything was new and exiting. We will have to socially distance in class, and we are still not aloud to sing in the choir. It is a total myth that singing spreads the virus. If you have proper breath control you will not spread it. Mr Hardman-May proves this on youtube when he sings and the candle does not go out, but the government do not believe him. Fortunatley we will be back to normal by Christmas, the PM says this, so fingers crossed he is right, even if he is a Tory moron according to Leah (she keeps up with politics, I personally do not).

Moon Phase.

Waxing gibbous (85%)

Moon Facts

I have noticed that the date of the full moon gets earlier each month. This is due to the lunar month being shorter than the calender month. It gets earlier and earlier, so sometimes you get TWO FULL MOONS. The second full moon is called A BLUE MOON, which is why the proverb says 'once in a blue moon'. The next full moon will be August 3rd and 4th it will be called the 'sturgeon moon' in Native American, sturgeon is a type of fish. It is also the 'Barley Moon' or the 'fruit moon' or the grain moon.

P.S. I did not see the comet

P.P.S. There will be shooting stars on 11 august, so I will be sure to look out for them instead.

Back in Lindford, Freddie rinses the paint roller under the tap. Gonna look awesome. Blue, blue, blue. Like Chefchaouen, which he's always wanted to visit? Top of the list when all this is over, for sure. To live high up in the mountains, in a blue city – what's not to love? This is the vibe he's going for. Mixed the colours himself, with white emulsion and blue powder paint, like being back in school. Man, he *loved* art lessons, only Dad made him take something 'useful'?

He squeezes the water out of the roller and props it up to dry. Then he goes back upstairs to look. Yeah, all ri-i-ight! Oh, wow – what if he did the entire house like this? Wouldn't that be something? Makes him sad to think he's only just this week reached this point, after living here since February. Makes him even sadder that it took Dad telling him the best thing you can do with an ugly 60s house is pull it down and start over. And suddenly he's all protective of the house? Hey. Do *not* call my house ugly.

I'ma love this house to bits. Every corner. Every centimetre. Love it till it *sings*. He remembers suddenly this song his mum used to sing when he was tiny? Aw, sweet. Totally one for him and the girls on TikTok.

At the baby grand piano downstairs, Ambrose hears him, and starts to play along and improvise a harmony. Alfie lifts his head and joins in. Exactly. This *is* a very very very fine house. And when Chloe comes, there'll be two dogs in the yard. And who knows? Maybe another little person one day. Everything is good. Even though it's really not, it still is.

AUGUST

Grain Moon, Part I

'Whoa!' Ambrose jumps. Coffee slops over his hand. 'What the hell, Freddie?'

Freddie grins up from under the desk, where he's sitting cross-legged. 'Here to help out, dude. Like Dishy Rishi said?'

Ambrose guffaws. He puts his mug down and dries his hand. 'And is this what Dishy Rishi meant?'

'Huh? It's not?'

'I'm taking a wild punt here and going with "no", Freddie.' He sits in his chair and switches the computer on. 'Anyway, I've got a conference call right this minute.'

'So? Use your poker face, man. No one'll know.'

Fractional hesitation.

'Ha ha, you're thinking about it – you *so* want to!'

Ambrose points to the door. 'Go and finish packing.'

Freddie crawls grumbling from under the desk. He props his chin on Ambrose's knee and gives him an Alfie look. 'But I wanna go on holiday no-o-w. How come you're working Saturday? Dude, this here's our anniversary! How long's this gonna take? Are we nearly the-e-e-re yet?'

'The sooner you go, the sooner I'll be done, babe.'

'Fine.' Freddie hauls himself up and slouches off.

'I'll deal with you later,' adds Ambrose.

'You better, my dude. Coz third anniversary? Leather.'

Ambrose smiles. 'Oh, I'm across that, believe me.'

227

Overall, people have grasped the chancellor's *Eat Out to Help Out* scheme rather better than Freddie affects to have done. All across Lindfordshire, they are eagerly booking themselves tables at participating establishments ready to claim their half-price meals. Well, I say they've grasped it. Many will be wrong-footed when they discover it's just Monday to Wednesday, and they only get a fifty per cent discount on food or non-alcoholic drinks to eat or drink in (up to a maximum of £10 discount per diner). Swizz! But all the same, hoorah for Dishy Rishi jump-starting the economy. Those who are struggling to make ends meet, who fell through the furlough-scheme cracks and dream of being able to eat out – well, I expect they are being supported some other way. In claps and rainbows, perhaps. That should tide them over till Christmas, by which time the Prime Minister hopes there will be a substantial return to normal.

Both normal and Christmas feel a long way off. It's high summer now. August in Lindfordshire, 2020. We are now sanitizer connoisseurs. We can discern relative concentrations, and distinguish between slippery and sticky, perfumed and unperfumed. We learn the ways of the dispensers – foot operated, hand operated, automatic, and which ones will leave you wringing your hands for ten minutes, trying to absorb the equivalent of a shot of vodka into your epidermis. After some grumbling, particularly from glasses-wearers whose lenses keep fogging, we've grown accustomed to shopping in face masks. We have finally worked out that there is a correct way up for the disposable ones (wire strip at the top). Some of us have discovered by accident that the disposable ones are washable. A minority have apparently not discovered that your mask is supposed to cover your nose as well as your mouth, and they wander round supermarket aisles with the COVID equivalent of their flies open and Percy Pointer flapping in the wind. Most of us are settling on our mask of choice, be that Liberty print washable, amusing moustache/cat/maniac grin, black 'fashion' mask off Amazon (which pulls your ears forward like Mickey Mouse) or a simple hoiked-up scarf. Compliance levels are high. We've repurposed the excoriating English Glare (normally deployed to shame queue-jumpers) and direct it at non-mask-wearers. The Glare is a bit of a blunt instrument, unfortunately, and takes out people legitimately exempt from wearing a mask. We must be alert when glaring down Hereford way, in case we've unwittingly strayed into Wales, where bare-faced shopping is legal.

Apart from the pandemic, August commences as usual in Lindfordshire. The fields are turning white unto harvest. If we fly across the landscape now, among the swifts and swallows, we will see the farmland laid out below us like a Farrow & Ball paint chart, with many subtly different shades of white. Hay white, barley white, wheat white, oat white. Then there's sheep white, thistledown white, the white of the clouds reflected on lake and river. How long ago February seems, when much of this was lying under floodwater.

August brings crushing disappointments. There have been spikes of new infections. Greater Manchester is the epicentre this time. They're not put into full local lockdown like Leicester; but different households may not meet indoors or in private gardens any more. The government slams on the brakes nationally too, just as they warned us they would (with the 'nuclear option' of a return to full lockdown held in reserve). They postpone the changes promised for 1 August. Indoor theatre performances and concerts won't be taking place. Casinos and ice rinks will remain closed. And bad luck if you went ahead and planned a wedding reception with thirty guests. Mrs Logan is tearing her hair out over in her pretty wedding venue in Gayden Parva. Florist stood down, bunting and party favour production halted, gazebos and topiary pots loaded back on to the trailer.

Thanks, Greater Manchester. You are the individual ruining it for everyone else. The whole school has to stay in because of you. It's wise to resent Greater Manchester in general, because nobody wants to sound racist by saying out loud that *apparently* it's the BAME communities with their huge households and lack of social distancing that have brought this about. Here in Lindfordshire, the thought of accidentally saying something racist makes us uncomfortable, because we're nice people. God, we thank thee that we are not as other men are; bigoted, prejudiced, or even as this white supremacist.

Kat, the bishop's EA, would include fragile white on her paint chart. Still, she is on annual leave, so I'm pleased to say she's not having to

229

put up with a load of anguish on this subject around the Close. She is sitting up in bed with her coffee, looking at pictures of the crammed beaches of Dorset on social media. Yeah, right, we don't know how to socially distance. Show us the way, white people.

You will notice that Kat is sitting in bed, not in the airport. She and her partner Jo reluctantly cancelled their holiday in Nice. They could see which way the winds of COVID were blowing, and Jo couldn't afford to take a further two weeks off afterwards to quarantine. Oh well. At least they've got pain au chocolat. Jo is drinking coffee and scouring websites for last-minute alternatives, trying to find places where they'll feel safe and relaxed and not too stared-at as a gay black couple.

I fear that didn't occur to Bishop Steve yesterday when he blithely suggested destinations, as wrong-headed as an ignorant Sassenach who hasn't heard of midges. Kat listened and said thanks. Then Sonya popped in with commiserations and suggestions of her own, just when Kat was about to escape. I rather fear Sonya tries Kat's patience. (We pause here to thank the Lord that Kat never had to navigate Susanna Henderson's weaponized niceness and pastoral head-tilt.) Sonya hasn't a clue that she and Steve can travel anywhere they want on the Passport of Whiteness and feel safe. And the places where they wouldn't feel safe? Well, those aren't really the kind of places they'd want to go on holiday.

Kat and Jo have a different map of the world. Do they ever! Different map, different road signs. In the Penningtons' world, 'Can I help you?' is customer service, not 'Fuck off, you don't belong here'. But explaining all this is just so knackering, Kat can't always be arsed. Steve's not so bad. He's got better people skills. He can usually tell when he's done his white thing again somehow. And he also gets that he's not the one who dictates how and when she explains what he just did wrong.

'OK, so what about this?' says Jo. 'Converted goose house on farm, perfect for a romantic break. Private garden, parking, wifi. Look.'

'A cabin bed! Omigod! Look at the quilt! And a reading nook! So go on, whereabouts?'

Jo checks. 'Hmm. Somerset? Everywhere's booked solid. Shall I go for it?'

'Sure you don't fancy camping? Sonya's offered us their tent. And the cooking stove.'

'Aw, bless.' They laugh till the bed shakes.

Will they be OK? Will they get a warm welcome in Somerset? Yes, they will. As chance (i.e. your soft-hearted author) would have it, Jo has just booked ten days on the Hardman family farm – though nobody will work out there's a Lindchester connection until ages afterwards. You may remember that Freddie and Ambrose stayed in this very goose house, but that was before Ambrose's sister and mum did it up for paying guests, elevating it to swoon-making standards of Pinterest gorgeousness. You may be interested to learn that it even ticked Neil's exacting list of decor boxes when he spotted it on his own search – though he *might* have been inclined to go with salon drab rather than Hardwick white for the walls – but sadly there was no availability. Ambrose's mum is mightily relieved to see Jo's booking, after a last-minute COVID-related cancellation. It will be perfect. Forget France. There will be homemade scones waiting, and homemade gooseberry jam, some Wyfe of Bath cheese, fresh eggs, organic local cider, and (talk about Cottagecore) a bunch of dahlias in a vintage Kilner jar on the little kitchen table.

Ambrose and Freddie, on the other hand, will be camping. Not just camping, but *wild* camping. Wild camping and wild swimming. That's what Freddie wants (given that – sorry, babe – they really, really can't go to Chefchaouen in the middle of a pandemic), and what Freddie wants usually becomes the focus of all of Ambrose's fiendish scheming.

Ambrose makes his work call, ties up the loose ends, then puts on his out-of-office message, about being away from his desk without access to emails. This is a polite fiction, of course. We can always access our emails these days. It's not as though he and Freddie are time travelling back to the early 90s, even if they will be camping in some remote rural spot beside the Linden. What Ambrose means is that he *chooses* not to check his emails while he's on leave. Quite right too. His clients can manage without him. (And nobody wants their phone dunked in a fresh cowpat by their irate spouse.) It's been a nightmare year. Massive implications for financial reporting. Ambrose shakes his head. Some of the local businesses whose accounts he looks after won't still be going concerns on the other side of COVID. Vespas are going to struggle to keep their new Lindford branch. Unless the students are back in sufficient numbers when uni term starts.

He shakes his head again and logs off. Done. He won't think about work again until he's back in a week's time. My readers may envy Ambrose these robust watertight boundaries. He forged them early, in a prestigious accountancy firm in London, during his meteoric rise up the golden escalator from grad scheme to the lower rungs of senior management. Between ourselves, he was tipped for a top role nationally. Nobody could understand why he'd walk away from all that, aged thirty-three, to become a small-time accountant in a provincial town in the arse end of nowhere – where was Lindchester, again? – Norfolk or something? Weren't there choirs in London if he wanted to sing? Nobody got it, because although everyone liked him (apart from those who hated him for managing them out of their roles) nobody ever knew him, not really. Watertight work/play boundaries. Ambrose, the dark horse.

This was the long game he'd been playing from the start. To make enough money to leave London comfortably, become a lay clerk somewhere, settle in some gorgeous cathedral city, and set about the business of finding a life partner. That was his choice.

Not his choice to fall for Freddie May. Literally at first sight. In fact, a split second before that. He was on the threshold of the room – Chloe was with him – on the point of entering the welcome drinks party at the Director of Music's house, when he heard a voice in his mind say, *He's here.* Ambrose had never in his life had a premonition, but – crazy stuff! – he was actually shaking as he walked in. He scanned round, saw the back of a blond head. The head turned. *Oh shit.* That's what Ambrose thought. If it'd been a poker game, he'd have folded. No way would he have carried on playing when the stakes were so high and his chances so slim. Five years ago, nearly. The best, and stupidest, gamble of his gambling life was to go ahead anyway, and bet everything on that premonition. He still can't believe his luck.

232

GRAIN MOON!!!!!!!

I decided to go with <u>GRAIN MOON</u> because that is Old English. One website said it is called 'the moon where everything ripens', when I read that out Leah went, AKA <u>harvest</u> and roled her eyes. She makes a good point, dad said. Whatever, harvest moon is <u>September</u>, so I'm going with grain moon because of the wheat and other crops ripening.

I was scared it would be cloudy and this would be the first full moon I mist in 2020. Fortunatley it was not!!! So last night at midnight me and Leah went out of bishop Pauls cottage where we are staying in our bear feet, and walked onto the yard, it was a bit cold but not to cold. The yard is made out of black bricks with a crisscross pattern on, they are called 'Lindfordshire Patterned Pavers'. When Dad told us, mum and me looked at each another, like, That's where Leah get's it from, her and dad both have to know everything the entire whole time lol.

So Leah and me walked so we could see the moon coming up over the top of the cottage roof which is kind of zigzag, and I went 'They are actually called Lindfordshire Zigzag roof bricks' and Leah went No they aren't. Then she went SLUG! and I screamed but she was just pranking me. Mum opened their window and said Are you OK, girls? And I went Sorreeee. She and dad are having to share a room because there are only three rooms and me and Leah will only fight if we have to share (says mum).

The moon was beautiful as per usual, it was in a whisp of cloud. It was so so quiet. I whisperd Do you reckon they are getting back together again? and Leah went don't jinks it. Then I said You can wish on the full moon you know, and she went God you are such a baby sometimes. (Ha ha I bet she wished!!!)

Moon Facts

So you can wish on the full moon like I said, but there are neumerous other moon traditions, like for example 'a moon bath'. N.B. Moonbathing is not like sunbathing, we did not lay out under the moon to get a moon tan!!!!!!! It means if you take a bath at the full moon then it is super healing because mineral absorption is optimized. I was not going to tell Leah this or she would of gone first and used all the hot water, but then I did, and she went no, it's OK you can go first so I did, I used one of my Rainbow bath bombs. Hopefully I have absorbed rainbows LOL. Sometimes Leah is very thoughtful like that, she is an awesome big sister at the end of the day.

'So whaddya think?'

'Wow'. Chloe blinks. 'It's very . . . blue?'

'Ya like it?'

Chloe gazes round the spare room. 'It's amazing, Freddie!'

'Aw, gurl. Gimme a hug – oops, my bad.' He jumps back and flaps his hands like he's just grabbed nettles.

'Sorry, sorry, sorry! I'll have wall-to-wall hugs lined up when you guys get back from holiday,' Chloe promises. 'I'll be out of quarantine then.'

'Cool. Listen, you can do the extension out however the hell you want? I mean, like that'll be your space? I just wanted to make this, I dunno, heaven? Make sense?' He shrugs a big happy shrug. 'And hey, look at this – you can get out on to the garage roof?' He pulls aside the white muslin curtains. 'See? C'mon.'

After a bit of coaching, Chloe is out on the flat roof beside him. They stand looking over the henhouse, the garden fence. They can hear the mower next door.

'So this here's where your little house'll be? I mean, yours and the baby, if. Aw, can you believe, I'm totally blushing here? So yeah. With a little window about here? Gonna be awesome!'

'Well, I'm sure it will be,' agrees Chloe. 'But I can't really picture it yet.'

'Seriously? You've seen the plans, no?'

'Yes, but I can't think in three dimensions. I need to see the actual— Ooh, look! There's Miss Sherratt!' Chloe cups her mouth. 'Yoo-hoo, Miss Sherratt!'

Miss Sherratt turns on her terrace and shields her eyes. 'Yoo-hoo! Is that Chloe? What are you doing here? Are you back?'

'Yes! I'm dog-sitting and feeding the hens!'

'And supervising the builders!' calls Freddie.

'Jolly good!' trumpets Miss Sherratt. 'Would you like some tomatoes?'

'Yes, please!'

'I'll send Jack with some!'

'Jack? Jack from church? Yoo-hoo, Jack!' Chloe waves as though she's a castaway semaphoring passing ships from her island. Jack pauses in his mowing and raises a hand.

Ambrose, down on the drive packing the car, hears all the happy shouting. He smiles. Already Chloe's doing her ray-of-sunshine thing. Connecting people. Making a community. He wonders whether someone is watching out the back, through that crack in the blind. Whether that person has spotted Chloe and is thinking, There's someone who looks like me out there. That's what Ambrose hopes. He's hoping that somehow they can get a message through: You are not alone. We want to help you. And he's praying the police don't raid the place before they get the chance.

Grain Moon, Part II

Jane chafes. To be stuck in quarantine while August slumps replete across the landscape! The fourteen days of isolation pass slowly. Dominic has promised to pop over with his mum this evening if the weather stays nice. It's hot but humid, with the threat of thunder hanging over everything. If the storm keeps off, they will sit on the patio for a drink. True to her inner commitment to be more Spanish, Jane has decided to name the shocking truth: she doesn't like Prosecco. Tonight they will drink cava.

Well, at least she's got the garden to stroll in. She makes her way towards the bench with her coffee and a cushion (for white-linen-trouser-related reasons). The well-stocked borders are not as kempt as when Janet Hooty was in charge, but the hollyhocks self-seeded between paving stones are a triumph again. Bees rummage up the petals like Georgian rakes backstage at the opera. The apples are ripening. It's the archetypal lovesome spot, but God wot, Jane aches to wander the little lanes of rural Lindfordshire, to get up on to the heathland to see the heather, or to potter along the canal to recall her first ever date with Matt all those years ago.

Apart from having itchy feet, quarantine's not too much of an inconvenience, to be honest. Matt's had to cancel a couple of services he'd been due to take. Jane's work hasn't been affected, other than not being able to go in and help staff the clearing hotline. That alone makes the Spain trip worth it. Two idle weeks recharging in a village in Andalucia was a sheer bonus. Isolation also means she doesn't have to invent an excuse for not going to Aunty Betty's funeral, where in any case she'd only be taking up a valuable place in the crematorium that would be better filled by a close friend from the village. Jane suspects that her cousin Elaine, who's the one organizing everything, is relieved. No need for those whisper-bawled explanations for deaf old relatives: *It's Jackie, Eileen's girl. JACKIE. She's married to a bishop. Yes, A BISHOP!*

Jane is self-aware enough to realize that this is her shit, not theirs. That time she went back with Danny, everyone was kind and welcoming. She was never the centre of the family drama. It all carried on without her. Her bit-part was simple to summarize: the brainy girl who moved up and out. It would be nice to feel that she'd taken a less clichéd trajectory. One where contempt of working-class culture wasn't implied. She blamed Oxford for this, because it was easier than blaming herself. That said, what eighteeen-year-old can stand unperturbed and true to herself over against middle-class public school cultural hegemony?

She puts her cushion on the garden bench and sits to address an ad hoc seminar group of insects, who ignore her and busy themselves in the lavender, like students catching up on social media. Same old.

Take net curtains. The homes of her childhood all had them. You washed your windows once a week and your nets once a month. But at Oxford she learnt that net curtains were naff. This came with all the heft of a universal scientific law, as though the chemical formula of nylon itself was $Naff_2O$. Furthermore, *everybody who was intelligent and educated knew this*. Ergo, if you didn't know this, you were neither intelligent nor educated. White stilettos, draylon three-piece suites, Jackie Collins novels, framed reproductions of *The Hay Wain*, calling your grandmother Nan, artex ceilings. All these things shifted into the same category as gaffes and mispronunciations. Add to this all the cultural references you didn't get – brands you'd never heard of, places you'd never been, pastimes you'd never tried. Yes, and let's not forget the casual assumptions about what was expensive or affordable, what time you ate, what your meals were called. Jane's Oxford learning experience came with a generous topping of shame. Avoiding shame was a powerful incentive to assimilate. Resistance got you labelled as having a chip on your shoulder.

The bees murmur on. Jane drinks her coffee and stares at the sweet peas climbing the fence. When she was little, one of her ambitions was to own a miniature wishing well. She could buy one now and stick it in the garden, but only if she is being *ironic*.

Everything is still and heavy. Someone's mowing their lawn. The songbirds are silent. Just the occasional wood pigeon or clashing shriek of a magpie. A car goes past.

Elaine will be taking down her mum's nets before long, she thinks. Clearing the house. The house! Jane remembers playing round at Elaine's after school. *Scooby-Doo* on TV. Fish fingers, orange jelly and evap. That time Elaine was wearing a big orange plastic pendant and scooped it up with her spoon, thinking she'd dropped jelly down her front. The two of them laughing till they nearly wet themselves. She can still hear Elaine saying, 'I thought, Oops, Mum'll crown me!' Then playing out the back, going down the narrow garden, ducking under the clothes line, heading for the garages. The nettled path between pebble-dashed walls, concrete road, French skipping with knicker elastic, how it got caught on your sandal buckles. Clapping games. *When Suzie was a teenager, a teenager she was, she went-a Ooh, ah, I lost my bra, I left my knickers in my boyfriend's car!*

A van comes up the drive. Amazon delivery. She exchanges waves with the driver. Jane's treated herself to an electric pencil sharpener ahead of the new academic year. Showing herself a good time in quarantine, all right. The van drives away again. Silence. At some level, Jane knows she's grieving her aunty Betty. But when she goes looking for that feeling, it's missing. Like a volume stolen from a library shelf.

Well, on with life. She finishes her coffee, gets up and heads back to the house. A-level results day is looming, which promises to be another comprehensive cock-up, with the concomitant balls-up for universities. This strikes her as the appropriate male imagery for describing the omnishambles serially spunked out by the bunch of bell ends in Johnson's government.

The reader may be saddened and disappointed to witness Jane sliding back into the habit of vituperation she renounced in January. Father Dominic, you may remember, consoled himself with the idea that Jane had passed on her swearie mantle to Leah. But with all due respect to young people everywhere, the impact of a brilliantly crafted obscenity does tend to get lost in a discourse where the F-word is freely used as a mild intensifier. This effing linguistic tic is deeply shocking to older generations. They, in turn, deeply shock today's young by having no problem with phrases like 'half-caste' and 'that darkie lad', or even with using the N-word to describe a particular shade of brown cloth. Whether a linguistic tic is more shocking than unexamined racism, I leave for the reader to decide.

While we are on this topic of bad language, schoolteachers may be concluding that their own capacity to swear is no longer fit for purpose. If only they could hire some kind of cuss-o-gram to express their anger and frustration as the A-level results debacle unfolds like the slo-mo train wreck they've long foreseen. I am happy to report that here in Lindfordshire there is at least one acting Head – Mrs Hill has gone off with stress – who is in the happy position of being able to outsource her contumely to her next-door neighbour.

It's late afternoon. Unbearably hot, even with a fan. Rachel can hear Gayden Parva whistling. She peels herself from her chair, goes to her bedroom window and looks out. Gayden Magna is just setting off to walk the dog. And there's Parva's Panama hat passing between the gap in the orchard trees. She seizes her moment – and the pot of Mexican fleabane Mum has set aside for him – and heads round to the vicarage. The Logan family has been dying to hear what Gayden Parva makes of the Scottish exam results fiasco. Publicly, Ms Logan must confine herself to phrases like 'really challenging times in education, and we are committed to doing our best for our pupils'. She's very much hoping Neil can do justice to her true feelings.

I have chosen to draw a polite Anglican veil over this scene. Rest assured, Neil did not disappoint. If Rachel had been writing a school report on his performance, it would have been glowing. You must conjure for yourself the ingenious compound nouns, the juxtaposition of images never before united in the same utterance, the twang and smack of apt dialectal words – in short, all the linguistic pyrotechnics in the Ferguson repertoire. It will aid Rachel tonight, when the government decides (last thing on the penultimate day before results are due, and without consulting schools or universities) that mock results will be given as A-levels, if they are higher than exam board calculated grades. Not all schools do mocks. In others, the results weren't collected or standardized, and some – QM Girls in Lindford, for example – mark harshly to head off complacency. Exactly how much fun is Thursday going to be?

But this particular midnight lurch on the rickety DfE rollercoaster is still in the future. We will join them in the vicarage potagerie as the rant concludes. The cardoons are doing nicely, by the way.

'Och, well. Enough of that.' Neil takes off his Ray-Bans and looks at her. 'How are you doing, darling?'

The blue eyes are locked on hers. Rachel looks away, seized by the fear he's about to go religious. Like the Christian Union types at uni, awkwardly springing Jesus on you. 'Fine, thanks.'

'Don't give me that.'

'Well, fine under the circumstances. You know.' She glances round quickly for inspiration. 'Wow. Your cardoons are *huge*.'

'Oh, you!' He bats his eyelashes. 'All the girls say that.'

Rachel laughs. Jesus is apparently not lurking in *this* potagerie. 'God, isn't it stifling today?' She flaps her blouse. 'We could do with a storm.'

'Tell me about it. Listen, how about a wee cocktail?' He consults his Rolex. 'Will you look at that! It's five o'clock already.'

'Is it?' Rachel checks her phone in surprise. 'You liar. It's ten past four, Parva.'

'That's close enough. Sit!' He points at the reclaimed teak bench under the reclaimed teak pergola. 'Caipi, or mojito? Pssh! Reason not the need.'

'Ooh, get you with your *Lear* quotes!' She hesitates. 'Oh, what the hell. Mojito, please.'

'Coming up.'

'Don't make it too strong,' she calls after him. No answer. He's singing 'Brush up Your Shakespeare' while he picks the mint from his herb garden. Well, I tried. She sits in the blessed shade. The bench has a nice deep cushion. I won't tell you how much the deckchair fabric cost per metre, in case you stop liking Neil; but it's more than I'd contemplate spending on a deckchair.

Parva disappears into the vicarage. God, what an ugly house! Rachel sometimes feels a bit bad that her parents now own the Old Rectory, as though they'd ousted the Gaydens personally. Shame that the gracious days of Anglicanism have gone. She much prefers church to be a comforting Merchant Ivory wedding-day backdrop, with old traditional hymns and the King James Bible. Obviously, this is self-indulgent bullshit, but she hasn't got the bandwidth to challenge herself properly on the subject right now. If Neil does spring Jesus on her, she's going to have to stop calling round, which would be a shame, but there we are.

She draws a long breath. The smell of crushed mint reaches her. A chaffinch is twerping monotonously in a shrub. She lifts her damp hair from her neck. Oh God. It's going to be carnage on Thursday, isn't it?

Moon Phase
Last quarter (56%) It still gets me every time, I always forget that last quarter is actually half a moon, like last night, it was half an orange moon. I saw it from our garden because we are back at home now.
Teusday 11 August
Today we went shopping with mum for new uniform. Leah did not want new uniform, because it is waistful, but she has shot up again and her trousers have jack-ups. Nobody likes jack-ups, even if they are vegan and want to save the planet. Leah had this plan, she wanted to go round the charity shops and find some black trousers to upcycle. Her plan was to cut the red rose badge off her old trousers pocket and sow it on the charity shop one's. Mum said How about we donate the old trousers to a charity shop and not cut them up and destroy them, your old trousers might help out student's who can't afford new uniform. So Leah went actually, good point to be fair, and mum went thank you your majesty and so Leah got new trousers and shirts (but not a new blazer).

So anyway, Leah might of shot up but me not so much. I did not need new uniform because last year mum bought it with room to grow. Last year Leah went Omigod, she looks like a tortoise in that blazer, its mahoosive on her! Thanks for that, you only made me massively self

241

conscious on my first day, but I must of grown a bit, it is not so big this year thank God and Jesus. N.B. The uniform shop is called Thrashers which mum and dad find hilarious.

After Thrashers we went to M & S to get socks and mum went IN THIS LOUD VOICE let's see about some bras for you Jess!!!! Trust me I nearly DIED. Like I mean, couldn't we like get them online???? It's not like you can try stuff on in shops in Covid. Then Leah went (exactly as loud) FINALLY, Jess, do NOT let Mum force you into some pukey beige old lady MONSTROSITY and mum went Hey, they were ALMOND, so it doesn't show through a white blouse, and Leah was all, So? Who even cares if it shows?! and mum went, shall we actually let JESS choose??? And they're standing there yelling in there masks and I'm like la la, I am so not with these people, no way is this at all embarrassing.

So whatever, the floor UNFORTUNATLEY did not actually swallow me so I chose angel pink mix multipack because that is my preference. Leah did not say anything but I know she despises pink. Then mum said Listen why don't you go to Diggers for hot chocolate and cake and I will catch you up, so we did.

Turns out bras feel really weird? they feel like your wearing this belt round your chest. Leah says you get used to it. Then she went, like you get used to facemasks. So I said, Ha you don't wear glasses, they steam up when your wearing a mask. And she said don't worry, your bra wont steam your glasses up – unless your wearing it on your face!!!! And she grabbed one of my bra's and put it on like a mask and we were killing ourselves. Then she went wait, I'll upcycle my old lady bra into a mask!!!! And I went You mean TWO masks!!!!

Then she went all serious and said you do realise why she sent us to Diggers – she wanted to buy some new underwear because you know. And I went no. And she went Well think about it, so I thought about it and still no. And she whisperd For dad. Then I was like, why's she buying him underwear? she roled her eyes and went Look forget it.

Moon Facts

If you take a full moon sacred ritual bath your meant to put your head under the water and say your intentions for the coming month, like maybe 'I intend to be my best self and live my best life'. I told dad and he said I hope the moon can understand bubble talk. It's like he does *not take this 100% seriously, and when I said you are not being very respectful of my beliefs here dad, he went I'm sorry darling, those are good intentions. So I will try this at Harvest Moon next month.*

All across Lindfordshire we are trying to be our best selves. We are trying to live our best lives. Under the circumstances. Everywhere, babies are starting to crawl, crawlers are starting to toddle. Children are growing up. Trying on their first bras. About to start new schools. Hair grows long, turns grey, falls out. People retire with no proper farewell. Accidents happen. Explosions rock distant cities. Local businesses go under. Relationships are foundering (or perhaps, tentatively, mending themselves?). Distraught schoolchildren are getting exam results. It feels to them as though the world has ended. What will happen to their plans now?

It's a mess. The days are drawing in now. Brexit slouches to Westminster to be born. The US presidential election gears up. The UK is on course for the worst recession in Europe. Worst death rate, worst recession. What's wrong with us? Can't we get anything right? It's too hot. Our clothes stick to pub and restaurant seats. Varnished tables grow tacky from over-wiping with alcohol spray. When will the storm break? When will this all be over? The summer has passed and we have not been saved!

People are dying. New babies are born, or planned. In an ugly 1960s house in Lindford, scaffolding goes up round the double garage, and a skip appears on the drive. A young woman talks to the hens and takes some eggs round to the homeless man in the garden next door, where a wind-up gramophone plays on a terrace and a stout old woman shows off her black bottom moves, and they all laugh. The world is falling down. It always has been.

Far away in a quiet rural corner of the diocese, Freddie floats naked in the Linden. In a nearby field, alpacas graze among the sheep. High noon. The water is dark. A buzzard circles and calls *kee-oo, kee-oo*. Freddie drifts downstream, among fallen leaves and snowy swan feathers. Now and then, an acorn falls with a plop. Silence. Twofold silence. He tingles with song. Every pore, every follicle fizzes with music.

Ambrose sits on the bank. An old crack willow has split and a huge branch lies across the water. If there's a storm tonight, the bough will probably get swept downstream, where it will catch, take root and regrow. Ambrose knows this. Things mend, given time. At his feet, along the river edge, tiny fish teem silvery. A dark brown froglet, no bigger than a pea, limps its way across the pebbles. They are as big as boulders to the froglet, those pebbles. Ambrose doesn't know how the poor thing will ever make it, wherever it's heading; it's so small and frail. But it keeps struggling on. Ambrose watches, as though this means something. As though his hopes are pinned on this working out OK, on this tiny little thing making it to its destination.

Grain Moon, Part III

The days are smoky now. Late August gestures towards autumn. Storm Ellen lashes the country, with Storm Francis in hot pursuit. We are rattling through the storm alphabet this year. A month of rain overnight. Landslides, blocked roads and railways. What were all those other storms called, the ones we had in February? We can't remember. Wildfires blaze in California now, like those fires in Australia. The worst in living memory. Everything is the worst in living memory this year. We tell ourselves it's just this year, as though once the pandemic is over, climate change will have fizzled out too.

All across Lindfordshire, people get up to face their impossible tasks. Or they don't get up, because getting up is itself the impossible task. Every impossible task logically requires three other tasks to be addressed first. It's like moving house and trying to unpack, but it doesn't make sense to unpack the books until the shelves are up, and there's no point assembling the shelves until the walls have been painted, but you can't get to the walls to paint them because of all the boxes of books in the way.

The whole world has moved house. We're all living in Pandemic Mansion, where there's no logical order in which to do things. Every option is wrong as we weigh up lives/livelihoods. People are doing their best. Who would deliberately do their worst at a time like this? Therefore, the Prime Minister and his Cabinet must be doing their best, even if their best looks scurrilous to us. Maybe we've lost a common vision of what 'best' looks like. We only agree that it can't look like this. This catalogue of cock-ups and U-turns, cover-ups and finger-pointing. We'll just have to carry on as though we're camping out temporarily, clinging on to the thought that the Best Is Yet to Be. That in the end our old house will be there waiting for us. It has to be there, or how will we manage to keep on going?

Jane is out of quarantine and waiting at Martonbury Station for the little trundler to Lindford. She needs to call in at Poundstretcher to pick up a new work laptop, which will be pre-loaded with all the software that will make online teaching a seamless and joyful experience. She's also planning on swinging by her office to collect some course notes. In theory, she'll be teaching partly on campus this term, but Jane isn't holding her breath. Who knows how that will work out in practice when 15,000 young people descend on Lindford from all over the country in a couple of weeks' time? The plan is to keep students in bubbles of twenty, but these aren't bubbles in the official COVID sense of household bubbles, which float as it were in the summer air, sealed off and self-contained. Call her cynical, but Jane notes that Poundstretcher has yet to come up with an effective way of stopping students smoking outside the entrance to the Fergus Abernathy building. The minute they leave the university's scrupulous one-way systems and socially distanced lecture rooms, these student bubbles are going to end up as clumps of foam in one big social bubble bath.

Jane is the only person on the platform. This is the first time she's made this journey since March, back when everyone was still controlling the virus by coughing into their sleeves in jam-packed carriages. She feels surprisingly weepy – though come to think of it, that's not surprising at all. What can we do but weep for our poor world and everything we've lost? She wanders past the metal seats she's not allowed to sit on. Signs at regular intervals tell her to wear a mask, avoid peak-time travel and not eat or drink on board. The sky is blue, with white clouds drifting. There's a pair of buzzards above the wooded rise. They hang almost motionless up there.

The train arrives. Jane puts on her face mask and gets on. Just one other passenger at the far end of the carriage. She sits, and puts her bag beside her. How nice to hog a double seat without having to feel bad about it. The train stops at the little stations on the way to Lindford. A few people get on. They sport a range of face masks or carefully arranged scarves. Everyone is complying. Jane gazes out of the window. Fences, hedges, little lanes. Streams rushing brown and furious after the storm. I've missed you all, she thinks. You bracken fronds, you self-seeded sycamores along the embankments, you distant heathland pink with heather. She sees a huge oak with a fallen bough, white wood showing like a broken bone. It's all so sad, but never mind – the mask will soak up her tears, tra la! Nobody can see her chin trembling, her bottom lip gripped in her teeth. In fact, masks are brilliant. She can safely blow kisses at strangers, or gurn like a lunatic. Of course, smiles must be amplified by crinkly eyes and exaggerated head nods, in case the people we can't hug don't realize we're pleased to see them.

She will try this out on her poet pal Spider when they meet later on. He's been shielding for months on account of his Marfan syndrome. They're going to risk a coffee in Diggers, if it's not too crowded.

We will join them later. But for now it's high time we paid a visit to the Close, if only to check that the cathedral hasn't fallen down in our absence, and that no ghastly Trollopian bust-up has occurred to set our friends at sixes and sevens. Work continues on the scaffolded spire. Gavin the deputy verger is mowing the bishop's lawn. Gavin is one of the few cathedral employees who weren't furloughed. He's been mowing steadily since March (and having illegal bonfires of lockdown Amazon packaging, to relieve the Close's wheelie-bin crisis). Most of the furloughed staff are now back, though some heart-breaking decisions about redundancies had to be made and implemented.

Lindchester Cathedral is open for worship again. But oh, it's not like it was! If we stick our heads in now, we will see that the chairs have been sanitized to within an inch of their varnished lives, and laid out in a grid two metres apart. Given that cathedrals famously attract people who just want to slip in, enjoy the service and slip away without having to make eye contact or be invited to join an Alpha course, you might think that this new-look worship would be a dream come true. No post-service mingling! No sharing the Peace!

But cathedrals also famously attract people who want everything done as it was back in the glory days when William of Lindchester was a boy, and who would prefer there to be preservation orders on the very cobwebs in the clerestory. We must imagine, therefore, the silent weeping into masks during every Said Eucharist, over these bare ruined choirs where late the sweet birds sang.

Let us also imagine the endless meetings and discussions between Dean and Chapter, music department and cathedral school over how and when they might safely bring the choir back. I have not been privy to these conversations or to any sharing of best practice between Lindchester and other cathedrals. This narrative does not pretend to press its ear to every vestry wall. I will merely tell you the good news: the lay clerks will be singing (safely distanced from one another) at the Sunday Eucharist on 6 September. The boy choristers will be back two weeks after that (alas, if only they still boarded, they could form a proper bubble and life would be simple!), and the girls on the first Sunday in October. Of course, all this planning is precarious. Who knows whether the cathedral school will have to quarantine a year group, or close entirely, because of an outbreak? Not forgetting that we could all end up in lockdown again, if new infections rise exponentially as winter approaches.

There's no denying that COVID-19 has wrought merry havoc with cathedral revenue streams. Happily, the Church Commissioners have stepped in, like a band of Anglican Dishy Rishis, to help fund cathedrals and choirs during the current crisis. But how are we going to continue funding the cathedral choral tradition long term? Where is the money going to come from?

Up here on the Close, even to ask this question is tantamount to torching the organ and gleefully tossing copies of Stanford in G into the blaze. We know what lies behind it! We can already picture those hateful evangelical iconoclasts ripping up the choristers' surplices to dust their beastly guitars and drum kits. It's Cromwell's soldiers all over again, stabling their horses in the quire and pissing on the altar! If the money question were at all honourable, it would depart forthwith, tail between legs!

Gentle reader, I know you love dear old Lindchester and all it stands for, and I would shield you if I could. Let us stroll now under the shadow of the cathedral, round the cobbled Close. Let us note the immaculately mown lawns and gorgeous old canonical houses, the palace, the scarcely less palatial deanery, the splendour of the Old Palace (now the school), the Tudor Song School, the sweet little half-timbered houses in Vicars' Court, the venerable mulberry where King Charles may or may not have done something. Let us relish all these beloved places, for they are brimming with history and replete with tradition. But can we not sense the metaphorical late August of the C of E gesturing towards autumn? Is it not lurking in that smoky quality that has crept into the light, in the crisping of leaves in the lime colon-nade, where seed pods pop under our feet as we pass beneath their boughs? Everything seems bathed in a final gathering golden glory. We may avert our gaze, but the leaves of the money tree have been quietly falling for decades. It might be that 2020 is the sharp frost that ushers in winter.

Let other pens dwell on decay and misery. We will pop in on the bishop's wife. Sonya is in the episcopal kitchen being very domestic. Another subliminal memo has gone out to the nation, whether from the House of Bishops or Downing Street we cannot say: *Organize Your Utensil Drawer – Control the Virus!* Spring-cleaning and storage solutions are the new sourdough. Sonya is responding like a faithful soldier and servant. She's been on Pinterest learning how to fold carrier bags into tiny neat triangles (and discovering to her surprise she's been peeling bananas wrong all her life). Her current focus is the Aga.

The Aga! Always so much more than just an oven. For Sonya, it represents all that was so glorious in her predecessor and so woefully lacking in herself. It is always hard to follow a paragon. The reader may remember how Sonya was minded to get rid of the Aga alto-gether. She was told that this was, of course, *her decision*. It *could* be removed. But perhaps future bishops of Lindchester and their wives might want an Aga, and sadly it would not be possible to install a new one, because installing a new one would be prohibitively expen-sive, far more expensive than maintaining the one currently in situ. Though it was, of course, *her decision*. The thought of condemning the See of Lindchester to a bleak Aga-less existence in perpetuity was too much for Sonya. So she's forced to live with a permanent reminder of Susanna Henderson glowing smugly in her kitchen.

And she has to clean the flipping thing! Sonya has a dim sense that it ought to be shiny. Obviously, she gives it a wipe every few days, but surely when they arrived it looked . . . I don't know, shinier? She resorts to YouTube. A gentleman demonstrates how he keeps his twenty-five-year-old Aga pristine and gleaming. He lays out his equipment: cleaning products, a stout oven glove and a special scraper. Oh, so *that's* what that weird flat Stanley knife thingy is – the one she found in the bottom drawer when they arrived! With a sense of triumph, Sonya digs it out and gives the Aga top a tentative scrape. My days! Look at all this gunk coming off!

It's so exciting that she has to go and fetch Steve.

'Look! Look at this! It's like peeling off sunburn!'

I honestly think that if it weren't for shielding and social distancing considerations, Sonya might have invited all the canons' spouses round to enjoy some fat-chiselling and a glass of wine. And they would have come (bringing a far superior wine as a hostess gift, in Gene's case). It took a long time for poor Sonya to find her level on the Close. The secret turned out to be the very one your mum always told you: just be yourself. Oh, the relief of abdicating, of giving over pretending to be anything more than an authentic big-hearted and occasionally blundering human being. Whether the assembled spouses would have had a naughty giggle at Susanna Henderson's expense, we do not pretend to know.

'I ran slap bang into my nemesis,' says Jane.

They are sitting at opposite ends of a sunny bench, with takeaway coffee and vegan falafel wraps, because Diggers (down from fifteen tables to four) was already full.

'The Quisling!' says Spider. 'God, I'd love to run into my nemesises. Nemeses? Weird, the way I've missed them. Skype for Business isn't the same.'

'No, but at least you can mute them if they're pissing you off.'

'I worked out why it makes me feel even more lonely and paranoid,' says Spider. 'It's because I'm sitting on my own and they're all sitting opposite me. Like a giant interview panel.'

'Exactly. But listen, I fell prey to a strange impulse. Ah, dammit. I may start crying.'

'Go for it,' says Spider.

Jane manages to rein it in, however. 'So there she was in the corridor. We both hesitated, then I blurted out, "Look, Elspeth, I acknowledge I've been a dick over the years. Shall we call it quits?" And she burst into tears, then *I* burst into tears – aargh, dammit!' Jane holds up a hand, draws breath. 'It's OK, I've got it. Anyway, we stood there, two metres apart, flapping about like Fanny Craddock's pastry and—'

'Like what?'

'Fanny Craddock's pastry. Celebrity chef in my youth. Something my aunty Betty used to say.' She watches Spider get his Moleskine notebook out and jot this down. 'You'd better put me in your acknowledgements, you thieving magpie. Anyway, we were both sobbing, "I *would* hug you." Turns out her mum died back in April, and she couldn't go to the funeral because she had symptoms and was isolating. God. This world.'

'I would hug you,' repeats Spider, writing it down. 'Good poem title.'

'Help yourself. Are those new glasses?'

'Yes. Broke the others three weeks into lockdown. Had to tape them up and limp on till I could get an appointment. That was my first outing after shielding: Specsavers.'

'Did it feel safe?'

He shrugs. 'Who knows? Plastic aprons, visors, everything sanitized. But then the air con was blasting away? Isn't that meant to be dodgy – airborne particles or something?'

Jane shrugs back.

They settle down to bitch about the Tories, the exam debacle and Poundstretcher's decision not to ask students to wear face masks in seminars. Later, Jane will get back on her little train home to Martonbury. She will be alone in the carriage and she will cry all the way, until her disposable mask is wringing wet and she has to replace it. Then she will cry into her second mask. She will weep for Poundstretcher, its staff and students, for this poor country, this world, for Elspeth and her mum. And finally – she will see it coming in, relentlessly like a weather front – for Aunty Betty, and her own mum and dad, for herself as an orphan, and oh, for all that she has ever lost.

August BANK HOLLIDAY WEEKEND

Monday is Mr Hardman-Mays birthday, he will be 30, Leah and me will bake some cookies and take them round. Mr Ambrose has organised a surprise party to which we are invited to!!!! It will be in there garden which is allowed, there can be up to 30. Leah says it is an honour to be invited because Freddie has loads of freinds. (NB she is aloud to call him 'Freddie' because he is not her teacher.) It's a surprise party like back in the day when I was only young and we made him that humungus cake who's name I forget, it was French and Mrs Littlechild and us made it, with sparklers and everything. The boys and girls choir and the lay clerks have all recorded happy birthday, to send in the morning so he will think that's everything that will happen, it will totally throw him off the scent!!! Mr Littlechild will fake an appointment to keep Mr H-M in Lindchester while we get stuff ready. The appointment will be about . . . wait for it . . . . . .

GOOD NEWS!!! Mr Hardman-May will be taking over the girls choir again from Mr Gladwin (no offence but Mr Gladwin is just not the same), he will be coming out of the furlow scheme and so will the other lay clarks. The girls choir will be singing the service on the first Sunday in October. I am super excited for this because it will also be . . . . MY BIRTHDAY! Yay! I will be 12 can you believe it, and next year I will be a 'teenager'. We are singing with the men (Stanford in C and F plus we will do the dreaded JACKS ANTHEM, it will be like closure Mr Hardman-May says).

Moon Phase

Waxing gibbous (82%) Almost full moon time! It will be Harvest moon. Plus in October we get a BLUE MOON, it will be on Halloween. I so hope we can go out trick and treating but mum says not to get my hopes up, infection rates are rising and we just don't know what the autumn will bring. Plus mum said all the uni students will be coming back so who knows. THAT'S RIGHT BLAME THE YOUNG PEOPLE (yelled guess who because she is apparently pre-menstrual). And dad went it's human nature to blame others. Look at Genesis, God blamed the man, the man blamed the woman, the woman blamed the serpent and the serpent didn't have a leg to stand on! And I was AHAHAHAHA HA HA! Because serpents don't have legs but Leah was all Your not funny dad.

P.S. She is up and down and I know she will cheer up later on because she will be seeing you know who on Monday!

P.P.S Leah told me the goverment are planning for 85,000 deaths this winter which is super scary but dad says this is worst case scenario and it will not be that bad they are just being prepared.

Ms Logan calls round at the vicarage once again to ask for Neil's help in articulating her feelings about the new guidance for schools (issued late on Friday before the bank holiday weekend), telling them to develop a back-up plan in the event of local lockdowns. Protesters gather in Berlin to demonstrate against COVID restrictions. Another unarmed black man is shot by police in the US. There are further protests and rioting, and a white teen shoots and kills two people, while doing 'his job' protecting buildings. Everything is streaming past so fast. There's term looming, markets slumping, infection rates rocketing, winter coming. Fires are blazing out of control across California. Everything is out of control. The list of quarantine countries grows. France, Czech Republic, Jamaica, Switzerland. There are now 24.7 million recorded cases globally, and 837,000 deaths. They are running out of hospital beds in South Korea.

Has it always been like this? Can we say that it's just ups and downs, good times, bad times? Can we still go on telling one another, 'Relax. You got this'?

The Harvest Moon waxes to full. Same old faithful moon, still circling round, face always turned our way. Always there, even when our shadow blocks it. It rises golden orange now over Lindford, where twenty-eight people and two dogs wait in a back garden in the dusk. In the next garden, an old woman stands poised by the wind-up gramophone, ready for the signal. The yellow daisies and pale pink hydrangeas seem to glow, where Jack waits to light the rockets. Thirty of them. Fairy lights twinkle along the henhouse roof. There are candles in jars, and Chinese lanterns swinging from the trees. The last

253

rooks have racketed home to the roost. Owls call. Silence. The wind chimes ring softly, like church bells far away. A conker drops with a sploosh into the old pond. Then a car approaches. It slows, and stops by the builder's skip. One of the dogs whimpers and is shushed. There are suppressed giggles in the garden. A car door slams.

Ready?

Stuff will go wrong, but it will still be perfect. It's all there, waiting to happen, even if we can't see it. There is so much love, more than we can easily bear, always waiting for us to arrive.

SEPTEMBER

———◆———

Harvest Moon, Part I

E ach month the full moon arrives a little earlier. It does its own thing, keeps to its own time. Maybe we glance up from our electronic calendars and see it there, half, quarter, full. Unlike our ancestors, we don't actually need to know what it's up to. For them, celestial bodies were the only reliable measures of time. Suns and moons. Days and months. The seasons cycled round and the sun was predictably high or low in the sky – so predictable it was worth transporting whopping chunks of bluestone 180 miles from Wales to Wiltshire and setting up a monument aligned to the winter and summer solstices. The calendar, set in stone. But they will have spotted that the solar and lunar schedules didn't sync to provide a neat number of moons per year. The figures needed fudging. Thirty days, thirty-one days (except for February alone).

If we were young Jess, Googling *The 'orbits' of the Solar System* for our Moon Journal, we might be surprised to learn that the sun rotates (!!!!!). Not round us, of course, but it does turn. Each rotation takes 25 days. The earth, on the other hand, takes 24 hours to rotate, and 365.25 days to orbit the sun. Meanwhile, our moon's orbit round us lasts roughly 27.5 days; but because we are a moving target, it takes another couple of days for the moon to appear in the same place in our skies (29.5 days). What kind of a mish-mash of measurements is this? 24, 25, 27, 29, 365 – not to mention halves and quarters thrown in. Honestly, it makes pounds, shillings and pence seem like a walk in the metric park. I'm glad I'm not in charge. Imagine being Chief

Operations Manager of the solar system! It's bad enough keeping track of which bin to put out nowadays.

But here, right on schedule, is the Harvest Moon – possibly the only named full moon most people know without the help of Google. In the southern hemisphere, the Harvest Moon is in March – something else for the chief ops person to keep an eye on. Funny lot, down under. They do everything backwards, upside down and a day ahead, as though north isn't self-evidently top, as though Greenwich isn't prime and England the norm. Imagine living like that!

Father Wendy is always imagining other lives. This is partly what makes her a good priest – her ability to think her way into someone else's situation and anticipate their needs. It is also what makes her an insomniac. It's 2 a.m., and she's had to get up and make herself a mug of hot milk. Her mind keeps going round and round the plans for their return to the church building this Sunday. Is it all organized? Has she remembered everyone? Will the livestreaming work, for those who still can't make it to the physical building (they are still church!). What if someone's allergic to the sanitizer? Jason has dreadful eczema, poor love – should she buy a bottle for sensitive skin? Oh dear, she does have a tendency to over-identify! To think she's responsible for everything. She's even feeling bad for waking poor Pedro up. Not that Pedro seems bothered. He just raised his head when she came in, then settled again under his anxiety blanket. Good boy. He's been so much happier since they bought him that. If only she'd known four years ago, when he came to them.

She turns the light off again and takes her milk through to the sitting room. The moon is so bright it's casting window shapes on to the floor. She goes to the patio doors and looks out. There it is! Big and silver-white. A contrail, straight as a ruler, slices the sky above it, and there's one very bright star, a planet – possibly Mars? All over the world, people are looking at the same moon, she thinks. Except it won't be visible everywhere at this precise moment, of course. Dawn will be breaking somewhere already. It'll be midday somewhere else.

Wendy finds herself humming a song they used to sing in primary school back in the 60s: 'Remember all the people who live in far-off lands.' It strikes her suddenly how horribly Anglo-centric this is. Why are *they* far off, and not us? It's like her friends in the South – convinced it's somehow much further for them to travel to Cardingforth than for her to travel to London! 'When are you next in London?' That never seems like an unreasonable question to them. But to ask 'When are you next in Lindfordshire?' would sound bizarre. Why would they be in Lindfordshire, the back of beyond?

How did the rest of the hymn go? Something about strange and lovely cities, and children wading through rice fields. It would be interesting to look it up, to see exactly how terrible it is. Turning non-Europeans into exotic *Others* in need of our help. You never question it as a child, though. Or perhaps you do – if you're not a white British child? There was only a handful of BAME children in her school. She's never wondered before what that must have felt like. Playground insults (*Clive's got fleas! Julie smells! Inky-pinky-ponky!*) weren't all equal. Not at the height of 'Paki-bashing' and Rivers of Blood. So how did the hymn sound to them?

This is a far-off land, she thinks. From an African or Indian or South American perspective, *we* are the distant people in a foreign place. This is the sort of land you might pray God will raise up men and women to send there and serve him, because the natives are godless and need rescuing. (Don't we just!) Yes, to the rest of the globe, England is *there*, not here. Oh, but it's still home to me, thinks Wendy, and home will always *feel* central, even if we drop off the edge of the globe and history, just another tiny nation who once ruled the waves.

Pale moon shadows stretch across the lawn. They remind her of something. Ah, that's it – sunlight cast up from the Linden on to the overhanging branches. Dappling on the bark as she sits on her bench with Pedro each day. Reflections dappling. And moonshine is just reflected sunlight too. She gazes up, eyes beginning to swim with tiredness. There's our moon, shining with the sun, although the sun's nowhere to be seen. (Wendy files this away for a future sermon.) The vapour trail softens now, grows woolly, and melts into scribble. Well, she'd better get back to bed before Doug wakes and comes looking for her to see if she's all right. He needs his sleep, bless him. School term starts this week.

That's right. Schools will open across Lindfordshire tomorrow. The buildings wait in the moonlight, silent and ready – as ready as anything can be in the changes and chances of 2020. Ready with sanitizer at entrance and exit. Ready with signs: *Help Us STOP Coronavirus. Wash your hands regularly. Keep your distance from adults in the classroom. If you feel unwell, let an adult know.* Ready with masks and visors, with disposable aprons and gloves.

The moon casts more window shapes. They fall across the corridors with their lines of tape and one-way arrows and *Keep Your Distance* circles like stepping-stones. Light shines pale on the desks, where they stand separated, all facing the same way – serried rows again, like in the good old days of rote learning the Three Rs. In the canteens, there are moon shadows from the new partitions put up to keep the bubbles separate. Here, in a patch of light, we can see crosses taped on tables, so no child eats their lunch next to, or opposite, any other. In Cardingforth, a fox walks across the primary school playground, slipping in and out of the painted circles where the children will play, socially distanced.

The moon goes by the windows of all who sleep in Lindfordshire. It blesses those who work, or watch, or weep this night. All teachers and dinner ladies, cooks and caretakers, the crossing wardens, classroom assistants, the minibus and taxi drivers, PAs and school secretaries, all parents and children. The moon sets. The sun rises. Term begins.

'Leah, can you stand there, by the door?' asks Martin.

'Fucksake.'

'Please? I want to take a picture.'

'Fine.' Leah drops her school bag and stands, arms crossed, with the gusty sigh of a teen whom nobody understands, who has been forced to get up unconscionably early, and in any case did not ask to be born. 'Are we done now? You're forbidden from posting that anywhere.'

'Of course. It's just for me and mum.' He looks at the image and smiles. 'Have a good day, darling.'

'Grrr-aargh! Well, obviously I WON'T.' She snatches up her bag and storms off. At the last moment, she hesitates, veers close and bumps a kiss on to the top of Martin's head. Then she's gone. He hears her yelling goodbye up the stairs to Jess and Becky. The front door crashes shut.

Silence. Apart from Radio 4 quarrelling away in the corner. He could do without that, frankly. But getting up, crossing the kitchen and switching it off is too big a task. A bad day. He has bad days and less bad days. He can feel the patch on his scalp where Leah planted the kiss. It glows, seems to spread. As if she's literally planted something, and now it's sending out tender shoots and tendrils over his head and down his neck. He closes his eyes. He feels it fan out across his aching shoulders and down his arms. In a moment, he'll find the other photo – Leah on her first day at QM Girls four years before – place them side by side in Layout, and marvel. He remembers how he had to force himself to send the picture to Becky. Squeeze out his last dregs of generosity.

In a moment, he'll put them side by side.

He opens his eyes. There above the fridge is the lovely cross-stitch sampler Becky finished last week. Just back from the framer. She's so talented. *This is the day that the Lord has made.* It triggers a fragment of scholarship left over from theological college. In Hebrew, it's only two or three words: today, made, God. That's all. Today. God. Simple. *We will rejoice and be glad in it.* Today. Not in some future, when he's better. He can't do much any more, but he can marvel, he can be grateful. For a grumpy kiss. For an embroidered sampler. A warm kitchen. For his family gathered back under one roof, against all the odds. For the gift of life. He can put the old Martin and the new Martin side by side, and marvel.

4th September
It is Friday YAY!!! It was so fun to be back at school and see everyone again but at the end of the day it is still school and I for one am glad it's the WEEKEND!!!! It was weird to see the teachers in vizers and to only go one way, if you need the toilet you have to literally go round the entire school LOL. But soon it was kind of normal?

Tonight we are celebrating our first week back at school, we're having deliveroo. It was mums turn to choose, she chose Mexican!!! Leah is ok with this because she checked them out and they have vegan options plus they are plastic free and use cardboard. I'm having chicken chimmychanga and she is having a black bean burrito. Mum ordered and then her and dad both said this rhyme 'Beans beans good for your heart, the more you eat them the more you fart'. Then they laughed like it was hilarious? FORTUNATLEY nobody else was around. Me and Leah looked at them like Seriously guys? Sometimes they are like six years old, they are seriously embarassing sometimes, its like they don't care.

So the Girls choir rehearsed in the cathedral yesterday. We can't all be in the Song School together, it is to small to distance. Other times we rehearse in the school hall. In the cathedral we had to stand on the crosses on the nave floor to be sure we are distancing.

Mr H-M took the practice, he taught us this doofy song (his words), the song goes 'We're all together again we're here we're here.' We had to sing it in our choir voice, then in a 'cockny' accent and then in a Lady Totty voice off Wallace and Grommit. He whisperd you know, like Mrs Voysey-Scott, I did not just say that, girls, you didn't hear that, la la la. Next we had to sing it slowly like we were falling asleep and then super quick. It was so FUN and then we rehearsed THE DREADED JACKS ANTHEM. Ellie whisperd across to me from her place 'Queue the earth gets hit by A GIANT METEOR.' I did not laugh because Mr H-M gave us a look and I do not like getting told off. Don't get me wrong, Ellie is my BFF but sometimes she can be inappropriate and does not get when its time to focus.

It was eery to sing God be with you till we meet again and to remember that the last time we sang it was when the cathedral closed and the bells were ringing slowly. Plus we rehearsed Stanford obvs. Some girls had forgotten a shedload of stuff, but not me. I did not say this because nobody likes a showoff. N.B. I told mum and dad this when Leah was out walking Luna, because she would only of gone Stop going on about school FFS. Nobody cares Jess. I know she has feelings for you know who and wishes she could see more of him. I can't help it if he is my teacher and not hers, but is good to be tactfull when all is said and done.

Moon Phase
Full (96%)

So I was kind of disappointed this month? You expect that the Harvest Moon is going to be this humungus orange balloon, but it is white like *an ordinary moon. When it was nearly full it was orangy, like at Mr H-Ms surprise party, but I'm sorry to say it has not really lived up to it's expectations. I did not do my ritual moon bath and say my intentions (I totally forgot to be fair). On the bright side, next month we get TWO FULL MOONS!!! First we will have the HUNTERS MOON and then like said before it will be a BLUE MOON.*

Moon Facts.

Our word for 'month' comes from 'moon' it is from Old English and old German I believe. This year I started French. I will start German in Y9 but I can already count to twenty (dad is teaching me) and say 'ich heisse Jess' (my name is Jess). Later this term we will be learning 'How lovely is your dwelling place' in German!!! I am already learning it off Youtube. Mr H-M said it is super useful for singers to learn German, so much of the ~~repartoire~~*??? is in German. At that exact moment Mrs Littlechild was walking past and she said something to him in German (N.B. she is actually German) and he said, Oh, wow, that's so kind! Girls, Mrs Littlechild says she will buy you each a pony and a £100 iTunes voucher, say 'Vielen Dank', girls! LOL LOL LOL But he was only messing, I do not know what she actually said.*

DELIVEROO TIME!!! So I will love you and leave you now. Byeeeeee!!!!

Oh, Lindchester. Maybe you are my comfort blanket, the thing I pull round me at 3 a.m. so that this world seems a little less terrifying. I glide past your windows like the moon, looking down on your streets and fields, the Linden and the tributaries feathering out, Whistle Brook, the Carding. I see the sleeping rooks in the windy roost, the prowling foxes. The cattle on your hills, the dogs in their baskets, the hens in their coops. All schools and churches. All the houses and flats. The farms. The homeless shelters, foodbanks, shops and offices, the summerhouse in Miss Sherratt's garden. Pubs and restaurants. The vast hangar where the workers walk day and night. Sports centres and clubs. Nail bars and cannabis farms. Hospitals, care homes. And the people, remember all the people. The emergency services. Illegal ravers. Students. Volunteers. Dog-walkers. Lecturers. Vice chancellors and high sheriffs. Clergy. Street pastors. NHS staff. Homeless people. Bus and train drivers. Postal workers and parish nurses.

Social workers and car washers. Librarians. Have I forgotten anyone? MPs. Bin men. Builders. Shop assistants. IT support. Plausible young men on your doorstep selling you the world's most expensive duster. Hair stylists. Uber drivers, Deliveroo guys – I can't carry them all. People will slip through the cracks. My performance rating as Chief Operations Manager of Lindchester is sliding. Who will hold it all together, this mish-mash, where the moon does its own thing and we still think we are at the centre of everything?

Frankly, you are a pretty rubbish comfort blanket, Lindchester. Very poorly designed. It turns out you weigh far too much. You are meant to be all velvety and stress-reducing, like a night-long reassuring cuddle. You are not supposed to pin me down with dread because I can't see how all this is ever going to end.

In fact, I discard this extended metaphor. Let's go and visit Freddie and Ambrose. They usually cheer me up. After all, it's company we crave most in these difficult times.

'Ready, babe?'

'Hnn?' Freddie slips his headphones off and looks down from the top of the stepladder. 'Time is it? Shit! Gimme two minutes!' He leaps down, dumps the paint roller and scrambles out of his overalls. 'Just gonna wash up.' He disappears into the kitchen.

Ambrose waits in the living room clicking his fingers and gazing round. The builders have just finished for the day. He sees their van pull off. The air smells of fresh emulsion. Yes. It's certainly very blue. Walls, floor, and the ceiling Freddie has just abandoned. All these different shades of the same blue. You don't notice the 60s stone fireplace now. He never was a huge fan of those. His gran had one, and it was her pride and joy in the new build Grandpa put up, after demolishing the row of seventeenth-century labourers' cottages. Moving on.

He checks his watch. Then he checks his exasperation. Let it go. You can't change him. You can't control him. Ambrose goes to the far end of the room to take in the full effect. The scheme has even attracted the Neil Ferguson imprimatur of good taste. This is a bit of a mixed blessing. Neil's turning into a self-appointed project manager. Ambrose is standing by to tell him to wind his neck in if he starts bullying Freddie. Or if the budget looks like it will go through the roof, sourcing genuine lapis lazuli powder from Morocco!

Anyway, Freddie's happy so far, and this saves them having to rip the whole fireplace out. Ambrose smiles at Freddie's earlier plan to turn it into a toddler indoor climbing wall. Hey, any baby of mine's gonna have those spider-monkey genes. Freddie, Freddie. Let's take it steady. One step at a time. Ambrose can hear him swearing in the kitchen as he scrubs paint off his hands and arms. He looks at his watch again and sighs. They're going to be late for rehearsal.

He goes slowly towards the door, battling the urge to go and sit in the car. The whole house is turning into the Blue Grotto in Capri. It touches off something in him that he can't quite put a finger on. Like a particular note resonating? No, more a key he's never heard before, yet instantly recognizes. The key all keys exist in. Below above everything. Or to put it with Freddie's succinctness: heaven.

'Shit, sorry, sorry, sorry.' Freddie comes running. 'Just wanted to finish.' He cast an anguished glance back at the living room. 'Gah, hate that so much. Like not singing the last line, you know?'

'Still be here when we get back, babe.' Ambrose pulls the front door shut.

'Yeah, no, but I want resolution, man. I want that last chord?'

The car pulls out of the drive. The builders have been making good progress. Blue sky fills the roof space, where the timbers sketch out the top floor of the extension. Chloe is outside in the garden, finally taking down the bunting and *We Love You* banners after Freddie's party. She printed them off herself in a dozen languages (including Latin, because lay clerks, ha ha!). Every so often, her heart does a huge bump, like the moment you go over the top of a roller coaster after the long climb. Next week. Ba-doom! Aargh! The fertility tracker app says next week! I mean, obviously this doesn't guarantee anything, it's just a first try. Ba-doom! Aargh!

She stands with her hands full of love and paper banners. There's one she can't reach, fixed to the top of the henhouse. She'll have to leave it for Lanky. He put it up there, let him get it down. The hens are scratching around. Are they broody? Are they sad? Do they wish they could make babies? Ambrose always shakes his head if she starts

265

doing this, trying to Disney-fy them. But Freddie's on her side. He knows the girls all have different personalities.

She shoves the banners into the paper and card recycling bin, and goes back into the painty house. The living room's nearly done now. Next up is the kitchen. Good thing she likes blue! I mean, you *could* have too much of a good thing, maybe? But it's their house. And she can always do the entire extension pink, ha ha! She sticks on the playlist of happy vibes Freddie's done for her on Spotify, and starts thinking about tonight's meal. Not that she's going to end up doing *all* the cooking. No way. But after all these years of cooking for one, it's actually fun!

The cathedral clock chimes, and Freddie and Ambrose just make it. There is a pause. Sunshine falls on old stone. Stained-glass saints in their windows look down. Ah! It's as though the whole company of heaven lets out a long sigh. At last, the huge shell of the cathedral resounds once again with men's voices. We will rejoice and be glad. Today. God.

Harvest Moon, Part II

Leah grits her teeth. How's she meant to do her homework? Shut UP, Jess! She slaps her history book, then claws it with her bitten fingernails, like it's Amy Collins' stupid face. I DID control my temper. If Miss Coles thinks calling someone a total fucking moron is me losing my temper, she seriously has NO IDEA. That was me telling the literal truth! When someone says 'God, I wish someone would test positive in our class so we could all get two weeks off'. . . Hello? That *is* totally moronic.

OK, Leah gets Ms Logan's point that another way to look at it is to say it was thoughtless, and that Amy had forgotten Leah's dad nearly died of COVID-19. Ms Logan did not insist on Leah apologizing. Leah *chose* to apologize, and you'd think that any normal person would accept an apology graciously and then say, 'My bad, sorry I forgot about your dad', but no. Leah accepts that this is Amy's choice. Amy has chosen to be a bitch who apparently has put all this stuff on Facebook about Leah, but like who cares? If you've deleted Facebook to stop your personal data being manipulated, literally WHO CARES?

But Ms Logan is awesome. Leah is *so* fangirling here. She got a detention for writing FUCK BORIS on the whiteboard. So they had this talk about free speech, and insults and giving offence, and whether words can be offensive or if it's all culturally conditioned, and how if you look in the King James Bible you'll find the word pisseth, because piss wasn't offensive back in the day. Then Ms Logan got Leah to check out an online Shakespearian insult generator, and come up

267

with a list of ten best insults, and analyse them, and finally she let Leah write pages and pages of FUCK BORIS and then they put it through the shredder in the office so Ms Logan didn't get into trouble too. Best. Detention. Ever.

A movement. Leah whips round. Just an old couple going past. Aaaand breathe. She's only ever seen *him* twice, but every time there's a movement on the street, her pulse jumps, because this time it *could* be. Another squawk from downstairs. FFS! Yeah, I KNOW we all have to start somewhere, but that clarinet sounds like a fucking goose being strangled! Plus Mum and Dad are paying for her lessons, which is so not fair. Leah has to pay her karate subs out of her allowance.

Her heart squeezes at the thought of karate. She feels bad for Sensei, and keeps guilt tripping herself for not going every week, but excuse me? No contact? Which means no sparring, just kata and drills, and frankly, if you can't fight, what is even the point? She can do her katas in the garden for free and save £5. At least in the garden you can use your ki-ai. Obviously, she gets the airborne droplets thing, but a strike without a ki-ai is like playing a clarinet without actually blowing into it. Which would be an actual *improvement* in Jess's case.

Leah stands up and leans her hands on the windowsill. She gets a tiny sharp pain as the cracks in her skin open again. Fucking eczema. Thanks for *that* special gift from the gene pool, Dad. Even the sensitive sanitizer Mum got her sets it off. Don't scratch, don't scratch! If she concentrates hard, she can choose not to make it worse, she can be in control by distracting herself.

So I'm going to take something else up. Yeah. Something new. Like maybe wild swimming? Shit. Now her face is burning. If she had *real* control, she'd be able to stop blushing, but so far no luck with that. Anyway, so what if Jess gives her that super-irritating look, like *I know why*. It's a free country. It's not like *he* owns the copyright on wild swimming. Everyone's all about wild swimming right now, it's a thing, so what's the big deal? She could've got the idea from anyone, not from overhearing him talking about it at his party. Obviously, Leah would wear her school swimming costume, or maybe a crop top and shorts, not . . . Though that's more natural, being naked is natural, obviously. Lyds and her mum and Helene went to a naturist beach last year, but with respect, that's DEATH. I mean, with your *family*?

Or running. She could start marathon training. Mum's doing Couch to 5K and that's cool for older people like her, she's out there giving it a go, which Leah respects, but Leah's already fit, she can run 5, 10K already without training, probably.

She leans her forehead against the glass. Oh, *when* will this be over? Downstairs Jess honks out 'Mary Had a Little Lamb'. Oh God, and now Dad's going out. Fetching the wheelie bin in. He moves so slowly she can hardly bear it. He'll make a joke. Like, That's my exercise for the day! She should've brought it in when she got back from school, and not been all, Why's it MY job to bring the bin in? Why can't Jess do it for once?

Argh, stop scratching, idiot! She clamps her hands under her armpits.

OK, so here's the plan. She'll go on a super-long run, like maybe to Lindchester and back, along the river bank. (*I know why*. Oh shut up.) Maybe another time she'll see if Lyds wants to come too, but not being funny, Lyds isn't really built for running, so they'd have to jog re-e-eally slo-o-owly in the arbo and never get the endorphins, which would totally do Leah's head in, she needs to push herself. Because there's something inside her, like an animal, that needs to roar, and right now everything's closed in. School, home, her own head. She wants to burst out. She wants to win. She wants to kill. To fast-forward or burst into flames or fly away for ever, or something.

It's mid-September. I think most of us would gladly fly away. The swallows have left. Now and then in the woodlands of Lindfordshire we still get a snatch of chiffchaff song fretting away. Shouldn't they have gone by now too? Or has our climate changed enough for them to stay all year round?

A faux autumn rusts the blighted horse chestnut trees. Conkers thud down on to pavements. Vivid colour creeps along the Boston vines and Virginia creepers now, and the occasional cherry leaf is picked out in vermillion. There are painted ladies and peacock butterflies in the wild-flower mix along verges. Wasps gorge themselves silly on plums and damsons. Up on Cathedral Close, Sonya gathers apples in the orchard and puts them in a box at the end of the palace drive. *Help Yourself!* She decorates the cardboard sign with hearts and flowers.

Hearts and flowers. That's what we need right now, with rapidly rising infection rates and winter ahead of us. Town after town in the North West and the North East has extra restrictions slapped on it. Signs go up: *Don't Mix with Other Households.* Pubs and restaurants must close at 10 p.m. Mrs Logan is tearing her hair out again over the moving goalposts for weddings. Our government dreams dreams of a mass-testing scheme called Operation Moonshot, using technology not yet in existence, at a cost of £100 billion. That figure in the leaked document is not broken down, but I daresay it will include a white Persian cat to stroke.

The Rule of Six kicks in this Monday. Gatherings of more than six (including babies and children) are banned, with the exception of schools and workplaces. Oh, and grouse shooting. If I were making all this up, I wouldn't have risked that last detail, for fear my readers would never swallow such a clunky bit of social satire. But there we are. Up to thirty toffs may gather on a big estate and blast the bejasus out of bushels of birds, while you and I are expected to submit to a ministerial wigging from a simulacrum of a 1930s beak, for our 'endless carping' about coronavirus tests. All of which means that unless the Bishop of Lindchester borrows guns, deploys the vergers as beaters and releases grouse into the palace vegetable patch, he will need to cancel the marquee and caterers he's booked for the outdoor socially distanced ordination lunches for candidates and their families.

I fling up my hands. You'll just have to imagine for yourselves the pages and pages of rant generated by the likes of Neil Ferguson on this topic, and feed them through the shredder of your mind. In my wiser moments, I stand with Jane. Vituperation is part of the problem, not the solution. Impotent outrage will mend nothing. It is mere fat crackling in the gleefully stoked brazier of popularism.

The Harvest Moon wanes. It will be back next year, but that's it for 2020. Did we heed Gandalf, and decide what to do with the time that

270

was given us? No. We were eaten alive by the task of running up the down escalator of COVID-19. Staving off bankruptcy, trying to keep the show on the road, staying safe, navigating the regulations, fretting about loved ones, holding our mental health together.

There's a crispness in the air first thing. The bishop puts on a coat to walk round the Close one morning and finds a box of matches in the pocket. He has not worn this since the day of the Easter Vigil and the great paschal candle fiasco.

Puffballs bulge up overnight through Miss Sherratt's chamomile lawn. She sees them from her bedroom window, and for a moment takes them for pigeon eggs or golf balls. Jack gathers them, and cooks them on his little stove in front of the old summerhouse. He knows what's what when it comes to fungus. Which ones you can eat, which ones you *can* eat, but only once, as the old joke goes. The tasty ones, the trippy ones. Jack steers well clear of those.

The smell of cooking puffballs wafts across to the garden where Freddie is measuring his tallest sunflower with his phone. Wa-a-y taller than little Jess's, but he's not gonna tell her that. He shades his eyes and gazes up at the row of heads, big as satellite dishes, and wonders if you could harness the solar energy off them, if fields of sunflowers could ever be solar farms, and hey, what about that song from the *Spiderman* movie? He and the girls could do that next. He's meant to be digging into *Winterreise*, but if he lies low, maybe La Madeleine will forget she suggested it? Gah, he hates *Winterreise*, can't say that, but. So yeh, sunflower songs? It'll be something to distract him, fill the time while they're waiting, waiting, waiting to see *if*. Oh, let it have worked?

Man, that smell's making him hungry. Freddie shins up the scaffolding and whistles. 'Hey, Jack! Dude, got any to spare? Trade you some eggs?'

Harvest comes to Lindfordshire in a riot of fruit and fungus. Jane gets a whiff of stinkhorn from the wood on the way to the station. She notes the red of rowanberries, and rejoices that the season of boots and jumpers is nearly here. Nobody else on the platform again. It's Freshers' Week. What will a socially distanced Freshers' Week look like? It will either look nothing like Freshers' Week, or else it will look nothing like social distancing. Jane's money is on the latter, after a few shots have been necked. She has every sympathy. They're unlikely to get very ill, and frankly, what's their motivation for keeping the older generation safe, given the way we've systematically screwed them over and blighted their future? If that's *not* what they are thinking, then bless their hearts.

She will be teaching face to face once a week, with all her other sessions online. It's one at a time in the lifts. No paper handouts. A visor will be provided for her. Masks must be worn when moving around the corridors, though they're not compulsory in seminar rooms. How long this will be sustainable is anybody's guess. Whole year groups at local schools have already had to quarantine. Realistically, it's only a matter of time before there's an outbreak at Poundstretcher. Though perhaps Jane's chances of going down with it were higher back in March, when trains were crowded and nobody wore a mask? Who knows?

September 19th

Me and Mr H-M are having a sunflower competition! So we were rehearsing and the flower guild were doing the flowers in the cathedral, there were some sunflowers, and Mr H-M told us that he's grown like the tallest sunflowers in the UK, the tallest is literally 3m tall? And I shot up my hand and said Not being funny sir but mine is 3m 15? And he went No way, and I went Yes way, we measured it with the measuring app? (Obvs I have not mentioned this to Leah, I just told mum and dad. It is a sore point, because her runner beans have not done very well, plus the slugs ate the lettice, but what can you do if your organic, it is a difficult one.)

So yesterday morning I had my clarinet lesson YAY! My teacher is Mrs Lieghton, she says I am making good progress. This is due to practising, I practice all the time, I literally have this sore patch inside my mouth where my bottom teeth press on my lip I do so much practise, you have to press the reed against your lip when you play. Mum and dad say I will have to start paying for my own reeds if I carry on breaking them. They break super easy I regret to inform you. Like for example you can break them if you rub them the wrong way against your school jumper because you are looking *to check your fingers are covering the stops and you forget to watch out for the reed. I keep doing that!!!!! one time I went oh b*ll*cks and Leah went OMMMM! I'm telling of you, you sweared!' Like the little kids used to go back in the day in Cardingforth Primary LOL.*

   NB Leah is in a good mood because she went for a run and has endolphins. Plus it's DELIVEROO NIGHT! Then we are going to watch a movie as a family, we are watching 'On the Basis of Sex'. (Its not what you think, its about a lawyer Ruth Bader Ginsberg who has sadly just died.)

Moon Phase

New Moon (3%) Yesterday the moon was 0% which means it was totally in the earths shadow. Sometimes you can see the whole moon even when its not full, you can see the crescent and then very faintly the rest of the moon. This is called 'the new moon with the old moon in her arms', there is an old song about this, mum told me so I googled it, it is Sir Patrick Spens and it says

> *I saw the new moon yestreen (aka yesterday evening)*
> *With the old moon in her arm,*
> *And if we go to sea master,*
> *I fear we'll come to harm.*

NB This is because it supposably means bad weather is on the way when you see both moons.

Moon Facts

If you happen to google this phenomernon you will discover that it is called 'earthshine'. I for one did not know that the earth could make the moon shine. It is so amazing. So the crescent moon is caused by sunshine, and the paler shine (aka 'the old moon') is earthshine. I am eternally greatful I have kept on writing this 'Moon Journal' through thick and thin this year, because I have learnt a shedload of amazing stuff even if I missed out on some of my education due to Covid.

More Moon facts

I just randomly thought to myself oh I wish wish wish moonflowers was a thing like sunflowers so I googled it and . . . . LO and Behold it actually is???? There is a 'moonflower vine', it has an enticing scent in the evening. I so want to grow some next year it would be so awesome.

The Rogers family are not the only ones who are watching *On the Basis of Sex* this weekend. Up on the Close, Gene and Marion are settling down to a film night in the deanery, after homemade cottage pie and a bottle of Nyetimber Blanc de Blancs 2013.

'Don't you find it a delicious slice of Schadenfreude that the Champagne region is fast becoming too hot to grow Champagne grapes?' asks Gene. 'They're being forced to buy land in Kent and Hampshire. But they won't be able to call it Champagne, of course, because of their earlier fierce defence of the name.'

'Mmm,' says the dean. She's trying to get the film started on her laptop, but her work emails keep popping up on the screen. It's like an outward and visible form of her inability to switch off from the woes of work.

'What's that?' says Gene, peering suddenly. 'Performance Improvement Plan? For whom?'

'Look away!' Marion fumbles frantically to shut it down. 'That's confidential.'

The inbox finally vanishes. Marion wipes her face. 'Let's just watch the film, shall we?'

'But that looks *far* more gripping!'

'Sssh. It's starting.'

Over in Martonbury, the Bishop of Barcup isn't even trying to switch off. Sermon prep, then bludgeoning the inbox into submission. Or trying to. He's off to take a service at a newly reordered church building tomorrow morning. It's Back to Church Sunday, would you believe? He rubs his bald head and sighs. Can't credit he actually thought in March that this would be the big jamboree, with people flooding back after it was all over, like animals coming out of hibernation. Even next year's looking a tad optimistic, barring an effective vaccine. He does a cheeky check of the Fantasy Football League, then cracks on with his prep. Ordinations next weekend. Steve'll do the priests on the Saturday, and Matt's got the deacons on the Sunday. Busy time. No let-up in the foreseeable. Ten services, rather than the usual two. The trick will be staying awake in the sermon fifth time round.

I'm afraid that Back to Church Sunday has rather passed Father Dominic by this year. He's got his eyes on the patronal, Michael and All Angels. It will be a very subdued affair, but oh well, we can only do what we can do. The flower ladies will be round to pick Michaelmas daisies from the vicarage garden as usual, so at least the church will look nice on Facebook for those who can't come in person. He'll get a goose delivered from Wood's the butchers at Lindford's indoor market. Mother will tell him every five minutes that goose is traditional because Queen Elizabeth was eating one when news came of the defeat of the Spanish Armada.

Dominic glances over. Good. She's still engrossed in her jigsaw. In a moment he'll get up and draw the curtains. Look how dark it's getting! Where's the year gone?

He goes back to his plans. Still no singing allowed, but he's got a trumpeter lined up to play 'Ye Holy Angels Bright' and 'How Shall I Sing that Majesty' from the high altar. That should send a little shiver down the spine. Goody-good. He always invites Virginia for lunch after mass, but can they do that safely this year? Maybe if they put the table by the French windows and keep the doors open? They'll freeze! But perhaps they should wrap up warm and seize the opportunity, in case Lindford ends up like Barnsley and the like, with no meeting up indoors at all?

There's no point consulting Mum. She can barely hold on to the fact that they're in the middle of a pandemic, let alone grasp what a socially distanced meal's going to look like. Better just ask Virginia, and see what she thinks. She's the gal for rules and compliance, after all. Ever the eagle eye. She actually interrupted last week's mass, when she spotted he'd forgotten to re-sanitize his hands before the administration. Eek! By the time this is over, everyone will think this is what wafers are *supposed* to taste like – marinated in alcohol gel!

He reaches for his phone to text Virginia and invite her. The thought crosses his mind again that he should ask if she wants to be in a bubble with him and Mum. But she might think he's only inviting her so that she can take a stint of mum-sitting. He knows – does he ever know! – how easily single people are patronized and exploited. As if it's our duty and our joy at all times and in all places to serve the nuclear family! She seems to be doing fine, anyway. He's probably just projecting his own loneliness on to her. After all, she's out and about seeing people all the time. No, better to stick to a lunch invitation. He wipes his eyes. Lord, what a weepy old maiden aunt he's become. He burst into tears the other day when he caught a clip from a Peter Kaye tour. The packed venue! All those thousands and thousands of laughing people. Dominic's got a six-month backlog of love and hugs, and only Mum and Lady to lavish them on. Lord help his poor congregation when they're allowed to share the Peace again!

All this pent-up love. It has to burst out somehow. All over Lindfordshire my characters are leaving parcels of fruit and veg on one another's doorsteps. They are donating and volunteering. They are picking up litter, or leaving trails of painted pebbles in the woods to make it magical for tiny children. They are wearing masks and keeping the rules as best they can, even if the rules are stupid and other people flout them.

It's harvest festival season, reinvented, reinterpreted, like everything else this year. If only all was safely gathered in, free from sorrow, free from sin. Cardoons tower in the potagerie. Neil is running out of people to give them to. Dahlias brighten allotments and borders where people dug and planted so busily in lockdown, back when everything – it seems with hindsight – was heightened, vivid, etched in crystal. That time feels like nostalgic memories of childhood. Hopscotch in the middle of silent streets and clapping for the NHS. Did that all really happen? Was it only this year we did all that?

There is so much love. A sign still flutters on top of a henhouse. Someone reads it every day through a crack in the blind. The girl who looks like him could not take this sign down. He saw her try, but it was too high for her to reach, because the tall man put it there. And now it's as if it was a message meant for him, written in his own language. He knows it's not, but he reads it anyway. *We Love You.*

Harvest Moon, Part III

It's nearly Quarter Day. This means nothing to my characters, but their stout Lindcastrian forebears would not have been able to imagine a year without four pillars: the two solstices and two equinoxes. Since the Middle Ages, it was Quarter Day when servants were hired, rents due and term started. It was when accounts had to be drawn up and lawsuits resolved in the Court of Quarter Sessions. Traces linger to this day in our fiscal DNA – the new financial year starts on the pre-Gregorian date of Lady Day, 6 April – and in the calendars of traditional schools and universities, which still have a Michaelmas Term. There were stepping-stones to get you from one Quarter Day to the next – the Cross Quarter Day feasts that fell between: Candlemas, May Day, Lammas and All Hallows. So the year was divided into eight manageable chunks. That feels right at some deep level. It's the sweet spot, the Goldilocks portion of time. However grim things are, we can probably just about see our way to the end of the next six weeks.

This year, Quarter Day in Lindchester brings the Michaelmas ordinations. Ordinations normally take place at the end of June at Petertide, but 2020 has fried the calendar. There are no proper stepping-stones through COVID-19, no obvious six-week chunk before we get a bit of a breather. Christmas was dangled as the light at the end of the pandemic tunnel. Didn't the Prime Minister promise us a while back that we'd be substantially well on the way to normal by Christmas? IF everyone used their British common sense, that is. IF they controlled the virus. IF everyone went safely back to work, bought coffee and sandwiches, ate out to help out. IF schools and universities safely resumed face-to-face teaching. IF everyone used the world-beating track and trace. IF the R-rate stayed below 1. If and only if.

Do the sums, people. IF+IF+IF=YOU WERE WARNED. It is manifestly obvious that you *haven't* followed the rules, or infection rates would not now be soaring. Thus, you have nobody to blame but yourselves that Christmas is cancelled. *Quod erat demonstrandum.** New restrictions loom for the worst-affected areas. Pubs and restaurants will have to close at 10 p.m. No visiting other households indoors or in gardens. No staying overnight in one another's houses.

All the same, we can't hang about for ever, waiting for it all to be over. Life must go on. The ordination services will go ahead in Lindchester Cathedral this weekend, in small batches, without the happy crowds, the robed choir and the thunderous Widor climax, where the organ sails almighty victorious on the ocean of sound like a vast liner, and everyone pours out through the great west doors into the bell-trembling air. There will still be a group photo opportunity at the end of each day, of course, where the bishop and the newly ordained can arrange themselves in a socially distanced pattern on the lawn in front of the cathedral, and jump for joy. Honestly, I do wish they wouldn't do that. Don't you? Do they not realize that each time a toe-curling image of jumping deacons is shared on social media, another precious golden leaf falls from Queen Anne's money tree in the Oxbridge quad where High Elves gather to save the C of E, by shuddering with distaste?

Jane is hunched at her desk, probably brewing another migraine on account of her crappy neck posture. Matt's on the train to London for an actual in-person non-Zoom meeting of General Synod, in order to vote for a motion that General Synod doesn't have to meet in person and can meet on Zoom. Or something.

Oh, how she's missing her September bounce, her new-stationery boost of fresh starts and optimism, of being with colleagues again,

---

* A Latin phrase meaning 'This demonstrates that I am better educated than you'.

even those she hates. Wait, she doesn't hate anyone. She's friends with the Quisling, who from now on must be thought of by her proper name: Elspeth. The new academic year of blended learning is proving pretty hellish. Not as bad in Lindford as in Glasgow and Manchester, admittedly, where whole halls of residence have been forced to self-isolate and told not to socialize. But they may just be ahead of the curve. It's week two of teaching, and already one student in Jane's third-year seminar group has tested positive for COVID. So far she's OK, although her hypochondria is giving her real gip.

The only bright spot in her life has been the automatic sub-titling on Kaltura Lecture Capture, which turns out to be a brilliant surrealist poetry generator. She spent three times longer editing the captions on her Josephine Luscombe lecture than it took her to record it in the first place. Tempting though it was to leave some errors uncorrected. 'Josephine lust comes nurse in lego sea' almost made it into the final cut.

She's in the middle of feeding back on the asynchronous online activity she has devised for the new first-years, when her phone buzzes. It's a text from her cousin Elaine.

> Elaine: Hi Jackie. Hope alls well with U. Just going through mums stuff. Found a couple of boxes of your mum's stuff in loft. Photos letters odd n sods. Pls advise on what U want me to do. Exx

Jane's heart leaps. Oh my God! She's a different person from the one who told her aunt to sling the lot in a skip twenty years ago. Her thumbs – she's all thumbs! – stumble as she types.

> Jane: Hi Elaine. I'm fine thanks, hope you are too. Wow. I told aunty B to chuck them! Sounds like she knew I'd regret that. So yes, I'd love the lot. Can you stick them in the post and I'll reimburse you? Thanks so much. Jane xx

There's a longish pause. Letters, thinks Jane. Whose? Whose letters had Mum saved? Probably Jane's from Oxford. Back when you used to write letters home, because the only alternative was queuing in a draughty corridor for the college phone, jingling your handful of ten pence pieces. She's got nothing but a few emails and texts from Danny to show for his student years in New Zealand. And it's mainly

WhatsApp messages now. Nothing you can put in a box. All the photos of Jane's childhood! Not gone for good after all. Tears well up. Ah, thanks, Aunty Betty, you wise woman. Ghastly school photos. Black and white snaps. Possibly a reel of coloured holiday pics from Isle of Wight trips?

> Elaine: JANE!!! Soz, I forgot. Cd do, but there's quite a lot. I'm dropping Jack off at Brum uni next week. Meet U at pub somewhere near motorway on way home instead? Exx

Moon Journal

So I'm learning my Grade 1 scales and arpeggios, I can already play F Major and G Major (one octave) plus arpeggios. Next up is A minor harmonic and melodic, I tried to explain the difference to Leah and she went whatever. It is like when she tells me about karate to be fair, I hear her but I do not actually listen. It's my birthday on October 4th and I so so so want a clarinet of my own not a school one, but they are super expensive and mum and dad say its early days, let's see if you are still keen on the clarinet next year. They do not know how committed I am and will do anything to achieve my ambitions. Right now my ambition is to be a clarinettist in a world famous orchestra and to be a singer maybe in a famous ensemble like for example the Dorian Singers. I for one am not interested in X Factor or being famous via TikTok, not being rude or anything, but it is not my thing that's all. I prefer to be a classical musician.

Mr H-M does TikTok and YouTube, he has like a bazillion followers but his heart is not really in it. He told us that in choir practice. He is just doing it during Covid because everything else is cancelled. Then he sang a verse of this song, 'My Hearts in the Highland my heart is not here.' It was all on one note. I listened to a recording on YouTube just now, it is on three notes in F minor plus organ. It is by Arvo Part and it was super strange and sad to hear Mr H-Ms voice filling up the cathedral with literally one note? I started crying, and Ellie was all, are you OK? And I could not explain it. How can one (or three) notes do this? Music does this thing that I can't explain.

Moon Phase

Waxing Gibbous (89%). This means it is not long till the next full moon which will be the Hunters Moon. I have just been researching and the

Harvest Moon is the full moon closest to the autumn equinox so technically the NEXT full moon is the 'Harvest Moon' not the 'Hunters Moon'. And this month could be 'The CORN MOON' or the Barley Moon instead. It's complicated LOL. This is due to the luner month being different to the calendar month (I think?????) There will be 2 full moons next month as I have said before, so maybe the second full moon is like a mash-up, the BLUE HUNTERS MOON!!!!

Blue tits are busy at bird feeders across Lindfordshire. Rooks converse in gargled roars from treetops. Chestnuts drop, and the pavements below look like a shore strewn with green sea urchins. Some days are still, not a breath of wind, and the smoke barely drifts from your neighbour's leafy bonfire. Other days are crisp and breezy. It rains, then the sun comes out, and raindrops hang like crystal beads along geranium stems.

Winter looms already. Despite the sun and the tender blue sky, the days are getting shorter. Keep going. Don't give up now. Oh, but this is school cross-country misery. Mud and rain, and there's nothing for it but to get your game face on and keep slogging. If only it would rain so hard PE was completely rained off! But there's no downpour, just this relentless drizzle. No getting out of it, unless your mum has sent a note. No getting out of it, unless you know a short cut, where you can hunker down and wait till the fast kids have ploughed past, then slip in behind the mediocre majority and pretend you ran the whole way. But then you're so cold and wet from your half-hour hunched behind the bus shelter, you might have been better off running.

All over Lindfordshire, people are turning to handicrafts for consolation. Jumpers are knitted for toddlers. Patchwork quilts are pieced out on tables and floors. I daresay all the ancient accomplishments of corseted femininity will be revived before we've seen the back of COVID-19. We will be netting purses and doing pokerwork for Christmas bazaars that can never be held. Small decorating projects are also being undertaken. Bathroom and study walls go from duck egg to aubergine; from buttermilk to ink. Entrance halls are given a makeover, and fiendishly clever ways of banishing heaps of shoes are introduced. Oh, there's nothing like a canny storage

281

solution to lift the spirits. Back porches become mudrooms. After a couple of decades of languishing, the cheese plant makes a comeback. In fact, green houseplants of all kinds are now permitted again. We are transformed!

As you know, the 60s house at the far side of Miss Sherratt's garden is being transformed from one degree of cerulean glory to another. Neil has popped across from Gayden Magna to inspect the project. Ambrose is out taking the dogs for a long walk up on the heathland. Chloe is out too, covering some of the liaising and organizing work normally looked after by Martin, who is still signed off sick.

This means – perhaps you are ahead of me here, reader – that Freddie and Neil find themselves once again in an empty house. What's more, Freddie is literally in the same painty overalls that Neil once enthusiastically helped him out of some half a dozen years ago. They are both furiously pretending that this thought has not occurred to them.

'Kitchen cabinets next,' says Freddie. 'Got the paint mixed. All good to go.'

'Hmm.' Neil runs a hand over the nearest door. 'You'll be wanting to rub them down, of course.'

'Nope.'

'What? The paint'll not stick.' Neil wags a finger. 'Rub them down, prime them, *then* paint them.'

'Nah. Chalk paint, dude. Sticks to anything? You can literally paint it on with a hammer?'

'Excuse me? Chalk paint! You will not, young man! If a job's worth— Can I smell weed?'

'Not me. Next door.' Freddie nods at the wall. 'Brose reckons it's a cannabis farm.'

'No! Really? Shouldn't you—'

'Ssh.' He raises a finger. 'Hear that? Industrial fan.'

They stand in silence, listening. One of the girls chooks broodily in the garden. The fridge hums. In the background, another hum, on and on.

Neil's eyes pop. 'Shouldn't you tell the polis?'

'Yeah, only Brose reckons there's probably a slave in there? Sometimes the blind moves upstairs. Like, trafficked, probably Vietnamese?'

'All the more reason!'

Freddie shakes his head. 'Kinda hoping we can get a message through, that Chloe can help? Legally, I mean, with asylum. Otherwise, he'll just get arrested and yeah. Criminal not victim? She's seen it happen.'

The fan hums away.

'What a shitty world,' says Neil.

'Yeah, kinda. But also not so shit? Sometimes.' He hesitates. 'Listen, you remember that time you and Chloe were street pastoring and you saw me with, ah, some random guy? Coming out a club?' Freddie waves at the memory, like it's a fly or a bad smell.

'Yes.'

'So after I saw you, I like got a cab home? I mean, straight home? Then I totally ghosted him. The guy? So I'm saying, nothing happened.' Freddie clears his throat. Gazes out of the window at the faded sign on the henhouse. 'So yeah. Thanks. Coz at the time, you gave me this look, and I – ha ha – I full on *repented*, dude. I totally did that. So.'

Neil is studying the can of paint on the work surface. 'Och.' Now he wafts at the imaginary smell. 'Well, we both know I'm no better than I should be. And I should probably thank *you*, while we're at it. You did the Lord's work that, erm, other time, brother.'

'Yeah?' Freddie grins. A ghost of the old slutty grin. 'You were so pissed at me at the time! You were *that* close to bitch-slapping me! Oh *man*.'

'Yes, well, I wasnae saved back then. You make sure you rub those doors down properly, young man. I'll be back to check up on you.' Neil does another sweep of the room. 'Very good.' Then he points to a corner. 'An orange tree. In a terracotta pot. That's what it needs. Or a lemon tree. Wait – what are those Japanese lemons again? Yuzu, aye, that's it. Look it up.'

'Uh huh. Yep. Want some eggs?'

After Neil's finally stopped his bossing and driven off, Freddie goes back to the kitchen. So fucking *empty*. Worse now that someone's been and gone. Reminds him of how much he misses everyone. He walks up and down, one arm across his chest, like he's propping a baby there, its little head curled into him, like the way maybe his mum held him, or even – who knows? – his dad? He remembers the little dude he helped bring into the world. Up and down, up and down. Thinks about the guy next door, if there is a guy next door. Thinks about Brose, whose mood's seriously tanking over politics again. He sings softly as he walks. Sometimes it's the only way of keeping his shit together when he's on his own. While they're waiting to see if they got lucky this month, or if they're gonna get their hearts broken. If that's gonna happen month after month?

> I refrain my soul, and keep it low, like as a child that is weaned
>   from his mother.

The whole Psalter is engraved on his soul.

> My soul is even as a weaned child.

Jane lies awake at 1 a.m., brain whizzing like a toy train round and round the same loop of academic trouble-shooting track. She tries her old trick of counting to a hundred in French, going back to *un* every time she stumbles. This works better than counting sheep. *Dix-sept, dix-huit . . . dix-sept . . .* Darn. *Un, deux.* Her own particular mental flock are rubbish. They refuse to pass obligingly through a gate in single file so she can count them. They wander, like lost . . . *Trois, quatre . . .*

What's in those boxes?

Cinq . . .

Elaine has a lamb's tail from someone's farm. It's woolly and wiry. Farmers put a tight ring round all the lambs' tails. It stops the blood flow, and eventually the tails just drop off, dead. 'Don't be daft, Jackie, it doesn't hurt them.' (Auntie Betty.) 'I know, love, but long tails get covered in poo and the sheep gets fly strike.'

But Jackie's read *Black Beauty*.

'Oh well, if you're going to go reading *that*, no wonder, you daft ha'porth.'

Uncle Ken is behind his paper. He says, 'Better not tell her about the boy lambs.'

'Don't you dare.'

He chuckles.

Auntie and Uncle's house has a fox's brush dangling from the light-pull in the dim downstairs toilet which is the bathroom. The tip of the tail is white. You have to pull it to turn the light on, but Jackie reaches up higher so she can pull the cord instead. Uncle Ken shoots foxes on people's farms. You don't want them killing the lambs and getting the hens. Elaine makes beautiful Plasticraft paperweights with flowers in. The stuff smells plasticky and funny. She has a Shaker Maker too. Elaine's good at sharing, not like some of the girls at school, who hold their nose when Jackie sits on their table, because Jackie smells. Elaine says, 'My cousin doesn't smell, takes one to know one, Mandy Goodyear!' Elaine makes Mickey Mouse and lets Jackie make Donald Duck. They shake them and the models wobble, which looks rude. Next day the models are dry and they paint them after school. Jackie's mum says toys like that are a waste of money. Books are the only present worth having. Elaine gets *Mandy* every week. Jackie gets *Look and Learn*. Jackie is a member of the Puffin Club.

Maybe Donald Duck is in the box? All the lost things not lost, just waiting.

OCTOBER

Hunter's Moon, Part I

30th September

So today in warm-up Mr H-M got us singing The Big Ship sail's down the ally-ally-oo, because today is . . . wait for it . . . THE LAST DAY OF SEPTEMBER!!! How time flies when your enjoying yourself. NOT. Mum used to sing this song with Leah and I as we walked to school when we still lived in Risley Hill (I was in Reception.) That was before mum and dad split up obvs. Back then Leah didn't just yell at mum Your so embarrasing. We joined hands and swung our hands and sang it while we were walking along. I for one am internally grateful that mum and dad have kind of got back together, even if its only because of covid and early days. (FYI Leah still yells sometimes but it is what it is.)

Today was so wierd at school. Sometimes I'm scared I'm getting mental health issues like mum used to. Leah said don't worry its just hormones, probably your getting your first period soon, but she also said 'I am here for you'. That made me cry again, she is super understanding when all is said and done. She then proceded to grab my hands and start singing (totally out of tune) The captain said this will never never do!!! She swang me round and round the lounge then she tripped over the poof and I was literally ROFL.

My mood is ok now, but when we were singing the big ship in warm-up, I started crying again (like I did when Mr H-M sang my hearts in the highlands), because don't ask me why, the words seemed really sad? Like the ship is full of toys for me and you, and then it literally SINKS TO THE BOTTOM OF THE SEA! In my mind I was going, what is even WRONG with you, this is a song for little kids, its not a sad song!!! SMH.

It was chemistry today and Daisy Lowther got to close to the bun St Bernard and her fringe caught on fire (it went out again). The smell grossed me out, it really stank. Mrs Jones said no harm done, do be careful everyone. Leah is making vegan dirty fries for tea. I'm so so glad tomorrow is another day and another month.

Plus I am accentuating the positive like the song says and looking on the bright side . . . because on Sunday . . . ITS MY BIRTHDAY!!!!! I'm trying not to hope for a clarinet (but guess what, I still am). I SO hope and pray October will be better. I am looking forward to the Hunters Moon, it will be full on Thursday slash Friday. I will do my moon bath and say my intentions and maybe everything will be ok despite of covid and hormones.

I add my Amen to Jess's prayer. But as the first day of October dawns across Lindfordshire, I confess that I am not full of faith, even though the sky is blue first thing and a golden light blesses the trees. Do you want the good news or the bad news? Like sensible people, you want the bad news first, of course. 'At least, to know the worst, is sweet,' as poet Emily Dickinson said (renouncing the world entirely and seldom emerging from her Amherst bedroom). The bad news is this: the death toll globally from COVID-19 has passed one million, infection rates everywhere are climbing again, we are teetering on the brink of another lockdown, the track and trace system is still flaky, people are being sent hundreds of miles for COVID tests, unemployment is rising, Brexit negotiations are in tatters and winter is coming. The good news is, the steadfast love of the Lord never ceases.

'Morning.' Chloe enters the blue kitchen. She's dressed for work. Her arms are folded tightly, hands gripping her upper arms as if she's cold. She crosses to the kettle and turns it back on.

Oh no, thinks Ambrose.

'So.' She gives them a bright smile. 'I'll just grab a quick coffee and toast, and then I'll be heading out to the Hub. Is one of you OK to W.A.L.K. you know who?'

'Sure thang,' says Freddie.

'Um. And just to let you know, not this month, guys. Sorry.'

The kettle reboils and clicks off.

'Ah well,' says Ambrose.

'I know. Well, there we are.' Chloe smiles again and shrugs. 'Sorry.'

'Aw, babe, don't be sorry!' says Freddie. 'Not like it's your fault.'

Ambrose moves to restrain him, but too late. Freddie's up from the breakfast table and giving her a hug. Which tips her over the edge.

'Oh God! Sorry,' sobs Chloe.

'Aw, babe.' He rocks her and rests his cheek on the top of her head. He's leaning against the kitchen cabinet. The chalk paint has dried and is waiting for a coat of wax. Today's task. 'Hey, it's OK.'

Ambrose knows Chloe hates crying. The dogs don't like it either. They're starting to whine. They stand gazing up at her and Freddie, who has tears in his eyes too.

'Here, Cosmo. Alfie, here.' Ambrose clicks his fingers. 'Hey, hey, hey. It's OK, guys.'

Maybe Freddie's right – get the feelings out. Let yourself be comforted. On the rare occasions when Ambrose has sobbed in Freddie's arms, he knows he felt better for it. Probably. Except he flinches at the memory. It's like catching sight of a wound. Too intimate, too painful. He buries his hands in the dogs' coats, rumples their ears, lets them nuzzle his face. 'Good boys. It's OK. Daddy loves you.' He observes that he doesn't think twice about this. He's more instinctive with animals than people. Because he's never trying to figure out what a dog's game is?

'OK. I'm coming out of it now,' says Chloe. She reaches out for the kitchen roll and blows her nose. 'As you were. Aw, Cosmo! Here, boy. Mummy's fine. At least I didn't set the hens off, ha ha!'

Freddie sucks his teeth, shakes his head. 'Not broken it to them yet, babe.'

'They don't need to know,' Chloe whispers.

'Hey. We're all in this together,' says Freddie. 'Lemme grab you some coffee. C'mon, sit.'

Later, Ambrose is in the car driving to see one of his farming clients out at the edge of the county. This is the farmer who let the

Hardman-Mays camp on her land and wild swim in the Linden. He could meet with her virtually, but he's got a hunch that a face-to-face meeting will be timely. He's hearing it from all over – not just from his family – how catastrophic things are for British farming. The current Brexit uncertainty, which comes on top of the Beast from the East winter of 2018, then drought, then floods and now COVID. The truly scary number of suicides.

Fields of winter wheat, belted Galloways, low hedges, turbines turning. He notes the bursts of colour on the field maples and cherries, but it's all just landscapes passing by from old road movies he doesn't really care about. He could carry on driving. He could turn off the satnav. Close down everything, all his apps and devices and accounts. Drive on and on, and drop off the map entirely. He's done that in the past, trying to keep a step ahead of the darkness coming in across his inner landscape. It's not a black dog at all. Dogs are fine. It's more winter in Tromsø, when the sun never makes it above the horizon. He knows the symptoms. Detachment. Blankness. The scene in the kitchen just now. He was spectating a drama he's supposed to be part of.

He turns off the old straight Roman road on to a smaller road. *Shotton Edge Farm Shop and Alpaca Trekking*. He'll visit Lesley – socially distanced across the big farmhouse table – then drive back home to his husband and cousin and the dogs and hens. He won't vanish. All the same, he can feel himself dropping from view, going AWOL inside. Like he did four years ago – 2020 is the deadly second wave of 2016. Staring down the barrel of a no-deal Brexit. The Good Friday agreement practically dead in the water. Trump. Racism and nationalism on the march. Hate crimes going up. Global economy tanking. Another Great Depression somewhere down the road? And towering like a mushroom cloud over everything, climate change.

Ambrose grew up knowing where the guns were kept, and how to use them.

He turns down the track that leads to the farm, and stops under the old oak to open the gate, same as they did back in August. The muddy lane is studded with acorns now, green, yellow, brown. Another one drops with a ping on the car roof. There in the left-hand field are the alpacas in their woolly trousers, looking like a bunch of giant poodles. Six adults, three young ones and a few sheep. He shakes his head. Daft little faces under all that hair, daft creatures. The only thing dafter is a llama, but it's a close call. Freddie adores them. Shame the pandemic's putting such a dent in the tourist trade. Not many families coming to walk Fluffy and Alpacino this year. Ambrose leans on the fence and calls them. They don't come. More acorns patter down. In the distance, a gunshot. A pheasant whirls up from the hedge, clucking rustily.

He gets back in the car, drives through, then stops to close the gate behind him. He knows the sheep are there so that, legally speaking, it's a field of livestock, not exotics; which means Lesley can prosecute anyone whose dog gets out of control. Which she did, when she lost three alpacas a while back, after some idiot let a pair of hunting labs off the lead. Absolute carnage. Ambrose didn't tell Freddie that. He just told him the alpacas are there to give the foxes a kicking if they go for the lambs in the lambing season. Never mind the poodle trousers, they'll literally stomp the shit out of any fox that gets too close. Maybe it's a better solution than shooting. If you can be bothered with alpacas.

Ambrose parks on the yard and gets out into all the smells of childhood. Cows, fresh earth – potato-digging? – hay in the barn, apples in the orchard. He takes a deep breath. There's a blackbird somewhere, singing scrappily. Lesley appears in the doorway and raises a hand in welcome, and all the dogs come running to greet him.

Jane is also out driving in the wilds of Lindfordshire. In fact, she passes the sign to Shotton Edge Farm on her way home from meeting up with her cousin Elaine. Alpaca trekking? Aren't alpacas a bit small to ride? Maybe she's muddling them with llamas. She goes through this every time she's out this way, and then forgets to Google it later. She also thinks (every time) that Danny would love this, because every time, for a fraction of a second, she forgets that Danny is twenty-six, not six.

Jane is driving home with a boot full of boxes, and Blondie's greatest hits blaring. She's hurtling along the narrow lanes a bit too fast in her knob-head girl racer black Mini, I'm afraid. This is despite having it out with conscience this morning. Jane demonstrated conclusively that to go out for a pub lunch on a non-teaching day is perfectly reasonable, given that she's consistently worked fifty per cent over her contracted hours since mid-August. But conscience is clearly not the kind of girl who gives up just like that. 'No no, oh-oh-oh!' sings Jane. Conscience is saying, Get back to that desk as fast as you can, you workshy dilettante. But conscience is not the only one riding gunshot in this car. Curiosity is bouncing up and down on the front seat going, What's in the boxes, what's in the boxes? When Jane gets in, curiosity is going to make mincemeat of conscience.

(Apologies if your blood pressure is going through the roof, reader. Jane is not about to career headlong into a potato lorry, or collide with Ambrose, killing her instantly and leaving him on a life-support machine, so that poor Freddie has a heart-breaking decision to make in a month's time. They will both get home safely. Things are bad enough right now without me adding to your woes.)

God, I love my cousin! Jane thinks. Was that the pandemic speaking? Maybe she'd love any human being she was lucky enough to spend an hour with, socially distanced diagonally opposite, at a pub table, eating fish pie. Possibly COVID has amplified her capacity to love? Her heart, like that of the psalmist, has been enlarged. (Although Jane is well aware this means 'set at large', not 'made bigger'. She spent two years at theological college, remember.) Oh, to talk about old times, about family, to have shared memories – these things matter increasingly. Thank God Aunty Betty didn't throw everything out when Jane foolishly believed she had no need of family history.

'Did you keep the fox-brush light pull?' Jane asked.

'That manky old thing? Don't be daft. Mum chucked that out after Dad died. Why? Did you want it for the palace?'

'Ha ha! Imagine! Listen, I was remembering the other day how you stuck up for me whenever Mandy Goodyear said, "Jackie smells."'

'The Goodyears! Mum had no time for the mother – what was her name?'

'Mrs Goodyear. Grown-ups didn't have first names back then. Unless we knew them well enough to call them Aunty and Uncle.'

'Good point. I can still hear Mum muttering, "A bar of soap costs nothing!" if we saw them in the Co-op. You might be poor, but you didn't have to be *rough*.'

'God yes, the fear of being rough! My mum was in a permanent state of war with dropped aitches. That said, I probably did smell. Fag smoke. Mildew. Cooking fat. I had one school skirt and two jumpers. And I only had one bath a week.'

'We all did, Jackie. JANE! Sorry. You probably smelt of Aqua Manda. Maybe that's what Mandy meant. Or Styx.'

'Ha ha ha! Or Stowaway.'

'Stowaway! Sleepy Lagoons and Rio Nights – remember the Radio Luxembourg ad?'

'If you listen to Radio Luxembourg, you're stealing money from the BBC!'

'She actually said that? Well, Aunty Eileen always was a barrel of laughs, Jane. Ha ha ha!'

We've got the same filthy laugh, thinks Jane. She laughs again now, remembering how the people at the other tables turned to stare. Her eyes brim with tears as she hurtles along the old Roman road towards Martonbury. Fucking Oxford. I've wasted my adult life denying my roots. Ah, it's so good to know where you come from. To know who your people are. If I get nothing else out of this pandemic, at least I've got that.

My characters wake to the news that Trump is in hospital with COVID-19. This is a test of their spiritual mettle. Will they pray for his swift recovery to full health? Or will they punch the air with glee, believing they discern judgement at work? I hope that they have managed to renounce all ill-wishing, just as I trust they've renounced fooling about with beakers of hydrochloric acid. One of them (bottle of Champagne already chilling) amuses himself by supposing that there's probably a German word for 'longing for the opportunity to indulge in Schadenfreude'. *Schadenfreudesgelegenheitsehnsucht*, perhaps?

'Yes, dear,' says the dean. 'Or, in our more economical mother tongue, sin.'

Virginia is dabbing with her trusty Sticky Stuff Remover at the label on her old clarinet case. It feels symbolic to have peeled off her own name and address – or rather, her parents' address – ready to give it away. She's warned Becky that it will probably need new pads and a complete overhaul, but it's not a bad instrument. She'd love to say she got a lot of pleasure out of it, but did she really? Wasn't it just another target, getting Grade 8 so that her CV looked well rounded? After all, she's barely played it since school – which probably tells you all you need to know.

There. All done. She'll drop it round tomorrow, while Jess is at school. Virginia smiles as she pictures Jess's face. Bless her! One of life's sunshine characters. It will be nice to stay for coffee – socially distanced, of course – and chat to Becky and Martin about their plans. Cautious plans. To help them try to discern what they really want, whether this set of feelings will outlive the pandemic.

Oh, to be with people! Virginia has had her hair cut. She's given blood and been to the dentist for an emergency filling. Apart from that, she's touched no one since March. May God forgive her for her feelings about those who flout the rules, who won't wear a mask or who wear it below their nose. About her neighbours, who clearly can't count to six! She has buried parishioners who have died of COVID, and she fears she'll be burying many more this winter. And God forgive her for wanting to slap people who moan about their partners and children. She sometimes catches herself envying Dominic, even. At least he's got his mum and his dog!

Stop it, Virginia, she tells herself firmly (in her mother's voice, but she hasn't spotted this yet). You know Dominic is much worse off than you are, coping with his mum and her dementia. At least you managed a holiday in Norfolk. Snap out of it. There are people far worse off than you are. Go and do something nice for someone else, then you'll feel much better.

Virginia acquiesces to this inner admonition, because she thinks it's the Spirit prompting her, rather than just her mother (who is merely a churchwarden and not a member of the Trinity). She will bake an apple cake for Becky and Martin, and take it along with the clarinet. Good. It's a shame she can't offer to look after Dominic's mum, so that he can get a bit of time to himself. She'd gladly do that, but Mrs Todd has no concept of social distancing. She sometimes needs physically restraining, or steering back into the house, if she's trying to go shopping or to the library. It's a shame, but rules are rules.

Leah is busy wrapping her present for Jess in recycled paper saved from her own birthday. She's bought her some bamboo socks with sunflowers on, and two packs of clarinet reeds from the music shop in Lindford. Jess has no idea, but Mum and Dad have bought a second-hand clarinet off Virginia, who says she'll never play it again and wants it to go to a good home. Virginia was literally trying to *give* it to them, but Dad insisted on paying her a fair price. He won't tell Leah how much, because it's quote, none of your business, unquote. It better not cost more than Leah got for her birthday, that's all.

Anyway. That's pretty cool of Virginia. Leah admits it. She intends to like her more from now on, instead of thinking Virginia's basically channelling her inner teacher, the kind that's forever going, Perhaps YOU'd like to teach this class, Leah, if you're so clever. Or, Please show some respect. Hello? How about, *earn* my respect, and then maybe we'll talk about me *showing* some. Not that Virginia's ever said that, it's just her face. Plus she's really bo-o-o-ring. What Leah can't get is how come Father Dominic likes Virginia so much, when she's so fucking boring. Her sermons! Shoot me now, already. Bad luck for Jess she's got Virginia for confirmation, not Father Dominic. It was Father Dominic who convinced Leah not to be a pagan any more. Plus they have to use Zoom, so no pizza nights, no cinema, no indoor Winter Olympics with sock-skating, or curling with mops and cabbages down the vicarage hall. You've got to feel sorry for Jess.

Leah finishes wrapping the present. She hides it in the bottom of her wardrobe under her first karate gi she grew out of ages ago, but still keeps for sentimental reasons. That's where she's hidden the Red Box too. The Red Box is ready now. Mum just finished sewing a red fleecy cover for the heart-shaped hot-water bottle today. So they can go, *Ta Dah!* when the time comes, and give it to Jess, and it will be like a celebration, not like something shameful's happened to her.

The full Hunter's Moon sails over Lindfordshire behind a film of ribbed cloud. It seems to lie underwater in a patch of silver ripples, as though the night sky is a lake and we are gazing down into its depths. We who are insomniacs, and night-shift workers, police, road sweepers. The farmer checking her alpacas. Freddie checking the hens – why are the girls restless? Is it a fox? Why can't he sleep? He knows why. Because Brose is vanishing away, even though he's like right here in the house? The moon shines over the roof of the new extension. On the blank windows still with tape on. The builders are nearly finished. Just the snagging list.

Freddie goes back inside. Chloe's old German dictionary lies open on the table in the blue kitchen. It looks like homework from back in the day. A4 file paper. Pencils. Like a flashback to his younger self being crap at school. Or no, maybe a flash forward, to him helping his own kid with something, like his own dad never did. He was all, Work at it, Son. Don't be a quitter. Don't be a girl.

I so won't do that, he vows. If. Maybe next month? Anyway, so he's trying to do what La Madeleine says, No cheating, no Google translate, coz she's not given up on the idea. He's meant to dig right down into *Winterreise*, till the meaning's in his bones and he can sing it, interpret it, not just impersonate Peter Schreier, like a clever mynah bird – ye-owch that one still hurts. So he's trying, and God it's a fucking beast. The grammar? Yeah, he can sight-read German, pronounce it, no problem; he just doesn't know what it *means*, how it works. Clearly it works, but like, if it was an engine, he'd be shaking his head and calling a mechanic, not trying to take it apart and figure it out. Does his fucking head in. Spanish? No worries because he learnt it by ear mostly. With an Argentine accent, but yeah. He's got a feel for Italian, because Latin? But German? No-uh. Obviously, he can get the gist of the repertoire from the English translations, plus he can add *feeling* coz he's a clever fucking *mynah bird*, but La Madeleine can tell it's bogus, apparently.

It's nearly 2 a.m. Why is he even doing this? Because if he doesn't, what is there? Gotta keep on. *Muß selbst den Weg mir weisen/In dieser Dunkelheit.* I must show myself the way in this darkness. Except he can't, he's got no light left in him. Lighten our darkness, we beseech thee, O Lord. For a moment, he sees himself following this tiny light through a dark forest. And maybe if he can keep going, then Brose can hang on to him, and he can keep going too? And it will end. The night will end.

Hunter's Moon, Part II

raise him! Praise him on the high-sounding clarinet badly in need of a complete overhaul. Let everything that hath breath, praise the Lord! Perhaps gratitude is the answer. We could do worse than look to Jess for inspiration. She is beside herself with delight at her birthday present. It may be pre-loved and out of condition, but it is hers. She'd bravely resigned herself to saving up her birthday and Christmas money for years – but look! Here it is in her very hands! Tomorrow Becky will drop it off at the music shop for repairs, but today, today, today, Jess will make a joyful noise unto the Lord. The squawking is atrocious. *Frère Jacques, dormez-vous?* Not likely, with this duck-throttling racket going on! Leah has gone back to bed after the grand present-opening ritual and birthday breakfast. Her bedroom is above the dining room, unfortunately. She clamps her pillow over her ears. Fucksake, Jess!

Becky and Martin smile at one another across the kitchen table. How can they have reached this point? This impossible point of smiling across a table, with those two tiny babies fine strong twelve and fourteen-year-olds.

'Thank you for my girls. You're a good mother.'

'I've been a crap mother, Martin, and we both know it.'

'You're a good mother.'

'Well.' Becky's chin trembles. 'And you're a good dad.'

In the next room, Jess embarks upon Beethoven's Honk to Joy. They both grimace. Becky gets up and stealthily closes the kitchen door. She sits back down. They smile at one another again. This is crazy stuff!

'Obviously, Virginia is right,' says Becky. 'We need to take this slowly.'

Martin laughs. 'Just as well. Slow is all I've got.'

'I meant—'

'I know.' He puts his hand on hers. 'It's fine. Let me stack the dishwasher.'

'Go back to bed,' she says. 'I'll wake you in time for Evensong. Marion says we can park on the deanery drive.'

'Thanks. I may just do that.'

Smoke rises from bonfires. The last roses of summer droop on their stems. The days are drawing in. We scuff through fallen leaves. Drifts of yellow lime. Green sycamore, leopard-printed with blight. We pass under scarlet acers, like ceilings of stained-glass stars. Not long until the clocks go back. Normally the evenings would be resounding to fireworks by now, in the long run-up to Halloween and Guy Fawkes Night. Yet here in Lindfordshire, we've heard barely a volley since Eid and #ClapForCarers. During the day, pigeons make avian-whoopee fireworks of their own. They sidle along ridge tiles, they thrash and slap in trees, and emerge with flustered feathers. It seems as though there is no season of the year when a pigeon's fancy does not turn lightly to the thoughts of love.

It's all over between Freddie and Dishy Rishi, though. Freddie didn't take kindly to the suggestion that his singing career is not 'viable'. Wow. Like, just because it doesn't pay a living wage, singing is suddenly a hobby, not his whole fucking *life*? Truth to tell, it may well be over between Rishi and artists of every stripe. The suggestion that they need to retrain as dog-handlers or bomb-disposal experts has not gone down well with hard-working creatives who are already doing at least one other job alongside their vocation, simply to pay the bills.

Freddie just can't? This is wrong at so many levels. How can you un-become your actual self? The government might as well go, Soz, being gay isn't actually viable; you should retrain as straight? Because music is not some add-on, it's literally him? He is fearfully and wonderfully made by music. It's in his down-sitting and his up-rising, in his head, his heart, his lungs, throat, mouth, eyes and ears, in his DNA. Music is coded through Freddie's universe.

The lay clerks of Lindchester Cathedral and the girls' choir sing Evensong this Sunday as viably as they can, to a socially distanced congregation. I don't mean *to* the congregation, of course. It's an act of worship, not a performance. We may not be allowed to sit in the quire or sing hymns behind our masks, but we are taking part. Our souls are the sounding boards. We reverberate with praise and lament, we bounce it back up to heaven. Like the three things that were too wonderful for the proverb-writer, music does what words alone cannot achieve. Why else would we weep to hear the girls' clear voices soaring? 'God be with you till we meet again.'

Oh, that ill-fated Jacks anthem. Every time they sing it, the back-drop darkens. Merseyside is about to enter Tier 3, with Manchester not far behind. There are rumours of a national three-week circuit-breaker lockdown. Hospital admissions are close to the levels we saw in March, and 16,000 test results get 'lost' because of an IT 'glitch' (no doubt a distant second cousin to the 'mutant algorithm' that ruined A-level results through no fault of the government). Global death rates climb, climb, while despots strut like the apocalyptic little horn, uttering great things.

And yet.

> God be with you till we meet again.
> When life's perils thick confound you,
> Put his arms unfailing round you,
> God be with you till we meet again.

It's too much. Martin's glasses steam up. He takes them off and wipes his eyes. Is there a way to blow your nose without removing your mask? Beside him – at a distance of two metres, because that is how the chairs are set up – sits Becky, also blotting her tears. On his other side slouches his fierce warrior daughter. Out of the corner of his eye, he can see her vegan-booted foot bouncing up and down as though she'd rather be stomping off out of here, or perhaps patrolling the nave again for coronavirus compliance. She strode round before the service started, pulling up anyone wearing their mask incorrectly. 'My dad nearly died of COVID-19. The least you can do is cover your nose.'

Oh, Leah, you are a daughter of kings and a shield maiden of Rohan! I wish I had the courage not to die of Englishness. I notice that you've taken Ms Logan's detention wisdom to heart. You chose not to deploy the F-bomb, because you've worked out that for testy my-civil-liberties-are-being-eroded septuagenarians, the crime of foul language easily outweighs that of being a super-spreader. You're scowling now as you watch Mr Hardman-May conducting the girls' choir. That bouncing foot is a nice touch. People will think you're bored. Nobody can know that you're grabbing every detail, panic-buying, stockpiling the fleeting seconds to see you through the lockdown of unrequited love.

The weeks and months are flying past. What day is it again? Was it really only this morning that we went out for a run? It feels like weeks ago. Flocks of birds go blowing along the wind, rising and scattering, whirling and gathering again. We see them pass over gardens and parks. Ambrose on his long lonely walks watches gulls following the plough, and a flock of lapwings wheeling. He passes old laid hedges along ancient fields, where larks fling up into the sky, and sing in broken fragments.

Star tilts her head up to watch the birds pass as she walks through Lindford Arboretum on her way to work. A murmuration of starlings. A charm of goldfinches. She knows all the collective nouns. A mutation of thrushes. The thrushes come whirling down on to a yew tree, tall as a great pillar. They start to eat the berries and call out with a weird noise, like ice cubes blitzed in a blender when you're making a super-cold smoothie. Birds. That was her favourite ever project she did at junior school – Mum's still got it, ha ha! She keeps all Star's stuff, love her. The hall is full of all the framed Merit Certificates she ever got at school, plus every school photo from nursery to Year 11. She's even kept the crappy eagle kite from DT that wouldn't fly!

Star exits the arboretum through the main gates, where golden leaves are falling from the tulip tree. Five magpies on the grass, five for silver. Up they go, over the bandstand. Someone in Leeds had a hoopoe in their garden. Oh wow, imagine an actual hoopoe in your garden, with his crazy stripy crest and everything? Last night she had this really sweet dream. There were all these tiny little birds in Mum's rockery, and you could pick them up, they didn't mind, they let you do that. One of them was a teeny owl maybe three centimetres tall, with blue eyes, all fluffy and super-cute, and it was sat in the palm of her hand looking up at her? Bless.

Busy day today. People booking in suddenly. She's had three, no four, clients this week so far who've said, 'Cut it really short this time.' Because everyone thinks there's going to be another lockdown. If she could, Star would give everyone a tiny bird, their favourite choice of bird – robin, parakeet, skylark or— No, that's crazy, because what would they do with it? They'd be stressing over would it get accidentally squashed? Or they'd be thinking, Oh God, now I've got to look after this tiny bird as well. I mean, what does it even eat? Forget that idea. But she'd like to give them *something* to make everything not so bad.

Jane is one of those clients who asked for a short crop at Hair Works, on her way to the station after her weekly face-to-face teaching session. It's a bit breezy round the back of her neck as she waits for her train home. Still no major outbreaks at Poundstretcher, but Lindford's infection rate is the highest in Lindfordshire. If anyone drags the region into Tier 2, it's going to be Lindford. And without blaming all young people in a simplistic knee-jerk way, there's enough anecdotal evidence of large parties for Jane to join the statistical dots.

I daresay you're wondering what was in the boxes in the boot of Jane's car. What glimpses will they provide into what she was like as a child? We have observed on occasion that Jane sees something of her younger self in Leah Rogers. Perhaps the boxes contained journals from when young Jackie Rossiter suffered year-long crushes on older boys so inaccessible and unavailable they might as well have been David Cassidy himself. The latter's name did adorn the covers of primary school rough books, but none of these are extant in the archive. Unlike Star's mum, Eileen Rossiter was not one to hang on to a load of rubbish for sentimental reasons. So what has endured the ravages of time? Young Jackie was never a great journal keeper. There's a Letts Schoolgirl Diary from 1973, but it peters out mid-March and offers little insight into her life, beyond recording netball scores, adventures on garage roofs, and revealing that her favourite school dessert was treacle pudding.

I daresay Jane made various Mothering Sunday and Easter cards, but her mother apparently didn't keep them. But she did keep text-books, school reports and Jane's Oxford exhibition offer letter. Of course she did. To her credit, she also kept the letters and postcards Jane sent home from college roughly once a week (1979 to 1982), in chronological order. The different years are separated now by with-ered elastic bands. The evolution of Jackie into Jane can be charted in the shift from floral notepaper, via plain blue Basildon Bond, to Conqueror laid ivory. Jane has dipped into them. It's like reading a tedious unedited first draft of an epistolary Bildungsroman. Or one half of it. Her mother's replies do not survive.

Rather thrillingly, the collection also includes an old Saxone shoebox of ephemera, and a jackdaw file of photos. This is what sparked the most joy in Jane's heart. Let's struggle into our time-travelling wings and fly back to the moment last week when Jane interrupted the Bishop of Barcup's inbox-wrangling.

'Look at this,' said Jane.

Matt stared at the six-inch perspex dome balanced on his keyboard. Skinny toy cat inside. Velvet. One remaining green diamante eye, a pearl necklace, and something green and feathery going on in the tail department. Matt raised his eyes and checked Jane's face for clues.

'It's a cat,' he ventured.

'That is not just an ordinary cat, my friend. *That* is a Sophisticat!'

'Oka-a-ay.'

'A Max Factor Sophisticat! The pinnacle of my childhood covet-ousness. I begged for one, *begged*, I tell you. But Mum said they were a waste of money. She always bought me a nice book instead. So Aunty Betty got me one for Christmas. It came holding a little bottle of Hypnotique perfume. Which I never used, just sniffed and swooned. I was saving it for . . . I don't know what. Heaven? Wonder where it got to? You have *no idea* how magical this cat was. I can tell from your glazed expression. So I'm going to show you a selection of photos instead.'

'Hang on.' Matt lifted the perspex dome off the cat and examined it. Faint bells ringing. Maybe the big girls at school had them? Older cousins? Which reminded him. 'Crazy foam. And those drinking birds,' he said. 'Remember them? You balanced them on a glass.'

'Good grief! Yes, I do.' Jane laughed. 'Hey, I bet you had a chopper bike.'

'Certainly did.' He replaced the dome. His eyes darted to his computer screen. 'You said photos.'

'Yes. Come and sit on your episcopal interrogation sofa and look at them properly.'

His eyes darted to the clock. 'All righty.'

They sat. Jane gave a shiver. 'The very leather is impregnated with the cortisol of terrified clergy!'

'It's PVC,' said Matt. 'And I give it a wipe between sessions.'

'Very compliant of you.' Jane opened the folder. Matt stifled a tiny sigh. She knuckled his leg. 'I'm not going to make you look at all of them, you bastard. Pretend to be interested. OK. Me as a baby.'

'Hey, Silver Cross pram. Classic. Made myself a cracking go-kart out of a Silver Cross chassis once. Decent bit of kit.' The photo was whisked from his hand. '*And* you were a cute baby.'

'No. Too late. Here's me and Mum at Alum Bay. I didn't have enough money to buy a coloured-sand souvenir, so I collected sand samples with Sellotape and stuck them on a plain postcard.'

'You look like your mum.'

'Wrong answer.'

'You look nothing like your mum.'

'I know! I look like my dad. Here.'

Matt studied the blurry black and white photo. Guy standing in front of a car. Austin Somerset, judging by the grille and headlights. Kind face. Nice smile. Dark eyes like Janey, but that's as far as it went. He looked weary. 'Older than her?'

'Yes. He died when I was five. He was a boiler worker, so probably asbestosis. I wish I remembered him better. He taught me rude songs.' She laughed her filthy laugh. 'Singing Nelly hold your belly next to mine!'

306

'Any wedding photos?'

'Nope. It was a small ceremony. And I was never interested in any of that, of course.'

'Really?'

'So my mum always told me. "Oh, you don't want to know all that ancient history, Jackie."' Jane put her hand to her mouth and muttered sideways, 'I was already on the way.'

'Ah! Big-bouquet ceremony. I get you.'

She brought out another picture. 'The young schoolgirl.'

'Pah ha ha! I like the plaits. Hope the tooth fairy came.'

'In my house it was a ha'penny for the first tooth, and then nothing. And now, finally – after which I will let you get back to your inbox – a work entitled "The Working-Class Girl Makes Good". Ah ah – wait for it. Our hero sets off for scenes of Oxford triumph, in a nice frock, perm and white stilettos. Here.'

Matt studied the photo for a long time. 'Nineteen-eighty?'

'Seventy-nine.'

'I was thirteen,' he said. 'I'd've definitely followed you round showing off and trying to impress you.'

'By showing me your chopper?'

I will whisk you away, reader, as this scene is about to descend into the kind of vulgarity that I know some of you refuse to believe an Anglican bishop is capable of.

Moon Phase
Last Quarter (49%)

So Leah and me were gardening this afternoon, we were racking leaves because leafblower's are bad for the environment plus they make noise pollution. We racked them into the corner because we are going to make compost, it is more sustainable than burning the leaves, burning them releases CO2 plus there might be a hedgehog hibernating and it would burn to death.

So I looked up, it was a blue sky, and there was the half moon. This reminded me that YET AGAIN I totally forgot to do my moonbathing ritual. What am I even like???? SMH. FORTUNATLY I will get another chance at the end of the month because its the BLUE MOON. Then I can say that I do a ritual bath 'once in a blue moon'!!!!! LOL. To be fair one of my intention's was to own a clarinet of my own and that has been granted. I so so so wish it was back from the menders, it will be another week probably. I will practice on my school clarinet while I wait and I wont lie to you, it sounds better, it does not squeek. But my own clarinet will be super awesome when its been overhauled.

<u>*My other full moon bath intentions will be*</u>

1. That mum and dad get remarried to eachother by Christmas, that would be so cool. Leah and me could be BRIDESMAIDS!!!

2. That I will get to do more soloing, fingers crossed I will one day sing the Stanford in G mag, (I already know it back to front) (not literally!!!!)

4. That they find a vaxine for Covid-19

5. That the planet is saved from climate extinction for future generations. P.S. I used this exact same list in conformation class with Mother Virginnia, (obvs I did not share it in the chat, it is personal.) I explained about ritual moonbathing to the group, and Virginnia says in her opinion prayer is similar only you can do it anytime anywhere, its more convenient in a way. I take her point.

Virginia is preparing tomorrow's intercessions. Giving thanks that the US president has made a good recovery (slightly didactic prayer, to remind the congregation that we pray for our enemies). For next week's APCM (informative prayer, to remind the congregation to attend). She hesitates over how to respond prayerfully to the sheer awfulness of the ICSA report. For all victims of—

There's a soft thud. She turns. Oh no!

She washed her French windows this morning, and a bird has just flown into the glass. Virginia slides the door open and steps on to the patio. It's a goldcrest. She crouches beside it. There's no movement. She gets her phone out and checks what to do. Google says not to try to pick it up. To wait a minute or two and see if it's just stunned. Please don't let it die. Maybe it's already dead. So tiny. Oh, I'm so sorry.

Another minute, then she'll gently touch it. All she can do is stay and keep watch, in case next door's cat finds it. She starts to cry. Ridiculous that something like this can tip you over the edge. She's been battling her low mood all week. If you're feeling miserable, do something useful, Virginia. It almost worked. Cheerful sunshine through clean windows! Then that soft little thud. Her mother's voice has fallen silent. In a moment it will regroup, and start suggesting she should have thought of this. She ought to have bought some stickers to put on the glass. She should have shut the curtains. *Should*, Virginia. *Ought*, Virginia.

I can't do this, Jesus. I can't. I've got nothing left. I can't hold it together any more. I've run out of wine. There's a wedding at Cana, and there's no more wine.

Is it viable, this faith of ours? What if we run out of everything? Maybe we should all retrain as atheists and agnostics . . . If religion were an add-on, and God wasn't deep in our DNA. If the six stone jars weren't lined up outside in the dark, waiting.

Hunter's Moon, Part III

Neil is out running. *They that wait upon the LORD shall renew their strength.* Ha, you can take the boy out of Sunday school . . . *They shall mount up with wings as eagles.* Wouldn't mind. Pair of wings. Fly up this hill. He slows another notch and glances ahead. The top is in sight. Eyes down. Keep going, Fergie. There's another couple of runners behind him, chatting as they jog, if you please, and gaining all the time. But he's not proud. It's not a competition. He'll just plod on at his own pace, and let the youngsters scamper past. They'll be laughing on the other side of their smug young faces when they're his age.

But flying, though. Saw that new mountain rescue kit on the BBC – paramedics zipping across the Lake District in a jet-suit. Boyhood dream. *They shall run, and not be weary.* There was that homemade parachute once, mind you. Old tarpaulin. Let his pal Murray test drive it – off the shed roof. Broke his collarbone. 'If Neil Ferguson told you to jump off a cliff, would you do it, eh?' Well, that incident took the wind out of adult sails everywhere. Because there were boys daft enough to do just that.

Here we go. They're about to power past him. But no matter. *Even the youths shall faint and be weary, and the young men shall utterly fall.*

'Morning!'

'Morning!'

They prance by. White haired. High-vis shirts. Skinny matchstick legs, like a pair of mountain goats. It's come to this. Overtaken by day-glo fecking pensioners! The shame! But have *they* just landed a contract to revamp Turlham Hall boutique hotel and bespoke wedding venue, a hidden gem nestling in the heart of unspoiled Lindfordshire countryside? He thinks not. *And* he could take the both of them in a fight, while playing 'A Gordon for Me' on Uncle Jock's ukulele with one arm tied behind his back. (*If* he wasn't a licensed reader in the Church of England.) Och, it's no good. He stops, hands on knees, at the hill's summit, panting. He's really let himself go. This was going to be the year he turned it round. Got a grip, got into shape again. But along came lockdown, and all diet and fitness bets were off.

He straightens up and gazes round. You can see for miles up here. Villages dotted about. All the wee churches Ed looks after. Spires, towers above the trees. At the bottom of the hill, the red phone kiosk he's never persuaded Ed into. (Poor Ed regrets ever divulging that fantasy.) There's the Linden down there. Patch of water shining, off in the distance. He can hear guns popping like fireworks. Either they're bagging a helluva lot of birds, or they're really shite hunters.

Off again. His legs skitter about like Bambi on ice. Kinnel! Lungs wheezy as a broken football pump. Least it's downhill now. The geriatrics disappear round the bend in the road ahead. Coming up the slope towards him is the big blonde lassie, puffing and blowing. Each time he sees her, she's looking a bit more into it, a wee bit less like death. Couch to 5K probably. They grin and gasp 'Morning!' as they pass one another.

Then a voice in Neil's head surprises him: Are you enjoying the body I've given you?

Well. It's not so bad for fifty-five, thanks. Aye, it's all right, this body. In fact, it's still pretty amazing when you stop to think – all these years, never failed him. Heart still pumping. He needs reading glasses, maybe, but lungs, joints, digestion, nads and plumbing – even his liver. (Good work under heavy fire, Sergeant Liver!) We've had a lot of fun, the body and me. He's running downhill laughing now, and the auld pair and the big blonde seem pretty amazing too – the variety, all these different riffs on the same theme, no two alike and every hair counted.

He sticks his arms out like a kid in the playground being the Bloody Red Baron, and belts down the long slope towards the church and home. Knackers the knees, but so what? If it turns out there's no flying in heaven, he'll be having serious words with the Almighty. Here comes Ed in the silver vicar-mobile. Neil machine-guns him and sticks up two fingers. The car slows. A window slides down. SHIT!

'*So* sorry, Mrs Logan. I thought you were my husband.'

Mrs Logan laughs. '*That's* all right then. Do I gather Leo and Jennifer . . .'

'Aye! They've asked me. Thanks for putting in a good word.'

'You're welcome. Bye bye!'

She's laughing as she drives off. Rachel's going to *love* this story! She keeps saying how much she's missing the Gayden soap opera, now she's back in her own house.

Mrs Logan is heading for her wedding barn in Itchington Episcopi, with a boot full of ivy garlands, fairy lights, hessian bunting and newspaper flowers for tomorrow's scaled-down socially distanced reception of fifteen. Her clients have been absolute stars. No whinging. Just grateful they can get married and have *some* kind of a celebration. No thinking the rules don't apply to their special day. I regret to say that Mrs Logan experiences a fierce glow every time she reads about the police shutting down another wedding with a hundred guests, and fining the venue £10,000. She doesn't like herself for feeling vindictive, but it's so hard when you're killing yourself to keep the rules and other people are just flouting them.

Parva's horrified face just now, though! Mrs Logan hoots with laughter and bangs the steering wheel. To think how worried she and Malcolm were when they moved in last year! Picturing some pious twit for a neighbour. Praying for their souls, and his bossy wife popping round night and day, pestering them to donate to the jumble sale or whatever. The Gaydens never fail to entertain. Turlham Hall will keep Parva out of mischief. Jennifer's always been a bit of a Pollyanna – seeing the pandemic as a ma-aarvellous opportunity to refresh the dated 1990s decor, rather than the truth. That the bottom has fallen out of the hospitality sector, and we may never recover.

312

So sorry, Mrs Logan. I thought you were my husband! She hoots again as she parks up in front of the old tithe barn and gets out. It's the kind of laughter that could easily overbalance into tears, but at least there's *something* to laugh at. And we're still hanging on in Tier 1, thank God. Unless the government goes for a circuit-breaker lockdown, the rest of the weddings up to Christmas will be fine. So long as she and Malcolm stay well. The Eye Hospital isn't risk-free, but at least it's not intensive care. This winter's going to be tough, really tough. If he'd made a different choice back in medical school . . . She takes a steadying breath. The hawthorn hedge is bright with berries. There's the soothing waterfall sound of the breeze in the aspen grove. Always good for the blood pressure. The leaves – still green – dance on their stems. A flock of long-tailed tits twitters past. Well, well. It's not all bad.

It isn't all bad for Virginia, either. We left her in despair, crouched over a dead goldcrest on her patio. There was an outside chance that it was only stunned, so Virginia did what Google advised. She lined a shoebox with cotton wool, gently picked up the poor little scrap in a tea towel, and put it in the box. It was dead all right, but she put the lid on anyway – having carefully made air holes with a screwdriver first. She carried the box inside and placed it on the kitchen table (a quiet, warm, dark place away from activity). Then she got a grip and went back to her study to finish off her intercessions.

Before long her mother's voice piped up to tick her off for being a bit silly and self-indulgent back there, and to remind her that there were plenty of people far worse off. I KNOW THERE ARE! I'm sorry. I've got nobody to talk to. I'm desperately lonely, and I'm just *so tired*.

Well, I'm tired too. We're *all* tired, Virginia.

Virginia paused in the very act of setting up a Zoom Annual Parochial Church Meeting. The voice had broken cover. It was not possible to imagine that the inner prompting of the Spirit would sound so tetchy, so much like Mum on a bad day, bless her. Come to think of it, wasn't rather a lot of what went on in Virginia's head more like inner nagging than inner prompting? It was. For heaven's sake! How come she'd never spotted that before? She wouldn't dream

313

of talking to an unhappy parishioner that way, so why did she talk to herself like this?

Virginia leant back in her office chair and closed her eyes. She rested her hands, palms upturned, on her thighs. *What would I say if someone came to me and said, 'I feel like there's a wedding in Cana, and I've run out of wine'? Well, I certainly wouldn't say, 'It's your own fault. You should've thought of that. I told you to get more wine!' So what* would *I say?*

After a moment, the words came to her. Mary's words. The perfect disciple, as Father Dominic always said. 'Do whatever he tells you.' *That's all. It may look impossible. There may still be hard work ahead, wrestling big heavy jars down to the well and back. It could be that most people are blissfully unaware of the crisis, and only the faithful servants know what's happening. And it might still look like water in the glass until the last possible moment. Do whatever he tells you. When you've run out of everything, and turn to him in despair, that's when the miracle happens.*

Virginia opened her eyes. *That's* what I'd say. And then I'd say, 'How about a cup of tea?' She wiped her eyes and went through to the kitchen. She had just filled the kettle when she heard a tiny fluttering in the shoebox. Her heart leapt. It was alive! *Oh, thank you, thank you!* She picked the box up and carried it carefully out into the garden. It was getting dark. There were voices and laughter next door. The neighbours had family round again. She placed the box on her little patch of lawn, and took the lid off. The bird was sitting up now, not lying. It watched her with a tiny bright eye.

'Go,' she breathed. 'Fly.'

Her phone buzzed. A text. It would wait.

The goldcrest gave a little flutter, and rapidly preened its chest feathers. Then almost too fast for Virginia to follow, it was off, over the wall towards the trees at the end of the street.

Her phone buzzed again. She picked up the shoebox and checked the message as she walked back to the house. It was Dominic. Bother. He'd be wanting the Zoom link for the APCM.

Fr Dominic: Hello Mother Gin. I've been pondering this for ages and trying to find a way of asking.

314

He wanted her to resign!

> **So I'm just going to come out with it. Would you like to join me and mum in our bubble? Have a think. No rush, and it's fine to say No. Dxx**

Well, I'm very glad for Virginia – who texted back immediately to say *YES PLEASE!* I'm glad for all three of them. There were hugs and tears and Prosecco in the vicarage that evening, let me tell you. And because Dominic and Virginia are such nice people, there was self-recrimination that neither of them had broached the subject before. But perhaps they had saved the best wine till now? They had to navigate the inevitable Groundhog Day conversations with Mrs Todd about pandemics and social bubbles. They agreed repeatedly that yes, it was a bit like Eyam. Naturally, Virginia was not going to move in with Dominic and his mum. That would not be appropriate. But she could stay late, and pop in whenever she liked. And she could invite them round for a meal. Tomorrow! Sunday lunch! Settled. Goody-good! They ordered a Deliveroo Lebanese meal, and settled down to watch *Top Hat* on iPlayer. It didn't matter a bit that every twenty minutes Mrs Todd observed that Ginger Rogers did everything Fred Astaire did, only backwards and in high heels.

Behold, how good and pleasant it is. Good company and spreading the load are how we are going to make it up the long hill of COVID-19. Virginia has been shouldering the burden of funerals at Lindford Parish Church since lockdown. Now Father Dominic will be able to take his turn and try to manage those occasions when eighty mourners turn up, and he can only allow thirty into church. He will be the one trying to turn a blind eye to the mingling and mask-less hugging going on in the graveyard, and a deaf ear to conversations about the wake that will follow.

Moon Phase
New Moon 0%
Moon Myths
So some of the girls at school say that you get your period at the new moon. I asked mum and she said no, that's an old wive's tail. Unfortunately Leah appeared at that exact same moment and she went That is so sexist, why are you gender stereotyping older women?

so mum went Oh my mistake, I meant to say it's a load of bollocks, is that better? Then <u>dad</u> *came in, which was embarassing I mean is it too much to ask just to want a private conversation with your mum????? They don't respect my privacy plus they all think they are funny e.g. dad preceded to say That is sexist as well, you are using the male anatomy in a derogatry way, nobody says a load of old ovaries, I rest my case. Long story short, the girls at school are wrong. Another time I will just google it and save myself the hastle. I'm going to* ***

I put those asterixes there because I totally forget what I was going to write because Leah came in. She said she could see I was upset and sorry if she upset me. Then she said do not listen to the other girls, or if you do listen you have to fact-check. So I said FYI that's what I was <u>TRYING TO DO</u> *only you were all being really annoying? Then I only burst into tears 'again'. She put her arm round me and said sorry again, and I kept trying to say its not about that its about everything. Like everything is so horrible, Covid is getting out of control and that teacher in France, only I was crying too much, like hiccup crying if that makes sense. I could not stop thinking to myself, what if it was one of my teachers (like Mr H-M) just walking home and some islamist terrorist cut their head off?*

So Leah was all, come on we are going for a run, trust me you will feel better after. Promise I wont go too fast. Then she said, listen if you come I will show you a thing on tiktok, you will love it. Long story short, we went running in the arbo (I won't lie, it <u>totally killed</u>*), and 'the thing' was Mr H-M lip-sinking President Trump like Sarah Cooper does only in this super 'gay' way, and inbetween its him and his chickens plus Alfie (Luna's brother) singing 'If I only had a* ~~brian~~ *brain' off Wizard of Oz, ROTFPML. Seriously, I do not know how he even does that? Like is there an app?*

So anyway now my mood and wellbeing are better, so I will love you and leave you, because next up, Leah and me are making. . . . vegan chocolate mug cakes in the microwave YUM!!!!! (Fingers crossed LOL)

'Ha ha! How do you *do* this?' asks Chloe. 'Is that actually the girls, or is it just you making chicken noises?'

'Hey. Pur-leese. It's totally the girls. And Alfie? So I record them, build a tune from the sound files, harmonize? Yeh, so basically I cut and mix, fool around, add stuff, then do an edit, if that makes sense?'

'Well, I hope you're not planning a trip to the States anytime soon,' she says. 'They check your social media before they let you in, you know.'

'No worries, babe. Coz Biden's gonna win. What?'

'Nothing,' says Ambrose. 'Ready?'

'Two seconds. Brush my teeth?' He races up the stairs three at a time.

Chloe looks at Ambrose. 'All the polls put Biden ahead,' she says. 'Holy Mary Mother of God! You don't seriously think Trump's going to get another term?'

'Who knows? He's been busy laying the foundations for claiming voter fraud.'

After a moment, she says, 'You . . . sound like you don't care.'

He shrugs.

'Brose, you don't think it's time you—'

'I'm fine.'

'You're really not, though, are you?'

But they can hear Freddie coming back. He vaults over the banister, lands in the hall with a thud, and raises his arms like a gymnast nailing his dismount.

'Ready when you are.' He looks from one to the other. 'What I miss?'

'Nothing.' Ambrose tosses his keys up and catches them. 'Come on. We'll be late.'

It's nearly half-term. Next weekend the clocks will go back, and for days the good people of Lindchester will scare themselves by catching sight of the cooker clock and thinking they're late. If they have anything to be late for. A Zoom meeting, perhaps. Nobody can believe that the end of October is looming already. Halloween – there won't be much trick or treating this year. No parties. Or no legal ones, at any rate. New restrictions inch closer like an ever-tightening net. Manchester fights off Tier 3, trying to get a better deal for the North. What about all those election promises? Wales is about to go into a circuit-breaker lockdown. Maybe that makes sense. Will we look

317

back on this as a missed opportunity? There's a creeping fear that this is going to be March all over again – too little too late. Here we are, obediently wearing our masks and scanning QR codes on our NHS app when we visit the pub, the stately home, the car dealership, the hotel. Is this any better than washing our hands and sanitizing door-knobs, like we obediently did before lockdown – back when masks had no proven medical benefit?

Jane has an opinion on all this as she sits at her desk with a sore neck, gazing at the one-eyed Sophisticat. She's expecting Poundstretcher will have to switch back to online teaching before long. There's a walk-through test site in the Luscombe Sports Hall car park. Handy for Poundstretcher students. Jane sniffs her coffee again, to check she's still got her sense of smell. One of her colleagues has been working from home all term anyway, having been told by HR that she is not to come on to campus under *any* circumstances, because her partner is in the shielding category. The colleague's partner is a teacher at QM Boys' School in Lindford, however, and has been told by the government that he *must* return to work, because schools are COVID-secure. Yeah right. So far multiple year groups at both QM Boys and QM Girls have been sent home to self-isolate for fourteen days after outbreaks. And test and trace is a joke. Operation total moonshine.

But hey, it's nearly half-term. Or rather, Reading Week. Jane will put her feet up and read the latest Marilynne Robinson novel. Then she'll claw back some of those hours of unpaid overtime and make herself a proper family album. She'll begin with the old photos in the jackdaw file, followed by her own (sketchy) collection from Oxford, then the drawerful of Danny pictures she's never got round to sorting through, and finally the wedding and consecration shots. Now there's a proper COVID activity for you, given that she can't be arsed to paint her study or make a patchwork quilt.

Yellow leaves swirl across the road as Freddie and Ambrose drive home from rehearsal. It's starting to rain.

'Look, the reason I'm quiet all the time,' says Ambrose, 'is that I don't want to bring you down too. I'm just, I just . . . struggle with being optimistic, when everything's so . . . It'll pass.'

'I get it, babe. Everything's shit and you're being your best self. So you do you, and don't worry about me, 'K?'

Ambrose doesn't reply. Just nods.

'Hey. Chloe tell you tonight's the night?'

Ambrose nods again.

Freddie reaches over and grips his knee. 'Hey. No worries, babe. I can handle the optimism side of shit. It's gonna be fine, you hear me? Gonna be fine.'

So long as we take it in turns to hit rock bottom, he thinks. He starts to hum the anthem they were just singing. *Many waters cannot quench love, neither can the floods drown it.* Let it be fine. Please. If not this month, then maybe next, or next, or next?

Blue Moon, Part I

Ooh, look at me! thinks Father Dominic as he pulls out of the vicarage drive. This is his first solo trip since goodness knows when. January? February? Bless Mother Gin for offering an afternoon of mother-sitting. He left them tackling Virginia's 500-piece double-sided M&S 'Wellness' jigsaw. Apparently, it was a thoughtful lockdown gift from a dear (happily married) theological college friend, whose heart went out to poor Virginia in her isolated single state. Virginia admitted that until this afternoon she'd felt too affronted and patronized to open it – even though she knew it was kindly meant.

Wellness! What a word. Dominic is heading out to Martonbury for afternoon tea on the palace patio with his old chum Jane. Experience warns him that any wellness package dispensed by Jane is likely to feel more like a brisk slap than a pampering holistic healing retreat. But he's looking forward to it anyway. There's a misty drizzle, but no heavy rain forecast if you look at the right weather app. Afterwards, he's going to pootle across to Gayden Magna, to see Father Ed, and possibly Neil too – if he's not busy at Turlham Hall, consigning the innocent 1990s to the fickle dustbin of fashion.

Talking of things getting binned – poor old Lindford. It looks so down on its luck. Boarded-up windows at the Laser Quest place. Oh Lord, *and* the Steam & Bantam micro pub – gone bust before he even got round to paying a pastoral visit. Metal shutters with scrappy graffiti. Why can't we have decent street art, like Bristol? He drives past an upended sofa on the edge of the industrial estate. You could say poor old Midlands and North of England generally. There's such a sad abandoned feel to things, thinks Dominic. Like a Victorian gold-rush town after the boom has passed. Forget all those fine election promises; it's clearly still London and the South that count. How will things ever recover? Manchester forced into Tier 3, without the financial support Andy Burnham was fighting for. South Yorkshire and Nottingham likewise. And Lindford has just dragged the region into Tier 2. Who knows what this will mean for all the businesses in his patch; for the indoor market!

He snatches his thoughts back. Sufficient unto the day. He knows to look out for this – the longed-for breathing space turning into a worry-bog, greedy to suck him down. No wonder, in all honesty. He's been running and running just to keep ahead of the dreads, and now he's stopped, they're all thudding into him like daggers! No-deal Brexit. US elections. Climate change. He reaches across and turns on the CD player. Bach's *Christmas Oratorio*! Has it really been that long since he was out in the car alone? He switches the radio on instead. Music ripples out, like the lounge of a spa hotel. Ah yes, of course. That would be pre-lockdown Dom, bless him, trying out Smooth Chill Radio to calm himself down. The song ends, and a voice hisses, '*Chill!*' like the basilisk in the pipes at Hogwarts. He turns it off, and starts singing show tunes instead. Happy talk. Keep talking!

It's still drizzly, but Jane's got the episcopal gazebo up to shelter the table and chairs on the terrace. She's done everything in grand ironic style, with a proper teapot under a cosy (shaped like a mitre), china cups and saucers, and a three-tier cake stand groaning with treats. Teeny-tiny sandwiches (supermarket, admittedly, but lovingly cut into triangles), slices of Battenberg, Mr Kipling French fancies, chocolate-finger biscuits, Tunnock's tea cakes.

'Oh!' Dominic's dowager shriek floats over the garden. The bishop hears it from his study, and grins. 'The clouds drop fatness! You're spoiling me, Mrs Bishop!'

'Just like Mother used to open,' says Jane. 'Except she never did. One pack of Penguin biscuits rationed to last the whole of half-term – if I was lucky.'

'But you were happy – *because* you were poor!'

'Oh, how I miss the sweet nostalgia of food poverty.'

Yes, those brisk wellness slaps – always so invigorating. He sits on a wrought-iron patio chair. He planned ahead, clever old stick that he is, and he's in his long winter coat, so that the iron won't enter his soul via his nether regions. These chairs were cold enough in the summer that time he came with Mum after lockdown eased. He gazes round. There's a mound of dead sweet-pea vines stripped from the wall. A few roses nod. The pampas grass wags gently in the breeze.

'You never did hold a swingers' party,' he complains.

'Sez who? Maybe you weren't invited.'

'Oh, I'd've heard, don't you worry.'

'Tea, Vicar?' She pours him a cup, then steps away from the table and gestures. 'Help yourself. I wore rubber gloves, so it's all COVID-secure.' She sits in the other chair two metres away, then leaps up again. 'Bloody Nora! I'm getting a cushion. Want one?'

'I'm fine, thanks.'

'Don't blame me if you get piles.'

'What rubbish,' he says when she gets back. 'You get piles from sitting on radiators. Or is that chilblains? Now then. What's been happening? Tell me everything.'

'First, let's bitch about the government voting down free school meals in the holidays, when MPs' meals are subsidised by public money.'

'Oh God. Must we?'

'Yes. All power to Marcus Rashford's elbow. I had free school meals all through primary school, along with half the class. Then I opted for packed lunch when I went up to the comp, just to escape the stigma – even though it meant I was ravenous the whole time. Marmite sandwiches and an apple. That was it.'

'Darling! No protein? No cheese even?'

'Occasionally. I couldn't moan to Mum, because she'd only point out I *could* have school lunch. So basically, I was the class dustbin, eating everyone's leftovers. Looking back, it was a grisly symbiosis with borderline anorexics on permanent diets.' Jane pauses to chomp a sandwich.

'I had no idea! You've never told me all this before, Janey.'

'Yeah, well, it's called *shame*, Dommie. And as for "virtue signalling"!' Jane has hit her stride now. 'Another conscience-cauterizing product straight from the Department of Useful Platitudes. It replaces "throwing money at the problem" as the go-to method of supressing outbreaks of common decency. I hope you got that memo.'

'Snowflakes aren't on their database, I'm afraid.' He peels the foil off his tea cake. 'Do you object if I nibble all the chocolate off first?'

'That's how we roll here in the palace,' says Jane. 'Then you have to slurp the marshmallow off in one go.'

'If I lick it suggestively, can I come to the next swingers' party?'

'Show me? Ha ha ha! OK. If Sonya-Sonya drops out, promise I'll squeeze you in.'

'Naughty-naughty. Is the ranting over now?'

'—ver-now. Yes.' They smile at one another, and sigh happy sighs. 'It's so good to see you, sweetums.'

'You too, darling. How are you doing? What's new?'

'Ah, now – brace yourself. I have old photos and sixties memorabilia to show you.'

It's half-term in Lindfordshire. Tier 2 means no holidaying in Tier 1 regions. Plans have been adjusted at short notice. Poor Rachel Logan, for example, had been bound for an off-grid Scottish break, but there is no over the sea to Skye for her now. She's ended up back in Gayden Magna at Hotel Mum and Dad – which admittedly is a lot more boutique-y than the croft she'd booked. And she gets the Gayden soap opera thrown in for free, so there's that.

The tier system sounds eminently sensible. Don't stick the whole school in detention because one or two individuals are smoking behind the bike-sheds. Focus the tighter measures in the areas where cases are rising exponentially. But as we saw when Leicester got stuck in lockdown, it's tricky to implement. There are places where it's Tier 2 at one end of the street and Tier 1 at the other. Scotland have a five-tier system, which adds to the fun. Bad luck if you booked a half-term break in Wales, as now they're in a two-week 'firebreak' lockdown, and non-essential travel in and out of Wales is banned. There are houses in the Welsh Borders where one room is actually in England, so technically you could go and stay there. Say what you like about the first lockdown, at least we all understood what we were flouting.

Despite the eminently sensible-sounding tier system, cases rise inexorably. The door of the empty stable creaks in the wind, and Captain Hindsight straightens his epaulettes once again in the Department of Useful Platitudes, ready to be deployed when everyone realizes that the time for a second national lockdown was late September, just like the scientists warned. Bloody scientists, with their *science*. What do they know? Was it not the goddess Rhamnousia herself who once said, 'The people of this country have had enough of experts with organizations with acronyms saying that they know what is best and getting it consistently wrong'? Bloody acronyms, bloody SAGE.

Half Term

I'm not going to lie to you, so far this half term is a big dissapointment, we were going to go and stay with Gran and Grandpops (mums parent's) but they live in Tier 1 in Hartfordshire so it is not allowed We 'could' go and meet them in a park, but at the end of the day it is a long drive to go and see them for like just an afternoon. Dads old boss who is the former ex bishop of Lindchester (bishop Paul) kindly emailed that we could go and stay in their cottage again (like we did before). I was super excited for the cottage but then dad googled it, it turns out it is just over the boarder in Tier 1, I was gutted. Leah was all, that is so dumb! Plus whose even going to know? Mum went 'The rules apply to everyone' and Leah yelled I KNOW THAT FFS and went out for a run. Long story short we are having a Staycation here in Lindford.

Mum is doing her best to keep our spirits up, we are carving pumpkins for Halloween. We are also doing a spooky window display, it will look cool, but there is no trick or treat this year. I am sad for all the little kids who will be gutted they can't get a shedload of sweets off people. FYI Leah and me did not go out trick or treating when we were young, we were not allowed because dad was all about All Saints Day instead, we had to go to the Light Party and dress up as saints and heroes and not celebrate evil. Plus you've got to remember elderly frail people who get petrified by people banging on there doors in scary masks. I totally get this, but part of me was always jealous even if it is cool to dress up like an angel. Leah obviously had to under-mine it by going as Judith with fake blood everywhere and a severed head but nobody could complain, it is in the Bible (well the ~~apochrophor~~ apocrypher????).

But at the end of the day, we are in the middle of a global pandemic, it is important to remember this perspective. Plus it is good to look on the bright side and accentuate the positive, so guess what . . . ???? My clarinet is overhauled and mum and me went to collect it, it sounds AMAZING!!! I have made great strides (NB my teacher says this, I'm not being bigheaded or anything), soon I will be learning the upper register, I've been watching all these YouTube clips about going over the break so I will be ready when the time comes. It is good to have 'an attitude of gratitude' so I am super grateful we are not in lockdown like they are in Wales. If we lived in Wales I could not of collected my clarinet till after lockdown, because music shops are 'none essential', even if Music is actually essential for wellbeing. That is what Mr H-M always says and I for one agree with him.

Moon Facts

Another thing I am grateful for is the Blue Moon. The blue moon is literally full on Halloween itself (NB this is rare), so not only is it a full moon for Halloween it is a full blue moon, that is super rare and will not happen again in my lifetime. I keep checking the forecast to see if it will be a clear sky. So far so good finger's crossed!!!

Jane clears away the tea things, then goes back to the dining room, where she's sorting through the photos for her family album. A posh book has arrived from Etsy, with marbled paper covers. May as well do the job properly. She opens the old envelope containing pictures of her parents from before she was born. A couple of Dad with an old car. A Morris of some kind? Matt will know. A series of Mum on her own and with two other young women. Audrey Hepburn slacks and headscarf. Quite a looker, back in the 50s. There's a patch of water behind, possibly a pier. Where? A holiday? Day trip to Scarborough? She turns them over to see if there are any clues. Nope. Even more tantalizingly, one of them has been cut in half. Ha, this doesn't altogether surprise Jane – Mum excising someone for failing her loyalty test. Three strikes and you were out, in Eileen Rossiter's friendship book. It seems to be from a separate roll of film, mind you. The finish is different. Another occasion, despite the same headscarf?

325

Matt comes in. 'Deliveroo?'

'To be honest, I'm still stuffed to the gills with French fancies,' says Jane. 'I'd be happy with cheese on toast.'

'All righty. How's it going?' He leans over and looks at the photos. 'Oh, still sorting through. What kind of car is this?'

'Austin Somerset.' Matt reaches out and picks up one of the seaside photos. 'Is this Mum?'

'Yes. I wish I knew where. Scarborough?'

'Hmm.' Matt studies the others. Then taps one. 'That looks like a ferry.'

'Aha! Isle of Wight, maybe?'

'Nope, too small. Looks like a river ferry.' He straightens up. 'Right. Well, I'm having a beer, anyway. Want one?'

'Yes please.' She squints at the picture, trying to make something new come into focus. Matt's humming in the kitchen, 'Ferry Cross the Mersey'. Everything slows down. How weird, she observes. Everything's slowing down. Like a déjà vu. Or as if she's about to make a momentous discovery. She waits. Something Cousin Elaine said? Then Matt comes back with the beer and everything's normal again.

Father Dominic and Father Ed have decided to go for a walk round the little lanes of Gayden Magna. They can't meet up indoors, and it's getting a bit nippy for sitting in the garden. Once Dominic has properly admired the potagerie, they set off with Bear. Bear has found an abandoned face mask in the gutter to subdue.

'That dog is as daft as Lady, bless him,' says Dominic.

'I know. Drop it. Good boy.' Bear just pants and grins, mask dangling from his jaws. 'Oh, for God's sake. Drop it!'

'Have you caught up with the whole "COVID companion" thing?' asks Dominic. 'Pedigree puppy prices going through the roof, all kinds of skulduggery with puppy smuggling and illegal farms – not to mention flat-out scamming!'

'God yes. Neil's on high alert for dog-nappers.'

'Ha ha! It would be like that O. Henry story,' says Dominic. 'They'd end up paying *you* to take Bear off their hands.'

'Yes, you and I know that, Father. But Neil still believes the sun shines out of Bear's furry backside. He completely spoils him. See?

Now I'm going to have to bribe him.' Bear relinquishes his treasure in exchange for a treat. Ed picks the mask up in a poo bag. 'How are things in Lindford? I keep seeing headlines about student parties.'

Dominic sighs. 'Well, most of them have probably had COVID now, so I can see their frustration, poor lambs. Pubs and what have you closing at ten, so they just party elsewhere. But in general, everything's just so . . . I don't know. Sad and empty.'

They walk on in silence. The sky is inky, yet the light is astounding. The grass verge is emerald, and the low sun sets the trees ablaze, yellow, red, bronze. Beyond the low hedge, the rainy fields look like sheets of brushed white gold. The sandstone walls of Gayden Magna Church glow through the graveyard chestnut trees, as though they're wafer thin and radiant from inside with a thousand thousand hidden candles.

'There's going to have to be another lockdown, isn't there?' says Ed.

'Yes. Maybe they'll do it now, and then lift it a bit for Christmas.'

'God, I hope they don't ban us from going into church again. They won't, will they?'

'Probably not, this time round.' They pass under a horse chestnut tree. Dominic kicks a conker along the road, and Bear races off after it. 'Oh God, it's all so shit, Father. Everything's shit. Trump's going to get another term – I know it in my bones. Sorry.' He stops and blows his nose. 'Just had to say it. I spend all my time staying positive for Mum.'

'It *is* shit, Father.' He reaches out. 'Virtual hug.'

'Thanks.'

They walk on. With each passing moment the sky blackens, yet the light intensifies. Bear padding on ahead seems to be a blaze of copper, like an uncanny CGI labradoodle projected on the wet country road.

'Look at that!' says Dominic. 'There should be a rainbow.'

They pause and gaze all around. In the distance three wind turbines turn, white, white, biblically white, whiter than any fuller on earth could bleach them. Dominic and Ed look at one another in wonder. Then the church carillon starts playing like a giant solemn musical box.

'It's mended!' cries Dominic.

'Yes. Didn't I tell you?'

Abide with me, fast falls the eventide.

'Oh God,' says Dominic. 'Who had to go and choose that?' Tears start to roll down his face.

Ed gestures helplessly. 'It plays "When Morning Gilds the Skies" at nine a.m. too.'

The old friends stand in the lane two metres apart, with the miraculous dog still blazing, all unaware of his glory. Then Ed begins to sing along. After a moment, Dominic joins him. Softly at first, then loudly. Their voices carry over the fields.

> I fear no foe, with thee at hand to bless
> Ills have no weight, and tears no bitterness
> Where is death's sting? Where, grave, thy victory?
> I triumph still, if thou abide with me.

The final notes chime and fade. A flock of pigeons rises, wings winking, above the stand of trees on the rim of the hill. A faint smudge of smoky colour hugs the horizon.

'There's your rainbow,' says Ed.

'Such as it is.'

'It will be all right, Father. In the end.'

'I know, Father.'

The moon rises over Lindfordshire. The sun is setting, but still it transfigures the white letters chalked over the vicarage door in Gayden Magna: 20+C+B+M+20.

Blue Moon, Part II

Storm Aiden sweeps towards Lindfordshire, inaugurating the 20/21 storm season. In the good old days, weather was just weather, and Real Men laughed in the face of nameless storms. Nowadays, the names are selected by the meteorological agencies of the UK, Ireland and the Netherlands, from ideas submitted by the public. Well, you know the British public as well as I do, and won't be surprised to hear that a great number of Stormy McStormface-type suggestions didn't make it to the final cut. There will be no Storm 'Gnasher' or 'In a Teacup'. The alphabet waits ahead of us unused, from Bella to Wilson. How many will we get through? There's no saying, but we will doubtless end as we began, with storms bookending the drama of 2020.

Meanwhile, the moon does its own sweet thing. It's never a ghostly galleon tossed upon stormy seas – not really. That's just our geocentric poetical conceit. It waxes and wanes as heedless of our weather as it is of our calendar months. In 2020, there's a full moon at the interface where October meets November; the hinge between Halloween and All Saints, darkness and light. Come with me, and we will fly across the Diocese of Lindchester in the liminal light of this Blue Moon. At midnight, your witchy broomstick will melt away. But just as you think you are going to fall, a set of angel's wings will sprout from your weary aching shoulders. You will flex feathers of pure light; you will fly and never be weary, and trail fireworks of glory as you pass. (Unless you are a biblical pedant, of course. In which case you will have six wings like the seraphim, one set covering your mouth to prevent you from saying *Actually*.)

Look! See how the Blue Moon shines on the wet roads and lanes below us, turning them into rivers of mercury. Poor old Lindford, down on its luck, with its tower blocks and student halls, and the derelict Station Hotel. The hospitals, care homes, COVID test centres, rotting sofas on trading estates and the vast hangar of Mammon. Martonbury, with its posh little shops and quaint butter market, its Tudorbethan mansions and episcopal pampas grass. Cardingforth, braced for more floods, where the cooling towers send up smoke signals of the Apocalypse. Risley Hill (creepy vicar now moved on). The suburban sprawl of Martonbury, all neat hedges and fences, and net curtains drawn on many a secret. The Gaydens great and small. Turlham, with pretty churches and farms, and rows of gentrified labourers' cottages, and affordable housing for local people in the nearby town of Erewhon.

Further afield now, at the edges of the diocese, look down on the scalped hillsides of sheep-grazing and grouse-shooting, and streams boiling brown and furious. Ingregham Palace, now a luxury hotel and golf course, where once the bishops of Lindchester entertained kings and queens with ruinous banquets of bustards and peacocks and swans. And at the heart of everything, shining in our darkest dark, lies Lindchester itself, a city on a hill, where all the old pilgrim routes lead. It's all still here. This dear, dear land I've cobbled together out of memory and longing, with its toile de Jouy-ified colonial history; this England, this Laodicea, where now and then we catch a puzzling knock-knock at the door of our imaginations – what *is* that? Is it just the wind? Are we still safe?

Moon Facts
Full Moon 99%
Moon Age 15.1 days
So I saw the 'Blue Moon' last night YAY!!!!! There is a storm, 'Storm Aiden' and I was scared it would be too cloudy and I would miss the full moon and my ambition to see all the full moon's of 2020 would fail. It was shinning brightly behind some thin cloud, I could hear firework's going off and some little kids being super excited for Halloween.

Then I heard the owls hooting, it is a shivery sound if that makes sense?

This time I did not forget the 'Full Moon Ritual Bath', I just decided not to do it. Just because you say your going to do something does not mean you have to do it, I can be empowered to say 'I changed my mind'. Obvs it is good to be the kind of person you can rely on, like if I promise someone else I will go to there party or if I promise mum I will empty the dishwasher, that's different. It was a huge relief to me to realise I can change my mind, it does not make me a bad person. Plus anyway, moon baths are pagan and I for one am not a pagan, I am going to get confirmed, probably next year now, it all depends on guess what??? Covid-19. Mother Virginnia says we will have to wait and see because . . . .

That's right, there is going to be another lockdown ☺. It is starting on Thursday, the prime ministor announced this, he was late and mum went typical, but eventually he announced it. I am not going to lie, it is truly scarey, there could be 4000 deaths per day, it will be worse than March if we don't have another lockdown. Plus now there is this whole other virus in Denmark, it is from minx, and they are having to put like millions of them down, and it is all humanities fault for wanting fur coats, I mean what are people even like? I for one agree with Leah here.

So today was our last choral service (it is All Saint's so it was sung eucharist not evensong), it is so so sad. From Thursday churches and the cathedral will have to not do public worship again unless its livestreaming. Livestreaming is problematical for the cathedral, don't ask me why, it is to do with 'public performance rites' so now they can only do none-choral services. This is super disappointing and Ellie wanted her and me to ask Mr H-M privately after rehearsal what's going on, but I stopped her because I was nervous, it was like a massive row had happened? I have antenni for that, if you happen to have parents who got divorced you are super good at knowing these things and you know to be tactfull. Hopefully we can have choral services after lockdown ends, it ends on December 2nd so hopefully we can be back to sing the Christmas services finger's crossed.

Blue Moon facts

You may be surprised to learn that blue moons only happen on 30th or 31st of the month. However this is logical in actual fact, the lunar

331

cycle is 29.5 days, so if you are going to try and fit two full moons in the month you have to have one right at the beginning and one at the end. But get this, in times of your, they did blue moons differently, it was calculated by seasons not by months. Each season, like for example spring or summer, had 3 full moons. Sometimes though there would be 4, and then the third one was called blue moon. Don't ask me why it was the 3rd one, you'd think it would be the 4th I don't make up the rules, I only google them LOL.

Mrs Logan has surprised herself and actually gone to church for once. She'd intended just to pop in and add some names to the All Souls RIP list for Malcolm – not quite such a lapsed Catholic after all, are we, darling? She didn't say that. When you've lost a good colleague to COVID, any port in the storm. Maybe it was the carillon playing 'Abide with Me' every bloody afternoon that wore her down and made her want to stay for the service. Or else it was cumulative despair and weariness. All those cancelled weddings, just when she'd begun to unclench and hope again. Well, whatever. Here she is in the parish church, in her mask, on a slippery laminated sign taped to the pew: *You Can Sit Here*. There's about a dozen others dotted about in the gloom. Candles flicker. The wind roars outside in the huge graveyard trees.

She follows the words on the paper sheet, but doesn't join in. She's not a believer, but now and then it just feels good to go and warm your hands at the fire of someone else's belief, even if (ssh) they're totally deluded. Christmas, she usually rocks up to church for that, to sing the carols and hear the old (fairy) story again, and it's comforting, the way home is, or childhood memories, and old songs, old friends. Probably cheating, eating the icing and not bothering with the boring stale-cake bit of church life, but there we are. She'll be able to report back to Rachel on Magna's performance too.

Oh God, now it's the sermon. She shifts and crosses her legs. She likes Father Ed a lot, she wants to think well of him, but what if it's toe-curlingly awful? Don't let it be like those receptions where the nervous best man brays out a string of inappropriate jokes, while the guests are visibly praying, 'Please let this end.' She's witnessed that often enough, waiting to clear the tables so her staff can get off home. If only she could mute him.

In the end, it's not so bad. Short, at least. He tells them about walking with a friend last week, and everything was lit up with a glorious light, and then they heard the carillon. Aha, I noticed that too, she thinks. The hawthorn berries. The white paint on the old dovecote. Mrs Logan feels her toes uncurling.

'We stood in the lane and joined in,' Father Ed is saying. 'Where is death's sting? Where, grave, thy victory? I triumph still, if thou abide with me.'

He goes on to talk about the saints in glory, and the three Christians martyred just days ago in Nice. Things are dark, he says. No shit, Sherlock, thinks Mrs Logan. She doesn't need him to list them, thanks. Extremism. The divisive US presidential election. This horrifying second wave. Yes, yes. I came here for a boost, she thinks. I can stay at home if I want to depress myself with the news.

Outside the wind is blowing a gale. Fireworks knock and bang somewhere in the distance. A draught passes through the church. The candles gutter, and the lace altar cloth stirs. The doors must still be open, she thinks. Could it happen here? A terrorist coming in with a knife?

'But there are always pinpricks of glory in the dark,' says Father Ed. 'All Saints' Day reminds us of this. We're not alone.'

He really believes this, she marvels. She takes a sneaky look round the rest of the congregation. Probably they all believe it. Something like envy washes over her. Or nostalgia, as if for the magic of Christmas before you're disabused about Santa.

'Brothers and sisters, there are always things to cheer the soul. The prayers of the saints, good friends, acts of kindness. We need more than ever to stay tuned to that wavelength as another lockdown approaches. Today is All Saints, and the King of glory passes on his way.' The candle flames all shiver again in the breeze. 'There's always a sense of loving kindness drawing close, if we sit still long enough.'

The wind pauses. They wait in the sudden silence. And for a second, Mrs Logan can imagine what it might be like to believe there's something there, something immeasurably vast yet kind, that would bother to pause on its way and pay us some attention.

Young Jess's antennae were correct to pick up a severe weather warning from the adult emotions Met Office. She rightly registered that Mr H-M was barely holding it together. It wasn't to do with performance rights, though. She did not spot – why would she? – that the other Mr H-M was absent from the back row. If Ambrose had known this was going to be the last sung service for four weeks, he might have hung on. But he'd already arranged cover by the time the new lockdown was announced, so someone was depping for him.

Singing sacred music as an agnostic didn't normally present him with much of a cognitive dissonance challenge. Like Mrs Logan, he could warm his hands at the fire of faith glowing all around him. Long experience, man and boy: Exeter Cathedral chorister, Cambridge choral scholar, Lindchester lay clerk. He didn't one hundred per cent rule out the possibility of things one day clicking into place for him too; but he was not actually expecting this to happen.

What the hell, though? He's somehow floated off on his little ice floe further and further from the warmth, and now there's nothing but fathomless black on all sides. He can still see the golden town, hear them singing, 'He has put down the mighty from their seat.' But apparently there's no way of getting back from here – here where there's no Magnificat, just stupidity and cruelty and arrogance reigning unchecked. He just can't join in from this distance.

So he's out walking the dogs this All Saints' Day, up on Lindford Common. The wind hisses in the gorse. Cloud shadows chase by. Things must be worse than he thought for them to stage an intervention. If your husband and cousin are sitting you down to say they're worried, you should probably listen. He needs to talk to his GP, they're saying. To contact his former mentor to arrange a coaching session. And what can they do in the meantime?

What can he say? I don't know, guys. Find a vaccine? Arrange a Biden landslide? Wind back to the referendum and undo Brexit? End this nightmare, somehow – douse the hate, put the fire out, save the planet, make it so that it's not already way too late.

'Maybe we should . . . hit the pause button on making a baby?'

He'd unsay it, probably, if he could. Except it's the truth. How can the three of them, with a clear conscience, be trying to bring a child into this shit-hole of a world?

Yes. He'd unsay that. Or at least wait until he's sure Chloe isn't already pregnant – unlikely, but still theoretically possible. He knows how much that hurt them. So yes, he'll make an appointment with his GP. Yes, he'll contact his mentor. He hurt them, and it's not that he doesn't care; it's that he's got nothing to care with. Just a big pointless blank where feelings should be. And he doesn't even care about that, either. There's going to come a point where he can't summon the energy to remember how to act like he cares even.

The dogs chase one another through the dead bracken. It's getting dark. He whistles to them, and they head for home.

Star is heading for church. It's dark and it's already got that almost Christmassy feel you get from walking past all the houses and seeing in the windows. It's cosy to peek into all the different homes. You don't get that in the summer. Not long before the crimbo decorations go up. Shame they won't be doing the One Thousand Christmas Lights for St Lucy's Day this year, with the big service at the church to end up with. Well, maybe people can put lights in the window, but it's not going to be the same, is it? Maybe they can just have Santa Lucia riding on the back of the van along the pilgrim road? Just her, not all the other girls. Like an angel coming down to earth, with her crown of candles in the darkness.

The wind swooshes in the trees. Fireworks, *Wheee! Bang!* No big display, but Dad's got a box to let off in the garden on bonfire night. There's a carrier bag caught in the hedge and it's rustling like crazy. And the wooden fence is knocking away, knock-knock, like a joke, ha ha, who's there?

She starts to hurry, like her feet can't get there quick enough? All Saints. Do they get excited for the service too? Are they all there in heaven, like, Yay! Party time! Like when grown-ups are busy getting a surprise for the kids, for Christmas maybe, and they keep going, Sssh! And they're keeping it secret so it's the Best. Surprise. Ever. In her head, that's what it's like, but probably it's not like that really, it's more theological.

There's Nurse Madge in the doorway with her clipboard, checking names of who's there.

'Hiya, Madge!' Star fishes in her pocket and gets out her mask. It's navy blue with gold *stars* on, ha ha! She sanitizes her hands and goes in. All the candles! There's just time to go to the Lady Chapel to light her own. Aw, look, there's Chloe! She's kneeling down praying, so Star just quietly lights her candle and slips away again.

It was the depression talking, not Brose. Chloe knows that. But it seems to have cast a shadow over her heart too. Is he right? Should they stop trying? (Or is she . . . No. Probably not. Not even overdue yet.)

She looks up at Mary holding out the infant Christ. How long since I was last here asking what to do? Months. *He has put down the mighty from their seat.* Well, you say that, but has he? Oh, if only. Maybe a Biden victory would snap Brose out of it. Except that's not how depression operates. It's not a matter of snapping out of it, or pulling yourself together. She knows that really.

Outside, the wind surges and roars. She hears the tinkling crash of glass. Someone doing the bottle recycling at the White Horse. Last time for a while, probably. They'll be closing again on Wednesday night. Storms. Terrorist attacks. Earthquake in Greece. Thirteen million mink being slaughtered – who even knew that there were so many fur farms? He's right. What are we thinking, bringing a baby into this world?

And what were you thinking, bringing Jesus into this world? It comes to Chloe that Mary sang her Magnificat when Caesar Augustus was reigning and Israel was under tyrannical foreign rule. And Herod was on the throne. Maybe every age feels like this – like the end of the world. And every time, we're wrong. It's not the end yet.

NOVEMBER

Mourning Moon, Part I

onday morning in Lindfordshire. It's chilly and blowy;
pale blue sky behind smoky cloud, with watery
sunshine breaking through. The horse chestnut
branches are nearly bare now. All the red leaves have
gone from the Virginia creeper on the Old Vicarage at
Gayden Magna. Nothing but crimson stubble bristles from the sandstone walls. From near and far comes the bellow of leaf blowers and
the rumble of bins being wheeled back in. Children set off for school;
or else they stay at home isolating. Life has become an in/out, on/off
nationwide playground game with endlessly evolving rules and no
sign that the bell is ever going to ring to tell us it's over.

All Souls' Day. Father Wendy is in her study, reading through the long
list of names and praying for the repose of each soul. This year, she
won't have to worry about stumbling over the tricky ones. The service
will be led by Archdeacon Bea, because Wendy is isolating. There's
been an outbreak in Year 7 at Martonbury Comp, and Doug's last
lesson on Friday was double D&T with his lovely keen eleven- and
twelve-year-olds, busy with their touch-operated lantern projects for
the festive season. So far, he has no symptoms. They are just waiting
for the test results.

Will Bea know how to pronounce Oisín? Maybe Wendy should
email across a crib sheet. Grieving people are carrying such a load
already. The vicar saying the deceased's name wrong can so easily
be the last straw. Wendy catches herself. She rounds up her straying

thoughts and refocuses on her list of souls. Some feel like old friends, she's been remembering them for so long. Let light perpetual shine upon them. Those who died content and full of years. Those whose time was cut short by accident or cancer – oh, those heart-rending infant funerals! Baby Aaron. Little Elsie. And here she is – Laura Styles. Can it really be twenty years since her Laura was killed? Rest in peace, my darling.

And now this year's new names! She shakes her head. Over 2,000 COVID deaths across Lindfordshire, several from her group of parishes. A cluster from Greenacres Care Home. Two NHS staff. The dad of one of the Year 5 pupils at Cardingforth Primary – only thirty-nine years old! This terrible, terrible virus. How can there still be people who think it's all a conspiracy? Seven hundred at an illegal rave outside Bristol. No worse than seasonal flu – they *still* believe that, when the excess death figures tell us all we need to know?

Excess deaths. Now why does that phrase upset her? She turns it round in her mind, examining it from different angles. Like *excessive* alcohol consumption. The uncontrolled binge of COVID-19, like a rampaging ogre, cramming the human race into its jaws. It makes her think of a painting – by Goya, maybe? For years she's been resisting the cliché of death as the enemy – all the more urgently since her own cancer diagnosis. Patiently rejecting all the 'bravely battling' and 'losing the fight' imagery. No, she's always tried to welcome the idea of death as a friend. Our sister death – as the hymn has it – waiting to hush our latest breath and lead us home.

Excess *mortality*. Well, there's no denying we are excessively mortal. Frail children of dust, and feeble as frail. How ghastly that we catch this virus from hugs and hospitality, from company and good cheer. There's a terrible shadow pandemic of loneliness tagging along behind COVID. This second lockdown is going to be worse, thinks Wendy. Looking back, there was a novelty first time round. It was a national drama, almost. All the clapping for carers, and whole streets coming together. And the lovely weather, of course.

But now it's November. 'No sun – no moon! No morn – no noon' – November! She knew the whole poem off by heart once, from the time when her class was doing 'choral speaking' in primary school assembly. Choral droning, more like. And tomorrow is election day in the States. Will it be No Trump? Or No Biden? No glimmer of hope, no truth, no justice, no long-term future for this poor planet of ours after this November?

Come along, Wendy, she tells herself. This won't do. We are people of hope. Alleluia anyhow. She goes through to the kitchen to make a cup of tea and break this gloomy thought cycle. Pedro is napping in his basket under his weighted blanket. He's getting old now, poor boy. An image of Lulu flashes into Wendy's head. She can almost see her, lying in the patch of sunlight by the French windows, weary, close to the end. Oh, Lulu. Seven years ago now. Rest in peace, good girl, and rise in glory. Wendy doesn't understand, theologically, how dogs fit into the doctrine of the general resurrection. But she's discovered that sometimes you can trust to the quiet theology of the heart. It finds a back lane to the truth, even though your head is insisting *No Through Road*, and other louder voices are picketing the way with biblical texts. There was that day just after Lulu died, when she saw – she almost saw – her as a young dog again, bounding off along the path by the River Linden to greet a distant waiting figure, and her heart leapt to think it might be Laura.

'So, tonight's presumably something of a final choral hoorah, before we close again, Deanissima,' says Gene. 'I have to say, I've got a great inclination to be there.'

'Please don't risk it, Gene. Infection rates are through the roof.'

'Fie, Madam Dean! Surely your cathedral is COVID-secure?' He reads her face. 'Oh, very well. I'll stay at home with a glass of Pomerol and listen to my CD of Fauré's *Requiem*. Better still, I'll sit on my little balcony, swaddled in blankets, and see if I can catch the chamber choir wafting on the wind. Their voices, I mean, naturally. Some of those contraltos would struggle to get airborne with a rocket booster.'

I would love to tell you that Dean Marion has long since abandoned any attempt at remonstrating with her husband when he's off on one of his riffs. She ought to know by now that her stern look simply inspires him to add ever-greater baroque detail to his initial sally.

'Talking of bulky contraltos, I wonder whether your beloved PA will be singing tonight?' he muses. 'Is she in fine voice these days? Or has Dykey Dora from William House put her on a *musical* performance plan as well?'

'Stop it.'

I'm afraid Gene is still angling for more information about that confidential email which popped up embarrassingly on to the screen when the dean was battling with Netflix. So far, Marion has neither confirmed nor denied that his guess is correct.

'Will you be rid of her by Chri—'

'No. No, no, no.' Marion covers her ears. 'If you want to do something useful, why not pray?'

He snaps her a salute. 'Captain Useful reporting for duty, ma'am! And what *exactly* would you like me to pray vis-à-vis your PA,' he delved cunningly?'

'Well, Gene, I don't know. What about the prayer our Lord taught us?' She gathers up her notes. 'I'm heading across now. Back in about an hour.'

Gene did not go and sit on his little balcony. What, was he a madman? Storm Aiden was still plunging and rearing across the landscape. He did say the Lord's Prayer, however, as he stood at the deanery drawing-room windows watching his beloved battle against the wind on her way to the cathedral, cloak dramatically a-swirl, like a Scottish widow, or possibly the French Lieutenant's Woman.

Deliver us from evil. It covered just about everything. A prayer that stubbornly persisted, even when the corpse of faith had been serially incinerated in life's crematoria. A metal hip joint of a prayer, if you will. During the darkest hours of his anti-apartheid years, in grief and bereavement, through the recent valley of the shadow of chemo – still astonishingly fit for purpose. It was certainly better than 'Footprints'. Kind members of the congregation (bless their Fairtrade bamboo socks) had sent him so many copies that the entire metaphorical beach had been trampled by a thousand feet. He could practically hear Jesus saying, 'No, my child – that was when I took you to Durdle Door during a global pandemic.'

342

Somewhere along the steep and rugged pathway, Gene had stopped expecting his prayers to be answered. God was not curled up in the tabernacle like a genie in a lamp, waiting to be activated by a brisk prayer-rub. It was more that, now and then, Gene's prayer briefly fell into sync with those mysterious footsteps planted on the storm. Or so one hoped. And then the answer would not be 'Yes', as though God's arm had been twisted by human faith, so much as 'Yes, tiny mortal, you've dimly glimpsed the plan'.

Well, heavens to Betsy! Listen to him! He ought to be a priest. Why was his BAP not lined up already? His *remote* BAP – joyous concept! Gene clasped his hands as he pictured it, a shimmering mammary mirage leading him kindly on amid the encircling gloom. But soft! Maybe if he popped across to the palace now, with a bottle of 2008 Dom Pérignon, Bishop Steve might ordain him upon a frivolous instant in the episcopal study! Gene wavered, then repented of this blasphemous thought. No. In all conscience, a bottle of bog-standard Bolly would suffice. Steve was an Evangelical, after all.

Gene drew the crewel-work curtains closed with a swish, and went through to the kitchen, to begin the ticklesome task of boning a pair of quails and stuffing them with foie gras and chopped pickled walnuts for his deanissima's dinner. This was his true vocation. Outside, the wind bounced and buffeted. The CD played softly, and he hummed along. *'Requiem aeternam dona eis Domine.'*

The Blue Moon starts to wane. Only two more full moons left in 2020. Where has the year gone? Even if we wanted to – and we really don't – we couldn't stop the days and months passing. This year will slip away. We will all slip away. Tower and temple will fall to dust. There used to be a castle in Lindford, by the way. A huge one. It stood for five hundred years. During the Civil War, it went back and forth between Parliamentarians and Royalists, and was finally so knocked about, it was deemed not worth repairing. If you know where to look, you can still spot buildings made partly out of stolen masonry – not mentioning any names, but watch my eyes, Lindford Parish Church.

The castle footprint covers most of the town centre, and the heart of it lies under the new indoor market. All manner of interesting antiquities were unearthed when the foundations for that were dug. You can visit the permanent exhibition in Lindford Museum – if you're quick and book a slot before lockdown starts on Thursday.

Maybe at night the ghosts of knights and troubadours wander the market aisles, past the little shut-up meat and fruit stalls, the vacuum-cleaner parts vendor and Infinity Nail Bar. Perhaps moonlight slants down through the high windows, and passes through their silvery armour and silent lutes. Five centuries is a mighty long time to stand proud, then vanish almost without trace.

Outside the shuttered market the wind stirs, and the sign on the White Horse pub swings and creaks, swings and creaks.

Tuesday 3rd November
So today is like a momentus day, it is 'Presidential Elections' in the United States. Leah was explaining it to me at teatime, (vegan sausage cassarole) she said 'the future of the entire planet is hanging in the balance'. She is going to stay up all night and watch the results because it is earlier in the day in America than here. Mum went, You will be to tired for school if you stay up all night, and Leah went HELLO? My year is actually isolating in case you've forgotten there is no school. So obvs mum went IT IS STILL SCHOOL, LEAH. And Leah was all, whatevs, and carried on saying loudly how if Trump get's back in it is GAME OVER, he has already pulled out of the Paris agreement, no way will global warming be stopped if he is president for another 4 years.

In the end I said don't get me wrong, Leah, I totally get how this is important, only it really depresses me, can you please stop telling me this depressing stuff when there is nothing I can actually do about it, I mean its not like we get to vote? And she was like WAKE UP! But then dad gave her 'a look' and she went FINE and did not carry on telling me stuff and I went to practice my clarinet in the dinning room. I played all of my repatoire plus my scales and arpeggios. I am now learning 'Stranger on the shore' it is by Aka Bilk. I listened to him on Youtube and I do not get how he does glissanders, he is a total legend IMO.

344

<u>Moon Facts</u>
Waning gibbous (95%) The blue moon will dissappear by the middle of November then there will be a new moon and this moon will wax and be the next full moon. EXCEPT it is actually the selfsame moon all the time, it is just our perspective that makes it look like we keep getting new moons every month. It makes me think about the moon and the stars, and then What is man, that thou art mindful of him? I can't remember the rest of the psalm (NB it is Day 1). Mr H-M knows the entire whole psalmody. He told us that when we were just probs, then he laughed and said, don't look so scared, you don't have to learn it off by heart, I just have this totally freakish memory, like musical photographic memory? I so wish I had that too but so far no luck with that.

<u>November Full Moon Names</u>
In Native America the November full moon is <u>The Beaver Moon.</u> When I said this at tea, mum and dad full on giggled? Leah went, OMG I do not believe you two, you are so immature? She went, its slang for vulva, they are just being childish ignore them, beavers are a keystone species, they have been reintroduced in Scotland, here I will send you the link.

So I read all about beavers (THE ANIMALS!!!!), and I for one am glad that they are back in Scotland, it is sad to think they went extinct because humanity hunted them for their fur and for 'castorium' which you trust me you do NOT want to know about!!!!! It is used in perfume and some foods, and it will totally make you want to turn vegan if you read about it. Now I am sad again, I keep thinking about all the poor minks that got culled, like literally millions of them?

So there are other names for the November full moon like for example 'Frosty Moon' and 'Mourning Moon'. I will go with 'Frosty Moon' because it makes me think of Frosty the Snowman LOL and it gives me hope because of Christmas instead of crying the entire whole time because of hormones and covid and everything being so sh*t.

Miss Sherratt is out for her constitutional. Once round the block. She takes her cane with her. How one scampered in one's youth, with never a thought of falling. All those busy wards she navigated with nary a stumble or slip, even when she was dead on her feet! But now it's one tripping hazard after another – tree roots, kerbs. One's childhood terror of cracks in the pavement coming back with a vengeance. She minces down the slope through the slippery leaves. The time has not come for a mobility scooter, not quite. Though one might tootle up to church rather gloriously in one of those, rather than calling a cab. Perhaps with a rubber bulb brass horn to parp? Grandpa's old driving goggles and cape must still be in a trunk somewhere in the Sherratt Hall Museum of Edwardian Collectables – she could rather fancy herself togged up in those, with an ermine stole perhaps. No – terrible foolishness, trailing scarves and moving parts. One wouldn't want to end one's days like Isadora Duncan.

Miss Sherratt pauses to catch her breath before turning the corner and starting the long climb home. Climb, indeed! You are old, Mother Wilhelmina! Barely a slope. Why, one's toboggan always ground to a halt on Pendleton Avenue. Snowy days, frosty days – not had a single nip so far. November! Too warm. And here she is, calling this a climb. Does the road wind uphill all the way? Yes, to the very end.

To the very end. One couldn't help wondering when that would be. If it wasn't for this new lockdown, she'd have her will finalized. Not a radical rethink, but new threads to weave in, as it were. Parish nurses. Jack to think about. Doubtless it could be arranged over the telephone, or internet, or whatnot, no need to visit one's solicitor in person. How very strange it all is. Retired for longer than she worked. Still not exempt from worry – you can't retire from the world. Trump, incompetence in Westminster, shooting in Vienna. Lockdown – first Remembrance Day when she won't be in church. Still. Lovely day. Golden red sunrise this morning, and the moon still hanging in the blue. Is that a skein of geese? It is. Probably honking away, but Miss Sherratt can't hear them.

She pauses again by a gated driveway. Why, what's that? She breathes in. Jasmine! Still – in November? She peers into the garden. There it is. Pale stars. *Stars that shall be bright when we are dust.* Such sweetness. And a cobweb, shining with tiny diamonds. Come along, old thing. Stir your stumps. She sets off again, stick tapping. *To the end, to the end, they remain.* Not to be in church for Remembrance Day! But one can remember at home. Pray at home. Join our prayers

346

with Mary, Our Lady of Joy, Hail Mary. Tap tap tap. Up the hill. Pray for us.

And why, how very strange, for one moment Miss Sherratt is not walking, but being carried, carried along at treetop height, like a child carried by an enormous grown-up, even though she's just a heavy old lady, plodding along the road home, past the 1960s house now, where they've built an extension, where those nice young people live, she *must* ask them round for drinks as soon as ever all this is over. And it will be over.

Yes, it will be over. But everything is still being sh*t for poor Ambrose, I'm afraid. He did talk to his GP. A phone appointment, of course. But a phone appointment with your GP is not a court appearance. Ambrose felt under no obligation to tell the truth, the whole truth, and nothing but the truth. As a result of the conversation, 'mild to moderate reactive depression' has appeared on his notes, with a recommendation of some CBT resources, and a follow-up appointment in four weeks' time.

It will pass. Probably. It passed in 2016. But that was summertime. And he was falling crazily in love. He stares at his half-eaten toast. Work keeps him going. Numbers. Balance sheets. Strategic planning and problem-solving. And the dogs. Walking the dogs. One day at a time. And Freddie. Freddie and Chloe. They keep him going. Prodding him awake, so he doesn't fall asleep and just slip away from hypothermia. That's what it feels like. Prodding, when he'd rather sleep.

He's probably made enough of the right noises to head off another intervention – for now, anyway. But just as he's thinking this, here's Freddie coming in through the French windows with one of the chickens. Oh shit. Ill? Ambrose pictures himself putting her out of her misery, and Freddie distraught.

'Problem?'

'Nope.' Freddie dumps the bird in Ambrose's lap. 'Hen-power, dude. Good for wellbeing. This here's Fabiola, case you'd forgotten. She likes to be scritched. Gwan, you know you want to.'

Fabiola nestles down broodily. Ambrose shakes his head and starts to work his fingers into the glossy feathers.

'What are we *not* gonna do tonight?' Freddie asks.

Make love. Sleep for more than half an hour at a stretch. 'You tell me.'

'We're *not* gonna stay up checking the election results and getting stressed. 'K?'

'OK.'

'Cool. Gonna call your mentor today? Dude, you better, cos I'll be on your case till you do.'

'I will.'

'Good. So Chloe and me are collecting a whole bunch of recondi-tioned computers and printers from some office and taking them to the hub? Oh, and she's got this info in Vietnamese – her mum emailed it? About asylum, advice, legal shit, how to say "I claim asylum"? And I'm thinking, maybe I could, I dunno, climb across, tape it to the window, the one he looks out of? Cos maybe now he trusts us, like, a tiny bit?' Freddie waits. 'So? Whaddya think?'

'Um.' Ambrose stares. 'Sounds good.'

'Aw. Dude.' Freddie smooths his hair back from his forehead and kisses him. 'Was there anything else in the plan I forgot?'

'Sorry. I'm just . . . Yes, one more thought. We could get Bishop Matt on board. He may have contacts in the force. What we don't want is for them to raid the place without being aware.'

'Awesome. I'm on it. I'll ring him now.'

Chloe comes in. 'Ready when you are.'

'Catch ya later, babe.' He's off.

'Um, Freddie?' Ambrose points at Fabiola.

'Hey. Take her upstairs to work with you, dude. Company? Wellbeing?'

'Oh, you so should, Brose,' says Chloe. 'It's National Take Your Chicken to Work Day – didn't you know?'

'That is literally a shit idea.'

'Ha ha ha! You made a joke! He made a joke!' Freddie comes back and gives him another kiss. 'Aw, love you. Don't forget to call your mentor! Laters.'

When they've gone, Ambrose gets to his feet with the hen under his arm. 'Sorry, Fabiola.' He lets himself out through the French windows and deposits her back with the others in the coop. A cobweb

348

laden with dewdrops trembles as he closes the door. Maybe he will call Theo. If only to avoid the hassle.

He sighs and turns to go back to the house. High above he hears them honking, tiny, remote. He looks up. Long skeins of geese roping their way across the sky. And some feeling goes looping and roping its way across his heart. Love, maybe. It certainly hurts enough to be love.

Mourning Moon, Part II

Jane is part of the generation for whom the question 'Were you still up for Portillo?' resonates with a Magnificat thrill. Jane had always been a stayer-upper. Even if your side loses, watching it happen is preferable to going to bed optimistic, then opening your metaphorical curtains the following morning on scenes of apocalyptic devastation. (Have no fear. Jane knows what 'apocalyptic' *actually* means, but she's happy to use the word like a normal person.) Last December's General Election was the first time in her adult life she didn't bother watching the results come in live. An overwound political watch is what she is these days. Her mainspring's kaput, and the cost of mending it is more than the thing's worth.

Yet she stayed up in case there was a Biden landslide! Complete bloody waste of time that was. Ought to have remembered the lumbering machinery of US presidential elections. It's going to drag on for weeks. Judging by Trump's bad loser antics, it'll be like watching a Six Nations match with the TMO called in every twenty seconds, and each try contested. What a daft process. Yeah. Sez you, Jane, from the land of Screaming Lord Sutch and the Official Monster Raving Loony first-past-the-post system.

The days of early November pass. England goes back into lockdown. Stay at home. Work from home. No meeting up in houses or gardens. No unnecessary travel. All non-essential shops must close, along with gyms, hairdressers, cinemas, pubs and restaurants (apart from those selling takeaway food). No weddings, alas. But churches can remain open for private prayer this time round and for the purposes of live-streaming a service – which surely means the wolf shall lie down with the lamb on Anglican Twitter, the lion shall eat straw like the ox!

Lockdown 2: the disappointing follow-up movie. They've changed the theme tune and the soundtrack. There's no jaunty 'Thank You Baked Potato' playing. No heart-warming community singing of 'We'll Meet Again', no opera from balconies. The trademark eerie silence isn't there either. No atmospheric shots of mountain goats invading empty town centres. No badgers outside Debenhams. There's as much traffic on the roads as ever.

The same old blanket of restrictions lies across the country, only now it's frayed and threadbare. People are tired of it. The smell, the texture, the flavour of lockdown – it gets in our hair and clings to our skin. We can taste it in our mouths. The thought of our study or workstation fills us with dread. Years from now, we'll hear the word 'Zoom', or catch a whiff of sanitizer, and we'll get flashbacks. This long, slow deprivation we're enduring is our generation's Blackout, our rationing. Each day we have to reach for our British stoicism. Well, you've just got to get on with it, haven't you? Or else we resent it, this ratty old blanket. It itches. It stifles. People throw it off. It doesn't keep us warm, and anyway, we're not even cold! It's all a hoax, this #Scamdemic. The mainstream press and their COVID-19 orchestrated hysteria. Do you actually know anyone who's had COVID – no names, just yes or no? We're prepared to take our chances. We'd rather die than live like this.

Not much changes in Jane's daily life, because this time schools and universities 'stay open'. Teachers and lecturers (if they can still summon the energy) point out yet again that WE NEVER CLOSED. On Friday, Jane gets on her little train to work and delivers her afternoon seminar in a big lecture theatre to a dozen socially distanced students, poor lambs. Sometimes she sees a colleague. They stand in their masks two metres apart and talk hungrily, with pantomime nods to convey smiles. They're like long-separated siblings, one on the ship, one on the shore. It might as well still be the ocean between them. But even this helps a little.

351

This Friday, she seems to be the only academic around in the foyer. She chats with the guy behind the desk, then sets off for the station. The town centre feels like Sunday in the 60s. There will be no Christmas market this year, presumably. It's already getting dark at 4 p.m. On the station forecourt, she passes students in shorts and those sports mules nobody wore back in her day. Shorts in November! Though to be fair, it's uncannily mild. God help this poor planet if Trump gets a second term. And now he's gone and ruined the word 'shenanigans' for her for ever.

She hooks the elastic loops behind her ears and hoists her mask as she enters the station. The shutters are down on Upper Crust and Costas. She follows the one-way system to her platform. On the opposite side of the tracks, she sees little Jess, with her school backpack and clarinet case, just back from Lindchester. They wave, but Jane's train is groaning in, so they can't call across to one another.

The state of him, Jane thinks. Like the ruins of a heavyweight boxer, roaring and taking punch-drunk swings at democracy from the golf course. I'll see you in court, electoral system! She gets on her empty train and sits watching the messages scroll round. At one point, the electronic board says *You must wear a face*. She thinks about taking a photo, but she can't be arsed. The bleep sounds, the doors close, and they're off.

They trundle through the town, past the trading estate. The announcement is still urging her to report anything that doesn't look right. How can we judge any more? Nothing looks right. Her phone vibrates. She gropes it out of her pocket, but it's only a message from Matt asking her to pick up more milk. God, how many more days of jumping at every alert, hoping for good news from the US? Forget the tortoise and the hare. It's a two-tortoise race, with one inching painfully ahead – come on, come *on*! – and the constant fear that the trailing tortoise might rear up like a Transformer and put on a preternatural spurt. Or that someone, somehow, is going to burst out of the crowd, pick slowcoach up and run across the line with him, while the world looks on in disbelief. Could that happen? Oh shit, thinks Jane. The script of 2020 seems to demand it. For a ray of hope to pierce the gloom at the very peak of the year's narrative arc – that would be too corny for words.

The train stops at a station, and some schoolchildren get off. Thank God Danny's safe in New Zealand. If this had happened ten years ago, how would he and I have ever navigated home schooling? The doors close, and they rattle off again, past hedges and fields now. The canal glows, a long stripe of light.

She thinks again about the footage of Trump's spiritual adviser prophesying victory. *Victory, victory, victory, victory, victory*, like the White Witch lashing the reindeer as they struggle to pull her wallowing sleigh. The train goes rocketing through a tunnel. Jane stares at her reflection. Her weary, pouchy eyes stare back over her mask – which at least hides her incipient jowls, so a silver lining there. *I hear the sound of an abundance of rain*. Well, Jane saw some loopy charismatic stuff back in her slain-in-the-Spirit days – but this? *And strike and strike and strike and strike.*

What if Aslan *is* on the move, though? The train bursts out into the dusk again. Her ears pop. The first fireworks zizz up into the sky. A moment later she catches the tiny banging, as though the giant is making popcorn at the top of his beanstalk. Come on, count the votes, count the votes, Pennsylvania! Hope is killing me.

In previous novels, dear reader, we flew this jerry-built Chitty Chitty Bang Bang of a narrative in real time, scattering engine parts, panicking, not knowing what the following day held for us. Our camera was mounted on the bonnet as 2016 hurtled towards us. When we landed on New Year's Day, we climbed out shakily, and vowed never to take to the skies of Lindfordshire again. Our Anglican wings were stowed in the loft, and we all had a little lie-down and a glass of sherry.

Nevertheless, here we are again. You will recall that we posed the question in the introduction to this work: WWGED? We concluded that George Eliot would have made like the moon, looking down with a forty-year perspective on 2020. There will be COVID novels four decades from now, I daresay. Prizewinning historical novels, informed by political and cultural perspectives, all meticulously researched and brilliantly reconstructed from contemporaneous accounts.

We who are about to be scrambled salute you, future novelists! *Angels Four Zero!* Each week we take off and fly at an altitude of forty feet, with a couple of weeks' hindsight. We are flying, as it were, at rooftop height, camera trained on the pale horse cantering a hundred yards ahead.

Don't worry. In a moment I will stop rapping my knuckles on the fourth wall, and allow you the consolation of pretending this is real again. I will just pause to observe that our fortnight's hindsight means that you know already that Jane was not hoping in vain for the end of winter. The Aslan rumours were true. Well, whaddya know! Jane will think. The White Witch was right. The Lord did say, 'It is done.' You *could* hear the sound of victory, my scary prophetic friend. Those battalions of angels dispatched from *Africa right now, Africa right now, from South America* – they showed up after all. They showed up and voted for Biden. What must that feel like? Jane will wonder. To be so frighteningly wrong, when you've claimed the ground for Jesus and felt so unassailably right? And *then* to be proved right for the wrong reasons? It is the Emperor's deep magic.

Friday November 6th.
Today is a red letter day, literally. Well not <u>literally</u> literally LOL. It is an important day for me personally because I got my first period so in a way 'red' I guess. (N.B. this is not a 'bad taste' joke, it is symbolicalism.) At the end of the day it was not so bad.

So long story short I told mum when I got in from school, she went, Oh that is good news darling and she hugged me, and she asked are you feeling OK? Then she called Leah and said good news, Can you get 'the box'? And I was all, what box, what are you even on about? So it turns out they've been planning this surprise for me? Leah came in carrying a red box and she went 'Ta Dah!!!!!! This is THE RED BOX!!!! I wish someone would of done this for me, no offence mum, but seriously, you should of?'

We were sat in the kitchen, dad was asleep upstairs because of long covid, plus this is like a woman bonding thing, it is ok for him to not be there (says guess who LOL)
List of things in The Red Box
1. Hot water bottle, it is heart shaped plus mum has made a cover for it in case of cramps.
2. Iboprufen caplets

354

3. *A MOONCUP!!!! NO WAY am I using that, I mean, really?!!! Leah says you will, trust me. (Still no.)*

4. *Eco-friendly bamboo pads and storage bag.*

5. *Red fleece hoodie and bedsocks for loungewear*

6. *Homemade (by Leah!!!) epsum salts with lavender oil and dried rose petals in a glass jar.*

7. *Book called 'Period Power'*

8. *Big bag of fair trade chocolate buttons!!! YAY!!!*

9. *'Vulva' cookie cutter??? Um thanks I guess????????*

10. *Betty Crocker Red velvet cake mix*

11. *Lavendar candles.*

We made the red velvet cake, it was our dessert. I am very lucky to have a mum and sister who would thoughtfully do this, not every girl is so lucky. There is such a thing as 'period poverty' so me and Leah have decided to raise money to buy sanitry products to donate to the foodbank, food is important but there are other kinds of poverty too, we would all do well to remember this.

<u>Moon Facts</u>

Waning gibbous. Moon age 19.7 days. This proves that the girls at school are wrong LOL, it is <u>not</u> the 'new moon', which proves it is totally random when you get your period.

It is the day after bonfire night but there's tons of fireworks. It makes me think of when we were little and we used to play under the table that it was an air raid, and once Leah 'ran away' (NB she was actually in her den on the flat roof) and mum and dad were really scared, and so was I, but she came home again and it was ok. I am too grown up for that game obvs plus anyway its like we don't have to pretend, things are bad enough IMAO it is a global pandemic at the end of the day.

Funnily enough, Jane is not the only person musing about Narnia this week in Lindfordshire. It's Saturday, and Neil is in his workshop over at the Britannia Business Park on the outskirts of Martonbury. Life is more harmonious in the vicarage at Gayden Magna when Neil is not working from home. So here he is. Ghost town, mind you. The Taekwondo dojo next door has gone bust. All quiet at the recording studio too. It's the weekend, so the deli's not open. All he's got is his wee tub of quinoa salad and a bottle of water, which is what early morning Fergie decided would be enough. What a sanctimonious git early morning Fergie is. He needs coffee and pastry! And he misses the bustle of being with people, even if it's just the takeaway queue. Och, well.

He's playing around with ideas boards for the revamp of Turlham Hall. There are nine en suite bedrooms; ten if you include the bridal/honeymoon suite. At present they're done up tastefully enough – if your taste got parked in the early 90s. It's heavy on the Victoriana, and fair play, it is a Grade II listed Victorian brick mansion, so dark reds and greens (and antlers) is the obvious route to go down. But Neil can't look at his reflection in the gold-framed mirrors without tasting oaked Chardonnay. So he'll lighten everything up. You can't seem to go wrong with pale grey at the moment.

He stares out of his window and drums his fingers. Two squirrels chase through the empty branches. There's a smoky quality to the light. The sun angles down in shafts. He doesn't want to deliver the generic McHipster hotel you could find anywhere. He blames Freddie Hardman-May for this. (One of the boards is a shameless rip-off of the Chefchaouen idea, but he knows he won't be showing Jen and Leo that.) God, he'd *love* to do something off-the-wall, not off-the-peg. But the customer is always right. Even when they're visually illiterate.

Wait, though – what if every room was different? The Morocco Suite, the Rural Nook, the Cape Cod Beach House, the Art Deco Great Gatsby Honeymoon Suite, the . . . I don't know, Narnia Room? Oh my God, Narnia! You could literally have an old wardrobe with the back off surrounding the door to the en suite, and you'd go through into the bathroom, which would be a snowy forest, tree murals, lamp-post light. Oh, he would *so* book into a room like that!

Hmm. He taps his chin. But isn't it all going to end up a bit incoherent and *bitty*? So what would the overarching theme be? He snaps his fingers. Victorian cabinet of curiosities! Each room a treasure trove of magic!

He guns the engines of his imagination and he's away. He'll need to price it up later on, but right now he's ON FIRE. His quinoa salad sits uneaten. The sun is setting when he comes in to land again. All ten rooms conceptualized.

Will Jen and Leo go for it? he wonders as he drives back to Gayden Magna. Well, who cares? He's having fun again at last. The fireworks popping all around might be popping just for him. Judy and Barbra are singing 'Happy Days Are Here Again' from the car speakers just for him! He can always do Jen and Leo a nice safe hipster hotel if that's what they prefer. And then he and Ed can open their own hotel when Ed retires! And that's not so far off these days. He'll be sixty next year, love him. Fireworks blossom and shower down petals of light. Shout 'hallelujah'! Neil suddenly realizes that he hasn't thought about the virus all day.

Shout 'hallelujah'. Bang saucepans. Take to the streets. Toot your horn. Fill the sky with rockets. Biden wins Pennsylvania. He's actually done it! *They've* done it: Biden and Harris. Kamala Harris, the first ever female vice president. The first ever female, black and Indian-American vice president.

'I don't know why I'm crying,' says Jane.

'You don't?' asks Matt.

'Yes, of course I do. This is massive. I just can't believe it, that's all.' She blows her nose. 'You know what? I'm going to nip to the petrol station and get some Champagne.'

'We'd be fools not to,' says Matt. 'I'll join you in a glass when I've finished this.'

Jane cranes her head to read the title of the book on his desk. 'Is that what I think it is? Give it here.'

'Nope.' He puts a hand over the orange cover. 'Not officially published yet.'

'The bishops should've smuggled it out now, so it gets buried by Biden.'

Matt sighs. 'I thought you were buying Champagne.'

'So I was.'

Why am I not happy? she thinks as she drives. One of my tribe. A woman vice president. I should be happy. Maybe I'm just too fucking exhausted. It takes so fucking *long* for women to make up the lost ground on this so-called level playing field where everything's man-shaped. The starting blocks, the running spikes, the hurdle height.

357

Every fecking form, every process, every default assumption. Not just man-shaped: *white* man-shaped. Kamala, you legend.

Up on Cathedral Close, the Champagne is already on ice. It is of a rather better vintage than any Jane will find at her local petrol station, let me tell you. Gene watches the footage from the drawing room, where a fire is blazing and he can see his neighbours' fireworks without stirring from his chaise longue.

It's happening at last. That political skimmington ride he'd pictured back in April, when he clanged his cane on the balcony railings for the NHS. Moments like this come along every few decades. The Berlin Wall coming down, Mandela's release, to name but two. And as always, there's another reality, a topsy-turvy universe where this is a disaster, filled with distraught souls reeling from a swingeing blow. And like all parallel universes, it's separated from ours by a hair's breadth of a hair's breadth, he thinks. It's a mere airy tissue-paper width away from us. Or a trillion miles. Apparently, it makes no difference when you come to talk of other dimensions. Our poor Flatland human brains can no more conceptualize it than his beloved deanissima can distinguish between Fleur de Miraval and Tesco pink bubbly. Ah well.

Miss Sherratt comes out with her stick, and stands on her patio. She's wearing her poppy. The day is foggy and totally still. The treetops melt into a white sky. No mass today, now they're back in lockdown. No Remembrance Day service either. But she's still come out here to remember. There's Jack, standing outside the old summerhouse. He raises a hand. She can't make out from here if he's wearing his medals. Too misty. But he probably is.

They wait.

Then she hears it. Well, goodness me, the Last Post! Someone's playing it at the war memorial after all, and it's carrying up here. Must be a trick of the still air. The sound is so tiny. Like a miniature bugle, playing a very great way off, or a long time ago, and the sound is only just reaching her now, years and miles later.

Silence.

Rain drips from the empty trees. A magpie calls. One for sorrow. All my lost ones, my dear ones. The winged squadrons of the sky. So close, they sometimes seem. Not long to wait now, surely. Her hostas have all rotted away to beige slime. But she can see one bright red splash in the flowerbed. A single poppy still hanging on, even though it's November.

Her bones ache, but she carries on standing. In a moment, it'll be the Reveille. She leans on her stick, listening, listening.

Mourning Moon, Part III

hloe copes with the disappointment a bit better this time round. She gets her crying done in the privacy of the bathroom. Ah well. Yes, it's sad, but there's always next month. She splashes water on her face and pulls herself together. In a moment, she'll get dressed and go downstairs to let Eeyore and Tigger know.

Yes. It'll be fine. Isn't she Princess of Silver Linings? Moving-in day is this Saturday, and this means she won't have to dip out of the heavy lifting. Ha ha! That's a pretty rubbish silver lining, come to think of it, because Brose and Freddie are constitutionally incapable of standing by and watching a woman carry anything heavier than a handbag. Bless. Freddie's hired a van, and they're all going to pack up and clean her old house, and bring her stuff over to the extension. She's leaving the furniture and kitchen things, and letting the house furnished – hopefully via the council scheme – to asylum seekers. That should cover the mortgage. But how on earth is she going to—

Silver linings, silver linings! She steers her little boat past the treacherous rocks of money and finding a new job. There's plenty of volunteering at the hub. She's been keeping herself busy offering free legal advice. And this lockdown's so much less lonely than the last one. Then there's Biden and Harris! The vaccine! See? The year won't end as badly as everyone thought. Right! Come on, we're going to go and stand in our new little home, our little nest, and curl our toes in the lovely new carpet.

Chloe wraps her dressing gown round her and pads through to the extension. She opens the communicating door. There you are! New paint, new timber, fresh plaster! And no blue to be seen anywhere – aw, sorry, Freddie! There's the kitchen-dining-living room downstairs. And up here, bedroom, bathroom and box room. She steps into her new bedroom. Farrow & Ball's 'Hay'. Aw look, Freddie's already put up the curtain rail and assembled the new brass bedframe! Mattress should be arriving this week. In a moment, she will go and stand in the other room, and she won't cry. There never were any guarantees. All they're doing, with this rigmarole of fertility tracking and home insemination, is making it possible. They're clearing a space and just waiting. And if it's not to be, well. It will still be OK in the end.

Hope's such a funny thing. A thing with feathers! Was that a song? Maybe a poem. She hesitates by the box room door. Yes, hope's a bit like a robin in the winter. You see it, and you can't help cheering up a bit, and believing it will still be OK. At the same time, hope can feel more like a hawk. She saw one plucking a pigeon once – yeesh! They don't worry about a clean kill first, do they? Anyway! She opens the door and stands in the little 'Pale Hound' room that may or may not become a nursery. It's empty, apart from Granny Gno's rosary on the window sill – how did that get there? Not that Granny Gno would give her blessing to *this* enterprise. Unmarried! Baby on the way!

Yes, Granny, but what about the Blessed Virgin Mary? She wasn't married either. No, that wouldn't get past Granny. Comparing herself with Our Lady, indeed.

Chloe goes across to the window and looks out across the street. The radiator is warm. There's that faint ticking of expanding floorboards, as if the extension is alive, it's almost a person, waiting for her to come and live here. She picks up the rosary and her fingers start working the beads. Decades slip unspoken through her hands. The horse chestnut trees are bare now. There's a parked car with a man just sitting. Police? Bishop Matt's passed on their concerns, apparently. Will it make any difference? The envelope is still taped to the upstairs back window, untouched. Sometimes Chloe goes and puts her hands on the party wall and prays for whoever is on the other side. Somewhere in the world – in Vietnam? – there must be a mother

361

praying as well, for her lost son. And maybe for a moment their hands are touching virtually. If prayer is like that.

Blessed is she who believed that there would be a fulfilment of what was spoken to her by the Lord. Chloe keeps wondering about these words. Because believing didn't mean Mary had arrived. She still had to go through the whole dangerous thing, didn't she? Giving birth, fleeing to Egypt. Except Mary was super-faithful, and Chloe isn't! Did Mary *feel* faithful, though? Maybe she was nagged by doubt every step of the way. (Sorry, Granny. I'm probably not allowed to say that!) All the same, maybe you only have to believe *just enough* to say yes. And then carry on, one day at a time. You just have to keep believing that you heard right in the first place, and that you aren't crazy.

The days of November pass. Bright days, misty days. Sometimes there's blue sky first thing, and a radiant light glorifies the roofs and walls and houses of Lindfordshire. The silver birch trunks turn gold. By Martonbury Golf Course, a crow very high up harasses a sparrow-hawk and drives it off from the pocket of woodland. There's no golf in lockdown. The fairways are ceded to joggers and dog-walkers again.

Jane is up there, mooching. It would normally be a running day, but she pinged her intercostal muscles trying to tighten the strap on her sports bra without removing it first. Fer feck's sake. Why not make them adjustable from the front, not round the back where you can't fecking reach? Is that too much to ask? How many jockstrap-related sporting injuries are there per year, she'd like to know?

Where has the year gone? It'll be Christmas before we know it – whatever that's going to look like this year. A week of promiscuous mingling to undo all the good work of this lockdown? Excellent plan. But damage limitation's probably the best we're going to manage. There's no way everyone will comply with strict regulations. Let's hope the mass evacuation of students goes smoothly. Get them tested and home safely.

She passes the same bench she sat on illegally in the first lock-down to ring Dom. Too wet for that now. It might be a different golf course entirely, a different world. Red toadstools in the grass under the birch trees. Fly agaric – used as an insecticide. Also a symbol of good luck on Victorian Christmas cards. Jane laughs. She can almost see Danny rolling his eyes, the way he used to when she spammed him with trivia on the walk to school. The way Jane rolled her eyes when Mum did the same to her. Oh God – I *am* my mother! She shakes her head.

There are no willow warblers now; but there are still magpies, and the occasional thread of robin song. Yes, Jane thinks, there are always a few blessings to count, if you scour around. Government U-turn on free school meals. Dominic Cummings booted out of Number 10. And look – there's a blaze of blossom shining in the gorse thicket by the eighth hole. Well, thank God kissing's never completely out of fashion, she thinks, even in the heart's deep winter. Not long till her and Matt's anniversary. Six years. He'll probably forget again, the bastard.

'What the?' Freddie slips off his headphones. He stares down at the hen Ambrose has placed on his laptop.

'It's Fabiola,' says Ambrose.

'No it's not! Dude, this here's Ella, and what the hell? I'm kinda busy editing here.'

'Hen-power. Good for wellbeing.' He sits beside Freddie on the sofa in the blue sitting room. Silence, apart from the radiator ticking.

'Yeah,' says Freddie. 'I know. Bummer. Chloe told me?'

'Um. It's not that.'

Freddie takes in his expression. 'Oh shit. Here.' He hands Ella over, and moves his laptop aside. 'You're scaring me. Someone's got COVID? Oh God – you've been fired!'

'No! Stop catastrophizing.' Ambrose passes the hen back. 'There's something you can do for me.'

'Anything. You know that.'

'The *Living in Love and Faith* report. You said you were planning on reading it?'

'Aw, *man*, yeah no, I kinda was, only it's really lo-o-ong, and I dunno?' He lifts Ella to his face briefly, and nuzzles her. 'Is that bad of me?' Ella clucks gently. He snuggles her into his chest. 'Listen, maybe when Chloe's done reading it? She like has to, she's on General Synod? I mean, I get they want us to engage, but I'm like, engage? I'm only fucking *living* it. But yeh, if you want me to, I'll read it.'

'I don't mind either way.' Ambrose runs the back of his hand over Ella's silky feathers, then twines his fingers with Freddie's. 'But there's a video. By some Evangelical group. Which I really, *really* want you not to watch.'

'*What?*' Freddie pulls his hand free. 'Say WHAT?'

'You see? Even the idea has triggered you, Freddie.'

'I'm NOT fucking TRIGGERED!' The hen flaps and squawks. 'Sssh ssh, it's OK, sweetheart. Aw.' He soothes the hen, and whispers, '*I'm not triggered.*'

'Babe.' Ambrose shakes his head. 'Please don't watch it. I did, so you don't have to.'

'*Man.*' Freddie clenches his teeth, breathes out hard through his nostrils. 'You realize you've totally made it like Pandora's can of worms? I'ma *have* to check now. Got skin in the game here, dude.'

'Your call. But you need to know, I honestly won't be able to handle your distress levels right now, Freddie.'

'Fine, but I'm telling you, if Paul Henderson's in it—'

'He's not.'

Freddie slumps back and closes his eyes.

'So, promise me you won't watch it?'

Silence. Then Freddie rolls his head towards Ambrose and opens one eye. 'So. Promise, as in, "I promise I'll email my mentor and set up a session"? Hn?'

Ambrose blinks. 'I can definitely do that today, yes.'

'Yeah, you *can* do it, but you won't. You are *so* full of shit.'

'He's a busy guy. I can't expect him to drop everything. Even if I email him—'

'Whatever. There you go.' He dumps the hen on Ambrose's knee and reaches for his laptop. 'Gotta finish off. I promise I won't watch it. OK? And guess what? I actually keep my promises, and maybe one day this'll be a two-way street? You know? Babe, I get you're depressed, but you're also a total asshole. Just saying.' He puts his headphones on. 'Bye.'

Freddie picks up where he left off, but Ambrose continues to sit there. After a couple of minutes, Freddie sighs and slides his headphones down.

'What?'

'Thought you'd like to know, she just shat on my leg.'

'BAHA ha hahaha ha! You *go*, gurrl!'

He's still laughing five minutes later. Partly it's relief? Coz Brose was laughing too, and he's not seen him laugh in a lo-o-ong time. It's like maybe he's finally turned a corner, and he's coming back into the light after months of sitting in some dark cave where Freddie couldn't reach him? Maybe he'll even email Theo? Freddie's not holding his breath, though. Man, is his husband ever phobic about asking for help? I mean, why wouldn't you just ask? Freddie would totally get himself life-coached *to death* if he had an in like that with a best-selling motivational self-help guru dude?

But hey, at least now today feels OK, despite the downer of Chloe's news. He just needs to upload this online singing lesson to his YouTube channel? Then one last push and he'll be through translating fucking *Winterreise*. Last song, '*Der Leiermann*'. Old barefoot guy, playing his hurdy-gurdy in the ice, nobody wants to hear. But he's still playing? Freddie kinda connects with that. And maybe tonight he'll ask Brose to play the accompaniment for him, give it a run through? Talking of which. *Man* could he properly use some hard-core duet time, after weeks of playing solo!

Moon Facts

Waxing crescent (10%)

We are now onto 'the beaver moon' so-called for when the beavers build their damns before winter. It is aka 'the frost moon', but we have not had any frost yet because of climate change.

Moon Zodiacs: Capricorn

I still have literally no idea what this means LOL because I thought November is 'Scorpio'. At the end of the day I am not interested, mum and dad say we don't believe in all that, it is like tarrow cards, we believe in Jesus and the bible.

Wednesday 18th November

So todays big news is . . . . . wait for it . . . I'm having to quarantine!!!! That's right – Jamie Knight tested positive so my Year group have to isolate. You totally would not believe that on the exact same day Leah can go back to school, I have to stay at home. Mum says at least I can be trusted to get on with my school work (NB she said this AFTER Leah went to school, because she is not totally stupid!!!) I will also practice my singing and clarinet.

Attitude of Grattitude.

I have decided to write down the good news in this journal and be more grateful.

Number One bit of good news is that there's a vaxine!!!! Yay! It will be rolled out in January hopefully. I for one am glad about this, the UK death toll has passed 50,000 people. Last night Leah was like, if a school minibus crashes and 25 children plus there teacher gets killed, that is like a major tragedy and everyone is OMG that's so terrible and they tie boquets and teddy bears to the railings and stuff. Then she said, 'Well this is like TWO THOUSAND minibuses crashing! That is like 5 minibuses PER DAY crashing and killing everyone this year.'

When she said this I could literally see it, it would be like the girls choir and Mr Hardman-May on our way to do sing-up at a primary school or something and then we all get killed. Game over. It is so weird how when the numbers are massive it feels less bad, like you can't imagine it? You'd think you would get it when your own dad could so nearly of died but like I said, it is weird.

Number 2 bit of good news is that dad has been feeling better, he can go to the hub most afternoons to help out, he mainly sits and gives advice and helps people with their claims and prints stuff out for them on the printers. He takes Luna because people all love her, and dogs are good for mental health wellbeing.

Number 3 bit of good news is that it is nearly Advent!!!! We will have proper advent calenders with chocolate in this year, mum bought them already. So I will not just have a 'Climate Extinction Countdown Calender' made by guess who LOL. I so love advent because of the candles and the beautiful music. NB we will not be doing darkness into light in the cathedral obvs it is still going to be lockdown ☹ I love that advent is only a hare's breath away from Christmas itself when we get to hear the bible story of Immanual coming to be with us, it makes me cry happy tears.

It's the Sunday of Christ the King. Across the Diocese of Lindchester, hawk-eyed proofreading is underway, lest we end up celebrating Chris the King in our livestreamed service (or, heaven forfend, Christ the Kink). Back in the Good Old Days of the Book of Common Prayer, it was always called Stir-up Sunday. Ah, if only the C of E hadn't abandoned the Prayer Book and the Authorized Version of the Bible, then our churches would still be bursting at the seams. Isn't it obvious how to reverse the trend? Is it not true to say that for decades young and old alike have been flocking in their hundreds to the BCP 8 o'clock in every parish of the land, hungry for the beauty of the language? (I enquire rhetorically, in the spirit of Anglican stirring.)

Here and there across Lindfordshire, people more faithful than I are celebrating the day properly. They are making their Christmas puddings and cakes. Thank heaven there wasn't any panic-buying of flour and sugar ahead of this lockdown. Kitchens fill with the goodly fragrance of spice and brandy. Some people recite the collect for the day as they mix, beseeching the Lord to stir up their wills, that they might plenteously bring forth good works. Will there be a big family Christmas dinner this year, though? Will the happy throng cheer to see this pudding carried in, a-flicker with tiny blue flames?

In the vicarage kitchen in Cardingforth, a CD of Handel's *Messiah* plays. Father Wendy and her husband Doug have a mini-pud production line going. They will donate all fifty to the Cardingforth foodbank. That won't be enough, but others have promised to make or donate some too. Nobody in her parishes will go hungry this Christmas. With the help of God, nobody.

In the vicarage kitchen in Lindford, Dominic and Mrs Todd are making mincemeat and the Christmas cake, while Virginia live-streams mass from church. Christmas carols are playing on Dominic's phone – gasp! Yes, of course it's too early, but the old familiar songs keep Mum tethered. Otherwise she'd be off and away, like a child's helium balloon. The music keeps her feet on the ground. So do the smells. Grated nutmeg. Lemon zest. Mum wraps pages of the *Church Times* round the cake tin, and ties it with string, then puts it in the oven. Just like she's always done. Ah, the smell of baking newspaper is the smell of Christmas for Dominic!

'If I were a wise man", sings Mum.

Hah, if Dominic were a wise man, he probably wouldn't be bothering this year. It's not as though he'll be having the parish round for mulled wine and mince pies, is it? But he carries on tipping things into the bowl and stirring. In faith. Because it won't be wasted. He can give it away.

Dominic joins in. 'Yet what I can I give him – give my heart.'

The half-moon sets. Mourning Moon. The ghosts of long-gone beavers swim silvery in the Linden. Owls call, chilly, shivery. Nurses hold the hands of the dying. Slowly, the night shift passes. Day breaks. A tall man goes out to feed the hens. He glances up at the dark window and sees that the envelope once taped there has gone.

I can picture it – the hare Jess imagined. It's poised on a golf-course fairway as the sun rises red over Lindfordshire. Everything is still. The hare might be forged of copper and bronze, every whisker cast in pure silver, and its eyes of amber and jet. Look. Each breath is a tiny cloud in the dawn air.

So don't be afraid. That's how close it is.

Mourning Moon, Part IV

omfort ye, comfort ye my people, saith your God. Speak ye comfortably to Jerusalem. Father Dominic is in his study stapling and folding the handful of service sheets he will need for this year's pared-down Advent carol service. It will be livestreamed, with only seven people there: Father Dominic, the organist, two volunteers to read the lessons, two to do the techie stuff with iPads and whatnot – and Freddie Hardman-May, bless him, who has agreed to come and sing. There's no official number, according to Bishop Matt. Half a dozen, give or take. He'll turn a blind eye to a few more, but if it's twelve, that starts to look like an act of public worship, which gets tricky.

Oh, what bad timing this is, that lockdown should end the Tuesday *after* Advent Sunday. And now all the hoo-hah about lifting restrictions for Christmas, and whether that takes other faith communities properly into account. People have been trotting out the old 'this is still a Christian country' argument, where 'Christian' is a euphemism for 'racist'. They didn't pipe up about churches being closed during Holy Week, did they? And another thing: if this were truly a Christian country, maybe our leaders would show a bit more character and integrity. The home secretary might resign for breaking the Ministerial Code of Conduct. The Prime Minister might sack her. Instead, it's the person who led the enquiry that resigns! Quite what would constitute a resignation matter for Tory politicians in these days of Trumpist doubling down, God knows. Profumo must be kicking himself in his grave.

Eek! He's starting to sound like an embittered old crone. (No offence, Jane.) Time to look out of his soul's window, instead of moping indoors. He glances at the service sheet he's folding. *Speak ye comfortably to Jerusalem, and cry unto her, that her warfare is accomplished, that her iniquity is pardoned.* Will these words shimmer with hope this year as Freddie Hardman-May sings his aria? Or will they seem to mock us? Even with three vaccines now in the pipeline, our warfare doesn't seem anywhere near being accomplished. No-deal Brexit looking ever more likely. Trump with his blunderbuss full of lawsuits. Dominic reminds himself that those words were first spoken into the exile in Babylon. And then spoken again into the Roman occupation. Desperate times. Comfortable words in desperate times. Perhaps it's always like that? Perhaps—

A ghastly noise comes from the kitchen. Like crashing crockery – on and on! A tea trolley careering down the Spanish Steps! He drops the stapler and sprints through.

'Mum? Are you OK?'

'Listen to that!' She points to the washing machine. 'That doesn't sound right, does it? It must be broken.'

He lunges and turns it off. The clashing clatters to a halt. He squats and peers into the drum. The breakfast crocks. Damn. He can see his favourite 'More tea, Vicar?' mug in pieces. 'I see the problem. I think plates and cutlery go in the dishwasher, not the washing machine, Mother dear.'

'What? Did I— Never!' Her hands fly to her mouth. 'I must have had a complete brainstorm.' She peers in as well. 'Oh dear. Are they all broken?'

'I'll say!'

'Oh dear. I'm very sorry.' She wrings her hands in her apron. 'I don't know what got into me.'

'Not to worry.' He gives her a hug. 'It's confusing. They're both big and square and white. I'll stick a label on, so you know which is which.'

'Well, at least it's not the Crown Derby!' she says.

'A consoling thought,' he agrees. 'Except I don't have any Crown Derby.'

'Well, not any more!' she says. 'Can you glue it?'

370

'Hardly! Smithereens, my dear.' He fetches the washing-up bowl and starts picking out the fragments. 'I'll buy some more, so don't you worry.'

'What? It'll cost a fortune!'

'Nonsense. It's tat from IKEA. And the cutlery's unscathed. Look.' He holds up a knife.

'Crown Derby from IKEA! Tiddly, widdly, widdly, Mrs Tittlemouse.' She starts wringing her hands again. 'Oh dear. There's that china repair place on Corporation Street. They did a good job on your grandma's Royal Doulton teapot when she chipped the spout that time.'

'Decades ago in a different town, Mother mine.' He rolls the drum round. The last few fragments clatter. He picks them out and stands up. 'I'll just wrap these in the *Church Times* and we're done!'

Mum stares in the washing-up bowl. 'That's never Crown Derby.'

'You're right.' He puts the bowl on the worktop. Then he pats his chest and laughs. 'Good Lord! I need a lie-down in a darkened room! That sounded like the end of the world, Mother. Now I understand why the Midian army freaked out when Gideon's men smashed their jars. Imagine *that* on a dark night!'

'Ah, but they had trumpets as well, if I remember rightly.' She starts picking out shards of china. 'We can glue it back together if we're careful. It's like a 3D jigsaw.'

'No, leave it, Mum. I'll sort it out.' He steers her gently away. 'Why don't you make us a cup of tea?'

'Righty-ho!'

Once again, it's not the end of the world after all. But Advent puts us on high alert. The bridegroom might come at any moment. Or the thief. Get ready. Lamps and extra oil. Stay awake.

The waxing gibbous moon rides across the sky, and the first frosty night comes at last. Jack hears the gritters going up the road at 2 a.m. as he stands in front of the ruined summerhouse in Miss Sherratt's garden. The orange hazard light flickers through the bare branches. They'll be out across the whole region tonight. Bad time to be sleeping rough. He's lucky. He has shelter and safety. Nobody's going to piss on him while he sleeps, or try and rob him. And he's by himself. Like a hermit. Or he would be, if he prayed a bit more. Must be the only person not suffering from isolation in 2020. Solitude is what mends him. All the hostels he's stayed in over the years. Always somebody kicking off. But now he doesn't have to worry about other people's demons. Just his own.

All the stars. Faint, though, compared to the Gulf. Blew his mind, when he first saw the night sky out there. Clouds looked like black holes in a bright starry ceiling. Sirius almost blue. And the Milky Way. Bright enough to cast a shadow when there was no moon. Funny to think that would have been normal everywhere a century or so back.

A fox limps across the chamomile lawn. Had a couple of cubs this year. They'll be around somewhere too. Tawny owls calling. Males, mainly. Hoo-hoo-hoo-hoooo! The fox vanishes through the gap in the fence. She'll be sniffing around next door's hens again.

A light goes on in Miss Sherratt's bedroom. Jack watches. A moment later, the bathroom light. Then off again. Then the bedroom light goes out. The house is dark again. Good. She'll most likely get off to sleep again, not have to come down for Horlicks. Tomorrow morning, she's going to open her curtains and see the frosty lawn, and she'll be fretting about him. He's got it snug enough in here, but she's been offering him the old garage for the worst of the winter. He may have to take her up on it, but it'll be for her peace of mind, not his own comfort. Because he knows she can't bear the thought some-times. Her alone in that vast house, him bunking down in the old wreck. Like Dives and Lazarus. She told him that once. So he stuck his head into the garage the other day, just to oblige. She's only got a blue Morris 10 saloon in there under a tarp. Wouldn't mind checking that over, see if he can get it going again. The whole place is frozen in time. Like one of those vintage emporiums, with all the little stalls inside, full of junk and treasures.

The owls call again. A jet goes over, high up. Something triggers next door's security lights. The fox, probably. He can see his breath smoking. Then the light flicks off again.

She had all the old Christmas tree decorations out the other day. He's off to get her a tree once lockdown's over. Far too early, she says. But it'll cheer her up. A six-footer. Norway spruce. He tried telling her it'll shed, but she said they're the only kind that smell like Christmas. Fair play to her. For him it's satsumas. The smell of the peel, and he's

372

opening his stocking in the dark, aged six. He'll stick a mask on, go inside, and help her decorate it. She doesn't trust herself on a step-ladder any more. Glass baubles like his gran had. Original boxes, tissue-paper nests. Silky tinsel going bald. She's kept the lot.

But Jack – he's more of a snail than a squirrel. You need to be ready to clear out at no notice.

Miss Sherratt is not the only person who has decided to put her tree up early this year. Another of those subliminal memos has gone out from COVID Central, that this weekend is the time to deck the hall. Up to the loft and down to the basement go the good people of Lindfordshire to haul out the decorations. Artificial trees are assembled. Lights are strung along gutters and garages. Santa once again creeps like a burglar over the rooftops of Martonbury. Magnolias and conifers sparkle and flash. Stars, reindeer, snowflakes, twinkling wreaths – you name it. Except for Cathedral Close, of course, which is like the Highway of Holiness. Nothing vulgar shall pass over it, nor shall fools err thereon with inflatable light-up gingerbread men. The annual pop-up shop (The Tree Kings) has already appeared in the car park by the arboretum in Lindford, ready to open the day lockdown ends. Hurry, or all the three-foot trees will have gone, and you'll end up forking out £60 for a tree that's too big for your lounge.

It's Black Friday. Smoke rises from overheated credit cards and PayPal accounts. There will be no ugly scenes or supermarket stampedes in lockdown. All the bargains must be grabbed online this year.

A calendar alert pings into the Bishop of Barcup's diary: *Anniversary*. After the cock-up of 2016, he made sure he never forgot again. The first alert was two weeks ago. The traditional sixth-anniversary gift, the websites tell him, is sugar, or iron. The gifts are wrapped and good to go tomorrow. He's got her a bag of demerara and a box of forty-millimetre lost-head nails from B&Q. *You're so sweet I lost my head over you xxx*. And because he's not a complete numpty, he's also sourced a genuine Victorian cast-iron boot jack. (Matt is not to know, but this year Jane will forget and his victory will be complete.)

Over in the vicarage at Gayden Magna, Father Ed has bought a sixth-anniversary present for Neil. Beyond the basics of avoiding anything ornamental, or wearable, Ed knows he will never master the Ferguson rulebook of good taste. He has settled with some confidence on an expensive bottle of Mount Gay XO Peat Smoke rum. Whence this sudden boldness? How can he be certain Mount Gay XO Peat Smoke rum will not prove to be tacky, cheesy and irredeemably last year? Possibly because of the text message he received last week:

HINT HINT 6TH ANNIVERSARY GIFT xxxx

With a link to the Mount Gay website. From there, it was a straightforward matter of selecting the most expensive thing available. Ed has no idea what Neil's bought him. All he knows is that he had to be out all afternoon last Thursday, and he's not allowed in the garage until tomorrow.

Ambrose is out walking this Black Friday. He's taken a day of annual leave. After he spoke to Theo, he got in the car and drove miles and miles. He spotted the reservoir on the satnav. Non-essential travel, but there's nobody policing things this time round. He thinks of the man with the gun getting turned back, and all those dead lambs.

The path is deep in copper leaves from the beeches, and there are gold larch needles sprinkled over everything – the moss, leaves, roots, in the cleft of branches. It's totally still. Windless. No sound from the branches, no breeze in his hair, past his ears as he walks. No traffic, no farm machinery, no construction work. A woman's voice on the far side of the water carries clearly as she talks to the baby she's pushing. Quiet again. When was he last in a place so silent? He stops and looks at the water. The reservoir is full up and deep with sky. Blue, with flocks of cloud. An upside-down wood pigeon flies over. Or under. Off in the far distance, a dog barks. He looks round for Alfie, then remembers he's alone.

So what's the narrative, Ambrose? What are you telling yourself?

All the wisdom he's ever passed on to Freddie over the years, he learnt from Theo. Ambrose knows all the self-help stuff. He knows what to do, what questions to ask to flush out the truth. What he'd forgotten, apparently, was that sometimes you need to hear someone else asking you.

'What are you telling yourself?'

'I'm telling myself it's not OK to be weak. It's not OK to need help.'

'Is it OK to be human?'

Ambrose gasps again, like he did at the time. It sounds loud in the still wood, like the hoarse bark of an animal. Yep. That's the one. That's the right question, Theo. Floodgates. Ambrose suddenly remembers when he was about thirteen. The burst pipe. He stood with Dad, looking at the bulge in the lounge ceiling. Get a bucket, Son. Dad poking the ceiling paper with a bamboo pole. Whoosh.

Is it OK to be human?

Ambrose starts walking again. The path underfoot is a matrix of tree roots, like veins under skin. He's walking on the skin of a giant. He's a tiny animal, just a tiny human animal. He runs a sleeve over his eyes and sobs. If he could believe, like Freddie believes, he might take comfort in the thought that the creator became human. If it's OK for God to become human, then presumably it's OK to be human. It's OK to be weak, it's OK to be nothing but a little baby. It's OK, Brose. You're OK.

Saturday morning. The Bishop of Barcup clears his throat.

Jane rolls over in bed and groans. 'What? What time is it?'

He is standing by the bed with the breakfast tray.

'Shit! It's today.' Jane hauls herself up on her elbow. 'I forgot. Shit, shit, *shit*!'

Matt smiles like a man who has been playing a very long game and it has finally paid off. 'Happy anniversary, Janey.'

Over in the garage of the vicarage in Gayden Parva, Neil whisks the dust cloth off. 'Ta dah!'

Ed stares. 'Oh my God. You're mad.'

'Ah-ah.' Neil wags a finger. 'You said you fancied it.'

'Yes, but . . .' He laughs. 'I can't believe— Is it genuine?'

'Genuine?! Of course it's genuine! What do you take me for?' He opens the door. 'Heh heh heh. In you go, big man.'

Still laughing, Ed steps inside the refurbished red cast-iron GPO Trafalgar phone kiosk. Neil crowds in behind him. The door closes, and we will tiptoe away, dear reader, and leave them to negotiate the transition from cherished fantasy to reality.

November 30th

It is St Andrew's Day and the last day of November. Yesterday it was foggy and I was scared it would be foggy today, and I would not see the full moon, but I did see it, I am happy to say. Two full moon's in the same month is something pretty amazing IMHO. To be fair this could of happened in my lifetime before but I was not aware of the significance.

Moon Phase

Full (99%)

Moon Facts

Moon rise 16.01 Moon set 07.52

So I saw the full moon when I went out for a walk earlier with Dad. We went really slowly and we just went round the block to count the Christmas trees (14) like we used to when I was little, only now it was me slowing down and waiting for him. I am eternally grateful he is on the mend and can walk even this far, last month he sometimes couldn't get up the stairs, he used to sit on the little landing bit halfway up and have a rest. When I am at school (NB I am still isolating) I am like 'seriously guys you do not want Covid, it is really scary, plus you REALLY don't want your parent's or grandparent's to get it.'

So anyway the moon. It was MASSIVE!!! Like probably the biggest full moon I have seen, even if it is not an actual 'super-moon'. Yesterday we did the exact same walk and we saw people putting there trees up, like in one house there was a boy and his dad putting up a tree in the front room and upstairs we could see a little girl standing on a chair, she was putting pink tinsel on a white tinsel tree. That would totally of been me back in the day LOL. I have moved on from that now, my taste has matured somewhat.

I totally cannot believe it is nearly a year since we did the thousand Chrismas lights and Leah was Santa Lucia with candles (not real ones!!!!) on her head all round Lindfordshire. How time flies when your having fun!!! NOT!!!! I told dad and he said yes, the years go by quicker the older you get. And then he said will you sing me the Sankta Lucia carol, so I did, I sang it in actual Swedish, I can still remember all the words. It means 'There in our dark house walking with lit candles, Sankta Lucia, Sankta Lucia.' He squeezed my hand when I finished but he did not say anything. So I squeezed his hand back and we just walked home. The full moon kept appearing over the houses like one giant Christmas light.

Freddie sees the full moon too, as he walks the dogs. Whoa! Get a look at that. They say 'the man in the moon', but to him it's always more a woman's face, a mother's? Like he always thinks of Mary, looking down at Jesus when he was in the manger – that tender. Tired to death after labour but, you know, still keeping watch? The same moon has been keeping watch literally for ever? Crazy to think Jesus saw the same moon Freddie's looking at now?

He smiles. Lockdown ending tomorrow. And Brose is coming out of it, looks like. He spoke to Theo. Finally.

Comfort ye my people. Man. He could sing that on his head with his eyes closed? But last night it was like it suddenly lit up again, tingled along every nerve, and he was on fire? Ha, on fire in an empty church, but hey, least he was singing again, performing at last? First candle on the ring glowing. And he was aching with Advent suddenly. He totally got the whole on-tiptoe-waiting vibe. Like, please, *please* come. But now he's thinking maybe it goes both ways? Maybe Jesus was all, Please let me be one of them. I want to be with them, I want to rescue them. And the angels would probably be all, That's crazy talk; have you even seen what they're capable of?

Freddie reaches home. He can see Chloe and Brose in the kitchen cooking supper. Then they're all gonna start the next season of *The Crown*. Man, is Chloe over-invested in that series. But that makes him think about the angels again, warning God. Dude, do not get over-invested in humanity. But too late. The incarnation? God's got skin in the game now.

DECEMBER

Long Night Moon, Part I

I t's December. The sun rises just before 8 a.m. It comes up like a red balloon above the earth's rim, behind bare black branches. Children rush to open the first window on their Advent calendar. In pious households there is a Bible verse waiting for them. The rest find chocolate. In some houses in Lindfordshire all the windows will be open and every chocolate consumed by the end of the day. I'm sorry to say that this outrage against the whole concept of waiting in joyful hope will probably not be perpetrated by children. Children have parents around to impose restraint; adults have to fend for themselves. But there is help at hand from the Department of Useful Platitudes – the following self-exoneration slogan, which will remain valid throughout 2020: *IT IS WHAT IT IS*.

Yes, it is what it is. We are what we are. Since March, the COVID pixies have been busy in our wardrobes taking in our waistbands. They keep treading on the edge of the bathroom scales to make it look as though we've put on ten pounds. What if we have become equally unfit and flabby spiritually? It would be easier to cast off the works of darkness if we were confident that the armour of light would still fit us.

Lockdown 2 has ended. Infection rates have only gone down by thirty per cent, and a new tier system is operating. There are three tiers: medium, high and very high. There is no Tier 0, where the risk of catching COVID-19 is low. Nowhere to run, nowhere to hide. Lindfordshire is in the new Tier 2. Pubs and restaurants can open again, providing it's table service and they serve food alongside the booze. Scotch eggs have been upgraded from snack to substantial meal in order to facilitate this. There's probably a Knightsbridge clause that calculates how many scotch quails' eggs you'd need to eat to be compliant, but what do we know of Knightsbridge up here? As much as Knightsbridge knows of us. Down thataway they think Lindfordshire is the North. We are the people who walk in darkness. Galilee of the Nations. Can anything good come out of here?

Churches can open again for public worship. Don't forget to book a place at the carol service to avoid disappointment. Non-essential shops are open again too. If we felt like it, we could get there early to avoid queuing round the block, and bag a bargain from Debenhams before it closes its doors for good. No! Debenhams has gone bust? Even if we never shop there, it's comforting to know it's still trading and we could pop in. It's like the C of E. Are we on the brink of a retailing mass extinction? Perhaps department stores have been dinosaurs for a while now. The gentle herbivorous giants of the High Street, habitat steadily eroded by out-of-town malls and online shopping – then along comes the whopping asteroid of COVID-19. Please don't say M&S and John Lewis are heading the same way!

But at least Christmas is safe. The year will be crowned after all. People, look east! We will be allowed to sing carols outdoors, if we are socially distanced. Most joyous of all, up to three households can meet for up to five days between the 23rd and 27th. Trim the hearth and set the table! Nab that Ocado slot. Order that Norfolk Bronze turkey. Launch Operation Christmas Food Shopping List. And thank goodness we won't have to post those parcels to family after all.

Jane still has one parcel to post all the same. She stands in her disposable mask in the queue in Martonbury Post Office. She may have forgotten her own anniversary, but at least she hasn't missed the last posting date to New Zealand. Danny will have his customary rugby sock full of crappy gifts from Mum in time to open on Christmas morning. She gets a fiercely intense image of them all gathered on Mickey and Sal's deck, with the pohutukawa blossom red against the blue sky. Turquoise sea down in the bay. Maybe orcas. Damn. She blinks the tears away, and focuses on the here and now.

The place is decked with office-style red and gold foil garlands.

There are toys and children's books on a shelf over to her right. Rotating stands of cards and calendars to her left. A rack of padded envelopes. She reads the poster listing the items you can't send through the post. In front of Jane there's a girl returning clothes she's bought online, judging by the ASOS logo on the bag. Jane checks her symptoms. Good. Threat of audible sobbing downgraded to Tier 1. But oh God, let this terrible term end. I am so weary. Only a week and a half to go.

The shorter the queue, the slower the progress. Only one counter is open, and there's a pensioner getting money out of his Post Office account with a card. He chats about COVID to the woman serving. That's all we've talked about all year, thinks Jane. We'll know it's finally over when we're back to the weather again. She watches as he pokes the keypad with a trembling forefinger. There's a cash machine outside, for God's sake. But she's not much better herself, is she? She's never paid for anything with her phone, the way the youngsters do. To her students she's as big a brontosaurus as the man now folding the cash carefully into his wallet and tucking it into his inside pocket. He zips up his anorak and says goodbye.

The queue shuffles forward to the next circle on the floor. Then she gets it: this is a rare chance for social contact. He must be glad lockdown's over. She pictures him going to the butcher's, then the grocer's, shopping old-style, chatting to the owners the way we always used to. God, that was boring, though, when you were a child tugging on Mum's coat and whining to go home. The complex etiquette of not going into the baker's with bread you'd bought at the Co-op visible in your basket. Green Shield Stamps. The catalogues, drooling over the toys Mum would never let her have.

Her phone buzzes. It's a message from Cousin Elaine:

Hi Jane. Hope all's well. Just found a pic of your parents wedding. I'll stick it in the post xxx.

Just as Jane is wondering what it's like, another message arrives. Elaine is ahead of her, and has taken a photo. Wow. Dad in a suit. Mum in a sticky-out swing-style dress. Jane's three-month presence is not yet visible. It's black and white, but Jane knows the dress is pale jade. Well, that's what Mum always said. She hadn't expected it all to look so 50s. But it was only just the 60s, of course. January 1960 to be precise. Pre-mini-dress and floppy hats and white knee boots and the whole Carnaby Street vibe.

'*Next*, please!'

'Sorry.' Jane sticks her phone in her pocket and steps to the counter to put her parcel on the scales. 'New Zealand, please.'

She's going to need to study the photo properly on her iPad. Mum's expression so clearly saying, *Marriage? Yeah, right.* Well, *that* didn't skip a generation. There was some of that going on six years ago at the Lindford Register Office, as her own wedding photos attest. Jane fills in the customs label: *Sweets and toys, value £10.* And Dad was so much shorter than she remembered. Same height as Mum, in fact. Could he actually have been a short man? He'd always been a giant to her. Giant and champ. Best dad in the world. She gets a pang of loss. He might still have been around if working conditions had been better in the 40s and 50s. She can see him, in his 90s, getting money out of his Post Office account every week.

'Sorry?'

'Are there any batteries in the toys?'

'No.'

She pays with her card, sticks the receipt in her purse, and leaves. She must be a throwback, then. Either that, or she's got the NHS to thank for her height. All that rosehip syrup and free school milk. But dammit, she's going to have to rejig the album completely now to accommodate this new picture.

Advent wreaths have appeared on doors. In every church, some version of an Advent ring has been set up. In each case there are five candles. The central one is white for Christmas Day. The other four we are at liberty to argue over, and pour scorn on any ignoramus who thinks the pink one is for Mary. Christmas cards start to arrive. The Bishop of Barcup stands by to whisk away any envelope addressed to The Rt Revd and Mrs M. Tyler, so that Janey doesn't blow a gasket.

In the Bishop of Lindchester's office on the Close, Kat lines up the boxes of official cards for her boss to sign. This year she's had a standard message printed inside as well, so that the bishop simply has to write '+Steve', and he doesn't get RSI after four hundred cards with another two hundred to go. The address labels are all already on the envelopes. Once he's signed them all, she will drive them over to Martonbury for Matt to sign. Matt's PA will then post them.

Advent. Stay awake, for you do not know when the master of the house will come. Pray that justice may roll like a river, and righteousness like an ever-flowing stream. The US courts dismiss Trump's lawsuits as fast as they appear in this game of legal whack-a-mole. At home, Brexit negotiations are on a deal/no-deal knife-edge. 'Oven-ready' proves not to relate to a trade deal. Silly us. All 'oven-ready' actually meant was 'there's definitely a cooker somewhere, and I've sent my people out to locate a world-beating turkey'. The government cuts overseas aid to the poorest nations from 0.7 per cent of the gross national income to 0.5 per cent. A tiny but important gesture – from infinitesimal to infinitesimalest. It will have no discernible impact on our fiscal prosperity, but it *puts Britain first*. In this season of Advent, when we look for his coming in great glory to judge the living and the dead, at least we will know what to expect. The trumpet shall sound and the dead shall be raised, and Britain will be last in the kingdom.

Moon Phase
Waning gibbous (87%)

Yay for December and Christmas!!!! I am loving my calendar. It has chocolate plus I do not have to go oh look an endangered species every day in December LOL (no offence Leah but 'apocaliptic water warfare scenario' for window 24 is not very Christmassy!!!!). Guess what, it actually snowed today!!!! I was so excited for snowmen and snow-balling but it did not really settle, it was slushy and now its nearly gone. We saw it through the classroom windows and everyone was like ITS SNOWING!!!! (NB FORTUNATLEY I have finished quarantining, we are back at school.) Dad said 'There is something about the first snow which is allways magical'. I so hope we get a white Christmas.

Everyone is super excited for Christmas as well because they will get to be in a Christmas bubble and maybe see there grandparents. Three households can be in one bubble 23-27 December. Mum went 'That is complete madness' when she heard. I for one agree. If you boil it down in cold blood we would all do better to wait for the vaccine. So we will not be seeing grandma and gramps or granny and grandad (mums parents) because we know how serious covid is. Plus now there's a new avian flu AKA bird flu, it is not just minks getting culled, it is very sad.

December Full Moon name's

Surprize suprize, there are different names for the December full moon. It can be 'the Cold Moon' or 'the Long Night Moon'. Both of these totally make sense unless . . . wait for it . . . you happen to live in the southern hemisphere, it is summer down there! The full Cold/Long Night moon will be last one of 2020. I will be SOOOOOO mad and dissappointed if I don't get to see it, it will ruin my record of seeing every single full moon of 2020. Finger's crossed it will be clear at the end of the month, it will be full on 30th and 31st.

Interesting Moon Facts

I just discovered (from google) that the moon is not round it is egg-shaped!!! That blue my mind. You may wonder why it does not look egg-shaped. This is because the small end is always pointing our way so it look's round. You can check this out by holding up an egg, it will look round if you hold it with the small end pointing towards you. I proved this to Leah by using an egg from the fridge but she just said whatever. I regret to say she is suprisably uninterested in scientific facts, you'd think someone who cares so much about the planet and gaia would take an interest, but no. Well that's all for now folks, I will go and practice my clarinet and do my vocal exercises. Byeeeeeeee xxxx

Window after window is opened on calendars around Lindfordshire. Advent 1. Advent 2. The light shines in the darkness. Students begin their journeys home for Christmas, after mass testing. The vaccination programme is rolled out. The Bishop of Lindchester offers church buildings for clinics and test centres. The first nonagenarian recipients make the headlines and become internet sensations. People over eighty, those in care homes, NHS and key workers. That's the pecking order. What is this strange feeling? Could it be hope? Are we finally winning?

The sun rises and the sky is charged with pink. The very air seems magical in the gardens and parks of Lindfordshire this Saturday morning. Ambrose stands looking at the henhouse. He's been following the progress of bird flu on the government website and via updates from Mum and Dad. He's already got rid of the feeders from the patio and ordered a hawk kite on a pole, which he'll set up on the henhouse roof. Chloe is pretty heartbroken at the thought of driving birds away, but it is what it is. The henhouse mesh is fine gauge, so no problem with wild birds getting in there. The challenge will be stopping them perching and crapping on the wire roof of the run. Polythene is the best bet. They've got till the 14th to make sure their biosecurity's up to scratch and they're compliant. Freddie's preferred option is to bring the girls inside, put straw down for them in the dining room. Ambrose rolls his eyes. He knows where that would end – with free-range hens wandering through the whole house and perched along his bedhead every night. He's only just managed to reimpose the no-dogs-in-bed rule.

Freddie comes out through the French windows. Ambrose can almost feel it, the Van de Graaff crackle of his husband's mood.

'Did you explain?' Freddie asks.

'Explain?'

'The rules, dude. Gotta tell them the rules.' He squats down. 'Hey, listen up, girls. There's a virus. So no socializing, no mixing with other birds outside your household, OK? Wings. Beaks. Space! Just till Monday. Then you can all come inside for Christmas! Yay!' He stands up and grins. 'So they're cool with that?'

'Right,' says Ambrose. 'Well anyway, I'm off to buy some heavy-duty polythene sheeting and a staple gun, to cover the roof.'

'What? After I just promised them? Du-u-ude.' He punches his arm softly. 'Hey. Don't be too long. Busy morning ahead for you, babe. Chloe's out. Not just the henhouse needs seeing to, is all I'm saying?'

Ambrose shakes his head and smiles as he drives to the builders' merchant on the other side of town. He understands why Freddie is so hyper today. Third time lucky. Maybe *this* month? God, it's so *hard* to stand back and let Freddie manage his own hopes, and not be forever trying to shield him. He knows his perspective-bringing and realism just blight the present while being powerless to prevent the bad stuff happening. It's a pointless exercise. Worse than pointless. Ambrose doesn't need Theo to remind him that there's five decades of research indicating that optimists have better cardiovascular health, stronger immune systems, bounce back faster from surgery and live longer.

So what would optimism look like?

Suddenly, Ambrose laughs. It would look like him risking everything four years ago – his heart, his sanity, his future happiness. It would look like weighing up all the counter-arguments, the warnings, the projections, and saying, Fuck it, I'm going to marry this crazy lunatic anyway. Yep. It would look like that. He parks at the builders' merchant. And it would look like the stand-out best decision of his entire cautious calculating life.

But that still does not mean he's going to have chickens running loose about the house.

Tomorrow is Gaudete Sunday; the third Sunday of Advent. Rose vestments are brought out from storage. The pink candle will be lit on the Advent ring. Pink socks may be worn. It is also St Lucy's Day. How can it be a year since Father Dominic organized the Santa Lucia 'one thousand Christmas lights' all along the old pilgrim route? And in this Unprecedented Year, he will be holding the first of two Christmas carol services at the parish church. Christmas carols in Advent, Father? IT IS WHAT IT IS. The service will end in the open air, so that the congregation can sing 'Silent Night' and 'Hark the Herald' legally. A procession with candles and swirling incense will set off from church and end in front of the flats of the Abernathy estate. If people can't or won't come to church, then Dominic will take church to the people and bless them through his megaphone.

I happen to know that he will accidentally push the switch the wrong way and hit the siren setting. The megaphone will emit a brief but terrifying end-of-the-world scream. Startled by this solemn warning, the inhabitants of the Abernathy estate will rush to their windows. What the *hell* was that? High up and far off though they may be, the incense smoke will reach higher and farther yet. All will hear and receive the blessing and join in the singing – the righteous and the unrighteous alike, for all I know. I'm not the one who decides which story is beautiful and who is in and who is out. Things are what they are because God is who God is. The kingdom is always unprecedented.

Long Night Moon, Part II

It's Monday morning and Neil is in his car, stationary in a four-lane queue of traffic. It's so long since this has happened, he gets an absurd hit of nostalgia. It's like the M25! No, it's like Portsmouth, waiting for the car ferry to France (if you remember to renew your passport, grrr). The marshals in high-vis vests waving you into the right lane. Sitting there with the engine off, waiting, and wishing you'd thought to have a slash. He can see the long low tent with the row of stations that form the drive-through blood clinic. Drive-through – that's what fooled him. He thought he'd just drive up, get seen and drive off.

Halfway through December already. Unbelievable. It was all kicking off in China this time a year ago, he thinks. And we had no idea. Thought it was just another of those scares, swine flu, bird flu, not our problem. We were busy fretting over presents and Norfolk Bronze turkeys and church services. Maybe it's all kicking off again with this new variant and we still have no idea. All very Advent-y, isn't it? You don't know the day or the hour, you never do.

He gazes round the vast car park of Lindford Arena. The low sunshine is catching all the raindrops on the trees. If you squint, it looks like they're threaded with LED lights. Some kind of scaffolding construction going up. He can hear the clank of poles. There's a parked lorry loaded with aluminium chairs. Maybe there's going to be an outdoor socially distanced festive concert? There must be something planned, or they wouldn't be moving the test centre to the hospital car park next week. You'd think blood tests would trump concerts right now, but what does he know?

A car pulls away in Lane 1. He feels a little squeeze of dread. Is this the hour and the day for him? The whole queue follows. Then Lane 2. More cars arrive. Three cars ahead of him, Neil sees a hand emerge from a driver's window to tap ash off a ciggie. The guy in the high-vis vest says something into his walkie-talkie. Must be a dull cold job, marshalling. Day after day, standing two metres off, asking people if they've had COVID symptoms. At least it's not raining on them today. A fifth lane forms beside Neil. The car door ahead opens, and the driver gets out, mask dangling from an ear, to stub the cigarette out on the gravel.

And we're off!

Pulse of dread again. Neil's not *really* worried. But he's been persecuted by the auld NHS bobbing up in his Twitter timeline to say, 'It's probably nothing, but a tummy upset that goes on for three weeks and more could be a sign of cancer.' Which in Neil's mind at 3 a.m. obviously mutated into, 'It could *in theory* be nothing, but PREPARE TO MEET THY GOD, FERGUSON!' So he's had a phone consultation with the GP and here he is.

Another marshal in a mask steps forward and explains the system to Neil. He's to wear a mask, have his NHS number ready, then drive to the booth he's directed to, wind his window down and turn his engine off. Neil gives him the thumbs-up. Suddenly the *Match of the Day* theme tune blares from somewhere. Neil jumps half out of his skin. Feck's sake. Jangly, like the monster ice-cream van from hell. He drives forward and waits again. The tune stops abruptly in mid-phrase. Now he's going to have a fecking Sunday school earworm all week. *Why don't you put your trust in Jesus and ask him to come in!*

What if he *has* got cancer? Och, he hasn't. (But what if he has?)

He's waved forward to Table 3. He pulls up, kills the engine and opens his window. A woman in a mask stoops to greet him. Would you look at that! It's the blonde lassie. The one he sees out running. He reads her his NHS number off his phone, and confirms his name and D.O.B. She won't know him from Adam, in his mask and out of context. She's wrapped up nice and warm, but what a job, out here all day in the cold, not in her snug little room at some GP surgery.

He bares his arm and offers it through the window. Blue disposable gloves. The tourniquet goes on.

'Sharp scratch.'

'Heh heh heh. Was there a memo?' he asks. 'Telling you not to say "prick" any more?'

She chuckles, but maybe it's in that way you do when you've heard it a million times. Then he's ambushed by a wave of emotion, and he's gushing his thanks for all the NHS is doing, for her standing out here in the cold all day.

'Well, the way I see it, my grandparents' generation had the war. Air raids, rationing.' She changes the vial one-handed. 'Now it's my turn. If all I have to do is get a bit cold, well.'

He can tell she's smiling behind her mask.

'Aye, well. Thanks. You're all heroes,' he says.

'All done.' Blob of cotton wool. He always likes to see skill, the deft practised moves of someone doing their thing when they've done it so often they could do it in their sleep. Doesn't matter where they are, in their consulting room or in a windy car park. She goes back to her table and sorts things out. He slides his sleeve back down. When he glances up, she's bending to look in at him again, from two metres away.

'I can see you're down for stool samples too.'

'Aye. All sorted.'

'Good. Because we've got the kits here if you need them.'

'No, I'm fine.'

The look in her eyes is like a hand on his arm. Reassuring. Kind. She knows he must be scared. His tears rush up.

'Well, you take care,' she says.

'You too. Thanks. Happy Christmas.'

'Happy Christmas.'

He starts the engine and heads for Turlham Hall, to put the finishing touches to the first room makeover. He's got the projector in the boot. And there it is, that maddening earworm: *Why don't you take him as your Saviour, and let him hold your hand?* Is it nothing? he wonders again as he drives. This could be my last week of . . . It's probably nothing. But that experience just now was a foretaste of the kindness and uncomplaining heroism that will be there waiting for him if this turns out to be *something*. Despite the long queues and all the hanging about, he knows it'll be there. Tears well up again. He realizes he's still got his mask on. He tugs it off and tosses it on to the passenger seat. Follow-up appointment next week at the GP's. Not so long to wait for the results. *He will strengthen, help and guide you till you reach the Promised Land.* Aye, well let's hope that's still a long way off, eh?

All across Lindfordshire people are getting ready. We are over halfway through our Advent calendars now. How like a low-tech Zoom meeting they look. The robin in one window, the pudding in another. Nutcracker, holly sprig, shepherds. They look out from their little windows, while the other half still have their cameras off.

Christmas gleams ahead of us like the stable in Bethlehem, amid the sad and lowly plains of pandemic restrictions. We *will* meet again, just as the Queen foretold. Five whole days with our loved ones. Our hearts tremble with longing. We might be those trees in the arena car park, full of quivering diamond raindrops.

In every town and village in the region, foreheads crease over the Rubik's Cube puzzle of Christmas get-togethers and what constitutes three households. Do childcare bubbles count as one household, or two? What about single-person support bubbles? If (like the Penningtons) you have three children, can they all visit with their children during the five-day window, provided they don't all come at once? What size turkey should we order? What size ham should we bake?

Chloe prepares to clear out of her little flat in the extension, so her parents can come and stay. Obviously, she and the boys have to stay here for the Christmas services at the cathedral. But they might all head off down to Brose's parents' farm on Boxing Day, and ask Jack to feed the chickens. That should work, unless Brose's sister wants to see her in-laws as well as her parents, because that would add up to four households. Freddie's father has invited them all, assuring them that his place is easily big enough for everyone to socially distance. God only knows how much non-compliant coming and going of friends and step-siblings will be happening over in COVID-sceptic Mansion May, so no thanks.

393

Infection rates are soaring across the south of England. It emerges that this new strain of the virus may be far more transmissible. We continue to twist the cube this way, that way, singing a festive fa-la-la-la-la to block out the familiar sound of back-pedalling from Downing Street as the pandemic bike hurtles out of control once again. Ah yes, when we said three households for five days, that was supposed to be a limit, not a target. Of course, you *may* meet up with your loved ones, but please don't take advantage of the opportunity. Keep your windows open. Don't hug your granny. Stay apart, stay safe.

Surely they can't do a U-turn now? Not now we've bought the turkey and done the big food shop! Didn't we earn this? Didn't we save up for this present with a second lockdown? We were promised!

Not everyone is surprised. There are the steady souls who never bought into the family Christmas idea in the first place. Not worth the risk. We can have Christmas in May, when we've all been vaccinated. The Bishop of Barcup phoned his father a week back. 'We won't be coming to visit you for Christmas, Dad, because we don't want to kill you.'

'Much obliged,' said Mr Tyler Senior. 'See you when it's all over.'

Finally, it's the last week of school term. The Great Advent Antiphons are upon us. This whole year has been a long succession of Os. Oh no, oh shit, oh dear, oh well. In far-off London town (where the pale horse is currently kicking up its heels and having a field day), the government threatens headteachers with legal action if they revert to online provision. We must put our children's education first! Schools must stay open! Father Wendy conducts the funeral of one of her husband's teaching colleagues who died from COVID. From the safety of his home office, a journalist decides that nobody has had an easier more stress-free time of it during the pandemic than teachers. Meanwhile, in the US, a man without a PhD ticks off Dr Biden for not preferring to go under the title 'Kiddo Biden'. Another man combs through Dr Biden's thesis and finds two hundred typos. Important work, this. Science has shown that whenever a less talented man finds an error in the work of a woman, his prowess grows by 0.00001 mm. This cumulative increase may be cited as a marker of esteem for

REF purposes. Thank God for academic vigilance and courageous journalism. I nominate these three giants among men for the prestigious Sharpest Scratch of 2020 award.

Rachel Logan blows her nose. 'Sorry, Mum. It's been such a nightmare term, and I thought I was just crawling over the finish line.'

She's sitting at the kitchen table with a mug of tea. She has driven home to Mum. That's what you do when you've got nothing left and everything's shit and then the government drops the final straw.

Mrs Logan rubs Rachel's arm. 'Oh darling. They're such a bunch of gits. They're so . . . Oh, I don't know. Let's get Parva round. He says it so much better.'

Rachel sobs again. 'That's the Christmas holidays gone. How am I going to set up testing for the 4th of January for fuck's sake? Retired teachers! What if they're vulnerable? Who's going to sort out DBS checks? Oh, and thanks for the thirty-minute training video!'

'Maybe they'll get the army in to help?'

'Fuck Boris. Fuck them all. Is there any wine? I know there's school tomorrow, but fuck it.'

'There's always wine. But I've got a better idea. Come on. Finish your tea and grab a mask.'

'Where are we going?'

'It's a surprise.'

In the vicarage next door, Father Ed glances through the kitchen window and sees Mrs Logan's car drive off. Ed is not worried about Neil's health, by the way. Over the years, the medical profession has run a battery of tests. They are closing in on a diagnosis of hypochondriasis. You need not worry either, reader. I am not about to crown this *annus horribilis* with bad news about a dear friend. This has been the tacit contract throughout. You come to Lindford for the consolation of seeing our small fragmented stories embraced by a bigger narrative. They may still be in fragments, but we know whom we have believed, and are persuaded – just about – that everything is being kept safe against that day. Oh yes, everything's in pieces all right. This isn't a proper novel. It is not Stendhal's mirror being carried along the linear high road. We dropped that with a ghastly crash back in March.

Instead, we offer you an improvised disco ball, with tiny squares of reflection, little glimpses into little lives, and scraps of light floating all around like snowflakes.

'Oh my God!' gasps Rachel through her mask. 'It's magical!'

'Isn't it?' says Jen. She flaps her hands and does a little dance of glee. Rachel can tell she's longing to spam them both with pats and hugs. Her eyes sparkle over her woodland animals cotton mask as if she's *on* something. 'He's a total genius. I LOVE HIM! Can you believe he wasn't sure we'd go for it? I can't *wait* for him to do the other rooms. Thanks so much for recommending him, Elspeth.'

'My pleasure,' says Mrs Logan.

The three of them have just gone through the wardrobe in the hotel room, and are standing in the bathroom of Narnia itself. The bedroom was impressive enough, with its four-poster bed and velvet drapery. But this! Wow, just *wow*!

Jen carries on talking a blue streak, the way you do when you've barely seen anyone for weeks. She's telling them about the concept – Victorian Cabinet of Curiosities. Rachel isn't really listening. Mum can field it, the barrage. Jen's always been like it, but COVID has sent her into overdrive. All that pent-up hospitality she hasn't been lavishing on guests: total dam burst!

Rachel explores deeper into Narnia. The walls are dark blue, stencilled with snowy trees, and mirrors are set up at angles, so it's all receding into an infinite forest. A fox, a deer, a badger – everywhere you look there are magical details, trickery. You can't tell what's reflection, until you see yourself moving. Other trees, three-dimensional ones, stand in the two farthest corners, their branches meeting overhead, where stars gleam. The floor is white, and it glints and sparkles. There's even an old-fashioned lamp-post glowing. And look at that – there's a sleigh bathtub. Well, of course there is! All around, snow falls softly, cast by a projector in the corner.

'Personally, I'd be freaked out that Mr Tumnus is going to trot through,' says Mrs Logan.

'We charge extra for fauns,' says Jen.

'Where's the loo?' asks Rachel. 'Oh! Ha ha ha! Behind the mirror! Clever. And there's a shower! Look, Mum.'

'Well, let's hope Aslan doesn't come any time soon,' says Mrs Logan. 'It'd be a shame to melt all Parva's hard work.'

'Book me in as soon as you're open again,' says Rachel. 'I want to be the first guest.'

'You're on! Let me show you the plans for the other rooms. Have you got time for a glass of wine?'

Rachel and Mrs Logan exchange glances. They both know they shouldn't really be here at all, meeting up indoors. As it is, Jen's not managing to stay two metres away, is she?

'Better not,' says Rachel. 'School tomorrow.'

'No, we'd better be off. Another time,' promises Mrs Logan. 'Mwa mwa! Thanks for the sneak preview.'

Jen stands on the drive in the cold and waves them off. They can still hear her calling 'Bye!' as they pull out through the big gates.

'Technically, we shouldn't have done that,' says Mrs Logan. 'But sod it. It's not like it's Barnard Castle.'

'It was the perfect antidote. Thanks.'

They drive in silence. The sick dread is creeping back already, but yes, it was perfect. It reminded her of childhood magic, of Granny taking her to see Selfridge's Christmas windows. Followed by *The Nutcracker*. Rachel must have worried about stuff when she was eight years old. Hell, she must have worried about stuff last year! For the life of her, she can't think what it was, though.

The golden crescent moon is setting, with the old moon glowing ghostly with earthshine. They pass Turlham Church, all floodlit, and houses with Christmas trees in the windows. The Red Lion pub is all dark. Maybe they've gone bust. Icicle lights drip, drip from cottage gutters. A string of reindeer in a garden. Then dark country road. The car's headlights catch the eyes of a fox as it stands by the roadside. There's the moon again, and a pair of very bright stars.

'Damn!' says Mrs Logan. 'Now I want some Turkish delight.'

Moon Phase
First Quarter.
Today is the solstice, it is the shortest day, in fact you could almost say it was not a day at all, it was like the sun didn't rise. There was supposably this amazing rare conjunction of planets tonight but I did not get to see

397

it. The planets are 'Jupiter' and 'Saturn' and conjunction means they are close together. This does not mean literally close, they just look close in the sky . . . IF IT IS NOT TO CLOUDY AND YOU CAN ACTUALLY SEE THEM!!!! I am super dissappointed because this rare event has not happened since 1623, it is possible that this also happened 2000 years ago and this is 'the Christmas Star' that the wise men saw, so you will totally understand why I am dissappointed. If I'd known it would be cloudy today I would of looked yesterday. SMH. This just goes to show you should always be alert, like the bible says, it is an advent thing.

It has been a super dissappointing week in many ways I am sorry to say. The goverment have done another U-turn and we are not aloud to meet up with two other household for 5 days any more. NB we were not going to do this anyway, it is madness, but lot's of my friends are gutted. There is a new strain of the virus which you can catch like twice as easily, and now we have a new tear, tear 4, which is basically the same as 'lockdown' only the goverment don't want to call it that, (guess what, everyone knows). This time it is London and the south in Tear 4, not Manchester and the north like per usual.

Attitude of Grattitude

So I am trying to remember to be grateful and to 'accentuate the positive'. Here is my list of things to be grateful for:

1. My dad did not die of Covid thanks to the NHS, he is slowly getting better.

2. It is the school hollidays YAY!

3. There is a vaccine for Covid, we will all get it in the New Year. (The VACCINE, hopefully we will not all get covid in the NY!!!)

4. Mum and dad are back together and very amicable and we will have a family Christmas with real turkey (and Tofurkey roast for Leah obvs). Maybe they will get re-married????? I asked mum privately and she said, well we will take it steady, and see how it goes. (Finger's and toes crossed!!!!)

5. I have an amazing clarinet and I can now play over the break which is awesome, I can play high notes now.

6. So Father Dominick has asked me and Mr Hardman-May to canter at the Midnight Mass!!! We will sing some carols and I will do the descants, plus I will solo the first verse of Once in Royal, plus in O Little Town, I will sing solo in another verse which we don't normally

sing, which Father D wants me to sing. It goes 'Where children pure and happy Pray to the blessed Child' it is suited to the tamber of voice (Mr H-M said that, I am not being big-headed or anything) NB This is a great honour, I am super nervous but we will get to rehearse (Guess who will want to come along to 'look after me'? LOL LOL LOL)

7. Plus loads of other stuff I for one all to easily take for granted such as food and shelter and education and a good WiFi connection in a world where many go hungry.

8. ONLY 4 MORE SLEEPS TILL CHRISTMAS!!!!!!!!!!!!!!!!

> O Oriens
> O Morning Star,
> splendour of light eternal and sun of righteousness:
> Come and enlighten those
> who dwell in darkness and the shadow of death.

The day arrived – the way these days will – when they least expected it. It came while all three of them were out. Chloe was at the hub all day, offering legal advice, helping with forms and claims. Well, it kept her busy. Distracted her from obsessing about whether she was or she wasn't, from being ridiculous. I mean, come on, she was only about three minutes late, it was *way* too soon to take a test, her body needed time to build up detectable levels of HCG. And anyway, she probably wasn't.

Ambrose was off on a secret Christmas present-related mission, cunningly disguised as a business trip to Lesley on her farm. Freddie had taken both boys to get their hair and nails done ready for Christmas, over at Dapper Dogs in Martonbury. After that he swang by Janey's and Matt's to drop off their card and present, then shot across to Gayden Magna to give Ed and Neil their pressie, and then *maybe* he followed Neil's BMW to Turlham Hall, so Neil could show him the first stage of the makeover? Yeh, probably he shouldn't've. But you could say it was like work, ki-i-ind of. I mean, isn't Neil going to give him a job, soon as he's had the vaccine? He wore a mask obvs. And oh wow. He *so* wished he'd thought of this? Maybe he'll do a Narnia nursery, if . . . Coz fair play, Neil totally ripped off Freddie's Chefchaouen idea for one of the rooms? Like total piracy? Bastard.

The police came and went. The stench of weed is fading now. You can read about it on the *Lindford Echo* website: 'Officers from the Safer Neighbourhood Team carried out the raid. Hundreds of thousands of pounds' worth of cannabis plants were recovered from rooms specially designed for growing cannabis. Enquiries are ongoing. No arrests were made.' You'll see a stock photo of cannabis plants, and another of the front of the property. Just an ordinary 60s semi, on an ordinary Lindford street, blank windows with the blinds down.

Ambrose is the first home. The neighbour from opposite comes straight across to tell him about the afternoon's drama. Police vans. Door broken in. Unbelievable! Right here on our street. Ambrose agrees: unbelievable. Did you have any idea? the neighbour asks. Ambrose shrugs a helpless shrug. He goes into the house. It feels different, the silence. Then he works it out – the fan has stopped.

He goes through to the back door and stands in the garden. It's almost dark. Rain patters on the polythene roof of the henhouse. The hawk-scaring kite swirls and dips on the wind. He looks up at the silent house next door. The upstairs window stands open.

'Hello?'

Nothing.

'Hello?'

The rain patters. No, whoever it was will be far off by now and still running. It was only ever a long shot. Like opening a tiny window of hope, just opening it a tiny crack. If Ambrose could pray, like Freddie and Chloe pray, he'd send one up now. Go well. Be safe. Today's antiphon goes through his mind. No Evensong tonight, though. Those who sing pray twice. Except he can't even pray once. But singing is as close as he can ever get, so Ambrose sings.

> *O Oriens,*
> *splendor lucis aeternae, et sol justitiae:*
> *veni, et illumina sedentes in tenebris, et umbra mortis.*

Oh Morning Star. When we need it most. Oh, oh, oh please. The white breath of his prayer melts in the winter night.

All the wrong food is in the wrong pantries of our land. The wrong-sized turkeys in the wrong fridges. Hopes and plans must be downscaled or dismantled. Practically the whole country is in Tiers 3 and 4 now. The new strain is everywhere. O Dear, O Dear desire of every nation. Oh that you would rend the heavens and come down! We can only plod on and make our house fair as we are able. There will be a lot of solitary Christmases this year. And a lot of rule bending and breaking.

The diocese teems with secrets. Presents are wrapped and hidden in cupboards. Last-minute surprise bouquets and hampers are dispatched to the people we won't be seeing. There are virtual Secret Santa sessions on Zoom. Unlooked-for acts of kindness spring up everywhere. People donate their surplus stocks to food-banks. In supermarkets, distracted shoppers get to the till and realize they've left their bags in the car, they've not got their Club Card, they've forgotten their purse. What a frail thread their sanity hangs by. They would have lost it but for the patience of the people on the tills. How can they still be patient, still be kind, in all this – when hours are long and jobs precarious and customers so rude and frazzled? Let us salute these frontline workers, and the quiet armies walking the endless miles, up and down vast warehouse aisles, so that our last-minute 'arrives before Christmas' gifts will arrive before Christmas.

Shoppers queue in supermarket car parks. Lorries queue in Kent. Cars queue for the drive-through blood test centre, or the drive-through COVID testing centre. People wait, wait, wait. They wait for the green light over the Tesco doors, for the border to reopen, for the results. They wait for Christmas. They wait for the vaccine. For the back of 2020. For good news. O come, O come. The tiny flame of the Brexit trade deal gutters in the cold wind. Surely, it's gone out?

My, this is fun, thinks Jane. Just when we thought we might have turned a corner with these vaccines, COVID deals us one from the bottom of the deck! A sneak preview of the chaos we can look forward to in the New Year! We're pariahs. Country after country bans flights from the UK, and who can blame them? We've been shite at controlling COVID, with our trademark 'too little too late' shilly-shallying. France schools us in the art of controlling our own borders. Boom! Kent becomes a lorry park overnight. Now would be the moment to demonstrate how frictionless our world-beating customs and border checks are going to be; how seamless the transition will be on 1 January.

God, we're embarrassing, she thinks. Did we deserve this? Maybe this is the final inevitable excrescence of empire.

It's Christmas Eve 2020. Somehow we've made it this far. Looking back, I can't quite believe it. Miss Sherratt, home from the 4 p.m. Christmas vigil (the midnight was fully booked by the time she got round to it), pours herself a sherry and looks out across the dark garden. She can see her neighbours' fairy lights twinkling through the hedge. Then a light comes on in the summerhouse. The rickety old thing glows, glory seeping out through all the cracks. It looks to her like the stable in Bethlehem.

Neil is on his way back from the GP's. He weeps as he drives, because everything is fine. He's got the all-clear. That's when he hears the news about Brexit. The Christmas present the nation had stopped believing the PM would deliver in time. It is the thinnest of deals, but it is a deal. He pulls up on the vicarage drive just as the church carillon starts playing 'Joy to the World'. He stands and listens. The wonders, the wonders of his love. Everything is fine. It's not, obviously. But somehow it still is.

We have all been bent low beneath life's crushing load this year. We've been toiling along this climbing way with painful steps and slow. But come, it's Christmas Eve. Let us rest beside the weary road, and hear the angels sing.

Freddie and Jess stand in the organ loft. From up here they can see everyone sitting socially distanced and all the candles on the Advent ring flickering. The white candle for Christmas. Father Dominic has finished his homily. In the distance, the town-hall clock chimes midnight. Happy Christmas! In a moment they will sing 'O Little Town', and the hairs on everyone's neck will stand up as Jess's clear voice (that timbre!) sings:

Where children pure and happy
Pray to the blessed Child,
Where misery cries out to thee,
Son of the Mother mild;
Where Charity stands watching
And Faith holds wide the door,
The dark night wakes, the glory breaks,
And Christmas comes once more.

The house is silent now. No drone of a fan next door. Chloe stares. It is the thinnest, the faintest of lines. But it is a line. Oh God! It really is. She could go and bang on their door and tell them now. Or she could wait. She could tell them on Christmas Day.

Long Night Moon, Part III

I t's dark across Lindfordshire. The half-moon has set. For all our dreaming, it isn't going to be a white Christmas this year. I base this on the lack of snow across the region, on the evidence of my eyes, and the weather apps. Call me old-fashioned. It seems a dangerous business to me, dangerous and futile, to butcher the truth to fit my preferred narrative. Like old Herod in his palace, insisting he's the real king.

Lights twinkle in windows and gardens. They hang above the empty shopping streets of Lindford and Lindchester, of Cardingforth, Renfold, Martonbury, where the shutters are down for good on businesses gone bust. Dawn is still a long way off. Everything waits. Inside the houses and flats, stockings bulge with presents. Gifts are heaped under trees. There's tinsel wound round the walking frames beside care-home beds. Patients on intensive care wards sleep, or wake, and staff keep watch. They tend the sick, soothe the suffering, bless the dying. Night shifts end. Staff return to their cars in the hospital car park and find they've got a parking ticket. Merry Christmas. France has offered fast-track citizenship approval to all migrant frontline COVID workers, as a token of gratitude. Our chancellor promises that NHS nurses will be spared from a public sector pay freeze. Peace on earth and mercy mild.

Christmas Day 2020. Just one day. That's all we have for family get-togethers and mingling in Christmas bubbles. Children wake far too early, as children will, and race into adult bedrooms with the glad tidings of great joy that *He's Been*! How hard it was in some households to scrape enough together for presents this year. How hard, on the other side of the great divide, to resist the urge to go mad and splash out on ridiculous gifts, to offset the deprivations and disappointments of 2020. All the money saved on commuting and lattes gets ploughed into state-of-the-art air fryers, metal detectors, electric scooters, or luxury hampers for shielding parents. You can't take it with you, so why not splurge? In Gayden Magna, the cast-iron Trafalgar telephone box has been brought in from the garage and installed in the corner of the vicarage kitchen. Behold, a cocktail cabinet!

Ridiculous gifts. Things you thought you couldn't ever have, but still secretly want. Freddie knows he can't keep alpacas in the suburbs of Lindford. You need at least an acre of garden for that. He went through all that with Brose back in August. But what's this in his stocking? A framed photo? Say what? You're kidding me! Only his own pair of six-month-old baby boy alpaca cria? Turns out Lesley's agreed to keep them with the rest of her herd for a monthly fee. Freddie can go and visit them as often as he likes. He can drive over before breakfast while it's still dark even (because he's crazy), wrap his arms round their necks, lean his head against theirs, maybe cry on them a little? Then say goodbye and race back to church still smelling of alpaca? Gonna call the silver grey one Andy. Yep. Still working on the other name. It'll come to him.

The dawn breaks red this Christmas Day. Everything turns golden. Freddie's crying again as he drives home, coz Brose would actually do this for him? Buy him baby alpacas? Yeh, he gets why. In case there's no actual baby. Ha ha ha! Looks like you maybe jumped the gun a bit there, dude? Could've saved yourself however many hundreds, thousands? (Probably there's a tax angle here, knowing Brose.) Oh man! Chloe, knocking on their door at 2 a.m., whispering, 'Sorry sorry sorry. I was going to wait, but turns out I can't. Ta dah! Magic wand! Christmas present for you boys!'

Get *in*! He catches himself singing. *Winterreise*, FFS! He switches to 'Joy to the World'. Yeah, no, Freddie gets that it's early days. Like, one in four pregnancies . . . For sure, he gets that. But that's like *three* in four will be fine? May as well be happy, no? Not like there's heart armour that's gonna protect you. Like, yeah well, I didn't let myself believe it, so I'm exempt. Coz you can't not believe it, even if it's only a faint line, a faint hope. Nu-uh. Not possible. Like everyone is always all, Don't set your heart on the house until you've exchanged contracts, it could all fall through? That's crazy talk. I mean, why would you even be buying a house you haven't fallen in love with? The way Freddie sees it, there's no free pass on pain, not if you're invested, not if you love.

As he approaches Lindford, golden light flashes off the tower-block windows. Gah, he's doing it again. Singing *Winterreise*. He can see that fecking dictionary on the kitchen table! Maybe it's got into his bones after all? *When the snow flies in my face, I shake it off.* He'll be safe from feedback from La Madeleine till the New Year. Only sent the recording yesterday. But hey, it's off his desk and on to hers, and it wasn't late. Christmas Eve is before Christmas? So please God please, maybe he can escape Schubert in 2021?

'Well, I'll stay till New Year's Day, and then I'll head back.'

'That sounds lovely,' says Father Dominic. This is a good day. A Christmas miracle day! She knows who he is. They've made it this far safe and well. He can let the details slide. 'More coffee?'

'Ooh, go on then. I'll regret it when I need a tinkle in the service.'

'That's not for ages.'

Not long till daybreak. The sky through the vicarage window is charged with pink. They're in their dressing gowns, enjoying a Christmas breakfast of croissants and clementine juice. Bach's *Christmas Oratorio* is playing in the background. *Jauchzet, frohlocket!*

'This was your dad's favourite,' she tells him. 'Oh, he loved his Bach.'

'You said.' A hundred times.

The air is already rich with the smell of three-bird roast. This is of interest to Lady, who is stationed near the oven, keeping watch, in case someone drops the lot on the kitchen floor. It has been known. They'll be eating it for days. He'll pack Mother Gin off with some, of course, but he'd ordered a whopper from Wood's, hoping Janey and Matt might join them. But they're doing Christmas *à deux*.

'It's very kind of you,' says Mum, 'inviting me every year. I don't take it for granted. I know what a busy time it is for you vicars.'

'You're welcome, Mother mine.'

'Well, I daresay, but I don't want you to think you have to saddle yourself with me. If ever you want a festive frolic with your friends, don't you worry about me. I'll be fine.'

'And don't you worry about me, either. It's my pleasure to be saddled with the old nag.'

'Stuff and nonsense. If you're saddled, *you're* the horse, not me, sonny Jim.'

Father Dominic whinnies. 'Call me Black Beauty.'

'More like Silver.'

'Oh!' He smooths his poor hair. 'That was uncalled for. On Christmas Day as well.'

'Pooh! At least you've kept it.' She gives him a pat and starts gathering up the crocks. 'I only hope Dominic takes after you, David.'

'Fingers crossed,' he says. 'You leave those, Mother.' She stares. Another slippage. 'I'll do it. Go and get washed and dressed. Shoo!'

'Remind me where I am again?'

'In my vicarage. On Christmas Day in the morning!' he sings.

'Oh yes. Well, I'd better get dressed then. Can't go to church in my dezza-bees.' She potters off to her room, singing, 'And what was in those ships all three?'

Will she hold on to the task long enough to complete it? He can't believe this is still viable, that he's not had to throw in the towel. He was only just in time to prevent her from hoovering the downstairs loo yesterday, instead of flushing it. Oh Lord! Something's going to give. One more plank in her memory is going to give way, and she'll plunge down into darkness beyond his reach. She'll start panicking, and fighting off this stranger who keeps appearing in the home she doesn't recognize. This has to be their last Christmas living in this house, surely.

Then enjoy it, he chides himself. *Jauchzet, frohlocket!* Your dad's favourite. Dominic can barely remember him. How curious to sense him now. It's as though past is collapsing into present. He glimpses what his parents' relationship must have been like. Tender, daft, constant. Oh, let the future collapse in us as well! The bright future

407

when this is all over – the virus, all sorrow and sighing. He wipes his eyes on his dressing-gown sleeve. Come on, this will never do. There's a three-bird roast to baste!

He shunts Lady aside and squats to peer in through the glass door of the oven. The dog pants in his ear. He rumples her ears and laughs. 'That's right. Glad tidings of good things, Lady!'

Celebrate. Rejoice. Is this still a good day? How can we be content with just one day, when the government promised us five? How can we still be joyful and triumphant in the middle of a global pandemic, with death rates soaring and people starving and homeless? When we can't meet up with our loved ones and sing carols together, when communion wafers taste of hand sanitizer and everything is shite and it's nowhere near over yet? Can we shake the snow of COVID off our faces and sing bright and cheery, and carry on with Christmas business as normal?

Joy always breaks into our world inappropriately. Like the heavenly host appearing to the shepherds. Or, to defamiliarize it for you, like angels appearing in the small hours on a bleak godforsaken northern industrial estate, scaring the bejasus out of the security guards. With 'Glory to God, and peace on earth!' booming out like the main stage at Glasto. Peace on earth in the middle of a brutal foreign occupation, where our hated overlords have a habit of nailing up protesters like moles on a fence, as a lesson to the rest of us. 'Good news! A saviour has been born for you in Barnsley.'

Is that the deliverance we were looking for? It's hardly allies with armoured divisions massing on the borders, destroyers and air carriers in the Channel, the messianic leader poised to coordinate the resistance and strike two days from now. A baby? What good is that? With the best will in the world, it's going to be decades before we see any results.

But the angels, though. There's no denying the angels. And doesn't a baby always melt your heart, even when it arrives at the wrong time, little, weak and helpless, when everything's in chaos and all plans have gone awry? Just look – will you just look at him? Aw. His little hands. Can I hold him? Give him here. Hush, hush. There you are. It's all right, it's all right.

Be near me, Lord Jesus. I ask thee to stay
Close by me for ever, and love me, I pray.
Bless all the dear children in thy tender care
And fit us for heaven, to live with thee there.

Giles Littlechild, the canon precentor, burrows through his Christmas vestments for the handkerchief in his pocket. Oh, for heaven's sake! He lowers his mask and blows his nose. The choristers finish the last verse of the carol as the administration of communion ends. Was there ever a hokier mushier set of lyrics? He adjusts his mask and looks out through misted-up glasses across the poor scattered flock. Giles has always loathed 'Away in a Manger' and vehemently contested any assertion it was penned by Martin Luther. Oh, but today it seems to say all he wants to say. Be near me. Bless all the dear children. God bless us, every one!

In many houses, lunch is finally ready at 3 p.m., just when the Queen is making her speech in her capacity as lead evangelist for the Church of England (though you would never infer this from the way the BBC reports it). Many a tear is shed as the NHS choir sings 'Joy to the World'. In other houses and flats, people are Christmasing alone this year. Maybe they are shielding. Maybe their families are too far away for a day trip. Some are in their jim-jams having a bacon bap and salted caramel ice-cream fest. The afternoon and evening will, or shall (let us slip into cod-Regency) be devoted to binge-watching *Bridgerton* on Netflix. The day shall swim by in a Prosecco blur of tight britches.

Other solitary Lindcastrians have risen to the occasion. They have dressed up, cooked properly, laid the dining-room table and lit candles. Miss Sherratt is one such. If we were to press our noses in vulgar curiosity against the windows of Sherratt Manor, we would see her sparkling in her highest hightum, diamonds twinkling, fringes sweeping, boas trailing. Watch that candle! Don't set fire to yourself, Tinkerbell! She's busy arranging a tray for Jack. She will leave it on the table on the terrace for him, along with a delicious mimosa waft of her vintage Caron Farnesiana. Miss Sherratt will dine alone this Christmas. Or will she? If she closes her eyes between sips and mouthfuls, the house begins to fill with memories.

Feet thundering on stairs. Squeaks and giggles. The cheeky faces at the window belong to her brother and cousins. Hide and seek. Can it be that she's the last one left? Has everyone else been found?

Her head jerks upright. I say, Belle, old thing! Whatever next! Nodding off over your food.

Jack can see the candlelight flickering from down by the summer-house. She's got smoke alarms, but he'll keep an eye as he stands eating his Christmas lunch. Best china. Monogrammed cutlery. It makes him want to weep, being trusted with the valuables. He eats too fast. Bad habit. But he's like those soldiers in the Bible, Gideon's men, the crack troops. Keeping an eye out as they drank from the river. Or maybe they were the ones that got sent home. He can't remember now. But it pays to keep an eye out. Means you're ready, you're looking the right way when needed. You can jerk your head and hold the door open, meaning *Quick! In here, lad.* Not that anyone followed him over the fence. Bizzies never came checking. Just cleared out the weed and the growing kit, and left. Investigations ongoing.

Poor lad. Never seen anyone look so hunted – not even back in the day when he was doing the hunting, checking bombed-out buildings.

Jack finishes the turkey, and goes and gets a slice of white to mop the gravy. Scrap of a thing, maybe sixteen, maybe twenty-six, there was no telling. Kept holding out a card with 'I claim asylum' on it. Thank God for smart phones and Google translate. Thank God for the Sally Bash, too. Yes, Jack knew who to call. They'll take care of him. Probably feeding him Christmas nosh now.

So that's another one. Another tick in the right column. Not that you ever cancel out the crosses. The three minutes looking the wrong way, and the toddler floating face down in the pool. You can't ever balance those columns of figures by yourself – he knows that. Come the day of reckoning, we're all in deep shit. But he'll carry on keeping an eye out all the same. Because looking back, there's always been someone keeping an eye out for him.

The presents have been opened now. Leah and Jess Rogers race their new scooters far across Lindford. Goodness, is that Mr Hardman-May's house? What a coincidence, nothing could have been further from Leah's mind. Poor Jess is out of breath, so there's nothing for it: they must rest and glance carelessly through the window, and be rewarded with the sight of the whole family, dogs and hens and all, gathered in the front room. Back at home, Becky and Martin sit on the sofa together. Becky admires her ring again. It's not an engagement ring. They've been engaged before. Is it a re-engagement ring? What's the word for it? They can't quite decide. But it keeps giving them the giggles as they sit there on the sofa telling one another to grow up, to stop it.

All across Lindfordshire people slump on sofas to FaceTime Grandma, and the siblings they won't meet this time. Then they wrap up warm and go for walks in fields and woods, where the merry bleeping of metal detectors sounds both near and far. They supervise the first outing on the drive of the sparkly princess bike, or the ride-on tractor. They Google *Are electric scooters legal in UK?* Followed indignantly by *Why are electric scooters illegal in UK?* The sun sets as it rose, in a glory of pink and gold. Anyone fancy a turkey sandwich? Christmas cake? These are blessed ones, the lucky ones, the ones who have not slipped down through the cracks of this COVID desert.

By evening, everyone must return to their own homes, for all the Christmas bubbles will pop at midnight. In theory. Is anyone really taking any notice of the restrictions? If we take to our Anglican wings and fly across the region, we will see rather a lot of extra cars parked on the drives and streets of Lindfordshire. On Boxing Day, we will see large groups out walking. That's never one household, is it? That's more than six people. That's less than two metres. Well, it's not our job to police other people. And anyway, how long is it going to be before we see some politician caught bang to rights, flouting the rules?

The days plod past. Lindfordshire is clinging on to its Tier 3 status. We can still shop, or get a haircut, or go out for a meal. The sales don't amount to much on the high streets of the region, though. Shoppers wander in masks through Lindford. Starlings muster in the trees to jeer and whistle, like a soundtrack of derision at the sorry state of things.

Star sees them at dusk as she tips the hair sweepings into the bin in the yard behind Hair Works. A murmuration, she thinks. She loves that the birds are always there, rain or shine, day and night. There's an owl in her neighbour's garden. She's never seen it, but it's right there, hooting away if you wake up in the dark and can't get back to sleep. Birds are like this alien supernatural race that share our planet with us, she thinks. Sometimes you can get really close to them? Mostly they are just doing their own thing though and who knows what they are thinking? Like angels, kind of. What if in actual fact they *are* angels? Obviously they aren't, but what if? They say, don't they, that if you find a white feather, that's a sign that your guardian angel is nearby? Maybe they're really close all the time, like birds, even if you don't ever notice?

Father Wendy sees the murmurations too, as she and Doug go for their walk with Pedro. No sons and grandchildren this holiday season, because they're all in Tier 4. It reminds Wendy of that Laura Ingalls Wilder book, *The Long Winter*. It's still on the shelf, with all the other Puffin books. It was her Laura's favourite, which is why Wendy has found it impossible to reread. But maybe the time is right? The little prairie town hanging on through seven months of blizzards until finally they celebrate Christmas together in May. It'll be a problematic read in other ways too. Hard to shut out the plight of the displaced indigenous people from the pioneering narrative.

The birds swirl and gather in the golden sky, like a black veil looped and swung on the wind by an unseen hand. Storm Bella is on the way. Oh, let it pass us by, prays Wendy. Spare us. Not another flood, on top of everything. Then she calls her anxious thoughts back, and squeezes Doug's hand. They've still got each other.

The last days of 2020 slip by. Strange to be stuck here in this rag-end of the year. We'd normally be off somewhere post-Christmas. Not a lot to do apart from go for a walk, and stuff yourself so that you have a real target to go at with the New Year resolution diet. What shall we do? Dunno. Fancy watching an old film? *The Great Escape*, maybe. If only we could escape! Fast away the old year passes. The end can't come quickly enough, frankly. Already on our little walks round the block we see the tell-tale sprinkle of pine needles that speaks of evicted Christmas trees. And I said to the man who stood at the gate of the year, Out of my way, moron! Can't you see I'm trying to get through?

Jane has always hated the week between Christmas and New Year. She generally spends it blocking her ears and barricading herself in a mental bunker with food and booze, to screen out the army of January dreads massing on the horizon. Her out-of-office message is on till Monday 4 January. Unlike Matt, she never gives way to a spot of cheeky checking of the work emails when she's on leave. She copes marginally better if she can go away somewhere. New Zealand, preferably. God, she's *ached* to be there this year. To be with her boy. To be in the sun. To be in a country governed by grown-ups.

To be with family. Now that's a new one. Or is it? No, it's an old one. Growing up an only child, with only one parent. Missing her dad, missing those imaginary brothers and sisters. Pretending she was adopted, or an Italian orphan (like Marianina Booth at primary school). And then spending adulthood as a single mother of one child. Marrying another only child. True, there's her cousin Elaine and her kids, aunties and uncles and second cousins. But 'tight-knit' doesn't spring to mind. Has it really taken a global pandemic to wake her up to her need for roots, for context? Maybe it's just an age thing. Denial has served her well for decades. But she'll be sixty next year. How many more years to go? Twenty? Twenty-five? She'd like a better grasp of what it's all about really, before she pops her clogs. Not to be on her deathbed wailing, 'But I still don't *get* it.'

Hark the glad sound of a Champagne cork in the deanery, where Gene and Marion are celebrating the final surprise gift of 2020: a resignation letter from the dean's PA.

'I imagine Dykey Dora's thumbscrews finally did the trick.'

'It wasn't like that, Gene. She's decided to take early retirement, that's all.'

'Of course she has,' agrees Gene. 'All those years of compassionately praying that God would open a door for her, who'd have dreamt it would turn out to be a trapdoor! And having observed your stern

413

expression, my lips are sealed on the subject henceforth and for ever-more.' He raises his glass. 'Cheers – 2021 now looks a little brighter.'

She shakes her head. 'I despair of you. If it looks brighter, it's because of the new administration in the States, and the prospect of the vaccine. And the grace and comfort of the Holy Spirit,' she adds.

'Not forgetting *that*,' he says brightly. 'Ah, remember when we thought 2016 was the year from hell? I look back on it rather fondly now. Has it occurred to you that 2021 might be waiting in the wings, saying, "Hold my beer"?'

'You are always such a ray of sunshine, darling,' sighs the dean.

29th ~~Januar~~ DECEMBER!!!!!
LOL that's a froydian slip, I must of been wishing it was already January. I for one am seriously sick of this year. I said that at tea and GUESS WHO said, yeah right, like 2021 is going to be better, WAKE UP! The virus has mutated twice, there is a new strain in the UK and another one in South Africa, plus there could be another virus that is MUCH WORSE before we have got through this one. So I went It is all humanitys fault to fall stall her. NB this did not work, she went off on another rant until dad said Who wants to come for a walk round the block. Normally it is me who says yes but Leah said yes and they went. Mum is watching 'Britches-Down' (says dad) on Netflix and did not want to be desturbed.

Moon Phase
<u>Full</u> (98%) I saw the moon just now so that means . . . . I have seen every full moon of 2020!!!! GO ME!!! It is the Long Night Moon or the Cold Moon, the moon and the whole landscape looked super awesome because . . . wait for it . . . . it snowed!!! I woke up this morning and opened my curtains and did a humongus gasp. WOW! I'm serious it was like Lucy going into Narnia I kid you not. The air was like this magical blue, and all the trees in the garden and all the rooves were white. The lawn was totally smooth because nobody had walked on it. NB the sky looks blue in the 'Blue Hour'. The Blue Hour occurs just befor dawn and then its the 'Golden Hour'. You can literally see this once you know to look out for it? It is an actual thing, the blue hour is 'twilight', it is due to the diffusibility of shorter wavelengths. There is also such a thing as 'nautical dawn and dusk' but you can look that up for yourself, I can't

414

be asked to write it down at the end of the day. So anyway, the sun came up and then it was the 'golden hour' and the sky was pinkish and the trees and houses went golden, trust me it is magical.

I regret to inform you that the snow started to melt, Leah and me only just had time to make a snowman, it is actually a genderneutral snowperson to be fair. We were finishing it when GUESS WHO came past with his dogs? You got it, only Mr Hardman-May. He got two baby alpacas called Andy and Theo for Christmas, sadly they can't live in his garden they have to live on a farm. I was all Squeeeeee that is so cute, I want one! He went yeah tell me about it. He was just going away again and Leah through a snowball at him and I went LEAH! so he through one back and we had this massive snowball fight, it was awesome, but then he went.

Believe it or not I have nearly finished this entire whole Moon Journal now with every single moon. It is kind of sad and happy at the same time. I have matured somewhat in this unpresidented year. I so hope and pray 2021 will be better but I am not a total moron (FYI Leah) I am aware there are difficult times ahead. But it is like the DREADED JACKS ANTHEM says, God be with you till we meet again.

Dad and Leah have just got back, we are now going to precede to watch 'Death to 2020', it is said to be very funny, plus dad will light a fire and we will make smores, it will be awesome, so I will love you and leave you.

Before long, I too will be loving and leaving you, dear reader. It is the final day of 2020. We began this tale up in the metaphorical loft, hunting for our fictional wings, with the distant rumour of a pale horse in some unknown province of China. We imagined it to be a topical detail enhancing the verisimilitude of the tale, not the entire plot, for heaven's sake.

The tale is only half told, I fear. It feels as though we are the disciples in the middle of the lake, rowing hard against the headwind. It's dark, and there's no going back. We are halfway through this pandemic, and the storm is getting worse. Right now, we're shipping green water. For all we know, the boat could break up and go down. So far 73,5012 people have died of COVID-19 in the UK. The number already goes off the edge of our brain, and it's still rising. WWGED?

415

George Eliot would not be writing this until lichen had blurred the name on the grave of the last person to die of COVID-19, and baby Hardman-May was forty years old.

Come, fly with me one last time over Lindfordshire in 2020. The vast full Long Night Moon has just risen in the east. The sun is setting in the west, equally vast as it goes down red behind tangled woods. Everything is coated with liquid gold – all the windows and gutters, the snowy fields, the signs saying *Logs and Kindling, Testing, Wreaths* and the chalked letters 20+C+B+M+20 above the vicarage door in Gayden Magna. Smoke rises from chimneys and bonfires. Look, the landscape stretches out, layer upon misty layer. Behind us, the moon sails up, and when we turn back, the sun has slipped below the horizon when we weren't watching.

At midnight there will be fireworks, whether for the end of 2020 or our final leaving of the EU, who can say? And that will be that. It will be cold. A man will stand in a snowy garden keeping watch over a dark house where Christmas tree lights shine. Moonlight will glint on the hoar frost, and moon shadows from the tall tree will stretch across the lawn. It will be the kind of night when joy could break in. The kind of night when we think we see a figure walking towards us across the lake. When those hokey mushy old hymns seem to say everything we want to say. Dear reader,

> God be with you till we meet again,
> 'Neath his wings protecting hide you,
> Daily manna still provide you,
> God be with you till we meet again.

THE END